THE
TEACHING

THE
TEACHING

A THRILLER

T.O. PAINE

DARK
SWALLOW
BOOKS

Published by Dark Swallow Books
www.darkswallowbooks.com

Library of Congress Control Number: 2021912989

Paperback ISBN-13: 978-0-9992183-2-7
Hardcover ISBN-13: 978-0-9992183-3-4
eBook ISBN-13: 978-0-9992183-4-1

For my blood family, my spirit family,

and everyone in between.

CHAPTER ONE

RAINE

When my dog ran away this morning, it was as if she took my belief in the Teaching and buried it in the woods.

"Java," I call. "Here, girl."

Somewhere out here, my dog is running around like an escaped mental patient. There aren't many places to hide in the desert hills of northern Nevada, but she's tricky. Brave bushes grow in shady spots, and Java can make herself small. I'm looking around every rock outcropping, every lodgepole pine, hoping this doesn't take all day. I could yell for her or blow my whistle, but I know better. I could run after her, and I'm in shape enough to run—really, I am—but Java is skittish. It's best to sneak up on her, let her think she found me, then coax her back to my cozy, A-frame cabin in the Haven.

This is how we always do it, Java and me.

But why did she have to run away today? While everyone else in our community starts their Saturday with prayer, I am out here, wasting my time hunting for my dog. Sometimes, I wish I could put her in a straitjacket and be done with it.

Don't get me wrong. I love that black and tan mongrel. If it weren't for her, I'd be all alone.

"Java?"

Dammit, where'd she go?

In the distance, an ATV rips through the forest, engine revving loudly. I hate hunters. The thought of them running over my Java spikes my anxiety.

I stop walking, close my eyes, and take a deep breath. The dry air warms my nose. Spring in these hills isn't green, but it is warm. Most people in our community don't hunt. For a while, when we had close to fifty families, the Pliskins wanted everyone to get hunting licenses so we could save on the community grocery bill, but Terry and Kattrice wouldn't have it. Guns destroy the future. The Teaching is about learning from one's past.

"Java? Where are you?"

The trail climbs up toward the firepit, weaving between scattered Junipers and pines before cresting the hill. We used to go up there when were teenagers—Zack, Shayla, David, Monica, and me . . . sitting around the fire, drinking Red Stripe, or whatever we could steal from the community store.

Now, with my thirties right around the corner, my closest companion is this furry lunatic. I shouldn't blame Java for being crazy. She spent the first year of her life living in the wild after a camper abandoned her. I'm grateful to have become her mom. Everyone I grew up with has married or left the Haven, but I know God will send my soul mate to me. Yet, it's hard. The men in town don't understand our way of life, and we're down to less than ten families in the Haven.

"Java, come on."

The firepit makes me think of David. I shouldn't, but I

sometimes wonder how things might have been. It's funny how facts don't change feelings, but I guess that's what Sebastian means by being in your mind and not in your heart. The fact is, David married Monica over ten years ago. *She's* his soul mate. His like-vibration in the universe. Sebastian said so. They have two kids and a decent marriage, but David would have been happier with me.

Stop it, Raine. Get out of your mind.

I know better than to do this to myself, but after every breakup, I go through a David phase. Warren broke up with me yesterday. I'm okay with it, though. We only dated for six weeks. He lives in Elko, and like others, he was never going to understand the Teaching.

At least I'll always have my dog. If I can find her.

"Java!" I yell louder.

I stop.

Something made a noise.

I listen.

Ahead, the trail snakes around a granite boulder. The rock juts out of the ground like a giant toe. Silver veins run down from its tip and touch the earth. Something moves on the other side.

I focus.

To catch her, I must go slow, act uninterested, and avoid eye contact.

I grasp my whistle and hold it still so it doesn't rattle. The boulder's surface is cool to the touch. The light brown earth beneath my feet is soft. Powdery. I step lightly before crouching, hiding, planning my next move—

A gunshot shatters the air.

I hit the ground and listen for Java, but there's no sound.

The shot should have scared her, and she should have come running around the boulder, but she didn't. She could be shot. Bleeding.

I listen.

All is quiet, except for her breathing . . . but that's not *her* breathing.

Java doesn't breathe. She pants.

Peering around the boulder, a teenage girl crouches next to a cluster of sagebrush. She shoves something into a large backpack—the kind for hiking, not for school—and her hands shake.

"Hello?" I say.

The girl jumps, putting her hand on her chest. "You scared me." She zips her bag shut.

"I'm sorry. Did you hear that?"

"The gun? Yeah, I heard it." She stands off-kilter.

"Are you okay?" I say.

"I'm fine."

She's not fine. Her face is red, and she keeps looking around as if we're not alone. "You're Samantha, right?"

Her backpack is overstuffed, and she leans away from me as if to run. There's a hardened look in her eyes. Two obsidian orbs glistening beneath a watery sheen. I ease myself around the boulder.

Pensive, she backs away, dragging her bag across the ground. "Yes, I . . . look, I—"

In the distance, Java lets out a stream of ferocious barks. Samantha startles.

"It's okay," I say. "That's my dog."

I scan the sparsely populated forest, searching for Java's black and tan fur between the trees, but the ridge blocks my view. The gunshot and Java's barking both came from the other side. She never makes a sound without a good reason. Given a choice between fight or flight, Java always takes flight.

Samantha puts her backpack on and grips the straps.

"My name is Raine." I hold out my hand. "We haven't officially met. Will you help me find my dog? Her name is Java."

"I'm sorry, I—" She starts to take off.

I grasp her arm. "Wait. We can help you."

"No. You're one of them." She pulls her arm free. "Please. Leave me alone."

"Someone's shooting a gun out here. It's not safe to go that way."

She breaks into a run.

"It's not safe!"

I chase after her. I don't want to scare her, but I'm not exactly at peace myself. Some idiot hunters are playing at being big men, putting our lives at risk. A stray bullet can kill the same as an intentional one.

My sandal gets caught in the weeds, and I fall. Samantha disappears over the ridge. I'm already out of breath, but I push myself off the ground and run after her. Her backpack was way too big for a casual hike. Maybe she's running away from the Haven. If she is, she has a long way to go. Elko is the nearest town with anything to speak of, and it's over thirty miles away.

At the top of the hill, my lungs revolt. My stomach muscles contract, I bend over, put my hands on my knees. Gasping, I lift my head and search for signs of life. Swatches of pine needles blanket the dry earth between clusters of sage and trees.

Samantha is gone and there's no sign of Java.

The stillness unnerves me.

When I catch my breath, a sterile scent pricks my nose. It's not natural. Was Samantha wearing perfume? In the woods? I sniff. Maybe she was meeting someone for a date, but I doubt it. I sniff again. The smell is masculine. Sophisticated.

It's cologne.

Maybe Samantha and the hunters aren't the only ones out here.

Java barks maniacally like she's cornered. She's somewhere behind me now. I glance at the trees ahead, hoping to see Samantha, but she's long gone. She was too fast. Too young. Even with that backpack on, she outran me up the hill.

Java barks again, and I head toward her. Toward the firepit. Rocks tumble into my sandals as I shimmy down the slope. I wish I'd worn my running shoes. She barks yet again, and I run as fast as my Birkenstocks allow.

I focus on my breath.

I focus on my stride, but my mind wanders.

Screw Warren. The next guy I find, I'm going to lay it out there right from the beginning. *Listen. The Teaching is the only life I've ever known, so love it like I do or leave.*

Maybe I shouldn't lay it out there. Maybe it's the Teaching that's the problem. Or maybe, as Sebastian would say, I'm *in my mind* about men. Playing little girl games instead of following my heart and getting closer to God. Being in one's mind is giving in to one's selfish ego. Listening to one's heart is fulfilling the will of God.

My lungs reach a new level of pain. I need to think about something else as a distraction.

Men. God. Warren. My thoughts swim. This is the opposite of meditating.

Java barks again, and I change course. She's not like me. She hates men. No, that's not true. My angel doesn't *hate* men. She's afraid of them. Someone abused her before God put her in my path. There hasn't been a man yet who doesn't send her running.

Not even David.

I come around a corner and skid to a stop, clenching my toes to keep from losing my Birkenstocks. Java stands there, bristling and baring her teeth. She sees me and skitters behind a tree. There's no one else around. I sink to the ground and roll onto my back. With my eyes closed, I put my hand on my chest and grasp my whistle.

I wait.

A soft breeze blows over my face.

The hesitant pitter-patter of Java's feet is music to me.

The faint smell of that strange cologne mixes with the sagebrush.

I feel Java's tongue slick my forehead, and I grab her by the collar.

She's mine.

When I was growing up, I knew every dusty inch of these woods. I could always orient myself by the position of Ruby Dome. That great bald mountain, looking down on us from the south. I could recognize each pine tree by the pattern in its bark and every trail by the distance between the sagebrush and the trees. Different areas had different smells. I knew where I was with my eyes closed. Now, I don't know if I've lost my senses or my memory, but all the trees and bushes look the same. And the smell of that cologne lingers.

Samantha is nowhere to be seen.

Java and I wander through the hills. Pebbles stick in

between my sandals and my feet, puncturing my soles. The knapweed scrapes my shins. My back begins to ache as more than an hour goes by. I wouldn't worry so much about Samantha, except I think she was living with David and Monica. They'll be upset if she doesn't come back.

We make our way past the firepit, trot onto the main trail, and follow it toward Control Road. In the shadows, there's enough moisture on the ground to show where the ATV bludgeoned God's earth with its knobby tires. Grinding my sandals into the tracks removes the traces of man. It's a little game I like to play, and it helps nature be as God intended. Natural.

At the end of the trail, Monica stands in the middle of the road, her hands cupped around her mouth. "Samantha. Are you out there?"

Monica doesn't see us as we approach from behind. "I saw her."

Monica turns, flashes her smile—the one that says, *hello, my sister*—and rests her hands on her hips. Her bright red leggings clash with her pale blue sweatshirt.

"She was up by the firepit."

"Oh, thank God." She exhales. "I've been looking everywhere. How have you been?"

"I'm—"

"Wait. Are you sure it was her?"

"I think so, why?"

"I'm surprised you'd recognize her. You haven't been around much, Raine. I haven't seen you in forever."

"It hasn't been forever." Six weeks is not forever.

But Monica is not entirely wrong. I haven't been around much. Six weeks ago, I started spending all my time convincing

Warren to be in the Teaching, but Mr. "I'm sorry, I just don't believe in ghosts" wouldn't listen. Sebastian is not a ghost. There's a big difference between a real spirit and a ghost.

"Why'd you stop coming to Trance?" Monica asks. "It's not good to miss Trance."

"I know. I've been busy. Have they said anything about me?"

She gently grasps my arm and smiles. "I have news. David and I are adopting Samantha."

"What? You're kidding." Holy shit. Monica and David already have two kids of their own, and goddammit . . . she has David. "Why didn't you tell me?"

"If you weren't such a recluse, you would have known. Sebastian announced it in Trance two weeks ago. Haven't you seen your mother? Honestly, Raine, you need to spend more time with the women."

The women. I love them, but I've wasted enough of my life sitting in on the older generation's Sunday brunches, listening to their endless stream of gossip. Debating who is, and who isn't, *in* the Teaching.

"Are you sure it was Samantha up there?" Monica asks.

"Long, blonde hair. About fifteen years old, right? She was carrying a backpack."

Monica's lips tighten.

"Is everything okay?" The fright in Samantha's eyes comes back to me.

"We had an argument this morning, and she took off. It's not a big deal. Why?"

"She looked upset, but that could have been because of the gun."

"Gun?" Monica's face reddens to match her leggings. "She had a gun?"

"No. We heard a gun go off and it startled us. I think there is a hunter out there riding around on an ATV."

"Why didn't she come back with you?"

"I wanted her to, but she ran away."

"You just left her there? Alone in the woods with guns going off?"

"No. She ran."

"Raine? Why didn't you do something?"

"I had to find Java."

"Your dog? You left Samantha alone in the woods to find your dog?" She huffs.

I want to cover Java's eyes.

Monica, my good friend and sister in the Teaching, is embarrassing herself again. She's always been so uptight. "Yes, my dog. I had to find my dog." With a deep breath, I speak slowly and demonstrate what serenity looks like. "I tried to help Samantha, but she ran away. She's fine. Look, I'll bet she walks out of the woods any minute now."

"She's not fine," Monica says. "We were going to adopt her, and now she's gone."

I kneel and stroke Java's fur.

Monica puts one hand on her forehead and rests the other on her hip. Her sweatshirt hangs on her narrow shoulders, flowing down over her pot belly. Child-rearing hasn't been kind, and neither have the mimosas at *the women's* Sunday brunches. I know better than to pass body judgments—David loves Monica for who she is, the way the Teaching tells him to—but she's changed over the years.

He would have been better off with me.

"Hey" She regains my attention, squinting as though she just read my mind. "Can you help me find Samantha?"

"I can't. I have to—"

A second gunshot pierces the air, echoing over the hills. Monica ducks.

Java lurches away, breaking my hold on her collar. She escapes down the road, and I bolt after her.

"Wait," Monica says. "I—"

"Don't worry," I shout. "It's just hunters."

A Birkenstock flies off at a bump in the road, but Java slows down near my cabin, and I catch her. When I turn to look back, Monica disappears into the forest.

A breeze sweeps dust toward me, and its warmth reminds me spring is here.

Spring.

A time for birth and renewal.

Not a time for hunting.

Hunting season doesn't open until autumn.

CHAPTER TWO

DAVID

David Johansen shifts into second gear and guides his truck down Control Road into the Haven, praying his transmission doesn't lock up.

The grinding sound torments him until he releases the clutch.

After wasting another Saturday morning working on his father-in-law's toilet, David drove out on the highway to clear his mind. The rush of flying down the road, the hum of rubber on pavement—these excursions never fail to free him from the earth plane, but now, drifting off the pavement back into the Haven, guilt consumes him. He doesn't have the money to risk this kind of selfishness, pushing his old Ford up to eighty miles an hour, wearing out the transmission, all for some cheap thrill.

His tires crunch against the dirt road. He passes by the forest, glances at Raine's cabin, and sighs.

His throat is dry. He wishes he'd brought a water bottle. He wishes he'd never wasted money on painting the side of his truck. *Johansen's Electric and Plumbing.* The paint has faded, and he can't afford to have it redone. Working for free, fixing Terry's toilet as a service to the community doesn't pay the bills.

What a horrible thought—*working for free.* Service isn't *working for free.* It's working for God. For God's children.

But working on Terry's toilet feels like slavery.

The Windhaven's demands never end.

His parents-in-law are evil.

Ahh.

Another horrible thought. A sacrilegious thought.

Terry is a kind and gracious minister, but—

David considers turning around and heading back out onto the highway where he can escape his mind, but he needs to make sure the kids are okay. Monica was asleep when he left this morning, and Samantha might have gone to town or somewhere else. It's almost eleven. If Monica is awake, she's drunk by now.

His head aches.

Life is about service, not money—but who will pay to fix his truck when the transmission burns out? Sure, he's a "teacher" in the Teaching, and that's fulfilling, but his bank account is empty. He will have to borrow money from the community soon. From Terry and Kattrice. Everyone thinks he gets special treatment because he married Terry's daughter, but the truth is, if his father-in-law ever paid him for his "service"—all the times he painted the trance room or fixed the generator or replaced fence or fixed Terry's toilet—he'd never need to borrow money again.

He swallows hard. His throat burns and his stomach is empty. His kids probably haven't eaten breakfast either.

Accelerating out of a turn, something flashes in the trees. He glances in the rearview mirror and sees Jace run out of the woods.

Jace.

That runaway is another kind of service, but working with him should pay off someday, right? David is Jace's teacher, and the more David teaches him, the more he pays it forward. Jace *will* learn to be of service to others. When David fixes Terry's toilet, Jace will repair David's transmission. Karma. That's how it's supposed to work.

But it's not working. If it were, David's transmission wouldn't be on its last leg.

He looks in the mirror again and sees the lanky teen sprinting up the road the other way. He considers making a U-turn, but he's got to get home to the kids. The world rejected Jace, and the Teaching took him in. David took him in. Tattooed and drugged up, Jace was a mess when David found him on the outskirts of Vegas. Like other trips, that one took a toll on David's wallet, but the boy's progress over the past year has made it worth it. David feels closer to God, with or without being paid. He'd like to think he would have helped Jace with or without the Teaching, but he doubts it. The Teaching is his life, and it's a good life.

It was a good life.

He pulls into his driveway and looks out the passenger side window. The lock on the shed is there, hanging from a chain looped through the handles, guarding his mower. His tools. His sanity.

The shed is his personal shrine, though he has never left a letter to God inside it.

Jenny and Joseph bang against the driver's side door, and David smiles at them. He rolls down the window. "Move out of the way, guys. I can't open the door."

Jenny jumps back, greeting him with her freckled face.

The large freckle on her cheekbone, the one in the shape of Virginia, reminds David of Monica's mom, Kattrice. He sticks his head out the window and looks down. "Get back, Joseph." Joseph's nose curls upward like a ski jump, like his grandfather's nose.

"Daddy, look." Jenny holds up a drawing she made.

David opens the door and steps out.

Joseph gets that devilish look in his eyes. He grabs Jenny's drawing and runs in a circle, waving it in the air, keeping it just out of her reach.

"Make him give it back," she screams.

"Stop it, Joe." David cuts across the lawn, accidentally kicking over a box of crayons, sending a rainbow into the weeds. "Joseph." He snatches the drawing out of the little tormenter's hands.

Joseph laughs maniacally.

"Here you are, sweetheart." David hands Jenny the drawing, and she glares at Joseph. "Forgive him. You know how he is."

"He's a spaz."

"Yes, but he's our spaz."

"Do you like my drawing?"

She has drawn a brown horse standing in a field of yellow flowers. "It's very nice."

Joseph gets that look in his eyes again, and Jenny sees it, but she's too late. He runs to her drawing pad and rips out a page before she can stop him. Holding his arms out like an airplane, he circles the yard and delivers it to David.

This picture is unusual. She likes drawing her family—Mommy, Daddy, Joseph—standing in front of the cabin. David with a big smile on his face, Joseph wearing a baseball cap, and Monica with her hands on her hips. But there's an additional person in this drawing.

"Don't look at that one," Jenny says, running toward him.

On the edge of the paper, away from the rest of the Johansen family, Jenny has drawn the newest member, Samantha. It's only been a week since they announced the adoption in Trance, and already, Samantha has made it into the family portrait. Jenny did great with the likeness—long blond hair, about the right height compared to everyone else. But the flames at her feet and the big X through her face disturb David.

Jenny snatches the drawing away from him. Her upper lip quivers, and she looks at the ground.

"It's all right," he says. "Change is hard for everyone."

Joseph throws a rock at the shed and turns to see if David is watching. The devil is in the boy's eyes, but he's not evil. He's just an overenergized six-year-old looking for attention. David wishes he had the energy to play with his kids, but it's been a long morning, and Monica kept him up last night talking about the Haven's future. Terry's daughter, the princess. Sometimes she talks like the community belongs to her and her parents, but it doesn't. It belongs to God. To God's children.

David needs a nap.

He hands the drawing back to Jenny and walks up the steps. The sun has stripped the color from the cabin's siding, and the porch planks have begun to split. Another rock pings off the shed, but he doesn't turn around. The kids are okay, and that's what matters.

He opens the screen door. "Monica? Are you here?" He stops in the hall between the living room and kitchen. "Samantha?"

No answer.

Monica's tumbler rests on the kitchen counter next to her Tequila bottle. The tumbler is empty. The bottle is *almost* empty. The counter is strewn with empty frozen dinner boxes, wrappers, dirty dishes, and crumbs. He walks down the hall and checks their bedroom, but she isn't there. He knocks on the laundry room door.

"Samantha? Are you in there?"

No answer.

He peers inside. Samantha's futon is empty, and most of her things are gone.

This is unbelievable. Samantha is gone, and Monica left Jenny and Joseph alone. Back in the living room, there's no sign of the babysitter's things either. Maybe Cori is on her way, but she's certainly not here now. She always brings her backpack like she's going to study and then leaves it on the floor by the TV.

It's not there.

And where the hell is Monica?

He goes to the living room window, looks over the weed-infested front yard, and there she is, marching up the driveway, red-faced and breathing heavy. Joseph and Jenny make a run at her, then back off. She looks pissed. The cabin sways when her feet come down on the front steps. It's not that she's over-weight. The cabin is under-built. None of the places in the Haven have concrete foundations. Short four-by-fours hold the cabins one foot off the ground to avoid flooding from the monsoons. They're all weak, and David's is the weakest.

The front door slams open, and she bursts inside, heading for the kitchen counter.

"Where were you?" David says. "You can't leave the kids alone like this."

"I can do whatever I want. Samantha ran away."

David wants to say *good*. He wants to say he hopes Samantha doesn't come back. Not because they can't afford her—and they can't—but to smite Monica. She's only trying to score points with her parents by adopting Samantha, but points can't be traded in for cash. The Teaching says money is love in motion, and he's in the Teaching, but when your money is gone, it's gone.

"What happened?" he asks. "Are you sure she ran away?"

"She packed up her backpack and took off."

"Mon. Look at me. What did you say to her?"

She grabs her tumbler off the counter. "Nothing. She got angry and took off. I don't know why."

"You can't leave the kids alone like this."

"I wasn't gone long." She glares at him while she opens the Tequila and pours it into her glass. "You don't seem very concerned about Samantha."

"I am, but what if one of the kids got hurt? Joseph can't be left alone. You know he's—"

"Samantha is one of our kids now, too. What if she got hurt?"

This isn't worth the fight. Not again. "I'm tired. I had to go to town and pay for another kit to fix your dad's toilet. I'm going to—"

"Well, I hope you fixed it this time."

"I did. Have the kids eaten?"

"Yes, David. Of course they have."

He glances at the kitchen. Silver Pop-Tart wrappers lay in a pile by the sink. "I'm taking a nap."

"A nap? Oh, no you're not. Not until you've found Samantha."

"What?"

She leans forward, puts her weight on the counter, and sips from her glass. David wonders if there are any Pop-Tarts left in the box. He's so tired, he forgot how hungry he was.

"You're going to go look for Samantha," she says. "Something might have happened."

"No, I'm not." The floorboards creak as he crosses into the living room. The cabin sways. "I'm going to lie down while you make us lunch."

Now he's done it. Here comes the anger.

But it's worth it.

The couch feels so good, it's worth it.

Monica, glass in hand, stomps toward him.

The cabin shudders.

"The hell you are," she says. "Get up. Sebastian told us to adopt her, and that's what we're doing. You're her father now, so you better start acting like it. You better start acting like you're in the Teaching."

"I am in the Teaching." He stands. Careful now. Anger begets anger. "This has nothing to do with the Teaching. If Sebastian is right, she'll come back on her own."

"What if she can't? What if she's hurt? Or lost?"

"Why would she be hurt? Just because she took her things doesn't mean she ran away. Maybe she went to stay with Jace. I saw him come out of the woods when I drove by."

"Was she with him?"

"No."

"She doesn't want to see him. They broke up." She furrows her brow. "I bet you didn't know that did you?"

"I did, but it doesn't mean—"

"But if you saw Jace . . . " She turns away, thinking.

"What?"

"I don't like it," she says, stroking the side of her glass. "Jace is trouble."

"No, he's not. He's *had* trouble, that's all. I've been working with him a lot lately. He's coming around."

"I don't like this at all. Raine said she saw Samantha up by the firepit. If Samantha did go to see Jace, and you saw him without her, then she's alone in the woods."

"You saw Raine?"

"Dammit, David." She turns, spilling her drink. "Go look for Samantha. Now!"

"No. I'm eating lunch and taking a nap."

"No, you're not. For the love of God, I heard gunshots."

"So."

"So, if she's hurt, it'll be your fault."

Everything is always his fault.

He could argue the Teaching. He could say, *there are no dead, and there is no dying, so why worry if she got shot?* She'll return in another life. So some idiot was shooting his gun in the woods. So what? It's nothing to worry about, but with Monica, there's always something to worry about. There's always something he's got to do for someone. There's always service.

There are no dead, and there is no dying. There's also no peace and no winning. Not here. Not now. Not with her. Not ever.

"Well?" she says. "Are you going to look for Samantha or not?"

"I—"

"I'm your like-vibration. You have to listen to me. That's it." She puts her drink down. "I'm going to call Mom. She'll know what to do."

"No. Don't do that."

Monica pulls out her cell phone.

"If I go, promise you'll keep an eye on the kids?"

"Just go, David."

He swipes his keys off the kitchen counter. The Tequila is almost gone. Maybe Monica will take the kids to Shayla's and go to the store for more liquor. Maybe she'll pass out on the couch later, and he can have the bedroom to himself.

One can only hope.

David stands in the doorway, thinking about where Samantha might have gone. The clouds have overtaken the sky, spreading a shadow across the weeds, the road, the woods—everything. It makes sense Raine saw her by the firepit. Teens have hung out there since the dawn of time, but it's all the way on the other side of the Haven, and he's tired.

Jenny sits near the driveway, drawing pictures. Joseph picks bark off a tree. David lets the screen door slam behind him, and Joseph looks up. David wishes he could stay and play, but orders are orders.

He wishes he wasn't so tired.

He wishes the Teaching didn't require him to listen to his like-vibration.

His truck sleeps in the driveway, dented and dinged, but not down and out. Not yet.

He walks down the steps and turns toward the shed. He could go to it, unlock the lock, and take a nap inside. He has the key with him. He could pray. Relax. Meditate. He could recover. Find peace. Sleep.

He sighs.

A man shouldn't have to hide in his shed to sleep. He shouldn't have to, but—

This selfishness must stop.

These horrible thoughts must stop.

This thinking isn't "being in the Teaching."

A girl—not just a girl but his spirit daughter—might have run away, and all he can think about is sleep. And lunch. And how much money he'd save if she didn't come back. He can't afford to keep the cabin aloft on its stupid stilts or fix his truck or put food on the table, let alone take on another child. She's not even a child. She's like all the other runaways who come to the Haven. She's fifteen going on twenty-two, and she can take care of herself.

Horrible thoughts.

Monica is right. If he doesn't find Samantha, and something happens to her, it will be his fault. Kattrice will exact some sort of vengeance. His mother-in-law will make him pay, either in service or some other way.

It will be all his fault.

"Jenny, Joseph," he says. "Go inside, wash up, and get yourselves something to eat."

Joseph protests. "Right now? Why?"

"Just do it before your mom falls asleep on the couch."

"But," Jenny says, "I'm almost done drawing this one. Can't I finish it?"

"You can finish it later."

"Where are you going?" Joseph asks.

That's a good question.

David gazes at the road. Control Road. People in town think the name has something to do with the Teaching. They think David lives in a "controlling" cult, but he doesn't. He lives in the Teaching. The county built the road to control forest fires, not people.

The wind blows and dust sweeps over the road.

He *used* to live in the Teaching.

The road runs from here to the other side of the Haven, meandering past the Shrine, past Terry and Kattrice's house, then ascending to the trailhead by Raine's place. The trailhead leads to the firepit where the teenagers hang out.

"Daddy, where are you going?" Jenny asks.

He's going to look for Samantha, but maybe not. Maybe when he gets to the trailhead, he'll keep on walking down the road. And what if he did? What if he started running like Forrest Gump and never came back? What if he—

No.

There is no running away. He'd probably die in the desert if he tried.

Horrible thoughts.

The truth is, it's not the distance nor the climate nor the lack of money that holds him here.

It's the Teaching.

The Teaching is peace. It's love. It's all he's ever needed. It's all he's ever known.

"Daddy?" Jenny says.

The Teaching is his life, but it's gone now.

"I love you, sweetie. Go inside and eat something. I'll be back in a while."

CHAPTER THREE

NOAH

The sign outside Pete's Kitchen reads Saturday Hangover Special Until 11AM—Steak and Eggs—$12.99.

Inside, stainless steel stools with teal covers run around the counter in a classic fifties style. Hanging by the window, a metal print reading ROUTE 66 shows a family of four smiling and cruising in a red convertible. This place is nowhere near Route 66. The blinds are open wide, letting the morning sun shine in. A short-order cook scrapes a griddle in an open kitchen on the other side of the counter. Noah puts his notebook down, sits on a stool, and swivels toward the cook.

"What'll you have?" Grease blemishes decorate the cook's apron.

"The special, thanks."

A waitress rushes by, sticking a pen in her hair, and heads for the tables near the front window. The smell of pancakes, bacon, and eggs wafts over the counter. The cook throws on a steak. It sizzles. Noah opens his notebook and flips to where he recorded Samantha's timeline. He reviews when she left Las Vegas, arrived here in Elko, and met a boy named Jace.

"Mind if I sit down?" asks a dumpy little man. "This is my regular seat."

"Not at all."

The man has thick fingers and a dirty yellow jacket.

"The usual?" the cook asks.

The man nods.

Noah goes back to reviewing his notes.

Samantha ran away from home two and a half months ago. She met Jace in Elko, and he brought her to a place called "the Haven" up in the hills about thirty miles from here. Mr. Baxter Oakes, her father, hired a private investigator to bring her back, but she refused to come. Mr. Oakes went to the Haven on his own and pleaded with her to return to Vegas with him, but by then, she was brainwashed. She said her new family planned on adopting her.

"What're you working on there?" the man asks.

"Notes for school."

"Oh, yeah? You doing some online classes or something?"

"No, I'm a student at UNLV. I just came up here to do some research."

"In Elko?" He smirks. "What do we got?"

"I'm studying religion. Have you heard of a place called the Haven?"

The cook flips one of the steaks too soon. Noah knows from his restaurant days he'll be getting a bloody steak for breakfast. The eggs will probably be runny too.

"Yep, I heard of it. It's up by Ruby Dome." He sips his coffee. "I guess there *is* something around here worth studying."

"Have you ever been there?"

"Nah. I got no reason to go." He gestures to the cook. "How about you, Jack? You ever gone up to see the cult?"

The cook shakes his head.

Noah writes the word *cult* at the top of a new page. "Why do you call it a cult?"

" 'Cause that's what it is. You know, they live together on a compound. I don't think they're stockpiling guns or anything like that, but they're weird. They talk to ghosts and shit." He raises his hand. "Sorry. My language. I forgot—you're a religious guy."

Noah laughs. "No. It's fine. I'm not religious. I'm just studying religion."

"There was also that kidnapping, but they were cleared of that."

"What?"

"A few years ago, a kid went missing up there. Most people didn't even know about the cult until then. An Amber alert went out, someone tipped off the cops, and they went up to the compound. We all thought those kooks were trying to brainwash the kid, so we thought they got scared and hid her when the cops came, but we were wrong."

"It was a girl?"

"Yeah."

"How old?"

"Young, I think. Eight? Just a child. Anyway, like I said, most people didn't know about those weirdos until that happened. There was this guy, some sort of cult buster. He got on the news and said all kinds of things. He said those hippies danced naked in the woods under the full moon."

Noah can't contain his smile. "I doubt that, but—"

"No. Really. He said they were dancing hippies. That

they preach about peace and love, and they get people to join them. Then they tell all the women to have as many babies as they can." He cocks his head to the side. "Then they sell the babies."

The cook slaps Noah's breakfast on the counter. It's red and runny, but it smells good. "That sounds pretty far-fetched."

"I suppose so, but stranger things have happened."

"What about the girl? They weren't hiding her?"

"Nope. Turns out, her stepdad kidnapped her and took her to California. Or . . . maybe it was Idaho. Anyway, I guess he liked being her stepdaddy enough to take her. Something like that." The cook refills the man's coffee. "Thanks, Jack."

The waitress returns and sticks an order slip into the clip above the cook.

He pulls it down, sniffs, and cracks an egg.

Noah finishes writing in his notes and glances at the window in front, imagining Mr. Oakes's daughter, Samantha. He's never met her, but Mr. Oakes showed him photos. Noah pictures her walking down the street here, flowers in her hair, wearing a ragged dress like one of Charlie Manson's children—a stark contrast to the well-dressed teen in high heels and diamond earrings from the photos.

He digs into the steak.

The man holds out his hand. "My name is Edwin."

"Noah. Nice to meet you."

Edwin's hand is as thick as it looks. The cook places a bowl of oatmeal and a side of peaches in front of him.

Noah's steak is tough but tasty. If everything works out, he'll never eat a tough steak again. All he needs to do is bring Samantha back to Vegas. When Mr. Oakes sees what he is capable of, he'll make him his right-hand man for sure.

Glancing up, Noah spies a woman peering in through the window. She's wearing a knitted shawl, and her graying hair is long, which isn't something he's used to seeing on someone her age. She presses her nose against the glass, squints, and cups her hands to see inside.

A vertical scar splits her left eyebrow in two.

There's something familiar about her, but he's not sure what it is. Mr. Oakes had shown pictures of people praying and walking in nature on the Haven's website. Several of the women were dressed like her, and—

They make eye contact.

She grimaces and darts away.

"Did you see that?" Noah asks.

Edwin shovels a peach wedge into his mouth. "No. What happened?"

"Somebody was looking in here."

"They're probably hungry. I'd give 'em this oatmeal if they wanted. I hate it, but the doctor says my heart is going."

"I'm sorry to hear that." Noah puts a twenty on the counter. "Hey." The cook turns around. "Here's for my bill. Keep the extra."

Sunlight glances off the car windshields in the direction the woman ran. Noah can't see through the glare, but she must have gone north toward the Red Lion Hotel. He races after her but loses track at the first intersection. He writes her description down in his notebook—long gray hair, scarred eyebrow.

What has he gotten himself into?

The walk sign lights up, and he crosses the street.

If the old woman is in the cult, she could help him find Samantha. He's got to find her, or he'll end up in another dead-end job. Restaurants, hotels, golf resorts, convenience stores—he is so sick of going from place to place. At one point, he risked his life as a bike courier in downtown San Francisco. Exciting as that was, most of these jobs don't hold his interest, and something always goes wrong. Last week, he got fired from a motel. Under pressure, he skipped changing the sheets on one bed, in one room, one time, and a snooty lady found a hair on her pillow. Everybody in that place cut corners, but Noah was the one who got caught.

Thankfully, the next day, his uncle introduced him to Mr. Oakes. Told him the secret to success was strong relationships with big people, not weak wages from small businesses. Menial labor gets a man nowhere. Rescuing a runaway teen from a brainwashing cult—there's nothing menial about that. And, there's nothing menial about acting like a private investigator to get on Mr. Oakes's good side.

But it's more than building a successful business relationship with Mr. Oakes. Becoming a highly paid personal assistant.

Noah is in trouble.

He rubs the back of his neck.

It wasn't the first time he'd borrowed money for gambling, but it was the first time he couldn't pay it back. A month ago or so, he lost his patience at the tables. The worst thing a gambler can do. After his money was gone, he borrowed more. Then more. He found a loan shark named Titus. A tall man in a vermillion suit jacket who cleans up his own messes. Noah became one of Titus's messes. He arranged to pay back his debt in installments, but when he lost his job, he missed the first payment. He needs to become Mr. Oakes's right-hand-man. Fast.

Titus has a penchant for money and kneecaps. He loves money, but when he doesn't get it, he's just as happy breaking kneecaps.

Ahead, an elderly couple strolls along the sidewalk. The woman has short hair and a round face. She looks nothing like the pictures of the people on the cult's website. Edwin said the cult members talk to ghosts and shit. He must have been referring to Trance. The website described "Trance" as a way to explore past lives by listening to a psychic medium channel spirits from the other side. Like listening to a gypsy at a séance. Mr. Oakes said the people behind the website brainwashed Samantha and wouldn't let her leave the Haven. After some more digging, Noah discovered an email address and contacted Terry and Kattrice Windhaven, leaders of *The Teaching*. After convincing them he was a college student with an open mind, Kattrice invited him to witness the miracle this Sunday.

To witness Trance.

Tomorrow.

This job had seemed so easy on his way to Elko this morning. All he had to do was go to the Haven, sit through the trance meeting, spot Samantha, and bring her back to Mr. Oakes. But that gray-haired woman outside the diner . . . was she spying on him? Were they going to ambush him? Push him away?

He pulls out his cell phone and taps the contact list. His hotel is only a couple of blocks ahead. He speeds up. Maybe he should change his plans and go to the Haven tonight.

"Hi, my name is Noah Carlson. Is Mr. Oakes in?"

"Yes. I'll put you through."

A click, dead air, then, "What do you know? What have you found out?"

"Not much. I'm not there yet."

"I'm concerned, Noah. Every day that goes by puts her in deeper under their spell."

"I know. I know. I'm going to bring her back. Don't worry."

"Please. I'll be eternally grateful if you do."

"I have a question. When you sent that PI here, did he mention seeing anything strange before he got to the Haven?"

"Like what?"

"Well, I'm in Elko, and this strange-looking woman was staring at me. I think she is a part of the—"

"Be careful. I don't know how, but they knew when Vito was coming. After he got there, they wouldn't tell him anything. That's why I wanted you to get invited to their trance thing. You're sticking to your cover, aren't you? Everywhere you go, right? In Elko, too?"

"Yes. I'm a student studying religious organizations."

"Good. It's the only way. I thought about hiring a deprogrammer, but these Windhaven people have been running this scam for decades. They know everyone in the business of breaking up cults."

"They don't know me."

"Exactly. I barely know you. If they research you like I think they researched Vito, they won't be able to connect us." He breathes into the phone. "They'll do anything to keep my baby there. They're taking her away from me, you know that, right? You've got to bring her back."

"I'll do my best." Noah crosses the parking lot to his hotel. "I'll call you tomorrow."

"Wait. Before I forget. Sammy has been chatting online with one of her friends back here. Her friend's mother saw the messages and told me she might be staying in an A-frame cabin with a woman and a dog."

"A woman and a dog in an A-frame cabin. Got it."

"Thank you so much for doing this, Noah. I'm counting on you."

CHAPTER FOUR

RAINE

I'm a meat-eater—steak, pork chops, hot wings—you name it. My mother, Miss Ally Parker—emphasis on the "Miss"—doesn't eat meat. She quit again last week. This puts a damper on our Saturday night dinners at her trailer. Growing up, I endured many meatless months. It was miserable, but she was well-meaning. My mother is harmless, like a gentle bird, except birds eat bugs and worms, and she eats tofu and edamame.

This is my week to cook at her place. I made Thai tofu noodle bowls from a recipe on the internet. My mother won't tell me if it tastes terrible, and I won't ask. Next week, I'll pretend to like whatever she cooks. And the cycle will continue.

She sits over there with her back to the fake wood paneling, sipping her green tea. Her long hair rests on her shoulders like a judge's robe.

"How's the law office?" she asks.

"The same. Boring." I put the bowls on the table and sit down. Java lies near the front door. She sees me look at her and raises an eyebrow, but she doesn't get up. I love that she doesn't beg at the table.

"I wish your boss would give you purposeful work to do. It shouldn't be boring."

"Well, it is."

"Do you ever get to help people? Be of service?"

I bite into a cube of tofu. It's too soft, but the sauce I improvised is delicious. "If filing affidavits and making appointments is service, then yes."

"Your boss should give you meaningful work."

"He tries."

"You should find a job taking care of others. I wish you hadn't left the daycare."

My chair scrapes against the linoleum floor as I scoot forward. "I don't need a job like that to be of service. There's plenty of people here I can help."

She dabs at her food, picking through the noodles. "But you haven't been helping them, have you? You haven't gone to Trance in weeks."

"I've been busy."

"Filing affidavits? That's no excuse, Raine. Kattrice is worried."

"Kattrice is always worried. I'll go soon. I just need some time."

"Time is an illusion. You can have whatever you want, whenever you want it, you just have to—"

"Mom. I said I'll go."

"Tomorrow?"

"Sure." I put my fork down.

"I'm sorry about your breakup. How are you doing?"

"I'm fine. I liked him, but I knew it wouldn't work out. It never does."

"What do you mean?"

"It's the cult stigma."

She raises her eyebrows. The scar over her left eye frowns. I'm not in the mood for another lecture about men and God. "Besides, he had crooked teeth. I want a man with straight teeth." I pick up my fork and tap my mouth. "Perfect, white teeth, so hard, he can chew through a metal fence and leave bite marks on stop signs."

She laughs and puts her hands on the table. "Then you should write a note and put it in the Shrine. God will grant you a man with strong teeth if you ask him. I have no doubt about it."

"Right. Sure." It feels good to smile. "I'm not doing that."

"But what *are* you doing? You practically abandoned the Teaching dating Warren. You know, you could go the other way. It would be okay if you wanted to give up on dating." She lifts her fork and gives it a twirl. "Look at me. I don't have a man, and I've never been happier."

My eyes go to her scar. I can't help it. She's never told me how she got it, but I'm sure it came from my dad. I was three when he left. Or did *we* leave him?

"Why didn't you ever find someone else?" I ask.

With a slow, deliberate attention to detail, she folds her napkin and places it next to her fork. She purses her lips, then smiles. "Once I found the Teaching, I had everything I needed. It was my path. I already had you." She picks up her fork and dabs at her meal. "I didn't need men anymore."

"But haven't you been lonely?"

"No."

I doubt it. She's been lonely. It's not that she's lying. She's just in her airy-fairy mood, letting the Teaching guide her. Everything always turns out her way because she's so damn accepting. I always go back and forth between trying to get what I want and taking what God gives me.

"Raine." She reaches across the table and places her hand on mine. "I want you to have what you want, and I know you want a man. Don't let your father's karma take away your hope. I wasn't joking about leaving a note in the Shrine. It'll help, I promise."

"Don't worry. I haven't lost hope. And I'm not desperate for a man."

"Couldn't you find someone in the Haven to date?"

David loved me once, but—

Dammit, Raine. Let it go. He married Monica. Not you.

"No," I say. "They're all taken." I point at her bowl. "Are you finished with that?"

"Yes."

I stack her bowl on mine and pick up the silverware. She says nothing, but she watches me, reading me the way she does. I wonder if it was a beer bottle that split her eyebrow and made the scar. Or was it a fist? Whenever I've asked, she's always dodged the subject. The Teaching tells us never to speak ill of others, but she's just avoiding the pain.

"Something else is bothering you," she says. "What is it, honey?"

I head for the kitchen. Java stands up, hoping for scraps. The bowls clink as I drop them in the sink. "The only thing bothering me is the Teaching." I face her. "It's not that I'm alone. It's—"

"Maybe you won't be alone for long. Kattrice told me an outsider is coming to Trance tomorrow. She said he's about your age." She glances down at the table. "He made quite an impression on Terry."

"How so?"

"When he asked if he could observe Trance, Terry agreed on the spot. He never does that."

"What's his problem?"

"Terry's?"

"No. The outsider's. He must be pretty messed up if he wants our help."

"It's not like that. He's a student at the University of Las Vegas. He wants to learn about the Teaching."

My mother babbles on about this guy from UNLV while I soap up the dishes and scrub. I haven't missed going to Trance. Everyone goes and complains to the Spirit, but no one listens to him. It's annoying. But if I were to be honest—if I were to be *in* the Teaching—I'd admit I don't want to go because I'm afraid. The Spirit—Sebastian—he knows things. He knew my old Volkswagen was going to break down before it did. He knew the name of Shayla's boyfriend before she met him, and he knew she'd be verbally abused by him later.

Sebastian doesn't just know things. He knows everything.

I'm afraid he'll know I avoided being in the Teaching while I dated Warren, and I'm afraid he'll know I left Samantha alone in the woods. He must know Monica is angry with me over that.

"They said he's majoring in religion," my mother continues. "All religions. You should come and meet him, tell him what we believe." She smiles. "He's got great teeth."

"Really? How do you know that?"

She tips her head to the side. "You never know. He might."

"I'm not interested," I say, drying my hands on a towel.

"I'm worried about you."

"Don't be."

She stands. "I should ask Terry to give you a private trance session so you can talk to Sebastian alone."

"Why?"

"He can help you, Raine. Plus, there's something else." She averts her eyes. "I didn't want to tell you yet, but—no. I'm not going to. Just know that it's wonderful news. I promise. If I set up a private trance, will you come?"

"Whatever."

"Sebastian will show you the way. Promise you'll come to Trance tomorrow."

"I'll be there." I'm empty inside, despite the dinner. Tofu isn't as filling as real meat.

"Good," she says.

Java walks into the kitchen and pushes her head beneath my hand. "We should go. It's getting late."

"Be safe."

Java leads me down the hill, pulling on the leash, occasionally trying to dart into the woods like she always does.

I follow, walking fast.

Two mobile homes, a long, dark brown one and a white one with a milk crate for front steps, are nestled in the bend between Control Road and the road to my mother's. The brown home belongs to David's dad, though he doesn't live there. Over the years, David's dad has collected three properties in the Haven. He lets newcomers use them until they get places of their own.

Java doesn't look both ways when she takes a right onto Control Road, but we're safe. This time.

As the sun sets, shadows hide the potholes along the

road's border. I do my best to dodge them, slipping off the edge into the weeds from time to time. I grasp my whistle. My father gave it to me when I was three. I wish I could remember something more from the day he left. Whenever I think of him, I hear the whistle, a piercing high trill blocking out all other sounds. I think of all the nights my mother rushed into my bedroom to see what was wrong. Alone and afraid, waking up from a nightmare, I would blow the whistle, thinking my father would come to the rescue. I wish I could remember what he looks like. In my memories, he's a giant with dark hair and startling blue eyes like mine.

I give the whistle a gentle blow, just enough to rattle the ball inside.

Java and I cross over the road past the Shrine and head toward the trail. I consider taking Control Road to the end and around to my place, but it's shorter to cut through the trees. I've got my dog and my whistle with me.

A pile of rocks marks the mouth of the shortcut. We enter the woods. The early evening shade hides the trail, but it doesn't affect Java. She pulls on the leash like a crazy beast, but I slow down to watch my step. The shadows coalesce, blocking out the ground between the scattered pines. My thoughts drift to Samantha. I wonder if Monica found her or if she's still out in the woods somewhere. If she is, I wonder if she is still scared.

I'm not.

I tighten my grip on Java's leash and wrap my fingers around my whistle.

I'm almost to the road on the other side of the trees.

Something snaps behind me, and I spin around like an idiot because I know no one is there. It was only Java stepping on a branch.

Then, she barks, and I jump. "Stop it, girl. You're scaring me."

The edge of the road slopes up out of the trees. My heart has no reason to be pounding like this.

I stop and listen.

The hills beyond my cabin are black, but an orange light glows in the distance, and I hear laughter. Friday evening at the firepit. Those were the days.

I'm an old lady to those teenagers.

My A-frame is the last cabin before the trail to the firepit. Walking by the Pliskin's place, I take in the outline of their chimney against the darkening sky. I remember when I believed Santa could fit in a chimney. As a child, I used to confuse him with God.

He sees you when you're sleeping . . . he knows when you're awake . . .

God and Santa even look the same, but Sebastian says God and the souls in heaven have no form. Still, I picture spirits as clouds of white mist. Angelic cotton balls bouncing around in God's bathroom sink.

Approaching my A-frame, something rustles in the bushes. I stop and take out my keys. Java looks up at me like, *Come on. Why aren't we going in?*

I squint and lean forward, peering across the road. The bushes quiver violently before expelling a dark shape. It runs past my cabin, disappearing into the woods.

Java barks and pulls on the leash. "Hush."

I put my whistle in my mouth, make a fist with a key sticking out between my fingers, and march across the road. Footsteps drum from the forest. I reach my front yard and stop. Someone is running through the trees, crushing bushes, breaking sticks.

I wait.

I listen.

The only sound now is the distant teens' laughter, drinking and whooping it up at the firepit.

Java pulls me up the steps—*can we go in?*

An envelope is taped to the middle of my door. It has my name on it.

I put my key in the lock.

Java bumps into my legs and whines.

I unlock the door, grab the envelope, and switch on the light.

The handwriting isn't familiar.

I read it.

I read it again and again.

Thick black swoops across the page. Looping letters, delicate and disturbing.

> *God is watching you. Sooner or later, he's going to run you down.*

CHAPTER FIVE

DAVID

David crests the hill overlooking the firepit. The rust-colored land holds onto Jace and the other teenager's footprints, dipping and diving beneath empty beer cans. He picks up a stick covered in graying bark, pulls off a piece, and throws it into the wind. The sun settles over the horizon.

"Samantha?"

He spent the afternoon searching for her, saving the firepit for last. An hour ago, he stood out of sight, waiting in the trees, watching the teens sit on the rocks surrounding the pit. Talking. Laughing. The way he used to do.

Samantha wasn't with them, but that doesn't mean she wasn't watching from afar like he was.

"Samantha, if you're out here, say something."

He sits down on a rock and picks at the stick's bark. Blackened cans lay in the ash, blending in with the dead coals—remnants of teenage bravado lacking in the Teaching.

But those were the good days. The days before he became a teacher in the Teaching. Back when the sun would go down, the trees would disappear, and he didn't have a care in the world. The rock outcroppings, the dirt, the Haven—everything disappeared, leaving nothing but the fire and his friends faces, laughing and glowing in the firelight. Zack made jokes at Shayla's expense. Raine talked about traveling to Europe. Monica got smashed and tried to convince everyone to go skinny-dipping in the creek.

What sixteen-year-old boy wouldn't want to go skinny-dipping with Shayla, Raine, and Monica?

Monica's hair used to run to her waist, hugging the curves of her body. When she drank, she would say the craziest things about God and trancing. It was like she got high on the Teaching. She'd run around the firepit, tapping everyone on the back of the head, yelling, *angel, angel, angel . . . devil!*

David was always the devil. From sometime before grade school, she attached herself to him like a groupie to a rock star. All through their teenage years, she kept on him and on him, not stopping until he was hers. He loved the attention.

But that was then.

On the gang's last night around the firepit, David brought a bottle of Jim Beam. He knew his announcement would change things, but he didn't realize it marked the end of their Saturday night forays forever. He didn't know marrying the daughter of the Haven's leader would make the "good" in the good times go away.

He stood, raised the bottle, but Zack spoke first.

How many people in "the world" does it take to screw in a light bulb?

Who cares? They're all going to hell anyway.

Shayla laughed, but she wasn't laughing at her brother's joke. She was laughing because of the whiskey.

So was Monica.

The Teaching says God wants his children to drink. He wants his children to have fun on the earth plane.

Raine leaned in close to the fire and described a mountain she read about on the internet. It stood in the Pyrenees. When she spoke of it, she left her body and traveled across the ocean, her blue eyes dancing in the firelight. She claimed to have dreamed Sebastian hiked the mountain six hundred years ago.

Monica told her she was wrong. Monica said Sebastian never lived in Italy.

Raine said the Pyrenees were in France.

Raine was right.

Later that night, David raised the bottle and announced Sebastian had spoken through Terry and said Monica was his soul mate. His like-vibration. He announced they were getting married. He announced the end of everything good in his life, but he didn't know it at the time. He turned seventeen that May and married her in June, fulfilling Sebastian's premonition.

If only Sebastian had said Raine was David's soul mate. The "good" in the good times wouldn't have disappeared.

He rolls the stick between his fingers. Picks off another piece of bark.

No amount of whiskey can fix Monica.

But it *was* a beautiful wedding. Monica's dress flowed behind her as she walked with her father down the path to the trance room. Beneath the wedding arch, Terry gave her to David. Then, Terry sat on a pile of red pillows. His old-man frame arched, his legs crossed like Buddha, his eyes closed, and his hands reached to the heavens, his long white hair hung down his back, and he tranced Sebastian. Sebastian's voice came through him louder and clearer than David ever heard before or since.

Sebastian spoke of love and purpose and the Teaching.

They were wed.

David floated into his future on a wave of hope. He'd married the hottest girl in the Haven, and she loved him more than anyone ever could. She was his like-vibration. Terry and Kattrice agreed the Haven would loan him money to start his electric and plumbing business, and he agreed to pay it back by being of service.

Service gets you closer to God.

Now, David stares into the forlorn firepit. He stands, stick in hand. This place isn't the way it was back then. The shadows creeping over the woods, running away from the setting sun . . . they're not a prelude to fun. Nothing is. He breaks the stick in two and throws it into the ash. The trees hide in the night, and he is alone. Somewhere out there, Samantha is alone too. She might be halfway to Elko by now, or—

"Samantha?" he calls.

Silence.

He thought he'd have found her by now. If what Monica told him was true—someone was out here shooting a gun today—then Samantha could be hurt, but no. It's unlikely a stray bullet hit her. It's not even hunting season. Monica must have been hearing things, or she made it up to get him to go. Either way, there'll be hell to pay if he comes home empty-handed.

With luck, Monica will be passed out on the couch. If not, the arguing will begin. She'll say he didn't try to find Samantha. She'll say he didn't put any effort into it, that he's not in the Teaching, but who on earth is he to mess with someone else's karma? Maybe getting lost in the woods is part of God's plan for Samantha.

Sebastian speaks for God, and he said David and Monica needed to adopt Samantha. He also said Monica was David's like-vibration. That may have been true back in the day, but David doesn't feel it anymore.

He stands. Wipes bits of bark from his pants. Gazes at the firepit. It's a foreign land. He walks down the hill and takes a left, heading deeper into the woods, walking away from Control Road. The sun hasn't completely disappeared yet. He still has time. "Samantha? If you're out there, just let me know. You don't have to come back with me. We just need to know you're all right."

A rock spire protrudes at an angle from the hillside, casting a deep shadow over the ground. He bends slightly and steps around the protrusion, careful not to trip over anything he can't see, but it's so dark. His stomach groans. He hopes his kids found something to eat for dinner.

If he hadn't wasted time arguing with Monica about lunch, he would have gotten an earlier start searching for Samantha. He might have found her before she made it too far. Fear is the opposite of love, and if he had done what Monica told him to do when she told him to do it, he would have been home by now, sleeping.

The Teaching says men must listen to their like-vibrations, and David is in the Teaching, but lately, he hasn't been able to listen to Monica.

He doesn't know what God wants of him.

Everything is so . . . empty.

A man ought to have meaning in his life beyond his like-vibration.

Beyond being of service.

Beyond . . . the Teaching?

He puts his hands to his face. His palms are rough. He presses on his cheeks, pulling back the skin, making his eyes water. The trees dim and blur. Their pine needles turn a deep green, and their bark turns black. The night turns everything black, but beneath a congregation of sagebrush, one rock stands out from the others like a jagged yellow tooth.

He takes his hands off his face.

The other rocks are dark gray and maroon. Normal.

He lifts a sagebrush frond off the ground and stares at what he has found.

It's not a rock.

It looks like a toy, but when he picks it up, the weight and the cold steel tell him it's real. Had it been black like a normal gun, he wouldn't have seen it. The entire thing, both the grip and the barrel, is a dark golden tan color. Camouflaged for the desert. For Iraq?

The gun feels good in his hand.

He presses a button, and the magazine drops out of the grip.

It's loaded.

This gun was not made for hunting. Not for around here.

He can't imagine whose it is or what they were doing with it, but he doesn't care.

That doesn't matter now.

What matters now is . . . it's his.

CHAPTER SIX

RAINE

It's Sunday morning, and I'm standing in the doorway of the trance room, half-in and half-out. My A-frame lies on the other side of the pine trees separating my road from Control Road. Java sleeps inside. I'd rather be with her.

People come down the road from both directions, joining together at the path to the trance room. The path winds between scattered plants and weather-worn statues—Buddha, Jesus, an angel playing a harp. The figurines look more like lawn ornaments than tributes to holy beings. Short and cheap.

Finding that note taped to my door last night has me on edge—*God is watching you*—but it shouldn't. Of course God is watching me. He always has. It's stupid. Whoever was hiding in my bushes left the note and ran to the firepit. Teenagers playing a prank. For the most part, the younger people aren't in the Teaching. They're not capable of thinking clearly and being honest. Sebastian says our frontal lobes don't develop until the age of twenty-five.

Another one of God's little mysteries.

At age twenty-nine, my frontal lobes are overdeveloped. I can't stop thinking about the note. I've been deep in my mind, trying to decide if I should tell Sebastian about it during Trance. The older people are so sensitive to things like this. If I say something, the rumors will start. Before long, they'll be blaming everyone in Elko for accusing us of running a cult. The older generation will assume someone left the note in an attempt to break up our community. I want no part of that, especially since it was probably a teenager pulling a prank.

The Gates family reaches the entrance to the trance room first. I step aside. Jerry and Amanda have lived in the Haven for over thirty years, and it shows. They're happy in the Teaching, and they're not bashful about it. They grin all the time like they know some big secret to happiness. They sit in the shadows near the front of the trance room. Candles flicker along the walls. The aroma of Nag Champa incense relaxes me, but I'd rather be at home with Java. I regret promising my mother I'd be here.

"Hello, dear," says a voice behind me.

I turn around and see Mary, our daycare leader. She looks up at me, her face pink and smiling. Working with her was my first job. She lost her only child to cancer years ago—decades ago—which is why I think Sebastian told her to run the daycare.

"Have you been feeling okay, Raine?" Mary asks. "We haven't seen you at Trance in—"

"I know. I've been busy with work."

"Of course you have, you blessed soul."

Across the road, a man in a white dress shirt and blue jeans gets out of a dented minivan. He slams the door. The door fails to latch, and he tries again, swinging harder. This time, when the door hits the frame, everyone on the path stops and looks.

He blushes, makes a sheepish smile, and waves.

Everyone waves back, except for Kattrice and Terry. Those two are at the end of the procession. Terry walks hunched over with his eyes narrowed like he does when preparing to trance. He'll enter the trance room, sit on his pillows, and his soul will leave his body. While it's gone, another soul, Sebastian, will take its place. Sebastian will tell us what he sees on the other side. Give us the Teaching. He died over six hundred years ago.

He is old.

He is wise.

I can't wait for this to be over.

The man in the dress shirt joins the crowd. He's carrying a notebook and wearing a pleasant smile. His teeth are not straight. One upper tooth angles east while the rest point south. It doesn't keep him from smiling. His shirt is pressed and his blue jeans look new. Obviously, nobody told him this wasn't church. Most of the guys coming down the path are wearing holey sweatpants, flip-flops, and T-shirts. Only the older women—the *wise* women—make any attempt to dress nice.

"Come," my mother says, grasping my elbow. "I want you to sit with me."

She pulls me inside the trance room. Candles sit at the base of all four walls, barely lighting the folding chairs. We feel our way to the front near Terry's pillows. Why my mother is making us sit right next to Terry and Kattrice, I don't know.

I turn and face the back.

Mr. Crooked Tooth sits near the entrance. David and

Monica are near him with their backs against the wall, holding hands. Shadows dance on the deep purple enclosure. David played music by the band Deep Purple when he painted the trance room for Terry. He had tried to make a joke out of it, but no one laughed. David has always had a quirky, albeit dark, sense of humor.

A woman steps into the entrance, blocking the outside light. "Ally," she says, "aren't you sitting with us?" It's Gail Pliskin, my mother's cohort in the older generation. She always wears her hair tied in knots. I would call them braids if that's what they were, but they're not braids. They're ratty old dreads.

"Not today." My mother's eyes twinkle in the darkness. "Today, my daughter and I need to be close to the Spirit."

Something sick, not evil but sick, squirms inside me. The note. I don't want to talk about it. With any luck, everyone will use up the time asking about their past lives. Trance never lasts more than an hour. Terry's body can't handle hosting Sebastian's spirit longer than that.

We sit.

We close our eyes.

People take their seats. The chatter falls to a low hum, and the doors close. All is quiet except for a few hushed breaths. People blow out the candles, and the room turns black. It doesn't matter if I have my eyes opened or closed now.

Terry's pillows make a wheezing sound when he sits.

Kattrice's wicker chair creaks beneath her. "Please, let us begin."

We sing. "In the times of our lives, praise God, praise God, praise God. In the lives of our times, praise God, praise God, praise God . . . PRAISE GOD."

"Hello, me children." The spirit voice of Sebastian rasps from inside Terry's body. His old British accent warms the room. "I be honored to speak to you today. You be the old souls of the highest seas. For many of you, this will be your last life on the earth plane for many millennia. For others . . . " His voice cracks. It scratches the air. "For others, and you know who I be talking about, you be doomed to repeat what you refuse to learn."

In the silence, I contemplate what I have refused to learn. It's meditative, and the silence is—

"Me ship is vast, people," Sebastian booms, "it sails on and on. I keep it clean of the negative. Your mind and your ego have no quarters on me ship. I love you all. Remember, I be here for you, me children of the highest seas. God's children. You are welcome to sail with me."

In unison, we say, "Thank you, Sebastian."

"Isn't that right, Katt?"

"Yes, Sebastian."

"Do you like how I call me medium's wife *Katt*?" he says. "It be cute, I think, calling her a cat."

Together, we laugh.

"Yes. It be funny," he says. "Laugh and enjoy your time. It's what God wants. But don't let your mind keep you from seeing. Don't let your ego tell you what to do. Listen to your children. They have more to teach you than you know. And do not mourn, for there be no dead, and there be no dying. On me ship—wait. Hm. Um. There be someone new here. Katt, did you know this?"

"Yes, Sebastian," Kattrice says. "Terry and I invited a guest."

"There be someone new. I do not see him with me eyes,

and no, it's not because there are no lights and no windows."
He lowers his voice. "You know, blocking out the sun is on
purpose. The rays are tough on me Terry's body when he
trances." He raises his voice. "It's because I do not need eyes
to see. I feel. I feel the newcomer's energy, and oh, he be a
kind soul. Shy, maybe a little afraid, but I think that's cute.
Isn't that cute, Kattrice?"

"If you say so, Sebastian."

"Hm, mm. The newcomer's name be Noah. A good
Bible name. Noah, would you like to introduce yourself to
me children?"

I couldn't be happier. This will chew up a lot of time and
I can get out of here without talking. Whatever my mother
is planning can wait. She said she was going to arrange a
private trance with Sebastian anyway, so I don't need to share
my mind today.

Then, my mother puts her hand on mine.

"I'm not sure," Noah says. "I—"

"Go on, there's nothing to fear," Sebastian says. "I don't
bite." He laughs. "I'm a spirit. I don't have teeth."

A few older women laugh.

"Okay, here goes. My name is Noah . . . I don't know
what to say. I've never been to anything like this before. I—"

"He's studying for a college degree," Kattrice says.

"Ah," Sebastian says. "A learning man. You came to the
right place for learning. What do you wish to know?"

"I'm studying religion for my masters."

"Ha! I be studying for me masters too."

Laughter fills the room.

"I be kidding you, Noah," Sebastian says. "Let me see.
What can I tell you about religion? Hm. Mm. Becoming one

with God is all the religion you need, you know. People on the earth plane group and classify things, they pull the wings off God's insects to see how they fly. Have your fun, Noah. Call one religion Buddhism, and another Catholicism. Call Jesus a saint and Buddha a teacher. There be but one God for all of man's organized faiths. Do you know what I be saying to you?"

Noah doesn't answer.

"Listen, everyone," Sebastian says. "Listen to the newcomer's pen move swift. He be writing in his little book. He *is* a learner."

"Sorry," Noah says. "I think I know what you mean. Your cult—"

"We are *not* a cult, Noah." Sebastian's voice echoes off the walls. "Do not confuse us with Charlie's children or those crazies who tried to catch a comet or—what was that sad soul's name? The one in your Texas, I think?"

"Koresh," my mother says. "David Koresh."

"Yes. Thank you, Ally. That man lost his way and the government blew him up, I think. Mm. Do not confuse us with some cult you saw on your TV. Do not confuse us with manmade religions. Me children live together in the Haven and share the Teaching, but they are no different than anyone else. They drink the bad beer and watch the footy ball games like the rest of the world. Don't they, Kattrice?"

"Yes, Sebastian."

"Mm. Let me see your energy, Noah. Yes. You have had many past lives. You be a gentle, old soul. Welcome to the Teaching. I know so much about you. I should let you know about me. Listen, people, this is how we share and learn from one another. This is how you should live out your purpose on the earth plane.

"In me last life, I be called Sebastian Smalls. I walked the deck of a great ship. It has been over six hundred years since then . . . maybe more, maybe less. I'm not sure. Time is different over here, you know.

"I sailed the seas from Great Britain to Africa. We traded everything, even people. It was wrong, but I learned many lessons in that life. Be careful because your eyes and ears can blind you. Do you know what I be saying to you? We are not a cult. We live to serve God's children, Noah."

My mind drifts to the note. Whoever left it is one of God's children. I must forgive whoever it was. I need to find out who it was.

"When you talk to the people in Elko, Noah, they will tell you about a kidnapping that happened here years ago. Ask them your questions and listen to them carefully. We have nothing to hide. We have no reason to kidnap because we are not a cult. We do not recruit. Me children come for the Teaching, and I teach."

Thoughts of the kidnapping scandal scathe my peace. I don't know why Sebastian brought it up. Our community had nothing to do with it. About six years ago, a deranged man kidnapped his stepdaughter to get his wife back. The whole town blamed us until the man was found eating breakfast with the girl at a Denny's in Idaho. But, until the girl was found, people in Elko sent death threats to us. We hired bodyguards. We lived with a curfew for safety.

They left notes like the one on my cabin.

People in "the world" don't understand.

On the bright side, this newcomer really has Sebastian on a roll. If this keeps going, I won't have to talk about the note. I don't need to scare everyone by bringing it up here.

"Noah," Sebastian says. "We welcome you. Don't we children?"

"Yes, Sebastian," we say together.

"Noah, me children have been hurt by newcomers before. It's hard for them to trust, but this is something they must learn. Forgiveness. Promise you'll be nice to me children. Promise you'll keep blame out of your studies. Learn with your heart, not your mind. You, too, can be closer to God if you let go of your mind. Will you promise?"

"Yes," Noah says. "I promise."

"Good. He's good, isn't he, Kattrice?"

"You would know."

The Nag Champa incense is pleasing. I need to order some the next time I go on the internet.

"Me medium's wife isn't feeling well today, and I know why." Sebastian's voice drops low, snapping me out of thinking about shopping.

Something is wrong.

The energy in the room changes. Compresses.

He's going to talk to me. I can feel it.

He knows about the note. He knows about everything.

I'm a child hiding something behind my back, and I don't want him to see what I've got.

He says, "Kattrice is feeling bad because of a material possession. Oh, the things your egos do to you over possessions . . . I'm not feeling well today either, people. Someone has stolen from me medium. If 'twere a light matter, I'd let it go. I'd tell Terry to get over himself. I'd tell Kattrice—get over it! But today, I cannot. Terry knows he should never have kept it. Mm. Hm. He kept it to remember his father by.

His blood father. Oh. Oh, no. I do not like weapons, people. Terry knows I am angry at him, doesn't he, Kattrice?"

"Yes. He does."

"Learn from your medium, people. Do not hide weapons. Do not own weapons. Terry hid a gun away from me like a squirrel for thirty years, and now, someone has taken it."

Low murmurs and gasps, butts shifting in seats—everyone feels Sebastian's disappointment.

"Who," Sebastian says, "has taken me Terry's gun? He had it hidden in his house. In his bedroom."

Silence.

"I do not allow guns of any kind in the Haven. I am very angry with Terry for having had one for so long. Do you know what will happen if the people of Elko think we are hiding weapons? What was his name, Ally?"

"Koresh," my mother says.

"Yes. Koresh. Who has taken me medium's gun?"

No one says a word.

CHAPTER SEVEN

DAVID

David sits with his back against the trance room wall, holding Monica's hand. The air is stifling. It stinks of incense and candle wax. Her hand is cold and sweaty, but he doesn't let go of it. To reaffirm everything is okay, he gently squeezes her fingers, and she squeezes in return.

Sebastian's voice emanates anger. "I will ask but one last time. Who has taken me medium's gun?"

The Teaching tells David he should speak up. He should describe the pistol he found in the woods. But he can't. He won't. His ego talks to him, tells him no one needs to know about the gun. He should follow the Teaching and speak up, but, like the trance room, the Teaching has become stifling. It's hard to breathe in here.

"So, no one is going to confess today . . . " Sebastian's voice drips with sarcasm. "This is one hell of a service. I can't even get them to confess in the dark, can I Kattrice? Come on, people. You must grow up to grow out. You must grow out of everything except God. Isn't that right, Monica, me child?"

Fear stabs at David's heart.

Monica lets go of his hand. "Yes, Sebastian."

"Yes . . . " Sebastian says. "Well, then, I will wait for a confession. Sooner or later, people, God will run you down. Another time, perhaps."

David breathes a touch easier knowing Sebastian is letting the gun go for now.

"Okay," Sebastian continues, "who can I be of service on this beautiful Sunday morning? You know the Christians say this is God's day."

"Sebastian?" Jerry says.

"Yes, me son."

"It's Jerry. I just want to check in."

"You sound troubled, me child."

"Yeah, well, I—I guess I am. I hurt my leg last week."

"I know. I know. You need to be more careful. You're not—what do they say? You're not a spring chicken anymore?"

"Yes, heh. I guess I'm not." Jerry's voice shakes.

David's not exactly sure how old Jerry is, but he's definitely past retirement age. Jerry has worked at A.J.'s Construction since David can remember, and there's always something wrong with him. Looking ahead forty years, David realizes he will end up like Jerry. No one in the Haven retires. There's always service to be done.

"It's just that," Jerry says, "it hurts real bad, and it's not been getting any better. I got a castor oil pack on it, but I don't think it's helping."

"Have you had Ally look at it?"

"No."

"Ally, will you look at his leg?"

"Absolutely, Sebastian."

"Thank you," Jerry says.

"And, me son, take a whiskey shot each night before you go to bed. You know what I be saying to you?"

"Yes. I will do that."

Sebastian raises his voice. "Who's next?"

"Sebastian?"

"Yes, me dear."

"It's Donna. I was wondering if you could tell me about my past life?"

"Which one?"

Everyone laughs, except for David.

"The last one, I guess," she says.

"Um. Mm. I don't see them in order. Let me check . . . there. Yes. You lived in France, teaching the children, centuries ago. Your mother was a teacher too, but I'm sorry to say, she's dead now."

He waits, but no one laughs. "Come on people, I'm joking with you."

A few of the women giggle.

Even if David weren't empty inside, he wouldn't have laughed. Death isn't funny unless you're dead.

His ego cracks.

Guilt tugs on his mind.

He has a gun at home. Terry's gun. If he says something, it will sound like he stole it.

Sebastian will eventually tell everyone David found Terry's gun. He sees everything from the spirit world, but he must let his children live out their own karma. Yet, if David says nothing for too long, Sebastian will tell Terry. Then Kattrice. Then everyone will know. They will all wonder why David kept the gun.

He had to keep it.

He couldn't just leave it there.

A kid might have found it.

No.

David did the right thing, but—oh, the feeling when he picked it up. It was like it was made for *his* hand. A gift from God. More real than anything else on the earth plane. It's his.

"Donna, me dear," Sebastian says, "in that life, you pranced among the grape orchards, leading the children of France in song. It be beautiful. Don't you remember? No? Of course not, but that be why. It be why everyone has come to the Teaching, to remember. Listen, I want everybody to review their past lives and think about what happens when your mind goes around and around, avoiding what God wants for you."

David once lived as a black man who escaped slavery in the late 1700s by hiding aboard a ship bound for Nova Scotia. When he arrived in Canada, the crew discovered him and promptly sold him to the highest bidder. He couldn't get away. Sebastian has told him about his other past lives, but this one stands out the most. It follows him like a slow-burning fuse.

"Who's next?" Sebastian asks.

"Sebastian?"

"Why are you crying, Mary?"

"I don't know. I—"

"You don't need to suffer this way, me dear."

"I'm just so full of fear lately."

"The anniversary is coming up, is it not? I know you miss him, but you must remember, there be no dead, and there be no dying."

Mary sobs. "He would have been twenty-one this year. I would have taken him out to the bars, and we—"

"I know." Sebastian's voice soothes. "He is here with me now."

"He is?"

"Yes, aboard me ship in the spirit world. He be a cabin boy, a surly grunt who casts an evil eye now and then, but he be a good boy. He loves you very much. You know he loves you, don't you?"

"Yes. Yes, I know."

"Leave a note to him in the Shrine. He would like that."

"Okay."

Mary lost her son to cancer when he was six years old. She's been cleaning Kattrice's house ever since. Service. According to the Teaching, being of service puts pain in motion and turns it into love. It takes away the worries of one's mind and frees the soul. But no amount of service will bring Mary's son back.

David wrings his hands. Service has made him a slave. It has not freed him of his mind.

Sebastian says, "David. You are troubled, are you not?"

He bites his lower lip. "I don't know."

"How are things betwixt you and Monica?"

"We're doing fine—"

"We've been fighting," Monica says. "I'm not sure what's going on with him."

"I be proud of you both, me children. Fighting be part of the process, learning what you don't have in yourself by seeing it in someone else. You be like-vibrations. Everyone, listen and learn. You will fight with one another, but you must do so with love. You must love your children, and Monica and

David know how to love their children. They be adopting their spirit child, you know. Tell me—how Samantha be?"

"That's the problem," Monica says. "She's gone, and David doesn't care."

David wishes he stayed home or went to work on that project in town or did anything but come to Trance. He can't breathe in here.

"Samantha be gone?" Sebastian asks.

"Yes. She took her things and ran away yesterday," Monica says.

"And David doesn't care?" Kattrice asks.

"Kattrice, your children be scared. Monica be filled with fear. Love your children when they be scared. You know what I be saying to you?"

"Yes."

"David," Sebastian says. "Tell me, what has happened?"

"I don't know. I came home yesterday and—"

"He didn't even want to go looking for her," Monica says.

"Let your husband speak," Sebastian grumbles. "Listen to him."

"I—"

"David, don't use your mind to think about Samantha. Ask your heart. Where has Samantha gone?"

David leans his head back. Presses it against the wall. Sebastian is asking him to meditate on Samantha. He hasn't seen her since he left for work Friday. Saturday morning, he went to fix Terry's toilet before she woke up. Stop it. Replaying these events is how one's mind tries to solve things. Breathe. Let the feelings flow. Search for the energy around Samantha. Meditate. What did she feel when she moved into his house? What did she feel when she ran away?

Nothing comes. His mind is a wall to the spirit world.

"Sebastian?"

"Yes, me child."

"I'm too worried to know where she's gone. I'm too much in my mind over this." He leans forward and puts his head in his hands.

"Oh, no." Monica's voice cracks.

"What is it, me dear?"

"I just realized—after Samantha ran away yesterday, someone was shooting a gun in the woods. What if it was Dad's gun? What if someone shot Samantha with Dad's gun?"

"Someone is shooting me Terry's gun in the hills? This is serious, children. Let me see—U-m-m. M-m-m."

David needs to end this before it's too late, but he doesn't know how to explain why he's kept the gun a secret so far. He pictures Sebastian descending from the heavens dressed in a woolen pirate shirt and pantaloons, slipping between the trees, hovering over the dry pine needles, watching David lift the sagebrush. Watching David pick up the gun, hold it, caress it, and put it in his pocket.

Sebastian booms, "I see."

David sits up.

"I have seen," Sebastian says, "but I am bound by God not to block me children's learning from the mistakes they make. I be but a teacher, and it be hard for me when I see me children stray from the path of God, but I cannot endanger their karma."

Monica says, "Can't you tell us anything?"

"Yes, I can teach, but you must listen to learn." Sebastian's voice deepens. "Me children, I tease me medium's wife sometimes, calling her a cat because of her name. But cats are creatures, you know. Kattrice be a soul embodied upon the earth plane. She not be a creature. Not a cat nor dog. None of you be creatures. Cats and birds and dogs, these be gifts from God, not members of your spirit family. God put them here for fun, I think. Do you know what I be saying to you?"

A moment passes before Monica speaks. "I don't understand. What can we do to find Samantha?"

"It's not you, me dear, but someone—someone chose to love their pet more than Samantha. This pet, this dog I think, it ran away in the woods too, and someone chose to leave Samantha alone to find it. Someone chose a creature over one of God's children." The air thickens. "Listen to me, people, much guilt can be gone if the dog's owner speaks now."

Silence.

David doesn't own a dog. He didn't leave Samantha in the woods to go find a dog. What is Sebastian trying to tell him? Jenny and Joseph have begged for a dog in the past, but David never wanted to pay for one. Another mouth to feed. He loves his children, but dogs don't like him. Raine's dog won't even come near him.

Java.

Sebastian is talking about Raine.

Monica said she saw Raine in the woods after Samantha ran away. Raine must have left Samantha to find Java.

"No one?" Sebastian asks. "No one has a cute puppy they wish to talk about? People, the Teaching tells us lying be but a wall built around our hearts to protect our minds. Our egos. Isn't this so?"

Silence.

"David, you be a fine teacher. Help me. Lying be wrong, no? Keeping secrets hurts others. No?"

"Yes, Sebastian."

"David knows the Teaching well, people. Listen to him. He knows it as well as anyone on the earth plane can know it."

Pressure builds inside David's chest. Why doesn't Raine say something? The air is stifling.

"David," Sebastian says, "tell us. Can lies come from silence?"

"Yes, Sebastian."

"How?"

"When someone knows the truth and keeps it secret, they are telling lies in silence."

"I love you, David," Sebastian says. "I love your wife too. Do not worry. Samantha be found soon. She be found when the deceitful silence be broken, and the truths about the dog and the gun and the forest see the light of day."

David's lie has him shipwrecked, alone and clinging to a plank in the middle of the ocean. If he hangs on, he'll bake in the sun. If he lets go, he'll sink. He'll drown.

"Listen to me, people." Sebastian's voice shakes the walls. "If you abide by me word, you truly be me children, and you will know the truth, and the truth will set you free."

CHAPTER EIGHT

RAINE

Trance always ends the way it begins.

We sing.

"Praise God, praise God . . . praise God."

Thank God that's over. I made it to the end without talking, but Sebastian knows. He knows I saw Samantha in the woods. He knows I left her to find Java.

Me cute puppy.

Everyone sits in the dark trance room, praying. Waiting for Terry and Kattrice to leave.

I pray Samantha finds her way to safety. My heart sank when Monica said Samantha didn't return last night. David and Monica don't need any more problems in their life. I pray for them.

The door opens, and the sunlight invades my prayers. One by one, people file out of the room behind Terry and Kattrice—Lord and Lady Windhaven. I let my mother exit first so she can join up with the older women. They have plenty to gossip about now.

Outside, my eyes adjust to the Sunday morning sun. Standing on the steps, I strain to see over the crowd. The path to the road splits our garden area. Red rocks and purple-flowered cacti surround a picnic table. Small Buddha and Jesus statues sit randomly throughout the bushes and weeds.

People cluster on either side of the path, talking about Trance. I spring down the steps and walk around a group of older men, looking for the teenagers. One of them left a note on my cabin last night. Not only do I want to know who did it, but now I want to know if they saw Samantha. She's still out there.

Somewhere.

David walks by and nods at me. I nod back, smiling. He doesn't return my smile. He looks tired. Broken. I should have said something about Samantha during Trance. Offered some hope, but I had none to give. I tried to stop her, but she was too fast for me. Despite Sebastian's prodding, I don't feel guilty for searching for Java.

Java is one of God's children too.

I love her.

Besides, Samantha is probably at David and Monica's cabin right now, unpacking her things. The Johansens and the Windhavens tend to overreact. Drama. Had I not stopped chasing after Samantha, I might not have found Java. When the gun went off the first time, I thought she might have been shot. Samantha was okay, so when she outran me, I turned around and went in the direction of my baby's barking. Was that really the wrong thing to do?

Am I in my mind about this?

Finding Java was as much my doing as God's.

The teens usually hang out under the willow tree behind

the trance room, but they're not there. I return to the gathering out front and see them standing next to the outsider, Noah. His name—*a good Bible name*—fits him. His hair is dark blond, thick and lustrous. He's got his notebook out, and he's talking to Kyle, Simon, and the teen David's dad is helping out, Jace. They smile while Noah gestures and speaks with a child's exuberance. These teens don't usually hang out with adults, but they seem enthralled. It's odd. These are the kind of teens who smoke pot during the week and get warrior tattoos on the weekend. Especially Jace. He's the kind who would think leaving a threatening note was funny.

Noah appears perfectly comfortable in the Haven. It's impressive. Listening to a dead guy speak through Terry's body for the first time usually sends newcomers running for the hills, but that's not the case here. And Noah isn't a desperate runaway. He has nice clothes. A minivan that runs.

I hate it when my mother is right. As a student, Noah could come to understand the Teaching. He could accept me despite my beliefs. I could get used to his snaggle-tooth. Terry invited him to Trance after one conversation, so there must be more to him than the average guy. Terry doesn't trust easily, so Noah must be trustworthy.

But those teenagers aren't.

God is watching you.

I plot a path through the garden, weaving around the statues, and my mother steps in my way.

"Why didn't you say something in there?" she says.

"I—"

She grabs my elbow. "Come with me. Over here."

"Why?"

She gestures with her eyes and nods in Monica's direction.

We stop near a golden Buddha bird fountain. Buddha is holding a finch in one hand and gazing up at the sky. His head is bald and he has a ridiculously toothy smile.

"What is wrong with you?" she asks.

"Nothing."

"A child is lost in the woods, and you saw her last, didn't you? Sebastian was talking about you, wasn't he?"

"That was yesterday. I don't know where she went."

"You haven't been coming to Trance, and—your silence. You heard what David said about telling lies in silence, didn't you?"

I shift my weight and lean to the left. Over her shoulder, I see Jace talking to Noah. The other teenagers have left. That's strange. Jace isn't exactly an expert on religion. Why is Noah talking to him? Jace has only been part of the community for about a year. Before that, he lived on the streets, going from one shelter to another in Las Vegas. That's what my mom said, anyway.

"Raine. Are you listening to me? I want you to come to Ladies' Brunch."

"No. I'm not going to spend my Sunday morning watching those old women get drunk and complain about their husbands."

"It's not just the old—Monica is going to be there, and she needs your support. Aren't you two friends anymore?"

Noah looks up the road and points. Jace does the same as if he's giving directions.

"Raine," my mother raises her voice. "Are you listening to me?" Her gray hair flies with the wind.

Jace and Noah turn their heads.

Oh my God, they heard her yell at me. I shield my face

and focus on my mother like I hadn't been watching them. She raises her eyebrows, expecting an answer. For a fleeting moment, I wish she had a scar through her right eyebrow so it would match the left. It's always bothered me that they don't match.

"I'm worried about you," she says. "I think you're in your mind. Did you listen to anything Sebastian said today?"

"Yes. I listened. I'm not in my ego. I—"

"Is Java the *cute puppy* he was talking about?"

"You caught me," I say. "Yep. I was looking for Java, but I didn't do anything wrong. There was no way I could have caught—"

She puts her hand in my face. "I've heard enough."

I brush her hand away.

She lifts her chin. Cocks her head to the side. "I'll call you later and let you know when to meet Terry for your private trance. You'd better pray for release from your mind."

"Whatever."

She stomps away toward the older woman. The *wise* women. Their eyes on me like ink on glass. Soon, everyone will know the cute puppy in the woods was mine.

I turn to see if Jace is still here, but Monica blocks my view of where I saw him last. She's talking to Zack and Shayla. David hangs off to the side, hands in his pockets. This Samantha thing really has him upset. I'd go talk to him, but I don't want to deal with Monica's drama right now. I love her like a sister, but when she has a tragedy, everyone has a tragedy.

Shayla catches my eye and heads in my direction. The sun strokes her auburn hair and glints off her pearly whites. I used to be jealous of her teeth, but I got over it.

"Hi, Raine, how have you been?" she asks.

71

"Great." I lean to the left, trying to see past her. I can't tell if Jace left or not.

"It's nice to see you here."

"I know, I know. I haven't been around much."

"I didn't mean that. It's just nice to see you. Are you still dating that guy?"

"No. We broke up."

"Oh. I'm sorry."

Monica walks away from David. She joins Kattrice, my mother, and the older women, all heading to brunch.

"Was it the Teaching?" Shayla asks.

"What? Oh—the breakup. Yes, isn't it always?"

"People in 'the world' just don't understand." She looks down at the ground. "I'm single again too."

I step to the right and my foot catches on a rock, forcing me to step back.

"Careful." She puts her hand on my shoulder. "Are you all right?"

"Yeah, I—"

"We should all get together and hang out sometime."

I peer around her shoulder, searching the road for Jace. "Sure. That sounds—" Noah's minivan isn't there anymore. "Can I call you later?"

"Are you sure you're okay? You don't seem like yourself."

"I'm fine." I walk toward the road. "I'll call you, and we'll hang out."

"Promise?"

I break into a run. Jace and Noah are gone, and so is Noah's car. There's no sign of them down the road. No Jace. No white minivan. No dust cloud hovering beyond the hill.

Noah must have driven away right after my mother yelled at me.

I scan the crowd.

Jace isn't there.

David walks toward me, heading for his cabin.

We pass each other, say hi, and continue walking.

His energy—his profound, distraught energy—sinks my soul and pushes the note to the back of my mind. David is in pain over Samantha.

He needs my help.

The Teaching says I should help him. Sebastian knows I saw Samantha in the woods yesterday. He knows I haven't been in the Teaching lately. If only I hadn't put my life on hold when I met Warren. I should never have stopped exercising, going for daily runs. I could have caught up with Samantha and brought her back. If only I'd practiced the Teaching rather than preaching it to Warren for the last two months, I could have been of service to the community. To my spirit family.

To David.

I consider cutting through the lodgepole pines rather than walking down and around Control road to my cabin, but it doesn't save much time, and the trail is rocky.

But I might not have much time.

Beyond my cabin, up in the hills, Samantha is alone.

She's out there.

Somewhere.

CHAPTER NINE

NOAH

"Thanks for letting me ask you about the Haven," Noah says.

Jace presses the button to lower the passenger side window of Noah's minivan and nothing happens. "No problem, man. Thanks for taking me to Home Depot."

"Sorry, that window doesn't roll down. It's broken."

The minivan moans into overdrive as they cruise down the hill out of the Haven. Jace lays back and props one of his Nike Airs up on the dash. He's long and gangly. A tattoo of a spiderweb with some indecipherable word scrawled across it peeks out from beneath Jace's shirt sleeve. Adolescent pimples and blemishes on his face shine in the morning sun.

Noah never thought he'd end up giving a ride to someone like Jace, but he never thought he'd spend a Sunday morning listening to someone "channel" a spirit either. Sebastian wasn't what he expected. Sebastian sounded old and wise but also funny and, ironically, very down to earth.

The news Samantha ran away from the Haven, though, has thrown a wrench in things. He can't convince her to come back to Las Vegas if she's gone. He's not sure what to tell her father. The runaway has run away, and someone was shooting a gun in the woods. Mr. Oakes has been through enough already. Noah doesn't want to be the bearer of bad news.

"Why do you want to know about the community so much?" Jace asks.

"I'm writing a thesis on alternative religions."

"For what?"

"School," Noah says. "Aren't you in school?"

"No way." Jace glances out the passenger window. "The world is too big to waste time on that shit."

Noah focuses on the road, holding back a smile. "I avoided school for a long time too."

"Why'd you stop?"

"I got tired of working dead-end jobs. You can only clean so many hotel rooms before your mind begins to go numb."

"I guess."

Pretending to be a UNLV student comes easier now. The more he talks about college, the more real it becomes. He's lying, but it's for a good cause, and he's not completely lying. The dead-end jobs did numb his mind—cleaning rooms, bussing tables, emptying porta-potties, landscaping expensive golf courses for snowbirds and movie stars. Maybe he should become a student someday, but first, he's going to become Baxter's right-hand man. He's going to find Samantha and bring her back to Vegas so Baxter will hire him. And pay him.

Then he will pay Titus, that is if he wants to keep his kneecaps intact.

"How long have you been living in the Haven?" Noah asks.

"About a year."

"What made you come?"

"It seemed like a good gig. They set me up with a place to stay and . . . I don't know. I was fine living on my own. It's not like I had to stay. It's just easier."

"What did your parents think?"

"My parents? Who the hell knows. They're probably dead."

"I'm sorry. I didn't mean to—"

"It's all right, man." Jace's voice is flat. "It's not what you think. I didn't run away or anything like that." He shifts his weight and leans against the door. "I don't like to talk about it."

Noah avoids eye contact. He's never talked with someone like Jace before. The minivan's air conditioning is pitiful, but Noah turns it up anyway.

They exit the hills, and the high plains desert stretches out before them, baking in the mid-day sun. Jace turns toward Noah and narrows his eyes. "Aw, what the hell. I guess, for your paper and everything, I'll tell you. My parents are the runaways. Assholes. For my twelfth birthday, they didn't come home. I stayed there a couple of days until I ran out of bread and peanut butter, then I went to a neighbor's house. Next thing I knew, I was living in a foster home, but that only lasted a month. I was in and out of eight foster homes before I left the system."

"How'd you find the Haven?"

"They found me, but like I said, I was fine living on my own. I can take care of myself."

"Of course." Noah glances at Jace's jeans pocket. There's a bulge like he's got a knife. It's thin like a switchblade.

Jace leans back, folds his arms behind his head. "It seemed like an adventure, you know? Vegas was getting old and that Johansen guy saw me outside a Denny's and, I don't know. We ate, and he told me about Sebastian."

"Do you like going to the trances? I mean, wasn't it strange at first?"

Jace grins. "You're kind of freaked out by it, aren't you?"

"No. I—"

"You want to know if I think it's real, don't you?"

"I didn't say that, but—do you believe it?"

"It doesn't matter what I believe. Terry's not hurting anyone. It's a pretty good life living in the Haven."

This is how it happens. People build a "community" in the mountains, then go to Vegas and lure runaways with free breakfasts at Denny's. It's like a bad movie. "Did you believe in trancing when you first came here?"

"Ah, don't do that, man. I already said it doesn't matter. I've got a place to stay now, and I'm not doing drugs. You know I was offered meth in almost every foster home I stayed in? And when they weren't trying to get me high, they were trying to have sex with me. How fucked up is that?"

"I'm sorry," Noah says. "You're right. It doesn't matter." He brings the minivan to a stop at an intersection. "For what it's worth, I'm glad you found them."

Jace gazes straight ahead.

Noah turns onto Lamoille Highway and heads toward Elko.

"It's not a cult," Jace says, breaking the silence. "Whether you believe it or not, Sebastian is always right. He knows everything."

Curious. Jace talks about Sebastian as though he is a real person. How long did Jace live in the cult before he started to believe in spirits? Maybe not long. Partway through the trance, Noah felt an urge to ask Sebastian about his past lives. It *was* intriguing.

"What else do you want to know?" Jace asks.

"Huh?"

"For your paper, man."

"Right." Noah could ask a hundred questions about what it's like to be brainwashed, but he doesn't want to offend Jace. Intriguing or not, everything about that place, even Jace's story, screams cult. Yet Jace says it's not a cult. "It's great how they help people. I heard in the trance that someone was adopting a girl. Does that happen often?"

"You mean Samantha?" Jace furrows his brow.

"Yeah. I think that was her name."

Jace takes his Nike off the dash. Sits up, bends forward. "They offered to adopt me, but I'm seventeen, and I wanted to live on my own. I don't think they were too serious about it either, not like Samantha. They really wanted her. A few others have been adopted, I think. I don't really know. In a way, the community is one big family."

"So that's why they were so upset Samantha ran away."

"Yeah, but I'm not surprised she left. She was really messed up."

"Oh?"

"Yeah." He looks out the side window. "She was kind of a bitch."

"I see."

"No, man. Sorry. I shouldn't have said that. Especially since she's gone missing and everything. I should, you know, be in the Teaching." He turns toward Noah. "We weren't like lovers in a past life or anything, which is too bad. She's hot. I dated her for a while but had to break it off."

"Is that why she ran away? The breakup?"

"I don't know. Maybe. It doesn't matter. I'm seeing a new chick now."

"Where do you think she went?"

"Probably back to her rich daddy's place in Vegas." His voice is filled with envy, laced with vinegar.

Noah plays dumb. "She was a runaway, like you?"

"I'm not a runaway."

"Sorry, I meant—she ran away from Vegas? From her father?"

"Yeah. Just because she's rich doesn't mean her life isn't messed up. Her mom left when she was a kid. Some kind of crack whore, or heroin junkie, or meth head, or—something like that. Her name was Gina. Samantha always made this lame ass joke, calling her mom Gina the Vagina. I didn't think it was funny."

"What about her dad?"

"Don't know much about him. Some big business man or something."

"Why'd she run away?"

"I don't know. Hated him, I guess. She didn't talk about it much. We only met a couple of months ago." He grins slightly. "She followed me to the Haven."

Noah eyes Jace.

"I didn't make her come with me or anything like that. We don't recruit people, man. It's like how Sebastian says. People come because of attraction, not promotion. Something like that."

It's a cult. It's exactly as Baxter Oakes explained. Samantha ran away from home, went to Elko, and was brainwashed by a cult. Maybe she was attracted to the Haven, but it's more likely she was attracted to Jace. Nice girls always want bad boys. "Why would she hate her father? I mean, it sounds like her mother was the one with the problems."

"I said I don't know, man. She hated them both. Whenever she talked about them, she'd get all shaky and shit. Except when she was making that stupid joke."

"And now she's run away again." Noah tries to hold it back, but he can't help himself. "If Sebastian knows so much, why didn't he say where she went?"

"Sebastian knows everything, man, but if he told us everything, it would ruin our lives. It's like he's not allowed to spoil our 'fun' while we're living out our karma here or some shit."

"I see, but—" Noah brakes at the stoplight. Elko snuck up on him when he wasn't looking. "Where do I go from here?"

"It's straight-ahead three more lights, then on the left."

The light changes. Noah presses on the gas. "I'm trying, Jace, but I just don't get it. They think Samantha is missing in the woods, and someone stole a gun. Shouldn't they call the police?"

Jace sits up and puts his hand on the armrest. "She's not missing, man. She ran back to her daddy, that's all."

"What about the gun?"

"What about it? I don't know anything about it." His face turns red. "And you can forget about anyone calling the police. They hate the police more than I do. Just forget about it."

"But someone should do something, shouldn't they?"

Jace slams his hand on the dash. "No. That's not how things are done."

"I'm sorry."

"You can let me out here." Jace pulls on the door lever.

Noah hits the brakes. "Wait, why? We're almost there."

The mini-can comes to a stop.

Jace glances around, then opens the door and gets out. "I'll walk from here, man. Thanks for the ride." He slams the door.

"Wait." Noah bangs on the window and hits the button, but it doesn't roll down.

Jace runs across the street.

Noah pulls ahead, parks, and takes out his notebook.

A car comes around the corner, and Jace begins to strut, but the girl behind the wheel doesn't notice him.

What it was he said that made Jace so angry?

Was it the gun?

Or was it the girl?

CHAPTER TEN

DAVID

David sits on the cold dirt floor of his shed, his back against the workbench, his tools hanging from the pegboard like crucified slaves. Sunlight shines through the cracks in the walls, casting thin gold bands over his legs.

When he got home from Trance, he walked behind his truck, unlocked the shed, and slipped inside without the babysitter seeing him. Cori is waiting for him inside the cabin. After what Sebastian had said, after telling lies in silence, he needed some peace before facing his children. He needed to embrace the Teaching and accept, truly accept, Samantha into his heart. Into his spirit family.

He closes his eyes and meditates on what might have happened to her. An image of the young blond teen lying next to the sagebrush pops into his head. She's bleeding from a bullet wound. She's dying.

He opens his eyes and rubs his forehead, pressing hard to rid himself of the image.

If something happened to Samantha, Monica will blame

him for not finding her. Kattrice and Terry will blame him, too. Sebastian said Samantha is part of his spirit family, and spirit families are stronger than blood. He must find her, or everyone will make his life a living hell.

Monica went to Ladies' Brunch after Trance as she always does. He pictures her, drinking Bloody Marys and mimosas, gossiping about him. Telling everyone he couldn't find Samantha because he didn't care. Because he's not in the Teaching. The other women believing her, blaming him, cackling and laughing, turning on him and all the other men in the Haven for not being as close to God as they think they are, as they think "the world" should be.

Stop it.

There's no changing what they think. How they blame. How they control.

He draws in a long slow breath and closes his eyes.

God, show me what happened to Samantha.

He sees her in the woods, but his mind is making it up. Imagining it. The image is not God's doing. It's a false memory. But then, a real memory surfaces. Jace trudging out of the trees and running up the road in the wake of David's dust. David was driving home from Terry's yesterday when Jace appeared, and he didn't stop the truck. He didn't know Samantha had run away.

He didn't know.

It's not his fault she's gone.

He opens his eyes and stands. Wipes a thin layer of sweat from his brow.

Cori will wonder why he hasn't come back from Trance yet. She'll have seen the others walking down the road.

But it's so pleasant inside the shed. Dark. Quiet. Peaceful.

Nonetheless, he pauses outside the shed to lock it. The heavy chain rattles in his hands. Maybe he can return after Monica comes home. Take a nap.

He opens the front door to his cabin, and Jenny runs to him. She wraps her arms around his waist, and he returns her embrace. "Dad. I beat Cori at checkers."

"You didn't beat me," Joseph says.

Jenny flashes an evil look in her brother's direction.

Cori puts her backpack on and heads for the door.

"How'd they behave?" David asks.

"Fine. We played games."

Jenny beams. "Cori's got a boyfriend."

"Is that so?" David muses.

A pink blush blossoms on Cori's cheeks.

"His name is Jace," Jenny proclaims.

"Cori," David says. "Wait a moment,"

"I really have to go."

"Just a minute. Are you dating Jace?"

She opens the door.

"Don't worry," David says. "I won't say anything to your mother."

"We're just friends."

Cori's mother isn't only in the Teaching; she thinks she *is* the Teaching. She's lost sight of the true meaning.

Like everyone, Cori is on this earth to find her like-vibration and learn from him so she can become one with the astral when she dies. One with God. But her mother, like the other women at brunch right now, is filled with pious judgment. She would never approve of Cori learning from Jace.

"Listen," David says. "Jace has had a tough life. It's made him rough around the edges, so be kind to him, okay?"

"Sure." She bounds down the steps, letting the wooden screen door slam behind her.

"Do you want to play checkers?" Jenny asks.

"Not now. I need to lie down. Why don't you see if you can beat your brother again?"

"She didn't beat me," Joseph says.

Jenny argues. Joseph yells. Jenny yells.

David walks down the hall to the bedroom and lies on his bed. He prays for silence. He prays for guidance. Sebastian is everyone's spirit guide, but David can't go to him. Sebastian knows David is telling lies in silence. He knows David has Terry's gun.

The kids yell at each other in the living room. The Teaching says to listen and learn from your children, but David's not getting the lesson. He just wants them to shut up.

That's my gun, he thinks. *Finders keepers, losers weepers. My gun.*

He rolls onto his side and rests his hand on the nightstand. He'd feel better if he could go to sleep. Monica might stay at brunch all morning and into the afternoon, but she might not. He wishes he had the energy to take the kids and go somewhere. Entertain them. Have fun with them. He loves them so much, but the weight of the world holds him down, and he can't get up.

Monica will eventually return with her collection of judgments and pick a fight. Again. She'll demand he finds Samantha.

He drums his fingertips on the nightstand.

He loves Samantha like a father, the same as he does all of God's children, but he can only do so much. He searched the forest for her already, and she wasn't there. Should he force himself to go again? Monica wants him to, but what does the Teaching say?

Nothing.

A chill races down his back.

He feels nothing.

Is he not in the Teaching anymore?

This emptiness, this inability to meditate and feel God's presence, this growing hatred for his like-vibration—his heart is empty, and his cluttered mind sinks to the bottom of a stagnant pond. And it drowns.

He sits up and puts his feet on the floor.

He opens the nightstand drawer.

His Holy Bible looks up at him. His Holy Qur'an, his Holy Vedas, his notes from the Teaching—Sebastian's trances on old cassette tapes—everything God has to give stares him in the face, and he wants to run away. Head out on the highway at high speed.

"David?"

He shuts the drawer. Monica's back early.

"In here," he yells.

She steps into the doorway, her Sunday gown hanging down. "We've got to talk."

"About what?"

"The women decided we shouldn't keep waiting to find Samantha. She's been missing for over twenty-four hours now."

David wipes his face and stands. "Okay. What do you want me?"

"They said this is your karma. You haven't been doing enough service, and now Samantha is gone."

The scent of tomato juice and Vodka radiates off her like heat rising off the highway. "First, you're going to write a note praying Samantha is safe and put it in the Shrine. Then, Mom wants you to fix their toilet again. It's still not working."

David glances at the nightstand, then closes his eyes. Monica hasn't read the Bible or the Qur'an or the Vedas in years. She has no reason to look in the drawer. His gun should be safe beneath the holy books.

"After you fix the toilet, you've got to go look for Samantha."

David pushes past her into the hall. "No, I don't."

"Yes, you do." She follows him into the living room.

He opens the front door, turns around, and points outside. "Jenny. Joseph. You guys need to go outside and play."

"Why?"

"You can take your game with you. Just go." Despite his best effort, his voice drops on those last words. His anger threatens to spill onto his kids, but he keeps it at bay, biting his lip. He motions for them to leave. Jenny gets a fearful look on her face, and Joseph angrily stomps his feet as he follows her outside, carrying the checkerboard.

Monica puts her hands on her hips and glares at David. "Well?"

"Why can't someone else go look for her?"

"Like who? The police?"

"No."

She goes to the kitchen. "Honestly, you're a fucking idiot, David." She opens the cupboard above the stove and pulls out a bottle of Vodka. "You want the Elko PD up here investigating us? They'll accuse us of kidnapping her. You know that, right?"

He stands at the window. Jenny and Joseph are setting up the game on the edge of the driveway where the weeds are short. The glug-glug of Monica's Vodka bottle trying to breathe sounds miserable. He listens to it splash inside her glass tumbler.

"Besides," she says, "even if it weren't us calling the police, they wouldn't care. Samantha was—I mean, *is* a runaway. The police don't care about runaways."

He gazes out the window. "Remember when we were going to run away?"

"What?"

"Remember when you, me, Zack, Raine, and Shayla were planning to go to Europe?"

"That was Raine's fantasy, not mine. Besides, we were kids then."

"What happened?" he asks.

"We grew up and had kids of our own, that's what."

He turns.

She leans over the kitchen counter, propping herself up on her elbows and stirring her drink with her finger. "Wait. Do you think we're going to Europe now? You can't run away from this, David. We talked about it at brunch and decided you need to love Samantha like one of your own. You haven't been acting like you're in the—"

"I'm in the Teaching." He grits his teeth. "What I'm not in is a barrel of money. Look around. Do you really think we can continue to afford all of this month after month?"

"All of this? We live in shit, David, but"—she looks at the ceiling—"God will provide."

"Bullshit." He faces the window. Joseph picks up a checker and throws it across the lawn, causing Jenny to turn red and yell at him. She runs to get it.

"Money," Monica says, "is love in motion. Samantha is part of our spirit family. The community will support us."

To hell with it. The community isn't going to pay for anything.

"David?" she says.

"What?"

"Look at me."

Begrudgingly, he does.

She walks around the end of the counter, clumsily making her way to the couch. Her gown flutters around her ankles when she plops her ass down. She puts her tumbler on the table and attempts to fold her legs into the Lotus position. "I've been meditating a lot lately. I'm starting to trance."

This is unbelievable. She can't trance. There is no way in hell God would let one of his high-order souls speak through her. She closes her eyes and begins to hum. David wants to laugh and scream at the same time.

"M-m-m . . . Um-m," she says.

He swears to God, if she speaks in some fake voice, he's going to the bedroom, opening the nightstand, and taking out the gun—no.

He can't do that.

He'd never do that.

If she gets to be too much, he'll leave. He'll go to the shed and lock himself inside.

"M-m-m." She opens her eyes and stares straight ahead, focusing on nothing. "There. I see it. It's in the forest."

David clenches his jaw.

She says, "I hear it. Gunshots, like yesterday. I see a gun." Slowly, she raises her gaze. Their eyes meet. "Do you know anything about Dad's gun?"

His legs tense up. "No."

"You were at his house fixing the toilet yesterday, and you were there the day before that. His gun was in the back closet."

"What are you saying?"

She closes her eyes.

This isn't happening. She can't possibly know about the gun. He didn't steal it. He wouldn't steal it. He found it.

But someone else did steal it.

Jace?

Jace *was* coming out of the woods yesterday.

Dammit.

Jace must have stolen Terry's gun and gone into the woods to shoot it. He must have dropped it, or maybe he hid it under the sagebrush. David taught him better than this. Deception, in any form, goes against the Teaching. The Teaching has failed Jace, and . . . the Teaching has failed David.

Another chill shoots down his back.

Without the Teaching, what is there?

Monica rests the backs of her hands on her knees, tips her head to the side. Sways to and fro.

"Do you think I took the gun?" David asks.

"I'm not going to answer that."

"I didn't take Terry's gun."

When she inhales, David feels like he's going to suffocate.

When she exhales, it smells like the cabin is going to catch on fire.

She says, "The truth will set you free, David. It's like Sebastian said in Trance today, sooner or later, God's going to run you down."

CHAPTER ELEVEN

RAINE

Spring is here, but it's still chilly in the Haven.

I park my car at home, grab a jacket, and head for Terry and Kattrice's. My mother and I haven't spoken since she yelled at me after Trance on Sunday. The easiest way to end the silence is to do what she said. Meet with Terry for a private trance. I promised her I would, and it will make her happy.

I'm not late for my meeting with Terry, but I cut through the trees to Control Road anyway. The temperature rises and falls as I step in and out of the early evening shadows. Spindly old pine needles cling to dry branches, and the path is cracked. As always, we could use some rain.

I told my boss at the law office I had a doctor's appointment so I could leave early today. That makes me guilty of lying—even half-truths are lies—but I couldn't stay there another minute. Besides, I *do* have an appointment with a doctor. Sort of. Terry will trance Sebastian, and Sebastian *is* a doctor. A therapist. One on one, he helps people talk through their problems.

The path exits near the trance room, and I step onto Control Road.

Despite what my mother thinks, I don't have any problems to discuss with Sebastian. None I want to discuss. I've decided the note left on my door was a prank. I suspect Jace did it, but I don't know for sure. I never caught up to him. It could have been any of the teenagers, but it doesn't matter. Just kids having fun.

I guess my biggest problem is David. He was so distraught over losing Samantha Sunday. After I saw him woefully walking along the road, I went into the woods near my cabin and checked the place I'd last seen her last. Then I spent the afternoon searching the hills. Java had a great time, but I had no luck. I searched for her again after work on Monday and Tuesday. Asked around town. Nothing. Because I saw her last, I feel responsible, though her disappearance wasn't my fault.

Poor David.

She probably made it to the highway on Saturday, hitched a ride, and caught a bus to Vegas, making fools of us all.

Coming around the corner, I'm struck by the size of Terry and Kattrice's cabin. For some reason, it always affects me. Logs twice the size of any other place in the Haven hold up the three-story edifice. On the bottom floor, three picture windows look over a massive deck with wrought iron tables and chairs. Forest green trim borders the windows on the upper floors and silky, white curtains hide the inside. Their lawn is forever lush and runs along Control Road like an oasis.

By now, Terry will be getting ready for me, preparing to trance Sebastian.

My guess is my mom wants Sebastian to guide me on my purpose in life. She's wanted me to quit my job and work for someone in the Teaching for a long time, and the way this week has gone, I'm starting to agree. There's not much purpose in filing affidavits and making phone calls for whiny, lawsuit-happy money-grubbers.

The Shrine sits at the far end of Terry's property, surrounded by the tallest trees in the Haven. White gardenias surround the little building, hugging the walls. It's not much bigger than an average shed, and I'm sure outsiders mistake it for one when they drive by. Christ on the cross, a crescent moon mobile, a ceramic plate with an Aum on it, and a Star of David ornament hang from the peaked roof over the doorway.

The Teaching welcomes all faiths.

Being this close to the Shrine, I can feel the energy. Inside, tucked between candles and photographs of loved ones, hundreds of letters to God wait to be answered. No one is allowed to read them.

Only God.

Ahead, David comes down the front steps of Terry's cabin. He has his toolbox in one hand and a plunger in the other. His head is hung low. I wish I'd found Samantha. He heaves the toolbox into the back of his truck and looks my way. I wave at him, and he nods. His cheeks are sunken, and his eyes are listless like he hasn't eaten or slept in days.

I speed up, but he gets in his truck and pulls away before I get there.

Standing in the wake of his dust, I wonder what life might have been like if Sebastian hadn't said Monica was his like-vibration back in high school.

"Raine." My mother appears on the deck. She's wearing her Sunday best on a Wednesday. "Hurry, you're late."

Not true. It's only a minute past four.

"Terry is leaving his body. Hurry."

I follow her inside. Kattrice stands in the hallway wearing gray sweatpants, a matching sweatshirt, and a headband with the word *Hope* on it. If I'm not mistaken, it's her slippers that smell like potpourri and cheese.

"Can I use the bathroom?" I ask.

"Sure," Kattrice says. "But I can't promise you it'll work. Make sure there's a plunger in there before you flush."

"No," my mother says, pulling me down the hall, "we don't have time."

We scurry into the master bedroom.

Terry is seated in the middle of a canopy bed with his legs crossed, surrounded by red pillows. His long, white hair flows down over his thick, handwoven hemp shirt. The wooden buttons are unfastened, exposing a tuft of ivory chest hair. He moans and sways, his eyes scrunched tight.

My mother pushes me toward the love seat in the corner and tells me to sit down.

I smell bacon mixed with incense and notice the remnants of a BLT next to the bed. That must be Kattrice's side.

"M-m-m. Hello, me children of the highest seas. Be you well?"

His British accent never gets old.

"Hello, Sebastian," my mother and I say.

"Raine," he says. "Such a pretty name . . ."

"Thank you."

"And Ally, I feel your joy. It be so nice. How can I help your daughter today?"

"Work." I blurt it out like I'm in a hurry. "It's been . . ."

Boring?

That's what my mother wants me to say, but it sounds so stupid now.

"Work has been what, me child?"

This is harder than I thought. I wish I hadn't seen David outside. "I don't know, I—"

"Relax," Sebastian says. "I love you, you know. Your mother loves you too."

"I know."

"The problems at work be not your true troubles," he says. "Those problems be nothing more than your mind playing games with your time. They be temporary; they will solve themselves. I want to know about the problems that be keeping you from sleeping, me dear?"

He's right. I've laid awake each night, thinking about everything—the note, Samantha, David.

"Raine, do you hear me?" he asks.

"Yes."

"What be keeping you awake?"

"I'm worried about Samantha." I glance at my mother. "Is she all right?"

"I be worried about you," he says. "You do not sleep well because you be keeping something inside. A secret."

"I was the last to see her. I left her to go find my dog, but I've been looking for her everywhere since. Really, I—"

"I know, me child. I know."

The light from the hallway changes. Kattrice stands in the doorway, leaning against the jamb.

"Do not feel guilty, me child." Terry's head tips back. His eyelids flutter and his tongue lolls over his lower lip. "Guilt be self-serving. God's purpose be not to condemn you, nor be mine. Do you know what I be saying to you?"

"Yes. But I don't know what to do."

"M-m-m."

My mother grins. Why is she grinning? This isn't funny. She sees me looking at her and puts her palms together as if to pray, then she covers her mouth, but I can tell she's still grinning.

"Raine." Sebastian's voice makes the canopy shake. "Samantha must be found for reasons beyond your guilt. Beyond David's guilt. Beyond Monica's guilt. Samantha be important to the Haven in ways no one understands. Her blood family treated her very badly, you know. You must find her and help her."

"I tried, but I'll keep trying."

My mother bounces like a little kid about to go on an amusement ride.

"You looked for her, but there be another way. I have met your spirit guide, Raine. Her name be *Cecilia Roman*. That be a nice name, no?"

A tear runs down my mother's cheek. "Oh, yes." The joy in her voice irks me. "That's a wonderful name."

"Terry has agreed to teach your daughter how to trance, Ally." Sebastian's voice softens. "Cecilia wishes to speak through Raine's corporeal being to help us find Samantha. She is a very old spirit, and she is wise, much like me self." He laughs.

My mother clasps her hands together.

"Raine," Sebastian says. "Will you allow Terry to teach you the ways of trance?"

"I don't understand. I . . ."

My mother acts like I just got accepted to Harvard.

Me? Trancing? I'm not the most spiritual person. I cuss. I eat meat. I always fall asleep when I meditate. I—

"Raine," my mother says, "what are you waiting for?"

"I'm not the right person, Sebastian. I don't pray as much as I should. I don't know the Teaching like you think I do. David knows it the best. Maybe he—"

"Cecilia is *your* spirit guide," Sebastian says, "not David's."

My mother folds her arms and cocks her head at me. Behind her, Kattrice rolls her eyes and turns away. She walks down the hall like she has something better to do.

"I love you, me child." His voice is gentle. Clean. "Ask God for guidance. Pray to him tonight. Write a note and put it in the Shrine. Trancing be the highest service one can perform, but it does not come for free. Take time. You will make the right decision."

"Thank you, Sebastian."

Terry's shoulders hunch forward. "I must leave me medium's body now. He needs to rest. And—" Sebastian chuckles "—Raine needs to use the bathroom, don't you, Raine?"

"Thanks for reminding me."

"I love you me children . . . m-m-m."

Terry lies back on the bed, and Kattrice suddenly reappears in the doorway. She motions for us to leave the bedroom.

I don't look at my mother. My bladder is about to burst, and I don't want to have this discussion. It's my choice, and Sebastian said I have time. I race down the hall and duck into the bathroom.

I hear them talking.

"When someone offers you the chance to get this close to God, you take it," Kattrice says. "What's wrong with her?"

My mother's voice is soft, muffled like she's crying. I can't understand her words.

"We need the adoption to go through," Kattrice says. "That child belongs in the Haven."

My mother speaks up, her voice a set of shaky wind chimes. "I know. I'll talk to her. She'll make the right choice."

"She better."

I stand and pull up my pants.

"She will," my mother says.

The bathroom smells like lavender and potpourri and pee.

I've got to get out of here.

I've got to find Samantha, but trancing? Letting someone—some spirit—take control of my body so I can ask them where she is?

There's got to be another way.

I flush the toilet and the bowl begins to overfill.

I look everywhere, but there's no plunger.

The water pours over the rim and splashes onto my Birkenstocks.

This is unreal.

A LETTER FROM THE SHRINE

Dear God,

I've never believed in you before, but Sebastian told me to ask for your help. I want to stay in the Haven. He said I should always tell the truth, and the truth is, I'm scared. When they find out what happened, they'll hate me. I don't want to go, but maybe I should. If I do, I know I'll be okay. I still have a gun for protection, but I hate it.

I hate that it's his.

God, what should I do? If I tell everyone what happened, they'll blame me. Will you help them understand it wasn't my fault? Will you make it so I can stay?

Love,

Samantha

CHAPTER TWELVE

DAVID

David pulls into his driveway and sighs.

After he fixed the seal on Terry's toilet earlier today, he tested it, and the seal worked, but the toilet clogged. His auger wasn't long enough to unclog it. Rather than listen to Kattrice berate him for the hundredth time, he left without saying a word. She has two other bathrooms. She can wait until the next time he goes to Elko and buys a longer auger. It's only Wednesday. He's already put in thirty hours on customer calls and four hours on her toilet this week.

She can wait until he has rested. Until he's had time to sort things through.

Until he has decided what to do with his life.

What to do with the Teaching.

The kids aren't playing out front like they were when he left. He walks around back and they're not there either. He goes in the back door, tosses his keys and wallet onto the bedroom dresser, and heads for the living room.

"Mon? Where are the kids?"

He finds her on the couch with her eyes half-closed and her arm dangling off the edge. She's traded her tumbler for a 7-Eleven Big Gulp cup. It's been one of those weeks.

"Hey, are you awake? Where are the kids?" He pushes on her shoulder.

"They're at Shayla's."

He takes his jacket off and throws it over a dining chair on his way to the kitchen. It stinks like a dumpster in here. The counter is covered in bits of shredded cheese, lettuce, and broken taco shells. Beads of water cling to the blender. An empty ice tray sits cock-eyed on an opened Pop-Tart box. Silver wrappers are everywhere. The lid to the salsa rests by the sink, but the jar is upside down on the floor.

Her Tequila bottle is half full. She'll probably make herself another margarita before bed. Without ice.

He opens the dishwasher and puts some dishes inside.

Monica yells from the living room. "Did you get my dad's toilet fixed?"

"Yes."

"Did you put a letter to God in the Shrine?"

"Yes."

"Did you ask for a private session with Sebastian?"

David wipes the counter, catching bits of taco shell in his hand. "No."

"Come in here. We need to talk."

He tosses the taco shell bits into the trash, puts his hands on the counter, and closes his eyes.

"David?"

"What?" He shouts.

She marches into the kitchen.

He picks up the blender and turns toward the sink.

"Don't dump it—there's still some left." She raises her cup.

He puts the blender back on the counter.

She empties it into her cup.

He walks into the living room. "When are the kids coming back? Is Shayla bringing them, or do I have to go get them?"

"You really don't care, do you?"

"About what?"

"About Samantha. She's still gone, David." She peers around the corner from the kitchen, leering at him. "Why didn't you ask Sebastian for help when you were there?"

He sits on the couch. His knees hurt when they bend. "You mean Terry? He was busy."

"We've got to find her. I know you don't want her here because of money, but that's just you being in your mind—"

"Stop it." David bites his lower lip. He massages his upper leg, but he can barely feel his own touch. Pinpricks sting his skin. "You didn't want her here either."

"What?"

"You're jealous of her."

"I am not." She comes around the corner.

The cabin sways on its stilts, and David wonders if it would be possible to get a loan to pay for a new foundation. A loan from a bank, not the community.

Monica stands over him, cup in hand. "I'm not jealous."

"Oh, no? Why do you two fight all the time?"

"I'm her parent. She's out of—she needs someone who will discipline her. You're a pushover." She raises her cup and her drink sloshes onto the floor. "You need help being a parent. I want you to talk to Sebastian next time you go over there."

David picks up the remote control, sits back in the couch, realizes he's too tired to watch TV, and puts the remote back on the coffee table.

"Actually, never mind." She wipes margarita off her cheek. "You don't have to talk to him."

"And why is that?"

"I've been meditating. Trancing. My spirit guide spoke through me for the first time today. Isn't that great? You can get the Teaching from him from now on."

David looks at the photos hanging above the living room window. Jenny. Joseph. Monica in her white dress, standing beneath the wedding arch by the trance room.

"Look at me, David." Her eyes shake. "You don't get it. You're always so worried about money. Don't you see how great this is? Once I begin trancing, we can collect tithings. Everyone will come to me for help. We'll have more money."

She thinks she's going to be a trance medium. That's rich. She thinks she's going to help people like Terry does. Daddy's princess trying to be queen.

She puts the cup to her lips and opens her eyes wide as she knocks back another glug.

"I thought you were worried about Samantha?" he says.

"I am. That's why I'm starting to trance. I spent all afternoon meditating, and guess what I saw."

"I'm going to bed. Feed the kids when they get home." He stands up.

"Listen to me, David. My spirit guide showed me images of someone shooting Samantha. I heard a gun go off just like the other day. The day she disappeared."

He stops.

She laughs. "You should have seen the look on Raine's face

when we heard that gun. She jumped so high. Her and that stupid—she said she was out there looking for her stupid dog." Monica takes a drink then stares into her cup as if she's reading tea leaves. "What do you think Raine was doing out there?"

"Raine's got nothing to do with this. If she said she was looking for her dog,"—he grits his teeth—"then she was looking for her dog."

"I don't know . . . " Slurp.

He walks into the kitchen and grabs a glass. Goes to the sink.

"Where were *you* when I heard the gun?" Her voice echoes off the walls.

He fills the glass with water. "Drop it."

"I'm just asking. You've been acting really strange lately. You could have stopped on your way home from Terry's and gone into the woods and—"

"Drop it," he yells back, spilling the water. "I was on my way home. What were you doing in the woods? Maybe you—"

"I never went into the woods. Raine came out before I could go in."

"And then you heard the gun go off, right?" He comes around the corner carrying his glass of water. God it would feel good to dump it on her head. Put her fire out. "How could Raine have shot the gun if she was standing right there in front of you?"

She squints. "Okay, but you—"

"I was home before you," he says. "I couldn't have—"

"If you had anything to do with this, David. I swear." She swirls her cup. "You know what will happen."

"What?"

"If I can keep trancing, I'll find out who was shooting

in the woods. I'll find out what happened to Samantha. You better watch out. You're not telling me everything."

He turns, looks at the kitchen. The cabinet door by the fridge hangs askew. That's new. "It wasn't me, Mon. But I do have an idea who—"

"I knew it. I knew you knew something. Who?"

David turns toward her. She's red with excitement. "It doesn't mean he shot anyone, but he might have seen her. She might have told him where she was going."

"Who?"

"Jace was coming out of the woods when I drove by."

"He did something to her—I just know it." The glee makes David ill. "They had an ugly breakup. He's getting revenge. I know it. I just know it."

David charges down the hallway. "You don't know anything."

"I know what I saw when I tranced." She trudges in behind him, breathing heavily. "Has Jace been hanging around with you at my dad's lately?"

"No. I haven't seen him there." He reaches the bedroom and turns to face her.

She stumbles, leans against the wall. "Then how did he steal the gun? Did you take it and give it to him?"

"What are you on?" He points at her glass. "Did you put shrooms in there or something? I'm going to bed. I'll talk to Jace tomorrow and find out what he saw."

Her eyes begin to close, and she slides down the wall. Her body puddles onto the floor.

"Monica? What are you doing?"

She shakes her head. "I'm going to practice trancing my spirit guide." Her voice is slurred. "I'm going to be a medium."

"I wouldn't bother."

She looks up at him. "Why?"

"I just wouldn't, that's all."

He heads for the bed.

She struggles to her feet. "Why? Tell me."

"Because. I overheard Terry and Kattrice talking. They're going to teach Raine how to trance." David turns around in the doorway so he can see her reaction. "Terry's going to give her lessons."

Monica shakes. She tightens her grip on the Big Gulp until the plastic rim cracks. "You're lying."

He turns toward the bed, hiding his smile. When he pulls on the covers, something smacks him in the back of his head. Liquid runs down his neck, chills his back, and he turns to see her cup lying on the floor.

Her eyes are on fire. "You're not in the Teaching, David."

He gazes at the nightstand, wiping margarita off his shoulder. It would be so easy to open that drawer, reach inside, and take out the gun. But he could never go through with it. Even in moments like this, she's one of God's children.

There's a knock at the front door. Shayla calls out, "Hey. Are you guys here?"

Monica stumbles past David and flops onto the bed. "You get it."

David walks down the hall into the living room.

"Daddy," Jenny says, running past Shayla. She gives him a big hug around the waist.

"Thanks for watching them again, Shayla."

"Where's Monica?"

"She's taking a nap."

Joseph goes to the couch and turns on the TV.

Jenny joins him.

"Did you want me to tell her something for you?" David asks.

"No. I was just wondering . . . is she doing okay? I'm worried about her."

"I know. This whole thing with Samantha has her kind of messed up, but she'll be okay."

Shayla glances at the kitchen then focuses on David's shoulder. "Just so you know, when I picked up the kids, we had a fight. I told her that just because Sebastian says his children should drink as much as they want and have fun, it doesn't mean she should get drunk all the time."

"Oh, yeah? How'd she take that?"

Shayla casts her eyes down. "I just wanted to apologize. I shouldn't have spoken against the Teaching."

"You're okay, Shayla." He puts his hand on her shoulder. "I'll talk to her. She probably won't even remember it."

"Thanks."

David follows her outside and watches as she gets in her car and drives away.

Everyone fights with Monica. Everyone except Raine. It's something David has always loved about Raine. She only sees the good in everyone. She lives in the Teaching without having to try.

For David, being in the Teaching has always meant work—physically, mentally, and emotionally. This latest string of fights, the accusations, the Tequila—none of it will end until he finds Samantha. Monica will persist until she gets her way. She'll accuse him of not being in the Teaching, over and over. As Samantha's spirit father, David *should* find her. He should stop at nothing. But he's so tired.

She's not *really* his child. She shouldn't be his problem.

But that's a horrible thought.

But—it's only horrible for someone in the Teaching. Horrible for someone who truly believes in spirit families—the reuniting of souls who knew each other in past lives. It's only a horrible thought if David wants to be in the Teaching.

And if he doesn't . . .

He rubs his chin. His hands are dry and his whiskers are rough.

The Teaching is all he's ever known. If he lives outside the Teaching now, like someone in "the world," if he stops teaching the Teaching to newcomers, then who is he? And how will he stop Monica from making his life a living hell?

What rules will he live by?

If he's not in the Teaching anymore, then . . .

Then there's always the gun.

The stars are out.

He considers going to the shed, but he left his keys in the bedroom. The thought of going back inside and listening to Monica snore all night makes him want to kill himself.

It's quiet out here.

Serene.

Peaceful.

But the quiet doesn't last.

Somewhere up Control Road, beyond Raine's A-frame, up the trail past the firepit—a gunshot rings out.

CHAPTER THIRTEEN

NOAH

Friday evening in the Haven is nothing like Vegas. There's not a soul to be seen. No lights. No stream of cars cruising down the strip.

Noah drives down Control Road, heading for the Johansen's. It took him all week to set up an interview with David and Monica, and now he's late. The clock in the dash of his minivan says it's five after six. Every day this week, David canceled because of work. His plumbing business must be doing great.

Noah guns the accelerator.

If he misses his chance to interview the couple tonight, he might have to wait until Monday.

That won't impress Mr. Baxter Oakes.

A week has gone by, and Noah has nothing to show for it. Mr. Oakes nearly broke down on the phone when he found out his daughter ran away from the Haven. Once again, Noah promised to find her and bring her back to Vegas. Mr. Oakes offered to pay for Noah's expenses. He said money is no object. This was music to Noah's ears, but it was bittersweet. He needs money to pay off his gambling debt—avoid losing his kneecaps to Titus—but listening to Baxter's voice tremble on the phone got to him. So sad.

To become Baxter's right-hand man—his well-paid confidant—Noah must find Samantha and bring her back, but until then, he'll need to console Baxter every time they talk. He has worked a lot of jobs, but grief counselor isn't one of them.

He drives past the first cluster of cabins in the Haven and holds his hand up to block the setting sun. Thin lodgepole pines stretch into the sky, casting shadows across the dirt road, creating a strobe-light effect on his windshield. The route winds through the trees until straightening out in front of the Windhaven's cabin. Their residence takes up three lots and has the most beautiful lawn of any place he's seen so far. Unlike the other lots, theirs actually *has* a lawn. The other places have weeds growing through swaths of dry pine needles.

Terry and Kattrice are clearly the cult's leaders.

He's late for the interview, but curiosity compels him to slow down. He looks in the Windhaven's windows, hoping to see someone milling about. What do they do when the ghost of Sebastian Smalls isn't speaking through Terry?

On the edge of the Windhaven's estate, a copse of incredibly tall pine trees surrounds a shed with a cross and other religious symbols hanging from its eves. White gardenias grow in a horseshoe around the shed, and a string of white Christmas tree lights borders the open doorway. It's like a petite wedding chapel.

There is a touch of Vegas in the Haven, after all.

It's ten minutes after six now.

He guns the accelerator.

A dark shape runs across the road.

He slams on the brakes.

His chest hits the steering wheel as the minivan slides to a stop, sending dust up over the hood.

Whatever it was, he can't see it now.

A woman in tight white shorts and a blue top appears in the middle of the road. "Java. Stop."

A black dog shoots up over the grill and barks at Noah.

He jerks his head back.

Frothy drool drips onto the windshield.

"Java!" The woman pulls on a leash, and the beast falls off the hood.

He opens the door and steps out.

She kneels, restrains her dog by the collar, and strokes its head. She's wearing a silver whistle around her neck like a gym coach. It dangles freely, glinting in the evening sun.

"Stay back," she says. "My dog doesn't like men."

"I'm sorry. I didn't see you."

She stands up and brushes dirt off her shorts.

Noah is struck by the blueness of her eyes. It must be an illusion. He looks toward the setting sun and verifies the rays are coming across the Haven at just the right angle to make her eyes glow like sapphires.

Her dog breathes heavy, its tongue hanging out of its mouth. It's not growling, but it's not laughing either.

"You shouldn't drive so fast," she says.

Her dog bounds toward Noah, barking.

She pulls on the leash, but it's one of those retractable ones, and the line snaps. Noah grabs the door handle, but he can't get it open before the mongrel is on him.

"Java. No!"

The dog pushes him face-first against the minivan. He twists around, expecting to see bare teeth, gums dripping with saliva, but the dog backs off. It sits and pants, tongue lolling to one side. Happy.

The woman rushes over. "I'm so sorry. She doesn't like—"

Noah kneels and rubs the dog's ears. "It's a she?"

"Yes. I—this is amazing."

"What's her name?" He asks as he stands up.

"Java." The woman puts her hand to her head. "I don't understand. She hates men."

The dog's tan and black fur shines, and her soft brown eyes glisten. She looks up at Noah like she knows him. Like she's saying, *Hey, I'm your dog too.*

"She's beautiful," he says.

"I know. I got lucky. She was a rescue."

"My name is Noah." He holds out his hand.

"I'm Raine."

They shake hands and . . . it wasn't the angle of the sun. Her eyes *are* that blue.

He remembers seeing her after the trance last Sunday. The woman with the long gray hair he caught spying on him in the diner had yelled at her outside the trance room. If he hadn't wanted to interview that teenager so badly, he would have talked to her then. He'd also wanted to confront the older woman, but after what Mr. Oakes had told him about the cult, he decided not to. He didn't want to draw too much attention and risk being pushed out of the Haven like the private investigator Mr. Oakes originally sent.

"Do you live here?" he asks.

"Yes." She averts her eyes.

"Sorry again for not seeing you there. I'll go slower next time. Those Christmas lights distracted me."

"The Shrine?" she asks, pointing at the wedding chapel.

"Yes. I thought it was a shed, but . . . shrine, huh?"

"You're that student, right?"

"Word travels fast."

She smiles. "Something like that."

Noah glances up the road, looks at the Windhaven's cabin. There's still no one in the windows. "Again, I'm sorry. I better be going." He opens the driver's side door.

"Wait," she says. "Sorry. That sounded creepy. I heard you talking about school in Trance. You're getting your master's degree at UNLV, right?"

"Right. You've got a good memory. I'm doing my thesis on alternative religions."

She laughs a little. It's not the first time he's told someone here about his thesis only to see them laugh. At first, he thought it was the idea of going to school that was so funny, but after the interviews this week, he's decided it's the study of religion. The people here come from all different faiths— Christianity, Judaism, Islam. All they really care about is the Teaching, and the leaders insist the Teaching is not a religion. It's a way of life. This way, Noah realized on Wednesday, anyone can join. Or, more likely, anyone can be recruited.

"Hey," she looks inside the minivan, "is that it? Is that your thesis?"

She reaches across the seat, trying to grab the notebook. Noah lurches inside and gets there first. That was close. He raises the notebook and puts his hand on the small of her back, trying to get out of the minivan without pressing too hard.

She smells like lavender.

"Yes," he says, holding the notebook high in the air. "I'm not letting anyone read it until I've got my degree."

She jumps for it and misses, laughing. "Let me see it."

"No. It doesn't make any sense yet. It's just a bunch of notes from interviews."

She stops jumping and takes a step back. Java is at her feet. "Why haven't you interviewed me yet?"

"I . . ."

Noah remembers something Mr. Oakes said. He told Noah Samantha's friend had messaged her online. Something about a woman with a dog. Noah promised Mr. Oakes he would keep an eye out and get close to that woman if he could.

And here she is.

"I—"

"I can tell you anything you want to know about the Teaching." She grins. "I've lived here my whole life."

"Really?"

"Since I was three."

Noah didn't expect so many members to have lived in the Haven for so long. His impression from researching cults on the internet was that most only lasted a few years. Johnstown was an exception, and so is the Haven. Maybe that's why Samantha came here. Stability. "I'd love to interview you. I was just saving the best for last."

She cocks her head and smirks like she's holding back a laugh.

Nice one, Noah. How cheesy can you be?

He glances at the clock in the dash and jumps in the minivan.

"Where are you going?" she asks.

"Sorry, I'm really late." He puts the keys in the ignition.

"I'm interviewing the Johansen's tonight. David and Monica. Do you know them?"

She cocks her head and smirks again.

He starts the minivan. "Of course you do. Look, I've got to go, but I'd like to see you again.

Her eyes widen, and so does her smile.

"For an interview," he says.

"Are you coming back to Trance on Sunday?"

"I'm not sure."

"It's weird for you, right? Trance?" Her smile tightens.

"No, not at all. I mean—it's a little weird."

"I understand," she says. "I'm not going either."

Java jumps up against the door.

"Java. Get down." She pulls the dog off the minivan.

"What are you doing tomorrow?"

There it is again. Her eyes—glowing sapphires. "Are you asking me out?"

"No, I just have some questions I'd like to ask."

"Sure." She looks at me out of the corner of her eye. "Do you have any blank paper in that precious notebook of yours?"

Noah tears out a page and hands it to her along with a pen.

She begins writing.

It's been a long time since he's gotten digits. He's never been much of a player. In high school, he wasn't a jock or a partier or anyone, really. One year, he tried to be a bad boy, but the drugs made him sick. Studying wasn't his forte either. He never got good grades, and he never got bad grades. He's always been mediocre, and while he's had a few girlfriends, he's mostly gone unnoticed.

She finishes writing.

A co-worker once told Noah he was great at hiding in plain sight.

If he's going to find out what happened to Samantha, that's what he needs to do.

Hide in plain sight.

Blend in and gain the trust of everyone in the Haven.

Raine hands him her phone number.

For an instant, he feels like a winner, then he wishes the circumstances were different.

He wishes he could tell her the truth.

CHAPTER FOURTEEN

RAINE

Thank God it's Friday.

I grasp Java by the collar and watch Noah's minivan disappear around the corner. After failing to stay awake at work multiple times today, I'm refreshed. The weather has steadily warmed up every day this week, and tonight I'm going to eat bread. I love meat, but I also love bread. I'm going to eat lots and lots of bread.

"Come on, girl."

Java and I head toward my mother's trailer for our weekly dinner get-together. I haven't decided whether to take trance lessons from Terry or not. No one I know has seen Samantha. I talked to Monica on the phone last night just to be sure, and she said Samantha hasn't come back or called. I feel for Monica. She said she's been out searching every day this week while David has been too busy with work to help.

Poor David.

I didn't mention my private trance session. I don't want Monica to get her hopes up. Maybe I could trance a spirit who knows something about Samantha, and maybe not. The idea of it is just too . . . unreal. And scary. Sebastian said I could take my time deciding, and I am.

But I know my mother will pressure me tonight.

At least there will be bread.

The warm evening feels like autumn though it's spring. I'm walking without a jacket, and I'm wearing shorts for the first time this year. That's always a good feeling. It's still cool in the shade, and the sun is going down, so it won't be long before everything is cool, but I don't care because I'm warm inside.

I have a date tomorrow.

Noah called it an interview, but I saw the look in his eyes.

It's a date.

My whistle bounces against my chest as I stroll down Control Road. I grab it, hold it for a moment, and caress the smooth surface before tucking it back into my shirt. It must have popped out when I pulled Java off Noah's car.

The smell of freshly baked bread hits me as I walk inside my mother's trailer. The bread pans lay in a circle on the dining table. A clear vase with a single white Chrysanthemum stands in the center, and the oven light is on.

I love the smell of her bread. Some people live for beer, and others live for sex. For me, it's my mother's bread. There's a stick of butter and a knife on the counter. I'll worry about my weight on Monday.

Mom carries a large stainless-steel bowl to the table. "I'm glad you're here." She takes a handful of dough and plops it into a pan. "You can help."

Java finds a spot to lie down where she can watch the front door.

"How was work?" my mother asks.

"The same."

She glances at me. I know that smirk. "What's his name?"

"Huh?"

"His name, Raine. What's his name?"

"Can I have a piece of bread?"

She points at the loaf on the counter. "What's his name?"

"Noah." Gentle chills course through my body. I hadn't realized how happy I was. It must be the bread.

"The UNLV student?"

"You were right about him, except he doesn't have straight teeth. He has this one crooked tooth that—"

"I'm not sure I would trust him if I were you."

"What? Why not? You said Terry approved of him."

She returns to the kitchen and places the bowl by the bread kneader. "I said Terry let him come to Trance. But that was before."

"Before what?"

"He asks too many questions."

"He's working on his thesis. He's supposed to ask questions." My piece of bread is half-gone already. I need to slow down.

"You're going to have a lot of responsibilities soon, and I'm not sure it's a good time for you to start dating someone." She wipes her hands off on her pants. Her hair hangs down her back in a braid, and her shirt has flour all over it. "Besides, anyone studying religion will second guess the Teaching. I don't think he'll make it here after all. He's too smart." She puts on her reading glasses and looks at the recipe. "Smart people have a really tough time letting go of their mind and getting in touch with God."

"What if he's different." I bend over and pull a plastic bowl out of the cabinet. "You won't believe this, but Java let him pet her. She likes him."

"Is that right? Well . . . I don't know if it's a good idea."

I put the bowl in the sink and turn on the cold water. Java recognizes the bowl and bumps into me. She wags her tail. Her eyes shine. "Well, maybe it's not up to you."

"I'm sorry, Raine. I can see how smitten you are. I'm happy for you. Really."

Smitten? What is she, ninety years old?

I'll take it.

My mother can be so controlling sometimes, but she's trying to understand.

I put the bowl of water on the floor and scratch Java behind the ears while she drinks.

"If he is true of heart," she says, "I'll come to trust him over time."

"He is smart. And dedicated. He takes his notebook with him everywhere he goes so he can write everything down."

She loads the bread pans into the oven. "I don't know about smart men, but I do know men who work with their hands are better in bed."

"Mother!" OMG. I'm fourteen again. Old people shouldn't talk about sex.

"I'm kidding. I saw it on a shirt somewhere. It was at the construction site where Jerry works. I haven't been able to get it out of my head." She glances up. "God forgive me."

"Get what out of your head? The shirt or the saying?"

"What?"

"Never mind." I cut another piece of bread.

She saunters across the cracked linoleum floor and sits at

the table. She crosses one arm over the other. The Chrysanthemum blocks half her face. "Kattrice told me you haven't talked to Terry yet."

Trance lessons. Here we go.

"Why haven't you made a decision yet?" she asks.

"It's only been two days. Sebastian said I could take my time." I shove a piece of bread into my mouth.

She motions for me to sit with her. "What I don't understand is why you need any time at all?"

Her stupid T-shirt slogan is stuck in my head. *Men who work with their hands* . . . I remember shaking Noah's hand. It was soft. Gentle. "I'm not going to do it."

"What?"

"I'm not going to do it. I'm not ready to be a trance medium." Her expression flies from shock to disappointment to sadness. "I can't do it. You need to be deeply in touch with God for that, and I'm just not—"

"Aren't you meditating every day?"

"Yes, but I always fall asleep before I can—"

"Sebastian wouldn't have chosen you if you weren't capable."

"I don't have time. Work is—"

"You have no purpose at work. You know that. You said so yourself." She sits up straight, squares her shoulders, and stares me in the eyes. "You should quit your job. You don't need the money. Getting closer to God is more important."

My face heats up.

I look away.

Down the hall, my old bedroom has been turned into an art studio my mother never uses. The last time I went in there, I couldn't walk across the floor. She'd left newspapers, boxes, and old rags all over the place. She used to make me clean my room, but now she leaves it a mess.

"Never mind," she says. "It's not really up to you anyway."

"What do you mean by that?"

"It's up to God. It's his will, not yours."

That tired excuse. "Not everything you want is God's will, mother."

She clasps her hands together like a hopeful angel and focuses her attention on the Chrysanthemum. "I wrote a letter, put it in the Shrine, and prayed for you to become a trance medium. It will happen. Think of the service you'll be to others."

She has that starry look in her eyes. "I'll think about it. Just give me some time."

"I'm not sure how much time you have." She looks over at Java. "Sebastian says trancing Cecilia is the only way to find Samantha, and you're the only one who can do that. Cecilia is *your* spirit guide. She was you in a past life."

"It's hard to imagine, Mom. Me? A trance medium?"

"You've got to do it, Raine." She fixes her eyes back on the Chrysanthemum. "Samantha still hasn't come back, you know. Monica must be worried sick. And David . . . have you seen him lately?"

David.

"Yes." My heart sinks. "I've seen him." I take another bite of bread.

"You'll do what's right. I have faith in you."

I stand. "It's getting dark."

"What about dinner?"

"I've eaten too much bread already."

"Oh."

I grasp Java's collar. "Don't be disappointed."

"I'm not. You wouldn't have liked what I made anyway. I don't cook meat anymore."

"I know. Do you have any rope? Java's leash broke."

My mother stands. "I have some twine in my art studio." She disappears down the hall.

I wait and wonder. If God intended for me to become a medium, why did he wait until now to put it in my path? Why does Sebastian think I'm the only one who can find Samantha? I've had immensely powerful dreams in the past, so powerful, sometimes I felt as if I were there. As if the people I saw were real. Is that what trancing is?

I don't know.

Sebastian has spoken through Terry my entire life. It's just the way things have always been.

Mom returns with a wad of black twine.

"Thanks for the bread," I say.

She puts her hand on my arm. "Won't you consider taking just one lesson from Terry? It won't take time away from you and your new boyfriend."

"Noah's not my boyfriend. We're just going on a—he's just interviewing me. That's all."

She removes her hand. "Then why won't you take a lesson? I don't understand why you're so resistant."

"Mom. I'm not ready. And if I do date Noah, then—"

She raises her voice. "Then what? You'll choose him over getting closer to God? Over saving a girl's life?"

"Come on, Java."

We bound down the steps.

Java veers and runs into my mom's old rocking chair.

"Raine. Wait."

I grab Java and fasten the twine to her collar.

My mother stands on the porch, looking down at us. "I'm sorry."

"Why do you always have to be so dramatic?" I ask.

"I just want you to do the right thing. I—"

"I will."

A thin red line runs across the horizon, broken by the silhouette of her trailer. I pull my whistle out and let it hang above my bread-filled belly. It sparkles in the twilight—my whistle, not my belly.

"Be careful walking home," she says.

"I will."

"Raine?"

"What?"

"Is that the whistle your father gave you?"

"Yes."

"It still looks new." With a flick of her fingers, she undoes her braid. Her silver hair falls onto her shoulders. "You know, I remember that day. The day he left."

"I don't."

"I'm sorry I judged you," she says. "I didn't mean to. There was a time when I chose your father over God, and I guess I—." She touches the scar on her eyebrow. "Just be careful walking home, okay?"

"I will."

Java leads me down the hill toward the mobile homes by Control Road. A light outside the dark brown mobile home shines, but none of the lights are on inside. The dilapidated white double-wide is also dark, but that's to be expected. It's a cheap summer home owned by someone outside the community.

I pull on Java's leash to keep her from darting into the middle of Control Road. A car is coming fast. She resists, then succumbs, panting and staring up at me.

I glance back at the brown mobile home. David's dad has let Jace live there for over a year now. I wonder if Jace pays rent.

We stroll along the road, following it around the bend, past the Shrine, past Terry and Kattrice's cabin, to the trance room. I grasp my whistle and suffer a quick shiver. The temperature has dropped along with the sun, and I regret not wearing a jacket.

The shortcut through the trees begins just past the trance room, but we stop here. As much as I've tried, I can't imagine myself sitting in there, cross-legged with my eyes closed and my palms up, trancing a spirit. Terry makes it look so natural. I'd make it look stupid.

Java pulls, and I follow. We take the shortcut through the trees.

The community comes first, but my needs matter too. I'm fine living alone. Java is all I need, but I couldn't help flirting with Noah this afternoon. It was so much fun. Something about his nervousness made me want to tease him. The moment Java let him pet her, I felt like I'd known him for a long time.

Am I rebounding?

No.

If Warren had come around to the Teaching, I might have fallen in love with him, but I was never head-over-heels. Noah, on the other hand, has a head start on the Teaching.

We exit the woods and walk toward my cabin. A fire dances in the distance, flickering through the trees from the firepit. Another Friday night party.

A few brave stars pierce the blackest part of the night sky directly overhead.

The Haven is my home.

I mentally prepare myself for Noah's interview tomorrow.

What do you do for a living?

I work in a law office as an assistant, but it's a dead-end job. My mom wants me to be a trance medium.

You mean like Terry Windhaven?

Yes. I'm going to loan out my body to a past-life spirit so it can speak through me and tell us where this missing girl is.

No.

I can't go there.

I'm not going to take lessons from Terry. Not yet. Maybe Noah is the beginning of a serious relationship, and maybe not, but there's no reason to scare him away on our first date. I don't have to do everything my mother says, and the beauty of free will is, none of us must do what Sebastian says. If I can find Samantha on my own, then everyone will drop this whole trance medium thing. Maybe, if the "interview" goes well, Noah will help me search for her.

Java pulls me up the steps to my cabin.

I forgot to turn the outside light on.

There's an envelope with my name on it taped to the door.

Java barks.

I drop her leash, charge around the corner of the cabin, and gaze toward the firepit.

The teenagers aren't making a ton of noise tonight, but they're up there.

The fire is burning.

Inside, I tear open the envelope.

The same delicate and disturbing writing disgraces the page.

Cursive black swoops.

> *God doesn't want you here. Leave the Haven now, before he runs you down.*

CHAPTER FIFTEEN

DAVID

It's Friday night, and David's week isn't over yet. Until Samantha is found, Monica will give him no peace.

He avoids shifting his truck into second gear, choosing to cruise slowly through the Haven. The transmission is nearing the end of its life, and he's got to make it last as long as he can. The old Ford has been with him since he got married, but unless he does something, it won't be with him when his marriage ends.

It will be dead.

He pulls up to Jace's mobile home. The lights are off, but the ATV is there. Jace has been in the Haven close to a year, but he hasn't started tithing. It's time he started paying his fair share. David wonders if his dad should ask Jace to give the ATV back. Some pressure might encourage the boy to embrace the Teaching at a higher level.

There's no answer when David knocks on the door. He knew the chances of catching Jace at home on a Friday night were slim, but it was a good place to start. With the ATV here, Jace probably isn't far away unless he got a ride into town.

"Jace? You out here?"

David walks to the mobile home next door. The lights are off. He gazes into the woods, up the hill toward Ally's trailer. Jace isn't here.

Slowly, he drives down Control Road, casting glances left and right. The older men are gathered on Terry's deck, drinking whiskey and playing cards. Max, Frank, Terry, Jerry, and Tom. They wave as he drives by. Sometimes they allow younger men to join, but apparently, not tonight.

At the end of the Haven, the road swings around and goes past Raine's A-frame. She walks inside. He stops the truck. Up in the hills, an orange light flickers through the trees, and he knows where Jace went. A beer would taste good right now. It would taste better, sitting around the fire, watching the embers fly into the air. Laughing with friends.

But there's no going back. It's another generation's turn.

David grabs a flashlight from the glove compartment and heads up the trail. Raucous guffaws flow down the hill in ribbons. He wonders if he'll ever laugh that way again. He passes the huge silvery boulder and crests the hill. On the other side, Jace and several other teenagers stand around the fire, drinking and laughing. David steps on a stick, and Jace looks his way. Cori quickly lets go of Jace's hand, and the others drop their beers.

"Jace," David says. "We need to talk."

Cori distances herself from Jace. He says something to her, and she backs farther away. It makes sense now why Shayla has been watching the kids so much. Cori's been busy with Jace.

"Now?" Jace asks, gazing up from the pit. "Does it have to be now, man?"

"Yes, now."

"I'll come over in the morning."

"No. Now."

He throws his beer into the fire. The other teens stand around with their hands in their pockets. They probably wish they hadn't dropped their beers. It's easy for kids to get beer here, but it's still a waste. Sebastian wants all his children, young and old, to have fun. Underage drinking is illegal in Nevada, but not in the Haven. Not according to Sebastian.

Jace trudges up the trail. "What do you want?"

"Walk with me." David starts down the other side. "If you were drowning in a lake, and I threw you a rope, what would you do?"

"Not now, man. Can't we talk about the Teaching tomorrow?"

"What would you do?"

"I'd grab the rope."

"Then what?"

"Hang onto it, I guess."

They reach the main trail, and David stops. "What else?"

David aims his flashlight so he can see Jace's face without blinding him. Frustration builds on the boy's brow as laughter pours over the hilltop.

Jace says, "I don't know, man. Why don't you—"

"You would pull on the rope, wouldn't you? Wouldn't you try to get out of the water?"

"Sure."

"Okay, that's the first thing I wanted to talk to you about. You need to start pulling your own weight. It's been close to a year now, and you're not paying my dad rent, and you're not trying to get a job. You haven't worked since—"

"I worked."

"You were fired."

Jace looks away.

"A big part of the Teaching is loving one another. Money is love in motion. I want you to get a job and begin tithing to the community."

David senses Jace's energy—pure hatred—but that's okay. It's part of learning, and Jace bears it well for someone who's been through what he has in this incarnation.

"I'll try harder on Monday," Jace says. "Can I go now?"

"No. There's something else."

"What?"

"When was the last time you saw Samantha?"

The boy's hateful energy intensifies. "I don't know. We broke up. Why? Hasn't she come back?"

"No."

"Who gives a fuck?"

The muscles in David's neck tighten. "I do."

Jace steps back. "I don't know where she went, man. She ran away."

"Do you know that for sure?"

The teens erupt in more laughter, and Jace glances up the hill. His face is pained. "Because she couldn't stand living with you and your bitch of a wife."

"Hey." David grabs Jace by the collar and pulls him off balance. "Don't you ever talk about another man's wife that way."

Jace stumbles backward and sticks his hand in his pocket like he's going to pull a knife. He hangs there, stooped over, glaring at David like a caged badger.

"I'm sorry," David says. "I shouldn't have done that,

but I need to find Samantha. Do you have any idea where she went?"

"Don't ever touch me again."

"Where's Samantha?"

"I already told you. I don't know. She probably ran back to her rich daddy."

"Vegas?"

"Yeah."

"What about her mom? She never talked about her. Could she have—"

"Her mom's a crack-whore. She's probably dead somewhere. Look, man, I'm sorry I called your wife a bitch. Can I go now?"

"When was the last time you saw Samantha?"

"I don't know. A couple of weeks ago."

"Are you sure?"

"Yeah."

David stares at Jace, focusing on each part of the boy's body. He looks for rapid blinking, hands rubbing together, a sudden itch that needs scratching—anything that would indicate deception, but Jace does none of those things. He's stone-cold angry, but he's honest.

Jace lumbers up the hill.

"Wait," David says. "Have you heard any guns go off tonight?"

"No."

David raises his voice. "Did you hear any guns go off last weekend?"

Jace stops on a steep part of the trail. He rests his hand on his knee and looks at David. "No."

"You wouldn't know who took Terry's gun, would you?"

Jace suddenly scratches his cheek. "I've got no idea, man. I haven't heard nothing."

"Why don't you come back down here?"

"Come on, man."

"Jace. Stop lying. I saw you coming out of the woods last Saturday, and I know you heard a gun. Samantha went missing right after that."

"Oh, yeah? You got me. I heard a gun, but guess what? So did your bitch of a wife. Why don't you ask her about it? She was out here running around last weekend too." He waits for a response, but David doesn't bite. "That's right. She's a bitch."

"You saw her *in* the woods?"

"That's right."

"Are you sure? Are you absolutely sure it was her and not someone else?

"Yeah. Why?"

"She hates the woods." David rubs his chin. "She said she didn't leave the road."

"Really?" Jace crests the hill. "For somebody so enlightened, your pretty fucking blind, man." He disappears over the other side, and his friends cheer his return.

Monica told David—she explicitly told David—she didn't go into the woods. It's not that she lied that bothers him. It's why she lied. Why would she?

Monica said she saw Raine coming out of the trees and never went in. Jace could have seen her down the road, but from where David saw Jace—no. It was too far for Jace to have seen Monica on the road. He must have seen her in the woods.

David's thoughts collide—the past, the present, the future.

He shimmies down the trail, careful not to slip on the steep incline.

Laughter follows him through the trees. The night is young for Jace and his friends.

David is old. Tired. His knees ache. His hands are cracked and rough. He feels older than a man ought to feel in his early thirties. If it's going to be like this—if it's going to get worse, year after year—what will it feel like at forty? At fifty? Sixty?

He exits the woods and slides onto the front seat of his truck.

No one would know until tomorrow. Monica is passed out by now, and the kids are at Shayla's. No one is expecting him on a job in the morning.

Tomorrow's Saturday . . . it would be noon before anyone noticed.

He stares out the windshield.

His hate for Monica grows by the minute.

A light comes on inside Raine's A-frame.

She stands in the kitchen.

David watches as she takes a glass from the cupboard and fills it with water.

In another life—in a past life, maybe—he could have stood there with her. They could have lived in an A-frame cabin in the Pyrenees, in the mountain town she always talked about.

He could have lived in peace.

With her.

CHAPTER SIXTEEN

RAINE

The midmorning sun lights up my map of the world.

I'm lying on my futon in the loft, staring up at the map. It's folded to conform to my A-frame shaped ceiling, one corner hanging down, undone. A single blue thumbtack sticks out of the middle, marking the little French village in the southern Pyrenees.

Bugarach.

I lived there in a past life. Sebastian says he first met me in Bugarach, in person, hundreds of years ago. The village lies at the base of an "upside-down" mountain bearing the same name. It is a spiritual, holy place, touched by the hand of God. Bugarach is the "upside-down" mountain because the rocks at the top are older than those at the bottom. It's not just what Sebastian says. It's a geological fact.

I've always wanted one of those rocks.

I roll over and my legs tangle, trapped beneath the sheets. Java lies next to me, holding the covers down. What a miserable night. I couldn't fall asleep until after three because of the note.

God doesn't want you here. Leave the Haven now, before he runs you down.

If I had to leave, I'd go to Bugarach.

My dreams were scattered and short. I piece them together, stitching sequences in order, but nothing makes sense. Samantha is in the woods, except she's smiling instead of crying. A gun goes off, and Java stands perfectly still at my side like she's deaf. Another gunshot sounds, but now, a man stands next to me. He's a hunter, but it's not hunting season. He's a poacher. He's a killer. He aims his gun at Samantha, and she laughs. She points her finger at me. She tells me to leave the Haven or she'll run me down.

The hunter's face is blurry.

My hands are sweaty.

I roll over in bed, untwisting my legs, trying to see the hunter's face. He hands me a note and pushes the gun's muzzle against the center of my forehead.

That's it. I'm getting up.

I kick the covers off, and Java jumps onto the floor. She looks at me with her sleepy eyes. Her hair is a mess. She shakes like she's wet, then does her favorite yoga pose—downward dog.

I throw a robe on and head downstairs. The dreams continue to invade my thoughts—Samantha maniacally laughing and pointing her finger. Telling me to leave the Haven.

God doesn't want you here.

I need to find out who left those notes. It still seems like a teenager, like Jace, playing a prank, but it could be more. I'm not sure how to find out without upsetting the community. I can't go around asking parents, *Hey, does your kid think God is going to run me down?* They would talk, and rumors would start.

There's no bread in my pantry, so I sit at the table with a bowl of cereal. Corn Pops. I read the note again and again.

If the older generation knew about this, they would panic. Terry would freak out. Everyone would relive the misery from when that little girl was kidnapped years ago. They would assume people in town were attacking us, trying to scare us away by leaving these notes on my door. They did things like this before—"go to hell" painted on our cabins, dead animals left in mailboxes, articles in the newspapers about the cult hippies in the hills, people whispering on street corners, dirty glances, terrified tourists staring at us before peeling out of the gas station between here and Elko.

No.

No one can know.

I finish my cereal. Drinking the sugary Corn Pops milk is my favorite part. I'm done with stressing over the note. The starchy white paper—smooth and crisp in my fingers—slides easily back into the envelope. I put it in a kitchen drawer and check my phone. Noah never set a time and place for the interview today.

Nothing. No text messages. No missed calls.

It's almost eleven.

Then, as if on cue, my phone vibrates, but it's not him. It's my mother.

"Hello?"

"I called to apologize."

"For what?"

"I had no right to judge you," she says.

"You already apologized for that."

"I know, but I needed to tell you again."

"Thank you."

"I'm also sorry I judged your new boyfriend."

"He's not my—"

"I had no reason to think he's not true of heart. I'm sorry. Sebastian tells us we must learn to trust outsiders, but I—I'm just concerned for you."

"Don't be."

"If you want to date him, it's fine with me."

"Thanks, but I don't need your permission." I walk into the living room.

"Honey—"

"Don't worry," I say, glancing out my front window.

"Why?"

"He hasn't called."

"Oh." She hesitates. "Do you think you'll take Terry up on his offer to teach you then?"

Java lets out a whimper. She stands at the top of the stairs, looking down at her bowl. She's hungry. I forgot to feed her last night after I found the note.

"Raine? Will you at least let Terry give you *one* trance lesson?"

"I don't know. Hold on."

I pin the phone to my ear with my shoulder and open a cabinet.

"You'll make the right decision," she says. "I have no doubt."

Damn her. She didn't call to apologize. She called to coerce me. It's just like last night.

"I just can't imagine why Samantha would want to leave the Haven," she says. "David and Monica were giving her everything."

"Maybe someone told her to leave," I say.

"What? Who would do that?"

I pull out a bag of dog food and pour some into Java's bowl. "I don't know. Maybe someone threatened her."

"No one would do anything like that, unless . . . do you think people in town know she ran away?"

"No. Never mind." I put the dog food away and gaze at the kitchen drawer.

"Raine. Noah is an outsider, and he showed up last week, right after Samantha went missing."

"Stop it. You're being paranoid."

But she has a point. Not about Noah, but about *why* Samantha left. If Samantha found notes like the ones I found . . . like the notes tucked inside my kitchen drawer. Like the notes that are giving me nightmares.

"Won't you please reconsider taking trance lessons, Raine? You could ask Cecilia so many questions, and—"

"Fine. I'll take one. But don't get your hopes up. I doubt I'm spiritual enough to do it."

"Nonsense," she says. "You're going to do great. This is so wonderful."

I hold the phone away from my ear while she celebrates, telling me all the things this will mean to me, to the Haven, to my relationship with God.

Java eats.

"I was really starting to think you weren't going to do it."

My phone buzzes. "Mom, I've got another call." I glance at the screen. *Unknown Number.*

"Okay," she says. "I'll let you go."

I tap the answer button.

"Hello?"

"Hi. It's Noah. Remember me?"

CHAPTER SEVENTEEN

DAVID

David thrusts the push mower over a depression in Terry's lawn. The rusted blades snag the grass, wrapping it around the spindle. His lower back threatens to seize. He pulls the mower backward and pushes it forward, trying to slice through a thick patch of grass.

Someone from the younger generation should be mowing Terry's lawn. Anyone one of those kids from the firepit last night ought to be here. Jace still doesn't get it. They're probably all sleeping in, hungover like Monica.

The rusty blades make the job twice as hard. David thrusts the mower forward and back, and forward. No matter how well he does, any grassy outliers will be used against him. It'll be as if he did no service. Kattrice will complain to Monica, and Monica will complain to him, and he'll be back here tomorrow, trying again. When he woke this morning, he'd had the fleeting thought that doing service today would make him feel better.

It used to.

The blades whir when he speeds ahead, and the wheels squeak when he forces the mower into a turn. He works the lawn from the outside in, making his rounds like water spiraling down a toilet bowl.

Terry's toilet is still broken.

Being of service never ends.

Sunlight glints off a rock in the grass.

David rushes the mower over the rock so he can watch it fly into trees near the Shrine. It bangs off the bark, and he stops mowing. Wipes his forehead.

The white gardenias around the Shrine wave in the wind, and he considers writing a letter to God asking why Jace doesn't have to do service, but he knows the answer. It's because he has failed Jace as a teacher. Jace stole Terry's gun, lied about it, and now David will be blamed for everything.

Or . . . he won't. Jace doesn't know he found the gun. No one knows.

He thrusts the mower over an anthill. The ants scatter, first away from the mound, then back again. They rush toward the entrance, toward the tunnel to their queen, climbing over each other as if there is nowhere else on God's green earth to go.

David takes his hat off, faces the sun, and gently runs his fingers through his thinning hair. The air this morning is cool. He takes a deep breath and tells himself to relax. It's going to be okay. No one knows he found Terry's gun in the forest. He's done nothing wrong. Everything is going to be okay.

A car cruises over the hill, leaving two dusty plumes in its wake. Raine waves to David from behind the wheel. He nods to her and puts his hat back on. She's the easiest person in the world to talk to, but he never has time.

Before he begins again, something moves in an upstairs window. A sheer white curtain shifts to the side. Kattrice appears, looking down at him, her fingers folded over the curtain's edge. Her face resembles a stone statue, something you'd see in an ancient cemetery.

She makes eye contact and then slowly closes the curtain.

He pushes the mower forward. Three more laps, and a run down the middle, and he's going home. That's it. The toilet can wait. He's not going to rake up the grass either. The wind can blow it away.

"David," Monica calls from the road.

He pretends not to hear her. He pretends not to have glimpsed her purple flip-flops kicking up dust.

"David, what the hell are you doing?"

She ought to be asleep. It can't be noon already.

He rounds a corner and pushes the mower in the opposite direction, wishing he'd brought his headphones.

She strides up the incline and shadows him from behind. "Stop. Listen to me."

"I've got to finish this," he says.

"No you don't. Stop. Now."

He speeds up. Grass flies from the blades, creating green halos around his legs.

"Stop mowing," she says. "This is serious." She tugs on the back of his shirt, then grabs his shoulder.

He breaks free from her grip and continues across the lawn. "Whatever it is, you can tell me while I finish."

She walks in front of him, and he stops. Her face is red and her chest heaves. She glares at him with bloodshot eyes, her neck throbbing. "Is there something you want to tell me?"

"No."

"Are you sure?"

"Yes." He angles the mower away from her feet and pushes forward.

"For God's sake, stop mowing."

"No. Just tell me what you want."

"I want to talk about the gun."

David stops cold.

He wishes she hadn't yelled. He checks the upstairs window. It's closed and, thankfully, Kattrice isn't there. She's not in any of the other windows either. The curtains hang listlessly in the morning sun. "Lower your voice."

"No."

"Look, I talked to Jace about the gun last night. I think he took it, but I don't think he—"

"Is that so?" She steps forward and leans, putting her face into his. "You're lying."

Her flip-flops are inches from the mower. Chipped, pink nail polish covers the upper half of her toenails. One quick thrust and—*snip, slash*—those little piggies went to market.

He pulls the mower away from her feet and runs down the last swath of grass. "I'm not the only one."

"What?"

"You told me you never went into the forest last week, but Jace saw you out there. You told me you didn't see Samantha after she ran away, but *you* were lying."

"But . . . I didn't see her."

David reaches the end of the row and turns around. "What about the forest? You said you didn't go in there, but—"

"I never said that. You're not making any sense, David. I was looking for Samantha, so of course, I went into the woods. I followed her into the woods." She talks so matter-of-factly as if she hadn't told him the exact opposite last week. "You and Jace are the liars."

"What do you mean by that?"

She purses her lips, puts her hands on her hips, and leans forward. She studies him like a bug. "The question is, David. What were *you* doing out there?"

"What? I wasn't out there."

She rolls her eyes and stands up straight. An eerie grin forms on her blemished face, then she glances up at the house and puts on a great big smile. The curtains in the middle window move, and Kattrice appears.

Monica waves to Kattrice.

Kattrice waves to Monica.

The sun warms David's face, but a cold shiver courses down his spine.

Monica speaks through gritted teeth, maintaining her smile. "You're in big trouble, David. I know you stole my dad's gun. I found it in your nightstand."

"Shh." All the air leaves his lungs. His mind races. She went through his nightstand. His things. He has—he has nothing.

She sneers. "You disgust me. Did you think hiding it under your Bible would keep God from finding out what you did?"

He lets go of the mower. The handle hits the turf, bounces once, and comes to rest at his feet. His fists tense, and he turns to leave.

"Hey, get back here," she says.

Hate fills his heart. There's no way to stop it. No reason to try. Not anymore. He feels disoriented, but he knows where to go. The dizziness is freeing. He slogs toward his truck. His keys are in his hand, and she runs after him, yelling, "From now on, you're going to do what I say."

He gets in his truck.

Kattrice is still watching from the window.

He starts the engine.

Monica plants her hands on the driver's door. She's shouting at the window, but David doesn't look at her.

It's a beautiful day for a cruise on the highway.

He puts the transmission in gear and pats the dashboard.

This old truck. His friend. It won't let him down.

It'll make one more run before the transmission dies.

Before everything dies.

CHAPTER EIGHTEEN

RAINE

Noah and I meet at a place called Pete's Kitchen for the "interview" in downtown Elko. It's kind of a diner for retirees, lounge lizards on a budget. The sign reads, SATURDAY SPECIAL STEAK -$12.99.

I love a good steak, but I order a salad.

No one in here owns a shirt with buttons. Noah is out of place in his white oxford and his clean blue jeans. His tight, clean blue jeans. He doesn't notice he's the only one with combed hair and a clean-shaven face. He doesn't notice because he keeps his attention on me the entire time, asking about my life in the Haven. It makes me realize what a blessed life I've lived. The Teaching is a blessing.

I push the notes to the back of my mind. I don't want to think about leaving the Haven. I also don't want to think about Samantha. When Noah brings up his interview with David and Monica, I tell him I didn't know Samantha well, which is true. He says David and Monica are distraught, and I can tell by the way he says it, he cares. He genuinely cares.

I do too, and I'm going to find her if someone else doesn't do it first. I need to know if she ran away because of notes like mine, but not right now.

Right now, I'm going to enjoy myself.

Live in the present.

Take in the view.

Noah.

He asks what my favorite kind of ice cream is. That's got nothing to do with studying religion. This interview is a game we're both playing.

He pays.

We walk outside, the searing Elko sun greets us, and I have an urge to hold his hand. We only just met, but after the way he listened to me talk about the Teaching, I feel a connection. He cared. He understood. If interviewing me is a trick to get to know me—to make me like him—then it's working.

He was hesitant to believe past-life spirits could speak through holy people like Terry, but everyone is at first. It's unlikely Terry will be able to teach me to trance, so I didn't tell Noah I plan to take a lesson. It's best to dole out the Teaching in spoonfuls.

We stroll across the parking lot. He has his notebook tucked under his arm. I wonder what he would do if I took his hand.

"Thanks for having lunch with me," he says, pulling out his keys.

"Want to come up to the Haven?" I blurt.

He grins, and his tooth, his adorable, crooked tooth, appears. "We're done with the interview. Haven't you had enough of my questions?"

"I thought you might want to know more." His grin

blossoms into a full-on smile. "About the community. I could show you around. We could hike up to the firepit."

I told him about my A-frame cabin and the firepit at lunch. I told him all about growing up in the Haven. The Friday night parties, the barbecues, weddings, community game nights—the walks in the woods.

He was *very* interested.

"Hey," he says, "look at that."

A gray sign with hundreds of flashing light bulbs looms over an artificial lawn across the highway. MEDI-EVAL MINIGOLF.

"You're kidding, right? How old are you?"

He grabs my hand and pulls me across the lot.

We run like schoolchildren on recess.

It feels so right.

Halfway to the entrance, I glance around, wondering if anyone from the community has come to town. I'd be embarrassed if someone I knew saw me acting this way.

The kid working at the minigolf entrance is unenthused when we crash his counter.

Noah plops down his notebook and reaches into his pocket. "Two," he says, pulling out a wad of cash. "All eighteen rounds."

"I'm not good at golf," I say. "Eighteen rounds will take a while."

"Don't worry, I'll help. I used to work at a golf course."

We begin to play.

He hands me his notebook and clears the windmill with his first shot. Amazing. Two shots later, his golf ball lands in the hole. I stop counting my strokes after eleven. "How long did you work on a golf course?"

"Just one summer."

"Wow. You're great at this."

We move on to the next hole, and he makes another great shot.

"Where else have you worked? Other sports places?"

"No. Just the golf resort. Before that, I was a cabbie, and before that, I was a bicycle courier."

"That's sportsy. Isn't that those guys who ride bikes in the middle of traffic?"

"Yeah. It's exciting but stupid. I worked in San Francisco, dodging in between cars, ignoring all the cab drivers honking at me. Then I became a cab driver and honked at all the bike couriers. It made me realize how dangerous I'd been." He eyes his next shot. "It also taught me to always try and see things from other people's perspectives."

"Sounds scary—dodging the cars."

"It was, but I didn't get it until later." He kneels down and gazes at the green. "Not until I stopped cycling and started driving a cab." He stands, tips his head forward, and rests the putter on the green. "But it was better than cleaning hotel rooms."

"You were a maid?"

He hits the ball. "No. The title is 'housekeeper.'" The ball bounces through a maze and pops out the other side.

I giggle. He was a maid.

"Hey, don't judge."

"How many different jobs have you had?"

"Not many. I haven't been an astronaut yet. But I wouldn't rule it out."

I mark his score one below par. Again. "I give up. You're too good at this."

His jeans stretch over his cute butt as he bends to retrieve his ball. I wish I were better at golf. It would help if I focused more on my shots and less on his jeans. Oh my God—am I smitten? That's my mother's word. Smitten.

Ugh.

He stands up straight, and the color drains from his face.

"What's wrong?" I say.

"Nothing, I—"

It's as if he's seen a ghost. "Are you okay?"

"Do you see that girl over there?"

"Oh, yeah. What a coincidence." Jace and Cori are two holes ahead.

"Is that her?" Noah's voice lifts, and he picks up his notebook. He takes out a pen. "Is that Samantha?"

"No. That's Cori."

"Who is—"

"She lives in the Haven. I would have thought they were too cool for minigolf."

Noah leans to the left. "Are you sure she's not Samantha?"

"Yes, I'm sure. You probably saw her in the Haven. She works at the daycare part-time." I place my ball at the start of the next hole. "Why did you think she was Samantha?"

He flips through his notebook. "I talked to Jace last week. He said Samantha had long blond hair and—" He stops flipping through the pages. "Here it is. He dated her when she first came to the Haven."

"Why do you have that written down?" He pulls out a pen and begins to write. "What does Samantha have to do with studying religion?"

He looks up. Hesitates. "I write everything down. This could be an interesting angle. How a unique religious community reacts when one of their own runs away." He finishes writing and picks up his putter.

We walk to the next green.

Smitten or not, I want to win. I need a hole in one. Cheating is against the Teaching, but Sebastian always says for us to have fun. The next time Noah looks away, I'm going to kick his ball into the water or something. Somehow, I've got to win at least one round.

I shoot.

My ball makes it over the incline but goes too fast and bounces off the dragon's tail.

"How well do you know David and Monica?" he asks.

"All my life."

"I hope I'm not overstepping my bounds here, but it seemed like there was something else wrong. Something more than Samantha running away."

"What do you mean?"

"Were they an arranged marriage?"

"No."

"Monica said they got married because Sebastian told them they were soul mates."

"It's not like that. They dated for a long time before David asked her."

"I see."

"Sebastian was giving his approval, not arranging a marriage."

He swings and misses his shot. I have a chance to beat him on this hole.

"That makes sense," he says. "I guess. Either way, they didn't seem like a married couple. It was more like they were pretending to like each other."

"They've been together a long time. Some couples get that way." I make a good putt.

We retrieve our balls and head to the next hole.

I love David and Monica, and I hate gossip. I tell myself Noah is only curious, but it feels like he is prodding. We each have our own lives to live, our own karmas, and I've always been careful not to interfere with David and Monica's. Especially David's. I dated him shortly before he asked Monica to marry him, and when Sebastian said David was put on this earth to learn from her, not me, I honored it.

"I don't want to be too forward," he says, "but—does Monica have a drinking problem?"

"What?"

"There were empty bottles all over their kitchen, and she had at least five drinks while I was there."

He drops his ball on the next green and lines up his shot.

"She's a drinker, but it's okay. God wants us to enjoy ourselves." There's that look. I used the G-word. Dammit. I'm trying to dole out the Teaching in spoonfuls, but I slipped. The world doesn't see alcohol for what it is. If Monica has a problem, if any of us has a problem, it's never with alcohol. Alcohol is the one reprieve God gives us from embodiment on the earth plane. Our problems come from our egos, not drinking.

It's too much to explain right now.

Spoonfuls.

"You're right," I say. "David and Monica have problems other than Samantha. They still have a lot to learn from each other."

"Interesting." His shot goes in. We have one hole left. "Is David always so, I don't know, not there? He acted like he had somewhere else to be the whole time. When Samantha came up, he got really nervous."

"He was probably tired. He works a lot."

"Do you know if he *wanted* to adopt her?"

"We haven't talked much lately. I've been—" I've been busy trying to convince my last boyfriend to love the Teaching the way I do. And now, I'm doing it all over again. "I've been busy with work. I didn't know they were adopting until last week."

"Do adoptions happen the same way as weddings? I mean, Monica said the spirit told them to adopt."

"Now you're accusing us of having arranged adoptions?"

"No. Well . . . maybe."

"David is a solid man. If he hadn't wanted to do it, then he wouldn't have."

"He wasn't happy Samantha disappeared, but he wasn't exactly upset either. I saw his 'tells.' "

"His tells?"

"Yes." He cocks his head. "David has a good poker face, but at one point, Monica said she worried Samantha might have been shot by a stray bullet or something. They started arguing, and I could tell he was bluffing."

"About what?"

"I don't know. It was strange." He hits his golf ball hard. It makes it through the double loop-de-loop and rolls right up to the last hole. "Whenever Samantha's disappearance came up, he changed the subject, like he knew something and didn't want to talk."

"David didn't do anything wrong." I snatch my golf ball from the tee.

"Aren't you going to finish?"

"No. You win. I give up."

"Hey, I'm sorry. I didn't mean to—"

"David is the most honest, spiritual man I know. He teaches the Teaching. He eats, breathes, and lives it." I head for the front entrance. "He's not hiding anything."

So much for spoonfuls, but this is how it begins. Something happens in the Haven, and an outsider shows up, asking questions. Noah is cute, and he's caring, but to think David did something to scare Samantha away . . .

The last note comes rushing into the forefront of my mind.

God doesn't want you here. Leave the Haven now, before he runs you down.

No. David would never leave a note like that. Not for me.

I dump my putter and golf balls on the counter.

"Wait," Noah says. "I'm sorry. It just seemed strange. Why do you think Samantha ran away?"

I face him. "Strange? It seemed strange? You know what's strange? Your fixation on David and Samantha."

He averts his eyes like a child.

"Do you want to know what happened to her?" I ask.

"Yes."

"Here's what I'm going to do." I put my hand on his arm. "I'm going to become a trance medium, okay? I'm going to let a dead person speak through me, and she's going to tell me where Samantha is. Then I'll tell you why she ran away. What do you think of that? Strange?"

The kid behind the counter grimaces, picks up my putter, and hangs it on a rack.

Noah stands there, motionless. Silent.

"Strange," I say. "You haven't seen strange."

CHAPTER NINETEEN

DAVID

The last person enters the trance room and closes the door.

Those people seated near candles blow them out.

The aroma of God's incense penetrates the air.

David sits next to Monica with his back against the wall. They are near the front, off to the side of Terry and Kattrice— Terry on his pillows, Kattrice on her wicker chair.

Sebastian is on his way.

It's Sunday.

David closes his eyes.

It's an empty, empty, Sunday.

Kattrice says, "Please, let us begin."

Everyone sings, "In the times of our lives, we praise God, praise God, praise God. In the lives of our times, we praise God, praise God—"

David doesn't join in. He stopped speaking yesterday after he got back from racing his truck up and down the highway, and he doesn't plan on starting again. He's not holding Monica's hand like usual. Now that she found the gun, she owns him like never before. The Teaching says he should seek Sebastian's guidance, but he can't. Not here. Not in front of everyone.

He opens his eyes, and it doesn't make a difference. The room is pitch black, but it feels like everyone is looking at him.

He is their teacher . . . he *was* their teacher.

He *was* the Teaching, but now he's a liar.

By not saying anything about the gun last week, he lied in silence.

He wipes his brow. His head is heavy. His heart is empty. He spent last night losing his faith in the Teaching. It's dead. He doesn't know why he's here. Sebastian only helps those who are in the Teaching.

The singing lifts in a crescendo. "Praise God. Praise God!"

Monica sings louder than usual. Her voice fills David with dread and disgust and fear. Like-vibrations are supposed to support each other, but it's like she's pointing the gun's muzzle at his head. *From now on, David, you're going to do what I say.*

"Hello, me children of the highest seas." Sebastian's words reverberate off the walls. "I be honored to speak to you today. You be old souls, sailing with me on a journey to God. To oneness with God. Oh, and what a blessed journey it be. You have all lived many times before, but you be back again on the earth plane, trying again. Trying to learn what your souls missed the last time around. It be a fun time, no?"

"Yes." The voices echo off the walls.

"I do not hear the joy I love so much. Me children should be happy, but I know why you be sad. Today be a low day in the biorhythms of our family. Not everyone sang, did they, Kattrice?"

"I don't know."

"Listen, people," Sebastian exclaims. "Me medium be full of misery and despair. Someone stole from him. They stole a lethal weapon, you know, like that movie . . . *Lethal Weapon?*"

A few strained laughs come from the suck-ups in the first row.

"You, many of you, live in your minds. You run on negative thoughts, letting them feed your ego and take away our joy. Negative thoughts and positive thoughts. You fool yourselves with things of the earth plane, clutching your little belongings and ignoring your karma. You clutch the things that do not matter. You hide these things away from others while you keep your hearts locked in iron chests. What be in you that God cannot understand? Why do you lock him out?"

David hears Sebastian's words, but he also hears breathing. His breathing. Monica's compressed breaths. Everyone sitting in the dark, pulling air in, and pushing air out. Everyone, breathing in. Everyone, breathing out.

"Kattrice, why have they asked me here today if they don't want to learn?" Sebastian says.

"I don't know."

"Sebastian, I want to learn," Jerry says. "My leg still hurts."

"Did you have Ally look at it?"

"Yes, but—"

"U-m-m. H-m-m. Your leg will be better in a week, Jerry. Keep the castor oil pack on it and stay away from red meat. It can cause gout, you know."

"Thank you, Sebastian."

"Who else would like to learn?"

"Sebastian?" Zack says.

"Yes, me child. How be you?"

"I'm doing good, I guess. I don't want to be in my mind about this, but it seems like—I feel like I've been selfish lately."

"You have been hiding your heart away, haven't you?"

"Maybe. The other day I was walking by a casino, and there was this guy slumped over on the ground. He looked real bad. I think I should have helped him."

"Everyone has their own karma. You shouldn't worry yourself over this man's life. He chose it when he reincarnated. He chose it before he be born."

"I know, but we have that extra room upstairs, and I was thinking I should've invited him to—"

"No one invites anyone here unless I have said so," Sebastian hisses. "The souls of Elko do not understand the Teaching. Especially now. Their energy be negative, filled with fear and distrust. I do not blame you, Zacharia. You be a kind, blessed soul, and you have done nothing wrong. Pray for relief from selfishness if you feel selfish, but do not think of recruiting as a way to God. Let God send his children here. Do not recruit. Do you know what I be saying to you?"

"Yes, Sebastian."

David thinks of Jace and the others. He didn't recruit them. Each time, Sebastian asked him to go to Vegas. He always had Sebastian's blessing.

"Does anyone else have questions? Anyone else feeling selfish?"

Silence.

"Anyone having trouble sleeping at night? Perhaps secrets be keeping you awake?"

We are only as sick as our secrets.

David is sick. Selfish. Keeping the gun to himself. The Teaching is dead to him, but Sebastian is right. Selfishness will make the world implode, one person at a time. David doesn't want to be that person, but the only way out is service. Could he do it? Could he tell the truth about the gun and be of service one more time?

Could he bring himself to fix that goddammed toilet? One more time?

"Does anyone have something hidden next to their bed, keeping them awake at night?" Sebastian raises his voice. "Maybe something in their nightstand?"

David wrings his hands. He should have come clean in Trance last week. He should have told everyone he put the gun beneath his Bible. His Qur'an. His Holy Vedas. He thought it was safe there. And yes—the gun kept him awake last night.

He doesn't know what to do.

No amount of service can change the past. No amount of truth can change the future. The truth wants out, but he can't speak. It's too late. He won't speak.

"Monica," Sebastian says. "You be suffering, me child."

"Yes. Samantha is still missing." She sounds like she is on the verge of tears. "I searched the Haven for her all last week, but she's gone. Do you think I should go to Elko and—"

"No," Sebastian says. "They will not help you. Do not go to Elko looking for answers that be here in the Haven."

Monica stammers, "I've been praying all week, too. I've meditated and asked God for help trancing my spirit guide."

Kattrice lets out a chuckle.

"Me dear," Sebastian says, "you be a wonderful mother and a spiritual woman. You know how to have a good time while living out your karma. Drinking the alcohols. Love your life as it be, and find Samantha in the human way. You were not put on this earth to trance. Do you know what I be saying to you?"

She shifts in her seat. Bumps up against David's thigh. Her body shakes. "Yes, Sebastian. It's just that I—we need to get Samantha back." She grasps David's hand and squeezes it hard. "Is she okay?"

"I will check." Sebastian falls into a deep hum, changing tones in a wordless chant.

The energy in the room changes. David's blood pulses to the rhythm of Sebastian's humming. He sees Samantha in his mind. Monica's hand feels like it's going to burn him. He sees Samantha running through the forest with her backpack. He's meditating. He's leaving his body—

"Samantha"—Sebastian booms—"is not okay."

David opens his eyes. The room is darker than his mind, and the image of Samantha fades to black.

Everyone around him gasps. They shift in their seats.

"David." Sebastian's voice is ragged and loud.

David's throat tightens. He swallows.

"David?" Sebastian says. "Listen to me. Monica has been looking for Samantha all this week. What be your endeavors?"

He bites his lower lip.

"How have you been sleeping, David?"

His lip feels like it's going to split. He can't speak. He won't speak.

Sebastian, calmer now, says, "David? Be you with us?"

"He's here," Monica says.

A copper taste flows into David's mouth. His lower lip goes numb and his jaw relaxes. His head aches. It pounds with each heartbeat. His face goes numb. He prays for Sebastian to go away. He prays for everyone, and everything, to go away. *Everything . . . just . . . go . . . away!*

And then the answer comes.

He knows what he must do.

"David, me child. You must support your wife if you want to find Samantha. You must do what Monica says. She is your karma—your like-vibration. Do you know what I be saying to you?"

He knows.

Sebastian is speaking the Teaching.

But for David, the Teaching is dead.

"You know what you must do to find peace, don't you, David?" Sebastian's question hangs in the air like a soap bubble.

David knows what he must do.

Monica nudges him. "David, say something."

He knows what he must do, and when he is done, he'll never have to do what she says again.

Never again.

CHAPTER TWENTY

NOAH

The Sunday morning trance meeting started twenty minutes ago.

Noah accelerates down the freeway, rushing to get there in time, but his engine light comes on. He knows better than push it, so he pulls over. A belt has broken and wrapped itself around a pulley. The steering is stiff, but the van still runs. He turns back and finds a white, three-bay garage called Larry's Oil City & Auto Repair on the outskirts of Elko. The open sign is on, and two of the bays are empty. With any luck, Larry, or whoever is in there, can fix the belt fast, and Noah can still catch Raine after the trance meeting.

He needs to talk to her.

The way minigolf ended yesterday was horrible. She tried so hard to beat him but lost. It made her mad, which was odd because she doesn't seem like the sore-loser type, but maybe it was something else. When they returned the clubs, he had brought up David and Samantha, and that's when she really lost it.

What a shame.

Noah had been having such a great time with her, he'd almost forgotten why they'd met to begin with. Mr. Oakes had said Samantha might have stayed in an A-frame with a woman and a dog. Raine had said she lived in an A-frame, and Noah had seen her dog. At the start, he was only doing his job, interviewing her, but it turned into so much more.

He parks and rushes into the auto shop.

The man behind the counter wears white coveralls smeared with oil, and his name tag reads "Joe." He's got a scruffy chin and the lines in his forehead crease in the middle.

Noah places his notebook and the keys to the minivan on the counter and holds up the severed belt.

"Looks like you've got a broken serpentine there," Joe says.

"I'm parked right in front." Joe takes the belt, and Noah points at his minivan. "How long do you think it will take to fix it?"

"About twenty minutes, if we have one in stock, and I think we do. Problem is, there's someone ahead of you."

Noah glances at the middle-aged woman sitting in the waiting area. She browses through an old issue of Car and Driver, licking her thumb as she turns the pages. He leans over the counter. "If it's a quick job, could you work on my car first? She won't notice."

"I can't do that, but I'll tell you what. I'll get yours pulled in now, and we can work on them at the same time. I got another guy back there."

Noah glances at the clock above the counter. "Okay. Please hurry."

With his notebook in hand, he takes the seat next to the woman. He flips through the pages, stopping on one with the word *drunk* written in the margin. Monica had said Raine was in the forest right after Samantha ran away. Why didn't Raine say anything about Samantha's disappearance? She must have been the last person to see her.

Flipping back farther, he spots the word *medium* written in the margin. The leader, Terry, is a trance medium. Terry channels the spirit of Sebastian. Yesterday, Raine said she planned to become a trance medium and channel a spirit. She said the spirit would tell her where Samantha went.

Strange.

She completely believes Sebastian speaks through Terry. Everyone in the Haven believes in Sebastian. Raine is so intelligent and beautiful . . . could it be real? Other than living in a cult, she's everything Noah has ever wanted in a woman.

He laughs at the thought—*what he wants in a woman*. He hasn't been looking for a woman, and he barely knows her, and, like she said, trancing is strange. But if it's so strange, why does she believe in it?

Of course, trancing isn't all she believes. She also believes Noah is a college student.

The guilt hits him.

She's so trusting, and he's done nothing but lie to her.

A paper clip holds a photo of Samantha to the inside cover of the notebook.

Noah tells himself the deception is for a good cause, but the guilt doesn't go away. He tells himself Raine wouldn't want him to lose his apartment *or* his kneecaps.

He gazes at the photo. Samantha stands with her arm resting on a banister and her head tilted forward. She wears a black sequin dress, high heels, and a thin diamond necklace.

"Is that your daughter?" the woman asks.

"No, but"— he pulls the photo out and holds it up —"have you seen anyone who looks like her?"

The woman closes her magazine and squints like she needs reading glasses. "She looks familiar, but to me, they all looked the same."

"Sorry? They?"

"A week ago last Saturday. It was prom." She talks like a cowboy. "They were all running around in their outfits before the dance started over at the high school. I had to go to Mackey's Grill for dinner 'cause everywhere else was too busy."

"She wouldn't have gone to prom. This is an older photo."

"Is she missing or something?"

"Look closely at her face. Do you think you might have seen her somewhere before last Saturday?"

"Nope. Can't say that I did."

Joe returns from the garage. "Hey, buddy. I think we can get you going in an hour or two." He wipes his hands with a rag.

"You said it would only take twenty minutes."

"Sorry. Her car is a two-man job, but we'll get to yours. Don't worry."

The woman opens the magazine and gazes at a bright yellow '67 Camaro.

"Would you mind if he worked on my car first?" Noah asks.

"I don't want to be here any longer than I have to." She keeps her eyes on the Camaro.

Noah holds up the picture of Samantha. "Please?"

"If she's been gone over a week, then another couple hours won't matter." She licks her thumb and turns the page. "Besides, you said she ain't even your daughter."

Joe shrugs.

Noah stands. "You've got to be kidding me. This is my friend's daughter. He's worried sick about her, and I've got to—" His pocket vibrates, and he pulls out his cell phone.

It's Mr. Oakes.

"Excuse me." He strides toward the front door. "Joe. Just get me going as fast as you can, alright?"

"Sure thing."

Noah walks to the far side of the lot. "Hello?"

"What do you know? Has she come back?"

"No. I'm sorry. I talked to the couple trying to adopt her, but they haven't seen her. She hasn't come back yet."

"Has anyone seen her? What about the woman she was staying with?"

"She was staying with the couple, not that woman. I interviewed her yesterday." Lava rock separates the parking lot from the sidewalk. Noah paces along the edge.

"What did she say?"

"Not much. I couldn't tell whether she was hiding something or not."

"Stay on her. I have a strong feeling she knows where Samantha went."

"I'm trying. I was on my way to talk to her again today, but my car broke down. I'm at an auto shop in Elko now."

"I apologize, Noah. I don't mean to pressure you, it's just that—every day that goes by . . . do me a favor. Tell the shop to send your bill to my office, okay? I'll pay to have your car fixed. Do you have a pen and paper?"

"You don't have to do that."

"I insist. Do you have a pen and paper?"

A semi-truck barrels down the road. Noah covers his ear and raises his voice. "No. I'm outside."

"Okay. I'll text you the address to my office then. Have the bill sent there. What's this woman's name?"

"Raine Harkins."

"What does she look like?"

Noah remembers running hand-in-hand with Raine across the Medieval Minigolf parking lot. She looks like an angel. A beautiful, innocent angel. "She's got long brown hair and blue eyes. Not too tall, but athletic."

"Do you think you'll talk to her today?"

"Yes." He glances at the time on his phone. "If I can find her. I don't know where she lives, but the Haven isn't that large, so I—"

"She lives in an A-frame."

"I know, I just don't know which one. Don't worry, I'll find her."

"Please. I'm counting on you."

"Listen." He hovers right outside the front door. "I think she might open up to me more if I told her who I really am. If I explained who you are and why I need to find your daughter."

"No. You can't do that."

"But—"

"They'll stop talking to you. Trust me. They'll kick you out of the Haven."

"But Raine is different."

"You just said she wasn't opening up to you. She's hiding something."

"I didn't mean it that way. I—she might be hiding something because she doesn't trust me. She has a kind of sixth sense about people."

"Sixth sense? Like she can read minds? You're not falling for their spiritual bullshit, are you?"

"No, it's not like that. I just think she would open up if I told her the truth. I could ask her not to tell anyone."

"Don't trust her, Noah. They're all the same. They only want to find Samantha and brainwash her against me. Are they looking for her?"

"Yes."

"But I bet they haven't called the police, have they?"

"No."

"That's because they don't want anyone to know what they're doing. See? They're evil. Even this Raine is evil. Don't trust her. You've got to stick to your story and find my baby, okay? Can you do that? Finding her is the only thing that matters."

CHAPTER TWENTY-ONE

DAVID

Believers in the Teaching gather in groups outside the trance room like wasps on a rose bush.

David says nothing as Monica joins the older women heading to their ladies' brunch. Their drunken ladies' brunch. Terry and Kattrice stand at the end of the path, smiling and nodding to those who pass. Raine joins them. She looks happy.

David averts his eyes, steps off the path, and heads toward the road, crushing thistles and knapweed beneath his boots.

"David," Kattrice shouts, "are you coming over later? Our toilet still doesn't flush."

He marches over the culvert, his boots skidding on the pebbles.

"David?" she says. "Come back. We need to talk to you."

Farther away, he hears Monica yell, "Let him go, Mom. I'll make him fix it later."

The hell she will. She has no idea what later looks like. He's not going to fix Terry's toilet again. He's never being of service again. A wave of anger crashes over him, turning everything a beautiful shade of red. He loves his mind. Damn Sebastian for telling everybody to get out of their mind. Knowing what you can do on the earth plane, doing whatever you feel like whenever you feel like it is . . . it's beautiful.

Red.

It's beautiful, empty, and red.

David's back hurts less the faster he walks. Everything hurts less the more he focuses on the road. The rocks and dirt blur together. He stops at his yard and looks over all he has achieved in his life. Patches of weeds over two feet high. A cabin on stressed stilts. A dented old Ford with an expired transmission. His shed.

The lock on the shed hangs from the chain, fastened tight. His tools hang inside.

A breeze cools his brow, made colder by his sweat, but he still sees red on the fringes of his vision.

He bounds up the cabin steps and bursts through the door, causing Cori to jump up off the couch. She runs behind the kitchen counter, holding her hand on her chest, her long hair, like Samantha's, flowing behind her. "You scared me."

He stops midway across the room. "How were the kids?"

She creases her forehead. "They were good . . . "

"Why are you looking at me like that?" he says.

"Are you feeling okay?"

David relaxes his shoulders, lets them drop. "I've never felt better."

She narrows her gaze. "You don't look like yourself."

"Cori," he says, putting on a smile he doesn't feel. "You should go."

"Yeah, okay." She takes the long way to the living room,

giving him a wide berth. "I gave them a snack about an hour ago." She grabs her backpack off the floor. "Have a good day."

"I plan to."

Jenny and Joseph run down the hall.

"Dad, can I have a Pop-Tart?" Joseph asks.

David opens a cupboard. "Have whatever you want."

Joseph tears into a box, pulls out a shiny package, and rips the wrapping off.

Jenny places a drawing on the counter. "Do you like this one?"

She's drawn another family portrait. Just the four of them this time . . . no Samantha.

"Do you have a crayon I can use?" David asks.

"Sure. What color?"

"I don't care. The blue one."

She hands him the crayon.

"Thank you, sweetheart." He flips the drawing over.

Dear Jenny,

Believe in yourself above everyone else. It wasn't your fault. Always remember that.

Love, Dad.

She reads it and smiles.

He kneels. "Listen." He puts one hand on each of their shoulders. "I love you guys. I want you to be good."

Crumbs fall from Joseph's mouth. "What did we do?"

"Nothing. You've done nothing. I—"

"What's wrong, Daddy?" Jenny asks.

"Nothing. Listen, do you think you could go to Shayla's house for a while?"

"I know how to go there," Joseph says, pride pouring over his face.

Jenny rolls her eyes.

"Follow your sister, okay?"

"Why do we have to go?" Jenny asks.

"I have some things to—" David's throat catches. He clears it and tips his head back, holding onto their shoulders for balance. "Just go and stay at Shayla's until someone comes to get you. I have some things to do. You can't be here." Without looking at their faces, he leans forward, pulls his children against his chest, and holds them tight.

Joseph returns the embrace for a second, then wriggles free and runs out the door.

"Wait." Jenny breaks away and tears after him. "You'll go the wrong way."

David stands, takes a step back, and the floor creaks. The house sways. He sees flashes of red, turns, catches himself on the counter, gasps, and realizes he must have stopped breathing when he told his kids good-bye.

Slumped over the counter, he catches his breath. The red flashes vanish. An empty bottle of Jose Cuervo stares him in the face. The expensive stuff. The Princess always gets the expensive stuff. Well, not anymore. The bottle of gin next to the tequila is half empty. He chuckles. Maybe it's half full. Maybe he should drink it. That would send her into an unholy rage.

He grabs the gin bottle by the neck and throws it at the refrigerator. It bursts against the door, sending a barrage of glass ripping through Jenny's drawings, magnets crashing to the floor. He didn't mean to destroy her work, and it only makes him angrier. The bitter smelling gin runs down the olive-green door and puddles on the floor. His hands shake. Someone's going to have to clean this up, and it's not going to be him.

And it won't be Monica.

Dammit.

The kids can't see this mess. The smell.

This is all Monica's fault. She'll be worthless when she returns. Drunk.

What was it at brunch today? Mimosas or Bloody Marys?

Right now, she's getting sloshed on one or the other. Laughing and telling the older women what a horrible husband he is. Bragging about how she's got him under control. Announcing that he is going to do whatever she says because she is his like-vibration and, without her, he can't get close to God. Holding the gun over him. How, without her, he's not in the Teaching.

And she's right. He's not in the Teaching. Not anymore.

She's going to be surprised when she comes home.

David glances at the clock on the stove. It's always been wrong. He can't remember if it's twenty minutes ahead or twenty minutes behind.

It doesn't matter. This is it. It's time.

The hallway is tighter than ever. It's so . . . narrow. He ignores the haze forming on the periphery of his vision, letting it turn red as he enters the bedroom. Turning back now isn't an option. Going for another joyride on the highway isn't an option. The transmission is shot. His truck is dead. He could call Raine, but there's no reason to mess up her life. She has a future. It's not an option. There are no options.

It's time.

He opens the drawer to the nightstand and picks up the

Holy Qur'an. It was never his favorite. He drops it on the floor and picks up the Holy Vedas. The plain red cover never did this book justice. Jnana, bhakti, karma—the three roads to salvation through knowledge, devotion, and action. He opens the cover then stops. There's nothing inside it he hasn't seen before. He lets go, and the Vedas fall onto the floor next to the Qur'an.

In the drawer, the sand-colored handle of Terry's gun peeks out from beneath the Bible. David reaches for it and pauses. His hand hovers, trembling over God's big black book.

For I am convinced that neither death nor life, neither angels nor demons, neither the present nor the future, nor any powers, neither height nor depth, nor anything else in all creation, will be able to separate us from the love of God that is in Christ Jesus our Lord.

The writers of this book should have left Jesus alone. For two thousand years, they've done nothing but bother that poor soul. Praying to him at all hours of the day and night. He was just a man with a gift, like Terry.

Prayers to Jesus don't work.

Terry is not God.

The alarm clock on the nightstand has the correct time.

Monica will be coming home in an hour or two.

David takes the gun in his hand.

He squeezes the grip.

Nothing has ever felt this real.

Nothing has ever felt this right.

It's time.

CHAPTER TWENTY-TWO

RAINE

I sit down on a pillow by the white wicker love seat near the Shrine. My nerves are amped up, but I'm determined to go through with this. I'll at least *try* to learn how to trance.

Kattrice and Terry approach, strolling across the lawn from their house. Terry takes his place on the love seat. Flakes of white paint crack and fall from the rattan as he folds his legs into the Lotus position. The wedding arch stretches over him, and the light blue sky beyond is free of clouds. It's clear.

Peaceful.

Kattrice picks up a flower watering can. "I'll be around back." She winks. "Good luck, Raine. You're going to need it."

I wish Terry hadn't married her, but I shouldn't think way. Trance mediums don't think that way. Instead, I need to fill myself with love, peace, and understanding, or this will be a waste of time.

"Your mother is very pleased you've decided to let me teach you," Terry says.

"I'm pleased, too." A rock presses through the pillow I'm

sitting on. It hurts, but I want Terry to think I'm at peace. I shift and pull, but I can't get my legs to bend the way his do, and the rock continues to pain me.

He sees me struggling and smiles. "Relax, Raine. After today, you'll know peace like never before."

I give up and let my feet flop out in front of me. The rock shifts to the side.

"What do you know about trancing?" he asks.

"It's when a spirit speaks through you." He's got to be thinking I'm an idiot. I wait, and he doesn't respond. He just sits there with starry eyes and a grin. This might be a test. The right answer might be no answer at all. Patience. I rest my wrists on my legs, palms up, and touch my thumbs to my forefingers, just as he is doing.

His grin widens. "Yes, being a vessel for another's voice, that's the gist of it, but not all. To go into a trance is to completely leave your body. You become unconscious. Completely. Some trance mediums' hearts slow to a stop. This opens the door for a soul from the spirit world to enter you and, as you said, speak through you. Actually, *you* are gone. The spirit uses your body to speak."

"Your heart stops? You die and come back?"

"There are no dead, and there is no dying." He radiates comfort, swimming in his rough-sewn cotton V-neck. "I have never had my pulse checked to know, but don't worry yourself. You'll be fine."

"How many trance mediums are there?"

"Hundreds, over time. We go back to before the Bible was written. Most societies, in one form or another, have used trance for spiritual teaching and counseling. What I'm about to show you is a well-established practice. Have you ever heard of Edgar Cayce?"

"Yes. You've mentioned him before, but I don't remember much."

"He is perhaps the most famous medium of all time. When Edgar was a young man, he lost his voice. He couldn't speak for over a year. Desperate, he wrote a letter asking a friend to hypnotize him, and while he was in a deep trance, he began to speak in another voice. The voice told his friend to make a series of suggestions to Edgar's body. He asked for extra blood to be sent to Edgar's voice box and it worked. Not only was Edgar able to speak again, but after he came out of the trance, he had found his spirit voice. He learned how to leave his body on his own and went on to help hundreds of people. He healed them with the word of God."

"Where is he?"

"He passed away in the nineteen forties if I remember right. After we're through here, I want you to go home and memorize Psalm forty-six. Will you do that?"

"Yes."

"Okay. Let's begin."

"Wait. Why did you choose me? I don't know the Teaching as well as other people here."

"Knowing isn't everything. To trance, you must have devotion and action as well as knowledge. You are an old soul, Raine. I've seen you speak with nothing but your heart as if your mind wasn't there to filter your ego. You live in the Teaching without knowing it. I believe in you. I believe you will trance, and your spirit guide will help us find Samantha. Then, you will help me help others, the way Edgar Cayce did." He tips his head back and gazes at the sky. "Are you ready?"

"Yes."

I am *so* ready. Not just so I can ask my spirit guide about Samantha, but so I can find out about the notes. I don't believe God is going to run me down, or that he wants me to leave the Haven, but to have a spirit speak through me and tell me everything is okay . . . it would set me free.

"Relax," he says. "You're shaking. Try to relax."

I nod, rub my hands together, then put them back on my knees.

"Do you meditate often?"

"Yes, but I'm no good at it. I usually fall asleep."

"That's fine." He raises his arms. "It's getting warm out here, don't you think?" He removes his shirt. "The sun is hot." He squints. "Don't you think it's getting hot?"

"Yes."

"Warm, spring days like this make me sleepy." He yawns.

I yawn.

"Focus on my eyes as we begin this meditation." His voice soothes. "Do you see the whites of my eyes?"

"Yes."

"Do you see the blues of my irises?"

"Yes." His eyes are oceans, flooding my periphery. His face, the wedding arch, the mansion beyond, the sky, the earth—everything—it all fades away.

"Do you see a bright spot in the center, surrounded by black?"

"Yes." His pupils gleam. I feel lifted. Weightless.

"Relax. Relax your throat. Breathe. Breathe."

In through my nose, out through my mouth—I breathe. *Ohm.* The fragrance of the gardenias fills my head. I hadn't noticed the scent before. My hands relax and fall off my legs.

"Relax your throat. Do you want your spirit guide to come?"

"Yes."

"She needs your vocal cords to be limber. She needs you to leave them alone. Relax. She will enter. She will leave. She will speak, and you will listen. Do not try to speak to her. Do you promise not to speak?"

"Yes."

"You will not speak your questions, but do not worry. She will know the answers you seek. Are you ready?"

"Yes."

"See the astral in my eyes, swirling stars, heaven's lights." His intonation caresses the air. "Two bright spots. Two stars. Focus. Focus." His voice rises. "Focus. When I tell you to go there, will you go?"

I whisper, "Yes." I'm weak. My eyes want to close. I have no feeling in my legs because they're not there . . . neither is my body. Vaguely, I sense I'm still breathing, but the fragrance of the gardenias is gone. All there is—all I see—is the light in his eyes. Now, just the light.

He raises his voice. "Go! Go there now!"

Everything turns black. It's all gone. I'm inside myself, delightfully disoriented. I begin to think, and a tinge of red encroaches on my vision. Looking at the backs of my eyelids is a mistake. I'll wake up if I see them. They're physical things. I don't want to wake—

"In this astral"—Terry's voice sinks, becomes quiet and soft—"there is precisely one star. One star. One star. H-m-m. M-m-m. Focus. Focus."

There is nothing but darkness. Pure black, except for a tiny pinprick of light. I focus on it. I don't feel myself breathing and—I shouldn't feel myself breathing. I should focus. I should only see the star. I should go . . . go . . . go . . .

"Raine, my child." Terry's voice is so far away. "My child, there is a river whose streams make glad the city of God." He rasps, speaking in a British accent. He sounds like Sebastian. "The holy place of the tabernacles of the most high awaits you. It be time for you to go . . . to go . . . to go . . . "

Impossibly, the tiny star moves away from me. It's getting smaller, and I don't want it to go. I'm weightless. It pulls on me, and I move toward it.

Is this it? Am I trancing?

I shouldn't think. It'll ruin everything. I promised not to speak. Is thinking speaking? I—

"Raine." A woman's voice enters my—*what am I? Am I conscious? Who?*

"Raine," she says. "I have watched you from the time of your birth until now. You know this, no? Wait. Do not answer. Do not be afraid." She speaks with an Italian accent. "In my last life, they called me Cecilia Roman, and you will call me the same in this one, no?"

Peace pours over me, but it shouldn't. I shouldn't be at peace.

My heart has stopped beating.

"Do not be afraid," she says. "There are no dead, and there is no dying. And now that I'm here, there is no going back."

A LETTER FROM THE SHRINE

Dear God,

Thank you for creating this community. I am home, but I need your help. I want to stay here, but I don't love Jace the way he loves me, and I'm afraid of what everyone will think when they find out what happened. Sebastian said I should be strong and independent. He said I don't need a man to live, and I agree, but I need this place.

I hate men. You know why.

The truth is, I'm afraid of them. That's why I took the gun. I want to stay here. Please help me. I don't know what to do.

Love,
Samantha

CHAPTER TWENTY-THREE

RAINE

Am I still on the earth plane?

Cecilia told me to leave my body, and I think I did. Everything is black, but not really. Everything is *nothing*, except for her voice. She sounds deep and scratchy, yet gentle like tissue paper tearing. Things don't feel right. I shouldn't be able to think, but I am thinking. And if I'm thinking, I'm awake. And If I'm awake, I'm in my mind, but my body isn't here.

Where am I?

Am I gone?

"Go," she says.

I've got to stop thinking, but—visions come. Blurry at first, then I'm floating. I'm looking down now. The top of the Shrine has torn shingles. The gardenias run in an arch around it like a priest's collar. Terry sits on the white wicker love seat, his body slumped to one side. My body is on the ground across from him, slumped forward.

I'm rising higher. Uneasy. It's like I'm walking downstairs in the dark, not knowing if the next step is there or not.

I'm dead.

"There are no dead, and there is no dying," Cecilia says, pronouncing her Ds with a thick, stuttering lilt.

Am I imagining this?

The landscape below vanishes. Red and black ribbons entwine and spin around me. I think about the color blue, and I'm surrounded by a clear blue sky.

"Having fun?" Cecilia's voice breaks my concentration. Her accent is strange. It's a cross between Dracula and an Italian gypsy. "My mother greets you well and sends you God's blessing. In my last life, I did not know you, but my mother did." She chuckles. "My mother says you had the raven's hair, and you coaxed many a man to lay with you in the little village of Bugarach."

I think my spirit guide is calling me a slut, but—

"I carry no judgment upon you. That's God's gig, baby, not mine. Do you like the way I speak to you now? Can you understand my jam?"

I try not to think. This can't be happening. Somehow, I'm doing this to myself. My subconscious is a magician. It feels like I'm tricking myself.

"Raine, I have never embodied a magician. This is not a trick. You'd be my first, baby, but you're no magician." She laughs. "Oh, baby. Baby, listen to me. You've heard me your whole life, but you've never listened until now. Isn't it a gas?"

The blue around me disappears and is replaced by my mother's long, gray-streaked hair, but it isn't her. The woman's face is a blur.

"There is an empty chamber in your life, Raine. Do you know your father loves you from afar? He regrets leaving. He misses you."

Not true. My father hates me. He left before he could ever have loved me. He never loved me.

"Remember the tears your father shed the day he left?" she asks. "I was there with you. We didn't know adults could cry until that day, did we?"

What do you want?

"What do *you* want, Raine? Why have you opened your body to me?"

I'm blank. The reason escapes me. I don't want anything. My mother made me come here so she could get closer to God through me. I should want to get closer, but who is God? And why do I care?

What do I want?

I want to go home, climb into bed, and roll up in my blankets.

I want to hide.

"Raine, baby. You want to be held." She is tender. "You want to be loved."

That's enough. Trance time is over. I can leave anytime I want. All I have to do is click my heels together—suddenly, I see ruby-red sequins streaming down, floating, falling, sparkling throughout. The sequins clog my throat. I suffocate, but I'm not breathing. My heart is still. The earth plane doesn't exist.

"The earth plane has two kinds of love, Raine. One for all the glory of being human and one for everlasting life. The first is true, but the second is pure. True love is for fun; it's animal love, and you're an animal. God put furry dogs and wet frogs and flying birds on the earth for you to have fun with. For you to love. He also put men all around you for the same purpose. Go ahead, hold them, love them, be held by them, but do not regard this animal yearning higher than pure love. Sex is not pure love. Pure love comes only when you sacrifice yourself to save another's soul."

The red sequins disappear, and in their place, I see Samantha, crouching in the woods, crying.

I'm lost. Samantha's lost. I lost Samantha. It's my fault she's gone.

"Guilt is self-serving, Raine. Do not mourn Samantha, and do not surrender to guilt. And you must stop chasing after men. They're nothing more than fun animals. They can fill you with what you want, make you feel wanted, but those feelings are temporary. Hollow in the end. This Noah is pure of heart, but he is only a man."

I am not chasing after Noah. Or any man for that matter . . . but I do know loneliness.

"Your father loves you from afar. Please take this truth and stop chasing men, playing your little girl games. Do you have the whistle your father gave you?"

"Yes," I say out loud, feeling a tingle in my throat.

Oh, no.

I spoke.

Terry said not to speak. I've changed my mind. I don't want out, but my consciousness is returning. I remember what I wanted, what I should have said. I want to know who wrote the notes.

I tighten the muscles around my throat. I will not speak again.

"Keep your whistle close and stop trying to appease your selfish wants. You can only save yourself—you can only find the pure love you need—by saving someone else."

Samantha.

"Yes, baby. Find her. Bring her back to the community and teach her the Teaching."

My face feels warm except for a tear coursing down my cheek. My legs are dead asleep, and I smell the gardenias. My neck aches, and—someone is screaming.

It's a woman. "Dad. Dad. Dad."

My eyes fly open.

Cecilia is gone.

Terry stares at me wide-eyed like he's surprised I'm alive.

The screaming comes from behind the trees up the road. "Dad!"

Terry lifts his chin and shouts back. "We're over here. What is it?"

Monica sprints into view. She crosses the lawn. "Dad, come quick." Her face is redder than usual.

He lurches off the love seat and hooks it with his ankle. He stumbles, and I jump to catch him, but my legs cave, and we fall down.

Kattrice rushes out from behind the house.

Monica looks down at us. "We shouldn't have let him—" She puts her hand on her chest. Bends over. Gasps for air. "We—"

"Who?" Kattrice shouts.

"David."

Terry gets to his feet and puts his hand on Monica's shoulder. "What has happened?"

"What did he do now?" Kattrice puts her hands on her hips.

From somewhere deep in my mind, Cecilia says, *Ciao, baby.*

Monica stammers, "He's locked himself alone in the shed. He—" She looks at me like it's my fault. "He's got a gun."

"Where are the children?" Kattrice asks.

"When he wouldn't come out, I took them to Shayla's," Monica says. "They're fine."

Terry takes her hand. "It's going to be okay. Everything will be as it should. God has a plan."

Monica snarls. "Don't give me that bull—"

"C'mon," Kattrice says, waving her arm. "Let's go see what the numbskull is up to." She marches toward the road.

Terry and Monica join her while I struggle to stand. My legs are still asleep.

What is David doing with a gun? He's alone in his shed with a gun.

No.

He wouldn't.

I stumble onto the road behind them, trying to catch up. Kattrice leads the charge, her hands balled in fists.

David's been withdrawn lately, but everyone has bad days. He never said anything to me, but I haven't been around. Until last week, I wasn't even going to trance. I was so busy dating Warren, trying to pull him into the Teaching that I—

Oh, no.

Cecilia is right.

I've spent my life chasing every man other than David so I wouldn't be alone. Trying to fill a void. I've spent my life chasing after the *fun animals* rather than being there for my friends. For David.

David.

Kattrice suddenly stops in the middle of the road and

turns around. She points her crooked finger at me. "Where do you think you're going?"

"To see David."

She puts her hands on her hips. "Terry, can you take care of this?"

Terry turns and faces me.

Monica glares at me through her tears. The veins in her neck throb.

"Raine," Terry says. "This is a family matter. A *Windhaven* family matter. You understand, don't you?"

I'm speechless. I can't even stutter. An unexplainable emptiness invades my insides and turns into a rage so hot— so terribly hot—I want to attack them like a feral dog. I want to bite their faces off. I wish Java were here to attack them.

I may not be a Windhaven, but David is a part of my family. We're all in the same teaching. What the hell happened to the Teaching?

Kattrice and Monica turn to go.

I put my hand on my chest and feel for my whistle.

Goddammit.

I didn't put it on this morning.

Shit.

Terry gazes at me, his eyes streaming across the astral, his voice like a soft blanket. "It could be dangerous, Raine. David's got my gun. Go home and I'll call you when we know it's safe."

CHAPTER TWENTY-FOUR

DAVID

Years ago, everyone in the Haven got together and built David's shed in a day. They used to do things like that. Gatherings with purpose. The Haven was more like a family then. One summer, when David was young, they followed a carnival company from state to state, making bagels and selling them at state and county fairs. Sometimes at rodeos. They worked together, everyone in the Teaching, as one family.

Now, the shed's walls have turned gray. Crevices in the wood, etched over time, run from the rafters to the dirt floor like the grooves of an old record. Light seeps in through cracks in the boards, glinting off the steel lock. It hangs on the inside of the door like a medallion. He looped the chain through the hooks on the outside, then pulled the lock through a hole and turned the key after Monica threatened to tell everyone he stole Terry's gun. After he refused to go to work on Terry's toilet again. After he told her to go to hell.

She went to get help.

But David doesn't need help. Not anymore.

God answered his prayers last week when he found Terry's gun. He just didn't know it at the time. The Teaching is dead, but God is everlasting. He's grateful God put Jace in his path, here in the Haven, at this time in his life. It's fascinating how one person's karma can affect another's. Jace's karma led him to steal Terry's gun so he could hide it in the woods where David would find it. Then, Samantha ran away so David would go looking for her. So God could give David the gun.

God always has a plan.

David loves his children, and they love him, but Jenny and Joseph don't just belong to him. They also belong to God. Somewhere on the earth plane, they have a spirit family. There's solace in knowing they will find their spirit parents one day. They will. David and Monica are nothing but blood to those kids.

And like life, blood is temporary.

The light seeping in through the cracks cast crooked lines upon the ground. The air is warm for this time of year, but a cold wind has been building inside David for weeks. Maybe years. For him, spring never came.

But it doesn't matter anymore.

His tools hang from hooks above the workbench. Real men work with their hands in the name of God, like Jesus did. David is no Jesus. He sits on the ground with his back against the wall, his legs folded like he's about to meditate. The gun feels good in his hand. He squeezes the grip, savoring the feel of its textured surface. It's a sand-colored, 9mm Glock. He would have preferred black a gun, but who is he to judge God's creations? God's gifts?

He prays for a clear mind; one that will let him do what

needs to be done. God's will. He meditates. *Praise God . . . praise God . . . praise God . . .*

An image of Samantha springs to life and shakes David out of his meditation. She is his spirit daughter. Sebastian proclaimed it so. David didn't fulfill his karma with her. He failed as a teacher. As a father. As a husband.

And now, nothing matters.

God knows best.

He places the gun in his mouth. Having it there releases the cold wind, and it blasts him with shivers of excitement. He shakes. He shudders. His jaw muscles ache. His teeth clack against the metal as he aims the muzzle upward. He points it at his mind. God wants him to do this. God gave Terry this gun years ago so it could find its way into David's hands. It was meant to be. The gun has found its way into his mouth, and it's pointed at the source of all his misery.

His mind.

This is his destiny. His karma.

And besides, he's not going to kill himself. That's impossible because . . . there are no dead, and there is no dying.

Shh. Goodbye.

He squeezes the—

"David. Get your ass out here."

It's Kattrice.

"David, my son. We've come to help you."

And Terry.

David relaxes his finger on the trigger. Reality comes crashing down around him.

"David?" Terry pleads.

Hot tears stream from his eyes. Slowly, he pulls the gun

out of his mouth. His tongue touches the oily muzzle, and he retches.

"Dammit, David," Monica screams. "I can hear you in there." The door shakes. The chain rattles. "I'm ordering you to come out now. You have to do what I say."

He shoves the gun inside his mouth and presses the muzzle against the back of his throat. His thumb finds the trigger.

His hand quivers.

This must end.

"If you're doing what I think you're doing," Kattrice says, "then you're going against God's will. You should never make your medium's daughter suffer this way. My husband has given his life for you, you ungrateful—"

"Enough." Terry's voice fills the shed. "David. Listen to me. Listen to—"

A shadow crosses over the walls, blocking out the light. Something falls against the door, bending the planks.

David pulls the gun out of his mouth and licks his lips.

"H-m-m. M-m-m. H-m-m." Terry moans.

Something slaps the outside of the shed. The tools swing.

"H-m-m. M-m-m. I be here, me child. Do you hear me? It be I, Sebastian."

David's bowels clench. He wants to throw up. The tears come in waves. He's never cried like this before. His head is on fire. The heat courses through him, wiping out everything in its path. Everything that was ripped away—his purpose in life, hope for the future, belief in the Teaching . . . it all comes rushing back.

"I forgive you, David." Sebastian's voice cleanses the air. "Terry forgives you. Everyone forgives you. No one blames you for anything. I will not allow me children to blame you."

David drops the gun, leans forward, and collapses onto the ground. He breathes in and out, panting like he's just climbed Ruby Dome. Acid rises in his throat, and he swallows it back down.

"I cannot stay, me child. The sun be bad for me medium's body, you know. Always remember, I love you."

The door rattles.

"David?" Monica asks. "What the hell are you doing in there?"

"Shut your mouth, Monica." Terry's voice is dry and scratchy. "Go over there, or I'll have to—"

"No," she says.

Shadows move. Feet scrape on the ground. A loud *smack* followed by a whimper penetrates the shed walls.

Monica is crying.

David rolls onto his back.

He closes his eyes.

Smiles.

He waits until the crying outside dies down.

Air flows freely into his chest, and gravity holds him to the earth. It's solid. It's real. All is quiet. A minute passes. Then ten years. All is quiet while he lays there, becoming one with the earth. With reality.

All is quiet now.

David doesn't have to listen to Monica ever again. He doesn't have to kill himself. He's forgiven. Sebastian forgave him for everything.

"David?" Terry asks. "Will you come out now?"

David stands. He unlocks the lock, pulls the chain through the hole, and opens the door.

"I forgive you for taking my gun," Terry says. "I should

never have hidden in my house to begin with." He steps forward and wraps David in an embrace. "I'm so glad you're still with us. I forgive you. Will you forgive me?"

Monica stands at the edge of the driveway, leaning against the truck.

"There is nothing to forgive," David says.

The trees in the distance stretch up into the bright blue sky. His cabin stands strong. Jenny and Joseph's toys play hide-n-seek in the tall grass. The world changes before his eyes, and for the first time in a long, long time, he likes what he sees.

Terry whispers into his ear. "I know how you must feel, but you should go to your wife. She is still your like-vibration."

Monica's face is wet with sweat and tears.

David goes to her and takes her hand.

Her eyes dart over his, searching for something. Anything. He hopes they don't find what they're looking for because it doesn't live inside him anymore.

"I was so scared," she says.

"I know. I'm sorry."

"What do we do now?" she asks, looking at her parents.

"David needs to have a private session with Sebastian," Kattrice says. "He's obviously all screwed up. He's in his ego."

Terry doesn't acknowledge her. Instead, he walks inside the shed and bends down to pick up the gun.

David says, "I'll have a private with Sebastian."

"Good." Kattrice looks him straight in the eyes. "Then I want you to talk to those who are deep in the Teaching. Get help from the community. Do service for them."

"Okay," he says. "I will."

"When?" she demands.

"First thing tomorrow morning. I'll begin by talking to Raine."

Monica lets go of David's hand. "Why her?"

Kattrice flashes Monica a look. "No. Raine is a good choice. She's going to be a trance medium soon, so you might as well start with her. Give her some practice."

Monica's eyes narrow on her mother. Her face throbs, red from crying, red from drinking at brunch. The odor of Vodka and tomato juice poisons the air. She is David's like-vibration, but he's learned enough from her in this lifetime. The learning is over.

"I can't explain it." Terry walks out of the shed. He holds up his gun, examining the tan barrel in the light. "This is—"

"What is it?" Kattrice says.

"My dad's gun was a six-shooter. A black revolver." Terry turns the gun over, holding it at different angles. "I don't know whose gun this is."

"What are you saying?" she asks.

"This isn't my gun."

CHAPTER TWENTY-FIVE

RAINE

My mind is exhausted. Washing dishes, shaking out the living room rug, sweeping, trying to stay focused on a book—none of it helps. My thoughts switch from David to Cecilia to Noah to the threatening notes . . . to Samantha and back to David.

Terry hasn't called all afternoon, and Monica hasn't returned my messages. As much as I hate it, I must honor Terry's request to let the Windhavens take care of David. Besides, if something had happened, something serious, it would have spread throughout the Haven like a grass fire by now. My mother would have called me. On the information food chain, she ranks right below Kattrice.

I sit on my sofa and check my phone for messages again. Nothing.

I should finish reading my book, but I can't focus. I'm still not sure what happened during the trance lesson. Was I unconscious or asleep? My throat feels funny, but that doesn't mean Cecilia spoke through me in the physical world. At times, it seemed like I was talking to myself. It was like I had an imaginary friend over for a playdate, but at other times, her voice was real—scratchy, deep, and real.

She knew a lot about me. I'll give her that.

She knew all about my father.

And about Noah.

I regret the way minigolf ended. I shouldn't have left angry. Technically, it wasn't a date. It was an interview like Noah kept saying. My mind only turned it into a date because I was so hopeful, so happy. He genuinely wanted to know about the Teaching and me. Sitting here, alone in my cabin, I don't care what Cecilia said about "playing little girl games." Chasing after men for animal love instead of pure love.

I think I could love Noah.

He made me feel innocent and free for the first time in a long time. I just wish he hadn't said David was strange. He insinuated David had something to do with Samantha's disappearance, and I overreacted. I can be so impulsive sometimes.

I check my phone again.

No missed calls. No messages.

I've got to get up and do something else. I've spent too much time sitting here, being in my mind.

The loft is a mess. I could clean it, but I'm in no mood to haul my laundry over to my mother's trailer. If she hasn't heard about David yet, she'll want to hear about my trance lesson. Bask in the glow and talk about the wonders of God. It'll be hours before she'll let me leave.

I could take Java for a hike and look for Samantha again, but wandering around in the woods seems pointless. Samantha disappeared too many days ago. I'm starting to forget what she looked like.

It doesn't matter. I can't go. My cell phone has never worked in the woods, and I need to answer it when Terry calls.

Okay. That's it. I'm getting off my butt.

The bathroom it is.

Everyone's favorite room to clean.

I march down the hall and surprise Java. She jumps to her feet, and her fur stands on end for a second. I thought she was in her usual place, sleeping on her pillow in the kitchen, but she wasn't. There's a sick look in her eyes like she ate a dead squirrel or something.

"Watch out, girl," I say, pulling open the bathroom door, careful not to hit her with it.

Toilet brush in hand, I'm ready. I flip the seat up and examine the ring around the bowl. It's reached a dark, disgusting color only a strong cleanser can get out, so I grab a can from under the sink and begin scrubbing. The chemical smell stings my nose, but it's worth it. I'm already thinking less about David and the notes.

Then, as I scrub, I remember how Kattrice pointed her finger at me. How she ordered Terry to "handle me." How he said David locked in the shed was a Windhaven family matter. It's not fair. I've known David longer than anyone, yet here I am, relegated to cleaning my bathroom, waiting for a call.

I bet Kattrice isn't cleaning her toilet right now. She never scrubs. She always has other people always do it for her in the name of service. When I become a trance medium, I'm not going to make people work for free.

Listen to that—me, a trance medium.

Strange.

Hearing Cecilia's voice . . . that was strange.

I've never questioned listening to Sebastian. He's been

here my entire life, but Cecilia—she's new. She said I've been *hearing* her all my life, but I that wasn't listening. If I try to trance again, I'll have to get used to her.

I stand, brush in hand, ready to tackle the shower. Orange-green fungus decorates the bottom of my shower curtains. Next time I go to the store, I should get a spray for that. I pull open the curtain, and there's an envelope taped to the back wall with my name on it.

I drop the brush.

It lands in the toilet, splashing my leg.

I don't move.

It can't be.

How is this possible?

Someone would've had to come inside my cabin while I was sitting on the sofa, or before I got home, and they—

There's a tapping.

I scream.

Java barks behind me, and I scream again.

She comes to me, her toenails clicking against the tile floor. Tapping. It was only her. The skin around my eyes tightens, and a headache comes on. My mind is exhausted. Until now, there was still a chance the notes were left by teenagers on a dare, but if one of them tried to come inside while Java was here, she would have scared them away.

This is no prank.

Java looks up at me with the same sickly sadness in her eyes as before. Did someone poison her to get inside? I picture a man, dressed all in black, opening the front door and throwing a steak laced with Drano into my house. It had to be that way. Java would never have let a man come into her domain uncontested.

She hates all men.

All men except for Noah.

I snatch the envelope off the wall and go to the living room and look out the window. There's nothing but the road and the forest between here and the trance room. There's no one around.

No movement.

I open the envelope.

The starchy white paper crinkles when I unfold it.

The hand of God is coming, Raine. You should have run away with Samantha when you had the chance.

CHAPTER TWENTY-SIX

RAINE

I'm standing at the back door of my A-frame, staring at the forest through the window, clutching my whistle in one hand, the note in the other. I don't remember putting my whistle around my neck. The deadbolt isn't latched. I've never had a reason to latch it before now. I can't leave, but I can't stay either.

The hand of God is coming.

Sunlight fails to penetrate the late afternoon shadows between the trees. The land behind my A-Frame rises and falls for miles, gradually climbing over three major mountain ridges before emptying out near Hennen Canyon. I can't imagine hiking all the way to Elko through these unforgiving woods. Could Samantha have made it on her own? No. She must have come back, found her way to the road, and gotten a ride, but no one I talked to has seen her in over a week.

What happened?

The note says I should have run away with her when I had the chance. When did I have the chance? She ripped her arm free from my grasp and ran away over the hills into no man's land. I couldn't have caught her. I tried but—

The wind picks up. Branches sway. Pine needles shake and fall to the ground.

She's been out there alone for days, lost but—she wasn't alone.

Someone was watching her before the gunshot. Before I found her near the firepit.

Someone was watching *us.*

You should have run away with Samantha when you had the chance.

I lock the deadbolt, crumple the letter, and charge into the living room to lock the front door. Whoever saw us in the woods must have done something to her. Something horrible. They're not going to get me. I need to figure this out. Cecilia was supposed to tell me what happened. She was supposed to guide me to Samantha, but all she did was lecture me about love and men and—she said pure love comes only when you sacrifice yourself to save another's soul.

Samantha didn't make it out of the woods.

She needs me to save her soul.

I sit down on the sofa, uncrumple the note, and read.

The hand of God is coming, Raine.

Java climbs up and lies next to me. I stroke her fur, then rest my hand over her heart. I need to find Samantha, but I still don't know what happened to David. The note is messing with my head. I can't leave, and I can't stay.

My phone shows no messages. No missed calls. I call Monica, but she doesn't answer.

I'm alone.

Cecilia said she has always been with me, but where is she now?

Maybe if I meditate, Cecilia will come. I close my eyes, but without Terry here to guide me, I feel silly.

When I was little, David's dad always warned me about doing silly things. He'd say, *If you make that face, it might stick. If you cross your eyes, they might stick.* I'm too afraid to meditate because it might stick. What if my heart stopped and I needed Terry to bring me back?

I've got no one, except Java, but she isn't pure love, yet her presence consoles me. I don't care if she is just an animal. Noah is an animal, too, and I wish he were here. So what if I'm playing little girl games?

I miss him.

No I don't.

I can't miss him—I barely know him.

The swooping black letters taunt me. Whoever wrote the notes wants me to leave the Haven. They could be waiting for me in the woods right now, hoping I found the note in the shower. Hoping I leave to look for Samantha.

Hoping to prey on me the way they did her.

My head aches when I think about leaving.

Thumbing through my contact list, there's no one I can call. I truly am alone. Sharing the notes with the Haven would only cause a panic. When that little girl went missing up here years ago, the police accused us of being a cult. They searched our homes, and the town attacked us in the newspapers. Damn them.

Damn me.

Now *I'm* doing it. I'm blaming the town for accusing us of being a cult.

Evil begets evil. Blame begets blame.

But I need someone's help. Noah is the only one in the middle. He's not part of the community, and he's not from Elko, but I can't trust him. He accused David of hiding something. He asked me why David was so strange. He probably hasn't called because he thinks *I'm* strange. Or because I got angry on our date.

And it wasn't a date. It was an interview.

Dammit.

I should have listened to him about David. I should have gone to David and talked to him. Then maybe he wouldn't have locked himself in his shed. If I had reached out to him weeks ago, maybe he wouldn't have done something to make Samantha run away.

No.

That's not right.

He didn't do anything wrong. He wouldn't have.

But this note . . . someone wants me to leave.

I read it again.

. . . *You should have run away with Samantha when you had the chance.*

No matter how hard I try, no matter what rationalizations, explanations, or theories I come up with, there's no making it okay. Anyone could have left it.

My phone rings.

Thank God.

I snatch it up. Noah's number shows on the screen.

"I'm so glad you called," I say.

"You are? I thought you were mad at me. I mean . . . are you okay?"

"I'm fine." My heart races. "I was just thinking about you."

"Really?"

"Sure. I . . . I was trying to figure out how you cheated at minigolf. Nobody is that good." My throat tightens.

"You weren't bad."

I toss the letter on the coffee table and it lands face up. The writing is disturbingly clear—black on white. Supple and soft. Could a man have written it? The writing is delicate, but maybe a man with soft hands could have—

"Raine?" he says.

Again, I wonder how a man would have made it past Java to the shower stall. Noah is the only man she's ever let pet her, but he wouldn't have left notes, would he?

No.

Still, I want to ask him where he was earlier today. Ask him why he didn't come to Trance. Interrogate him like a suspect on a crime show.

The thought sickens me.

I hate crime shows.

"Raine? Are you still there?"

"Sorry, I—" Someone wants me gone, or . . . dead? That's what the note implies. It implies Samantha ran away because the hand of God was going to strike her down. "It's been an unusual day."

"Tell me about it. My car broke down on my way up there this morning, and this woman at the repair shop wouldn't let me—she was just really rude."

"Why?"

"I don't know how to explain it, just that—hey, you said you live in an A-frame, right?"

"Yes."

"I found one when I finally made it up there, but no one was home."

"I was at Terry's learning how to trance."

"Right." He pauses. "You were going to ask a dead person where Samantha went."

"I'm sorry how I behaved yesterday. I didn't mean to get so upset."

"It's okay. You're not still angry, are you?"

"No. Not at all. I—" I can't leave, and I can't stay. Someone wants me dead. My voice shakes. "Where are you?"

"At my hotel. Is something wrong?"

"No. Yes. I—it's David. He's got a gun, and he's locked himself in a shed." This comes running out of my mouth like water over a dam. "I'm afraid he's going to kill himself."

"Oh my God, that's horrible. Where is he?"

"At his house, maybe. I'm not sure he's still there. It's been a while, and no one is answering their phone."

"Does he have a history of—"

I cut him off before he can say the s-word out loud. "No, he's never done anything like this before. I'm sorry, I shouldn't have said anything."

"No, I'm glad you did. But, I've got to say, I'm not surprised." A chasm opens. "He was really depressed when I interviewed him last Friday. Do you think he went in there because of Samantha?"

"I don't know. I'm sure that's part of it." I wish I knew. I can't remember the last time David and I talked, just the two of us. I'm heartsick.

"He was really nervous whenever I brought up Samantha. If he did something to her, and I'm not saying he did—it could have been an accident—but if he did, the guilt might have gotten to him. Especially if he's never done anything like this before."

"You don't know him." I want to reach through the phone and force my words down Noah's throat. "He's never hurt anyone, not even by accident. He's the most caring, gentle person I've ever known."

"Then why does he have a gun?"

"I—I don't know."

He sighs. "I'm sorry, Raine. You're right. I don't know him the way you do. I shouldn't be butting in. I didn't mean to say he scared Samantha away."

The muscles in my jaw tighten. "I don't know why David has a gun. He—" My mind races, searching for an explanation. The truth is, David *could* have done something to scare Samantha. He could have, but he didn't. He wouldn't have. No. Not him. "No. He would never have written those notes." I pick up the paper. I'm shaking. The black words blur. "There's no way this is his handwriting."

"What? Notes?"

David—no. It can't be him. He would never want me to leave.

The hand of God . . .

If I had to leave, I don't know where I'd go—Bugarach? Shit. The Haven is the only place I've ever known. The world—the people in "the world"—they don't know me. They don't understand the Teaching. Noah can't understand. I've got nowhere to go.

"Raine?" he says.

"I can't talk right now."

"You're crying. What's going on? What did the notes say?"

"They said I have to leave, or else . . . or else—" I wipe my nose.

"Raine, are you—"

"I'm fine. I've got to go."

"You're not fine. Are you alone?"

Java has her eyes closed, sleeping next to me on the sofa. She's entirely at peace. "No." I grit my teeth. "I'm not alone."

"Good," he says. "I'm coming over."

"No. Don't."

The phone goes silent.

The screen reads, *Call ended: 7:02.*

CHAPTER TWENTY-SEVEN

RAINE

My doors are locked, and my curtains are closed. As far as anyone can tell, I'm not here. Anyone looking at my cabin will think I've gone for a walk in the woods.

I resent being scared into hiding by the notes.

And I don't want to see Noah until I've figured things out.

Outside, the world goes on without me, the same as any other Sunday evening. It's not fair. People eating fried chicken, preparing lunches for the week, mourning the end of another weekend—all the normal things I can't do because I can't let anyone know I'm here.

Dammit. I left the kitchen light on.

As I pass by the kitchen table, I hear a car pull into my driveway. I rush, flip the switch, and return to the living room. Carefully pulling the curtain aside, I peer outside. Noah's minivan stops next to my car. Maybe he didn't see the kitchen light go off. I press my back against the wall between the living room windows so he can't see me.

My house looks strange from this angle. I can see farther

into the loft than I thought possible. One of my bras is draped over the foot of my bed, and my laundry basket overflows with smelly clothes.

The minivan's door slams and, a moment later, he's knocking on the door.

Java barks.

I close my eyes. Please leave.

I told him not to come over.

"Raine?"

The last note lays on the coffee table. The other two are in the junk drawer in the kitchen. All three say God wants me gone. I don't even know if Noah believes in God. I need some time to figure this out.

"Raine? I saw the light turn off. I know you're in there. Why won't you open the door?"

I lift the curtain. He wipes his forehead and puts a hand on his hip. His blue dress shirt is stiff like he just ironed it. His jeans hug his hips, and he's taller than I remembered. He doesn't need that belt, but it looks good on him anyway.

He checks his watch, looks back at the road, then knocks again.

Java sniffs the door and wags her tail. She wiggles, looking at me, wondering what I'm waiting for.

"Hold on," I yell, brushing my hair back. It feels greasy, and my eyes must be red from crying. Clutching my whistle, I undo the deadbolt, take a deep breath, and open the door.

We look at each other.

The soft evening light blankets the road, the trees, the cabins in the distance. The Haven blurs behind him. His crooked tooth sticks out when he smiles, and I want to leap into his arms because . . . because it's him and, truth be told, I'm scared.

"Can I come in?" he says. "Are you okay?"

"I didn't want you to come over."

"I know, but—" He steps to the left, trying to come around me, but I hold my ground. "I—" Java forces her way past me and jumps up, playfully clawing at his belt. He drops to one knee.

"Java, no. Get inside." She ignores me.

"What's the whistle for?" he asks.

"Nothing." He must think I'm hideous, standing here in a dirty T-shirt and pajama bottoms. My face feels hot and wet from crying earlier. I wasn't going anywhere, and I hadn't planned on opening the door. My hair must look awful. I brush it back again.

He scratches Java behind the ears. "I drove by David's house on the way here. It didn't look like anything was going on. I thought you'd want to know."

"Thanks. I'm sorry for bringing that up. It's nothing. Look, I have work in the morning, so—"

"Have you had dinner?"

"No." I step forward and grab Java by the collar. She resists, and I stoop to get a better grip.

"Can I come inside?" He leans around me.

"Not so fast." I stand. "I'm tired and I have work—"

He reaches toward my cheek. "But you haven't had dinner." I step back.

"Let's see what you've got in there to cook," he says. "And you can tell me about those notes."

Java twists, and I lose my grip on her collar. She runs into the house.

"There's nothing to tell."

"Raine, there's something. You've been crying. Let's talk."

"Okay," I turn and walk inside. "But you're not staying for dinner. I'm going to bed early tonight."

He follows, and half-way to the kitchen, I turn around. The third note lays face up on the coffee table. I try to get there first, but he grabs it and holds it up out of my reach. "It's not as bad as you might—"

"Just let me read it."

I jump again, bumping against his chest. His cologne is hypnotic. It suggests I should stay close—very close—to his body. "Please." I try for the note again.

He puts his back to me and reads it. "Where did you find this?"

Defeated, I slump onto the sofa and clasp my hands. "That one was in my bathroom. Don't tell anyone, okay? It's nothing to worry about."

"This one? You mean there're others? Where?"

"In the kitchen."

He glances at the note again. "Someone left these in your house?"

"No, just that one. The others were outside."

"Raine, this is serious. You have to call the police."

"I can't do that. Please don't tell anyone."

He carries the note into the kitchen. "Where are the other ones?"

I get up, open the junk drawer, and take out the notes.

He waits by the kitchen table.

"Here. You can read them, but then you have to go. I'm alright. Really."

While he reads, I open the cupboard to the pots and pans.

"This isn't good," he says. "Why did they think you should have run away with Samantha?"

"I don't know. Maybe they sent her the same notes." I drop a pot into the sink and turn on the faucet.

"Who do you think left these? Do you think David—"

"No." Here he goes again, attacking David. I cross the kitchen floor and snatch the note out of his hands. "Look at the handwriting. Does that look like a man's handwriting?"

"He could have written it that way on purpose."

"Why do you keep blaming him? He's—"

"I'm sorry, but you said yourself, he's not stable. Did you find out what happened this afternoon?"

"He's fine or my mother would have called."

Noah steps forward. His cologne smells too good, too powerful, for him to stand this close. He holds up the first note. "Why didn't you call the police when you found this?"

I head back into the kitchen. "I thought it was a prank. You don't understand. When you live in a place like the Haven, you have to be careful. We've been burned by the police before."

"That makes sense."

"It does?" I put the pot on the stove.

"Sure. A guy in town told me about what happened. That girl getting kidnapped and—I know how people can get confused. You're probably right not to call the police."

I pull out a box of mac-n-cheese and open it. Noah amazes me. No outsider has ever understood the Haven this way. Not this fast.

"Still," he says, "how can you be so sure about David? You said he had a gun."

"If I tell you something, do you promise not to tell

anyone else?" I pour the noodles into the water and watch as they sink to the bottom of the pot.

"Absolutely. You can trust me."

"No one knows this, well, almost no one. I was the last person to see Samantha." He sits down at the table with the notes and his notebook, intent on listening. "Java got out, and I was in the forest looking for her. I hadn't officially met Samantha before, and I didn't know she'd been living with Monica and David. I didn't know anything about her." I put the empty box on the counter. "My point is, David wasn't there."

Noah gazes at one of the notes. "This one says you could have run away with Samantha." He looks up. "Someone was there, watching you."

"It wasn't David."

"How can you be so sure? Think. Do you remember seeing anyone else? Were there any signs or—"

"No."

"What was Samantha doing when you saw her? I mean, what was she wearing? How was she acting?"

"Why do you want to know about her? What does she have to do with your school or your thesis?"

He hesitates like he's trying to remember something. "I'm concerned about you. You said someone might have left her the same kind of notes. If so, she would have been scared. Did she look like she was running away?"

"She looked terrified, but that could have been because of the gun."

"What?"

"A gun went off right before I saw her and—she had a backpack. She was putting something into it or taking something out. I don't know." I lean my back against the stove, bracing myself with both hands. "She startled when she saw me. The terror in her eyes . . . I wanted her to come to look for Java, but she wouldn't do it."

"Do you remember anything else?"

It's all such a mess in my head now. There isn't anything else to remember. I had her, and she got away. End of story. "No. Maybe if I meditated, I could remember something. I could ask my spirit—never mind."

"What about the gunshot?"

"What about it?"

"Everyone I talked to in the Haven says guns aren't allowed here. I can't help it, Raine." He lowers his gaze. "It keeps coming back to David. You said he has a gun. Why couldn't it have been him in the forest?"

"No. You don't know him."

Noah stands. "Exactly. I don't know him. That makes me objective. I'm an outsider, remember? That's what you called me." He paces. "Someone is threatening you. For real." The pain in his eyes is real. He cares. "When I talked to David, he was utterly miserable, and now he might have tried to kill himself. I'm telling you, it could have been guilt. I already thought he did something to scare Samantha away, and now I think he was in the woods with a gun." He stops pacing. "Maybe he was trying to scare Samantha away, and when it worked, he felt horrible about it, and"—he rubs his chin—"I just don't know."

"David would never do anything like that."

Or would he?

"I'm sorry," Noah says. "I'm not trying to blame him. I'm just trying to understand."

"I think you should leave."

He steps toward me. "How do you know David didn't leave the notes?"

I grasp the pot by the handle and pull it off the stove. "Stop accusing David."

"No. You've got to listen." He steps closer. "I'm worried about you."

"Back off." The weight of the pot strains my wrist.

He doesn't listen and comes even closer.

"I warned you." In one motion, I swing the pot and twist the handle. He ducks and I drench him. Noodles fly everywhere. He steps back, realizes I never turned the burner on, and rushes toward me. Water drips from his chin. He grabs me by my upper arms and pulls me to his chest.

His cologne is hypnotic.

He holds me tight.

I slap his back and push on his shoulder. He's tall. Strong. He lifts my chin, and our eyes meet. When his lips part, I don't hesitate. I kiss him, reach behind his back, and run my fingers down his torso. My hands slide over his muscles, pulling his body against mine, holding him against my chest. Breathing him in.

We spin until my back is to the kitchen table.

He pulls away with a mix of fear and excitement on his beautiful face.

"I'm sorry," he says. "I don't know what came over me."

I caress his cheek. He has no idea how adorable his crooked tooth is.

A piece of macaroni is stuck in his hair.

"What's so funny?" he asks.

I pluck the pasta from his head and fling it across the room. "Nothing."

He runs his hand up my back, inside my shirt.

I undo his top button.

"Are we going to—"

"Shh."

I undo the next button . . . and the next. His shirt comes off, and he lifts me onto the table.

I wrap everything I have around him.

Everything.

CHAPTER TWENTY-EIGHT

RAINE

The early morning sun shines in through the front window. I gaze at the ceiling. I'm lying quietly next to Noah on the living room floor, careful not to wake him. I count the knots in the pine boards on the ceiling until I spot a spiderweb at the far end of the peak. I didn't know it was there, and I don't care.

I close my eyes and hang onto the moment. Savor it.

My head is cradled in Noah's shoulder. I can't imagine he was comfortable without a pillow, but he never complained.

He shifts and opens his eyes.

Our legs are intertwined beneath a blanket my mother made when she was in her quilting phase. The patches are beige, brown, and blue with yarn knots holding the corners together. I wish I could go back to sleep and stay this way forever, warm and content. My skin feels like it's glowing, and I count the spots where our bodies touch. Nine, including my hand in his.

Little girl games never felt so good.

But these aren't games. Noah could be the real thing.

He stretches his arms out over his head, and I feel his chest flex beneath my cheek.

"Was I hurting you?" I say.

"No." He lifts a lock of hair off my face and loops it over my ear. His touch is tender. We kiss.

It's heaven.

"Do you want to move to the bedroom?" I ask.

"That depends."

"On what?"

He grins and furrows his brow. "Are you going to dump mac and cheese on my head if I mention David again?"

I pull the blanket up. "I might. That depends."

"On what?"

"Are you going to accuse him again?"

He puts his hand on my cheek. "You're so beautiful. I think I . . . "

"You what?"

"I think I . . . I should stay here today. You shouldn't be alone."

"I have work in a few hours"—I pull him close—"you can stay until then."

"Maybe I should follow you to work."

"Why?"

"I had a nightmare about those notes." He looks away. "If whoever wrote them is spying on you, I might be able to catch them in the act."

He loves me. "I don't want to be followed. Not by you, or anyone else."

"I understand."

"I do wish I knew who left them, though. I wish I could ask Samantha if she was getting the same kind of threats."

"You think someone scared her into running away?"

"Yes."

"I think you're right. Do you have any idea who it could be?"

"No. Nobody in the Teaching would do anything like this."

"What about David?"

"Oh, no." I pull away. "Not that again."

"Wait." He sits up. "I don't want to accuse him. I'd just feel better if we could rule him out. If only you remembered something about the last time you saw Samantha. That could eliminate him."

"Noah, please."

"I'm sorry, but the fact is, he could have been in the woods watching you. He could be the one writing the notes."

"He's not, but I hear what you're saying." I pull on his arm, encouraging him to lie back down. "Let me see what else I can remember."

Patience, I tell myself. *Patience.*

He lies down.

I take his hand, put it on my chest, and close my eyes. I wish for my heart to beat slow and steady. I hope Noah can feel it. I'd love for us to drift back to sleep right now. I'd love to meditate. Let Cecilia enter my body, speak through me, tell us who wrote the notes.

But if her voice came out of my mouth, it would scare the hell out of Noah.

I take deep breaths anyway. I retrace the events leading up to when I saw Samantha, sorting through hazy images, asking myself, *what am I missing?*

The gate is open and Java escapes. *What am I missing?*

I follow the trail toward the firepit, examining every rock, every tire track. *What am I missing?*

The trees have gotten taller since I was a teenager. *What am I missing?*

Nothing. I'm missing nothing.

Dammit.

Patience.

It's not working. I'm not missing anything.

I try again.

I hear something on the other side of a boulder. *What am I missing?*

A gun goes off and—wait. Before that.

I sit up.

"What is it?" Noah asks.

"Someone was riding around on an ATV before the gun went off. There was an engine roaring through in the woods. I remember it because I was worried Java would get run over."

"Was that before or after you saw Samantha?"

"It was before. The gun went off right after I found her. Whoever was on the ATV could have parked it and then shot the gun."

"Yeah. They could have followed you on foot." He takes my hand. "And watched you."

Despite his warm touch, chills course through my body.

Someone was watching me. . . but it wasn't David. What a relief.

"Why are you smiling?" Noah says.

"David doesn't own an ATV."

"Hmm."

I run my fingertips down his arm. "Do you still think it was him?"

"I don't want to, but couldn't he have borrowed an ATV?"

"I don't know from who."

"How about renting?"

"You saw the inside of his house. He couldn't afford to waste money on something like that."

"You're right."

"His dad used to have an ATV, but I think he got rid of it. I haven't seen him on it in a long time."

"So, David *could* have borrowed one?"

"Noah,"—I roll closer, slip my leg over his thigh, and run my hand around his waist—"David wasn't there."

His eyes are deep brown, speckled with orange and turquoise dots. "Okay. I believe you. I won't bring him up anymore. I promise." He kisses me.

It's heavenly.

"But," he says, "someone *was* there."

"I know."

"Who else has an ATV?"

"I don't know."

CHAPTER TWENTY-NINE

DAVID

David strolls down Control Road toward Terry and Kattrice's house, letting the morning sun show him things he hasn't seen in a long time. Things he couldn't see from inside his shed yesterday.

The Shrine leans to the left. He remembers when he helped Terry build it. Either the wood is rotting, or the ground is giving way, but it doesn't matter. He's not going to fix it. Terry's lawn is short because David mowed it, but weeds stand matted against the foundation.

Someone else can get out the weedeater and take care of it.

Inside the house, he imagines, the toilet is clogged, brimming with waste. The Haven doesn't have a sewer system, only septic tanks. No one's toilet works the way it should.

But that's not David's fault.

A breeze whips dust across the road. The Haven is tranquil today, and the Teaching is hollow. It's empty, but not like yesterday. Nothing is, or ever will be, as empty as yesterday, sitting in the dark, pressing the gun's muzzle against the back of his throat.

No, today is empty like a concrete slab waiting for a house to be built.

He tips his head back and lets the sun warm his face.

He has always had a foundation in the Haven and a construction plan in the Teaching.

Starting now, he's going to build a new house.

He only hopes Raine is in hers.

He needs her help.

While some people struggle with life, spinning their wheels, trying to be *in* the Teaching, Raine has always had the Teaching in her. She knows what it is to truly be in the Teaching without knowing it. David thought he knew how, but he was wrong. He lived every day for others, being of service to God's children—Terry, Kattrice, and Monica—and it nearly destroyed him.

It drove him to suicide. The opposite of the Teaching.

He cuts through the woods, taking the shortcut Raine's A-frame.

A cluster of sagebrush reminds him of when he found the gun. He tells himself yesterday is over and all is forgiven. Terry and Sebastian forgave him, and Sebastian said David wouldn't be blamed for taking the gun and hiding it, but the guilt remains. The lies he told in silence cause pangs of remorse. The idea he could have tried harder to find Samantha rather than letting his selfishness take over fills his heart with stabbing needles.

Patience. God, give me patience.

He knows now, he can take the Teaching with him wherever he goes. Being in the Teaching doesn't mean forever sacrificing himself for the Haven. He is a free man. He could leave the Haven, go anywhere. Go to—where? Europe? Italy?

Maybe Raine would go with him. She has always wanted to go to Europe—to a mountain town in the Pyrenees. They could live there together in peace. But this flight of fancy vanishes as quickly as it comes. He could never leave Jenny and Joseph alone to live with Monica. No one deserves that.

He exits the woods and sees a minivan parked in the driveway next to Raine's car. It looks like the one that guy from UNLV was driving. Noah. Maybe he is interviewing Raine for his thesis but—this early on a Monday morning?

David ascends the steps, raises his hand to knock on the door, and it swings open, smacking his fingers. He winces.

"David," Noah says, "you scared me. You—" He holds out his hand and smiles. "We were just talking about you." He glances down at David's other hand, then at David's waist. "You look like you're alright."

David takes Noah's hand and shakes it. "Why wouldn't I be alright?"

"No reason."

"David!" Raine runs through the doorway and wraps her arms around him. He wishes he wore something other than his dirty work coat. She's wearing a long T-shirt, and he can feel her ribs through the thin cotton.

She pulls back, leaving her arms locked around him. "I'm so glad you're okay. No one called me back when I tried to find out what happened."

"Why wouldn't I be okay?"

Noah turns away, rubbing his neck. The stress in his eyes doesn't match the smile on his face.

"What did Monica tell you?"

"Nothing," Raine says. "I was at Terry's yesterday when she came running down the street, yelling for help. She said you . . . you locked yourself in the shed with a gun." She smells like cologne. "I guess I thought the worst. *Are* you okay?"

Every word she says comes out guarded, not wanting to offend or scare or hurt. She couldn't know for sure what he did, but she's so intuitive. "You thought right. It *was* the worst, but it's over now. I just need to talk to you."

Noah glances at David as if he was about to say something, then looks away again.

"Can we talk?" David asks. "Alone?"

"Sure, I'd love to." The words bounce off her tongue. Blue stars in her eyes.

Noah puts his hand on Raine's shoulder. "Will you be okay?"

Why wouldn't she be okay?

"I can come back," David says. "I didn't mean to interrupt anything." Raine's legs are bare and she's not wearing shoes. "I can come back when you've had time to finish dressing."

Noah blushes. "It's okay. I was leaving anyway. Good seeing you, David." He holds out his hand again, and David shakes it. "I'm really glad nothing bad happened. I mean—I hope to see you around."

"Sure."

Raine makes a tight grin as Noah heads for his minivan. She's found someone.

David is happy for her. Really, he is, but if she goes to Europe in the future, it won't be with him.

He'll have to find somewhere else to go.

"I'll call you later," she says, waving to Noah.

She takes David's hand in hers and leads him inside the A-frame. "I'm so happy to see you. C'mon."

The kitchen table sits at an angle, and the tablecloth only half covers the top. A plate and fork lay on the floor next to Java's food bowl. Java sits by the back door, cautiously watching Davis as he crosses the room. "Was there a fight?"

"No." Raine straightens the table. "We were just . . . uh—"

"I see you've got yourself a new man."

Raine beams. "Yes."

"That's wonderful. I'm really happy for you."

She stops rearranging the tablecloth and lifts her head, keeping her hands on the table. Her gaze reaches inside him, looking for something. God, he's missed her. His friend. She's just his friend, but a warm feeling comes over him, and he steps into the living room to get away from it. A quilt and a pillow lay next to the coffee table as if Raine and Noah had a campout.

"David, I'm sorry I haven't been around much. I—"

"Life takes over. I understand. We all get busy."

Her shirt sways over her hips as she crosses the floor. "It's no excuse. We should hang out more like we used to."

Monica would never allow it, but—it's not up to Monica. Nothing is up to Monica anymore. "Yes. I'd like that." Raine's laugh lines have deepened over time, but her eyes still dance. She's going to be a beautiful old lady someday. "You really like him, don't you?"

She puts her hand on her chest, and a smile takes over. "Yes. I guess I do."

"I'm so happy for you. Really, it's wonderful. I hope he's your like-vibration. Monica and I used to—" His throat tightens and, out of nowhere—maybe not nowhere, maybe from the astral—a vision of an open door appears. The word *exit* is painted in black. A brilliant light shines in, mixing fear with joy. There's a word for this door, but David has never allowed himself to say it. He's never allowed himself to think it because it goes against the Teaching. It goes against learning from your like-vibration.

Divorce.

He bites his lower lip.

I'm going to get a divorce.

He holds back a deluge of tears.

The inside of his nose stings.

Raine's glow dims. "David?"

He looks away, hides his eyes, rubs his nose. There's a piece of paper on the coffee table. "What's this?" He picks it up, and she grabs it from him before he can read the strange, black handwriting.

"It's nothing," she says. "Just some trash I found." She crumples the paper and heads toward the loft. "Let me get dressed, and we'll go for a walk. We should talk."

"Yes. I'd like that."

CHAPTER THIRTY

RAINE

Will miracles never cease? David is okay. Well, not *okay*. But he is out of his house, and he did come to see me. It was awkward until Noah left—there's still macaroni on the kitchen floor—but David gets it. When he says he's happy for me, he's happy for me. I believe him.

I wish he were happy for himself.

We step outside, and I stop on the porch. The sun greets me, shining bright, making everything look like it's on display. Even my car looks new. The Haven basks in the sunshine. I don't want to leave. Ever. This is *my* home.

My shoulders tense up when I picture someone writing those notes. Sneaking into my house. Into my bathroom. It makes me seethe.

I turn to lock the door.

"What are you doing?" David asks.

"I—" the sun hits my back "—I'm taking my jacket off. I don't need it."

Java rushes the door when I open it. I'm in no mood for her

to lead me through the Haven, jerking me this way and that. I need to focus on David. "Goodbye, Java. I'll be back soon."

I turn the key in the lock and test the door to be sure she is safe inside.

David walks to the road. His shoulders are slack beneath his grimy yellow work coat. He's going to get hot.

"Were you locking your door?" he asks.

"Yes." I nod in the direction of the firepit. "Teenagers. There's been some strange—some kids I don't know have been hanging around there lately."

"Oh. Do you want to walk that way and check it out?"

"No, let's walk through the Haven."

I can trust David, but I don't want to put him in a bad position. If he knew about the notes, he would want to tell Monica. I can't ask him to keep secrets from her, and if she finds out, everyone will find out.

We walk down the road toward the Pliskin's house.

Something's really wrong or David wouldn't have shown up at my cabin this morning. Watching him come face-to-face with Noah put my emotions in a tailspin like I had cheated on David, though nothing could be further from the truth.

"I heard you're going to start trancing," he says.

"You did?" If he knows, others know. My mother is probably bragging to everyone she sees.

"I overheard Terry and Kattrice talking. There wasn't an announcement or anything."

"I told Terry it should have been you."

He laughs, bends over, and picks up a stick. "That would have been something."

"Why not? You know more about the Teaching than anyone."

"No, it's not that. I don't care to learn about that." He holds the stick up, assessing the curvature. "You should have seen the look on Monica's face when she found out Terry was giving you lessons. She would have really lost it if I were the chosen one."

I laugh. "I'm not *the chosen one*. It's not like some epic fairy tale."

"You're going to be great, Raine." His gaze shifts far away, somewhere down the road. We stroll. "I don't have it in me. Not anymore."

"What happened yesterday?" There I go, blurting out the burning question. He stares straight ahead. I pretend to be interested in the Pliskin's roof, giving him time to answer.

He doesn't respond.

We stroll.

"You don't have to talk about it," I say. "I'm sorry."

"No. I want to. They told me to talk to you."

"Who?"

"Kattrice and Terry."

It's happening. One trance lesson and they're sending people to me. Not just people—David.

His face pinches for an instant. "I'm fine now, Raine, but . . . I was going to kill myself. I don't remember planning it out, but I must have."

I let it soak in. I knew it, but hearing it come from his lips—there's nothing I can say. The signs were there, but I ignored them. Maybe it's because I've never considered—seriously considered—doing anything like that myself. Everyone thinks about it, wonders about it, runs a list of ways to do it through their head, but no one I've ever known has ever gone this far.

No one until now.

I take his hand. "I would've missed you."

"I know. It's the most selfish thing I've ever done." There's a tremor in his voice. "I can't believe I was going to leave Jenny and Joseph."

"And Monica."

He blinks. Lets go of my hand. "Yes. And Monica. And Samantha. You know we were adopting her."

"That's what I heard. I'm sorry she ran away. That must have been hard for you and Monica."

"Not as hard as you think. I—dammit, Raine. I didn't care that she left." *Don't look up at the sky, David. I'm right here.* "I didn't want to adopt her. We couldn't afford another one, and—that's the definition of selfish."

I grasp his arm. "Is that why you—"

"No. It was part of it, but I just got to a point where everything was empty." He rolls the stick between his fingers, twirling it over his knuckles. I let go of his elbow. "When I was sitting in the shed, I blanked out. Everything went black. It was like I was dead inside."

On impulse, I say, "There are no dead, and there is no dying."

He cracks a smile. "That was one of my reasons."

"Oh, I didn't mean to say that. I'm—"

"It's okay. I convinced myself that if there are no dead, and there is no dying, then it wouldn't matter if I left."

"I see. You know, that's not what it's supposed to mean."

"I know. The real reason was my falling out with the Teaching. I haven't been in the Teaching for a long time, and yesterday was a new low. I don't know." He wipes his brow.

"I've tried so hard to be of service so long, thinking it would get me closer to God, but I haven't felt—I just never feel—"

"Happy?"

"No. Human. I'm a robot, doing what everyone tells me to do. It's like I've been programmed."

"Sebastian says computers and robots destroyed Atlantis." Why the hell did I bring that up? I'm flustered. David needs help. Real help. Not me spouting off weird things Sebastian says.

"Yeah. I've always wondered about that. There weren't computers back then, but if he's saying humans started acting like computers, then I get it. That would kill a civilization. Last night, when I was praying, I realized I'd been following the Teaching like a train on a one-way track. I stopped thinking for myself, and I stopped living. I'm afraid I never really *lived* in the Teaching."

"I try not to worry about it."

"Exactly. Worrying is a state of mind, and you—you're so—you have a big heart, Raine."

"Thank you." My cup runneth over.

We cross over the road near the Shrine.

"See?" He points at the little building. "I wrote hundreds of notes and put them in there because the Teaching told me to." He grasps the stick with both hands. "I never needed to write those notes." He breaks the stick in half and throws it at the Shrine. "I never needed to do service!"

"David," I say, dropping my voice. "They'll hear you."

He stops. Stands still. Tense. His eyes fixed on the Shrine.

I step ahead and turn to face him. "You're right." I take his hand. His rough, cracked skin is cool to the touch. I give a gentle tug to get his attention, but he keeps his gaze on the

Shrine. "You need to love yourself before you can love anyone else. Don't ever let anyone push you around."

I picture the second note—*God doesn't want you here. Leave the Haven now, before he runs you down.*

I'm being pushed around.

I will not be run out of my home. I will not be forced out of the Haven.

Unintentionally, I squeeze David's hand. I squeeze it hard.

He shifts his eyes from the Shrine to me. His face relaxes. He pulls his hand from my grasp and rests it on my shoulder. "Thank you, Raine. You've always known what to say."

We walk away from the Shrine, side by side.

It feels right, like old—very old—times. As exciting and provocative as it was to make love to Noah on the living room floor last night, I feel dirty now. Cecilia told me the difference between animal love and pure love. David feels like pure love, but that's not what she meant either. Like Noah, he's just a man. She wanted me to stop chasing men and truly be of service.

She wanted me to find Samantha.

"We should turn back," David says. "Don't you need to go to work?"

"No, I'm not going in today. Let's keep walking."

"Why aren't you—"

"David, I have something to ask you."

"What?"

"Where did you get the gun?"

He slows his pace and looks at me. "I didn't steal it from Terry."

"No, of course not. I thought maybe it was your dad's. Didn't he have a hunting rifle?"

"No. He's never owned a gun in his life."

"Hm." But he owned an ATV. "I must have been thinking of someone else."

"I found the gun in the woods last week when I was looking for Samantha." He fails to stifle a nervous chuckle. "It's ironic. I felt so guilty about not telling Terry I found his gun, and it turns out, it wasn't even his."

"Whose was it?"

"I don't know. We have no idea."

"We?"

"Monica and me."

"Did Samantha ever say anything about someone wanting her to run away? Maybe, threatening her?"

"No. What do you mean?"

"I don't know." I kick a rock into the culvert. "I saw her in the woods the day she left. She looked scared like she was in trouble. I was wondering if something happened before that, or if you saw anything strange."

"No. Monica said they got into a fight that morning, but that's normal. What did Samantha say when you saw her?"

"I can't remember exactly. I tried to get her to come with me to look for Java, but she refused and ran."

David stops. "So that's what Sebastian was talking about in Trance. You're the one who chose an animal over one of *God's* children."

"Yes. I'm sorry. I shouldn't have let Samantha go."

"It's all right, Raine. I'm sure you did nothing wrong. Monica said you saw her out there, but I didn't know she looked scared." He stops again. "Did you see Jace that day?"

"No, why?"

"But you heard gunshots?"

"Yes." The terror in Samantha's eyes when the first gun went off still pops into my head from time to time.

"How many?"

"Two. One before I saw Samantha, and one after I ran into Monica on the road. Why? Do you think Jace was shooting a gun?"

"I don't know what to think. I wondered if it was the same gun I found, but the one I had was missing three bullets."

"That doesn't prove anything, does it? It still might have been the same gun."

"Yeah. And I saw Jace by the woods that day, but he insists he didn't see her. He said he heard the gunshots too, and I kind of believe him."

"You're a good judge. Maybe he is telling the truth."

"Maybe."

Ahead, a cloud comes out of nowhere, shading the highway. "Do you want to head back?"

"Sure."

We turn around, but it's not long before the cloud's shadow creeps up behind us.

"I should've known the gun wasn't Terry's."

"Why?"

"Sebastian said Terry had been hiding it as an heirloom from his father since the eighties. The one I found was tan and modern looking like it was made for Iraq. Terry's gun is an old-time, black revolver with a wooden grip."

"Where is it?"

"Still missing, I guess."

"You think Jace took it, don't you?"

"I don't know."

Terry's house appears in the distance as we stroll around

the corner past the Shrine. It looms. The cloud that was following us now covers the entire Haven, casting a chill over me. I wish I'd worn my jacket after all.

"Let's cut through the trees," David says. "I don't feel like walking all the way around."

I rub the backs of my arms and nod.

Last week, I suspected the teenagers were playing a prank on me. I suspected Jace first off, but I thought it was just a prank. Maybe I should have followed my intuition. "Do you think Jace was out there trying to scare Samantha away?"

"Maybe. I wish I knew. He denied knowing anything about her, and I can usually tell when he's lying. I might have misread him. I just don't know. I just don't know anything anymore."

"I'm sorry, David. I—"

"No, it's okay. Jace is a good kid, but he's angry. He's been through a lot, and Samantha broke up with him right before she moved in with us. Now that I think about it, he probably blames us for the breakup."

"I thought he was dating Cori. I saw them playing minigolf the other day."

"He is. It doesn't take teenagers long to move on. I just wish it wasn't with her, you know? Cori deserves someone better."

"It's a rebound."

"Yep."

"So . . . he could still be angry over his breakup with Samantha."

"Yep."

We exit the trees and step onto my road.

David stops. "Not angry enough to shoot her if that's what you're thinking. He's not a bad kid. He just—"

"David?"

"Yes."

"Does Jace own an ATV?"

"Yeah. He's been using my dad's. Why?"

CHAPTER THIRTY-ONE

NOAH

After driving back to his hotel this morning, Noah waits until ten before going to Yama's Powersports. Elko has two places where someone could rent an ATV on short notice: Yama's and Ted's Tractors Plus. Yama's website shows the most promise of the two. More selection.

On his way, he counts the fast-food restaurants. Six. The Walmart and two grocery stores add to the rural ambiance, as does every jacked up, extended cab truck he passes. Gray dust clings to the storefronts and parking lots along Idaho Street. It's an ugly town, but he could get used to living here. If he could be with Raine, he could get used to living anywhere.

Kawasaki, Honda, Yamaha, Polaris—Yama's has them all if you go by the signs adorning the roof, but the small sign inside reads CLOSED MONDAYS. It would have been nice if they'd hung something more prominent out front so he wouldn't have had to get out of his car. It would have been even nicer if the website had shown the correct hours.

Standing with his back to the store, he pulls out his cell

phone, opens the maps app, types in *Ted's,* and auto-complete slaps "Ted's Burgers" into the search bar. The map loads. He hits the back button and gazes across the parking lot, waiting for the search screen to reload.

A faded blue Ford Taurus rolls down the street. The woman behind the wheel wears sunglasses. It takes a second to register, but Noah recognizes David's wife, Monica. He waves, but she doesn't wave back. Maybe she didn't see him, or maybe she didn't recognize him. She *was* hammered the other night when he was at her house.

Ted's Tractors Plus is on the other side of town, eleven minutes away. Elko is eleven minutes wide. How quaint. The wind blows dust across the parking lot, making a gray wave. The small size of Elko, the quiet—he could get used to living here if it meant being with Raine, but Mr. Oakes will want him by his side in Vegas. If only he hadn't borrowed so much money from Titus.

He glances up the street, suddenly nervous his loan shark might have found out where he went. He looks for Titus's trademark vermillion suit jacket, but no one's there. Driving across town, he keeps a lookout for Titus and, as always, Samantha.

Ted is a much smarter businessman than Yama, assuming Yama is a person's name and not some stupid twist on the Yamaha brand. The open sign at Ted's Tractors Plus is big and out front where it can be seen from the road.

He parks by the front door.

Business appears to be slow on Monday mornings. There's only one other car in the lot. The large windows reveal a showroom containing two tractors, a few ATVs, some lawn-mowers, and a row of bar-b-cue grills.

Noah quickly runs over the plan in his head, then enters.

The teenage kid behind the counter might as well have had a straw hat, overalls, and a weed sticking out of his mouth. Tractor place is right. He doesn't actually look like Tom Sawyer, but he *is* wearing a John Deere cap, an orange and black flannel shirt, and a stupid grin. His jeans hang off his waist, showing the tops of his boxer underwear. That fashion statement has never made sense to Noah.

"Hi," the kid says. "What can I do for you?" He's excited like he hasn't talked to anyone in days.

"I was wondering if you could help me track down a thief."

"Sure, I—what do you mean?"

Noah puts his hands on the counter and lowers his voice. He leans in. "Somebody stole my credit card and used it here. I'm trying to figure out who it was. Do you think you can help me?"

The kid lowers his voice to match Noah's. "Sure thing, sir."

"The charge was made on April twentieth. Can you look up the receipts for that day?"

"That was last month." The kid stands up straight. "Ted keeps all that stuff in his office, but he's not here right now."

Assuming Ted is the owner, if he were here, there's no way Noah would get him to share his records. This kid is Noah's only chance. "What about rentals? Do you have a reservation book or something?"

"Yeah, right here." He pulls out a red binder and opens it on the counter. "Let's see. April twentieth. Nope. We didn't rent nothing that day."

"How about the nineteenth?"

"But you said your card was charged on the twentieth."

"Yeah, I mean, it was, but sometimes it takes a day for charges to go through."

The kid grapples with the concept, cocking his head to the side.

"Haven't you seen that before?" Noah asks. "Someone charges something, but it doesn't go through for a day or two?"

"Sure, sure. Let's see. Looks like we had four rentals on the nineteenth. Friday's our busiest day. Here, take a look." He turns the binder so Noah can read the entries.

Hank Marles - Apr. 19-21 - Polaris Sportsman 570
Jake Allenton - Apr. 19-21 - Polaris Sportsman 570
Max Wilcox - Apr. 19-20 - Yamaha Grizzly 700
Noah Carlson - Apr. 19-20 - Yamaha Grizzly 700

Noah begins jotting down the names and dates in his notebook and drops the pen when he sees his own name. *Noah Carlson.*

The pen hits the floor.

"Is everything alright?" the kid asks.

Noah bends over. He's never met another Noah Carlson. This can't be a coincidence. "Yes. I'm fine. I just dropped my pen."

The kid swallows and squishes his eyebrows together. He closes the binder.

"Wait," Noah says, forcing the binder back open. "Where was that?"

The kid finds the page for April 19th. "Here."

"What can you tell me about these people? What were they doing? Hunting?"

"No, hunting season isn't until fall."

"Then what were they doing? Joyriding?"

The kid leans forward. "Don't tell anybody I told you this, but these first two, Hank and Jake, they go out there to get away from their wives. They rent from us year-round. There's always a case of beer in the back of Chad's truck. They go out there just to get drunk."

"And Max Wilcox?"

"Yeah. I know Max. We graduated high school together. Good guy. He was probably just bored. He comes in every couple of months."

Noah puts his finger on the last name. "And this one. Do you know him?"

"Noah Carlson," the kid mumbles. "Nope. Must be an out-of-towner. You think he stole your card?"

"Maybe. What did he look like?"

"I don't know. I wasn't working that day."

Noah glances at the back office. The door is ajar. "Any chance you could look up the receipts from last month?"

"I'm not supposed to go in there."

"I just need to know if this 'Noah Carlson' used my card."

The kid leans to his left and gazes at the parking lot.

"Please? How'd you feel if someone rented an ATV and made you pay for it? C'mon, help me out."

"I don't know."

"Here." Noah places a fifty-dollar bill on the counter.

The kid looks at the parking lot again, takes the bill, and vanishes into the office.

Noah rubs his forehead. His thoughts spin. Why would someone put his name on the rental log? Could it be a coincidence? He paid the minimum balance on his credit at the end of the month yesterday, and he had no charges for Ted's Tractor Plus. He always checks his bill for discrepancies.

The kid returns with a manila folder and flips through it, glancing back and forth between the front windows and the receipt slips.

Noah watches. When he sees the date April 20th flash by, he grabs the stack and turns away.

"Hey."

Noah finds Hank's slip, and Max's, and—the only other slip for the nineteenth reads, "Tom Johnson."

"Give those back," the kid demands.

The name, *Tom Johnson*—it's so familiar. He could have been someone Noah worked with at the golf course, or at the hotel, or . . . it could have been someone from anywhere.

Tom Johnson paid for an ATV rental in Noah's name. Why?

The kid comes around the counter and grabs the receipts. "Can you, like, leave now? I don't want to get in trouble."

"I'm sorry."

The kid rushes into the manager's office with the folder.

Noah tears a piece of paper from his notebook and writes his phone number down. "Hey, can you have whoever worked that day call me? Here's my number."

"Okay, whatever. Can you just go?"

"Sure. Thanks for your help."

Outside, the wind has covered his minivan with enough dust to give it that Elko-gray tinge. Noah gets in and searches for the name *Tom Johnson* on his cell phone. Hundreds upon hundreds of entries come up on Google. The guy might as well have been named James Smith or David Brown. He narrows the search to Elko and only three come up, but all three are aged sixty or older, and they have lived here for a long time.

Noah gazes at the parking lot through his windshield. A crack runs along the bottom near the wiper blades. In crime movies, detectives always imagine what might have happened. The imposter must have pulled into the parking lot in a truck or a car with a trailer. He would have backed in over there and loaded the ATV. Or maybe he didn't have a truck or trailer. Would Ted have let him walk up and drive an ATV off the lot? Could someone drive an ATV all the way to the Haven? Not likely. Bleak farms in the desert wastelands surrounding Elko are cordoned off by barbed wire fences, making it hard to go cross-country. The imposter would have had to take the highway, and twenty-five miles is a long way to go out in the open, especially if you don't want to be noticed.

Noah gets out of the minivan and walks to the entrance of the parking lot. Across the street, an RV park filled with mobile homes and trailers lies beneath swooping power lines. One block away, a four-story building overlooks the mobile homes. HAMPTON INN & SUITES.

Tom Johnson could have stayed there.

Noah heads for the hotel.

The building looks new. Decorative wrought iron fencing and professional landscaping with bushes pushing up through lava rock surround the clean beige exterior. It's sorely out of place in this otherwise rundown section of Elko.

The automatic doors slide open, and the air conditioning blasts his face.

A clerk sits behind the counter, hunched forward, staring at a computer screen.

Noah waves his hand. "Excuse me, could you—"

The clerk jumps to his feet. "How many nights will you be staying with us, sir?" His thick black hair is full of product, and his uniform is spotless. He smiles like he's in a toothpaste commercial.

"No, I'm not looking for a room. My credit card number was stolen."

"Oh, I'm sorry to hear that."

"Thanks. Whoever it was used the number to reserve a room here, and I was—"

"We can't give out any information on our guests. Hotel policy."

"But—"

"I'm sorry sir, but if you would like a room . . . "

"No. Are you sure you can't help me? The person who stole my number wasn't necessarily a guest. He might have only placed a reservation."

"All information is protected by our security policy. I'm sorry."

Noah takes out his wallet. "What if I showed you the card with the stolen number? In a way, if there was a reservation placed with my card, I'm the guest."

"I still can't give out any—"

Instead of pulling out a credit card, Noah puts a fifty-dollar bill on the counter.

The clerk's eyes open wide. "I'm going to need to call my supervisor."

"That's okay." Noah grabs the fifty. "Never mind." He shoves the bill back into his wallet.

The clerk punches numbers into the desk phone.

Noah heads for the parking lot, but the automatic doors are slow to open.

"Yeah," the clerk says into the phone, "this customer just tried to—"

Noah makes it outside and hustles across the pavement. He can't afford to get into trouble. If the police hauled him in, they would ask questions. Look up his history. His cover would be blown, and his true identity would get back to the Haven.

To Raine.

She would find out who he really was. She'd find out he's been lying to her.

The back of his neck tightens, and he rubs it as he looks over his shoulder, fearful a security guard will come running out of the hotel any moment, but no one is there.

How ridiculous.

He takes a deep breath and wipes his forehead.

The clerk didn't call the police. No one is coming after him.

Still, he checks his back one more time.

All clear.

He nears Ted's tractor place, and a blue Taurus parked near the RV park hugs the curb. He slows down and looks for a clue, some identifying mark that would prove it was the same one Monica drove earlier. Red dirt clings to the wheels. The dirt could be from the Haven.

He crosses the street and strolls up to his minivan, and as he's unlocking the door, he glances through Ted's showroom windows. Monica is inside. She takes off her sunglasses and shakes them at the kid behind the counter. Noah's heart races. He climbs inside the van, lowers his head behind the steering wheel, and peers over the dashboard. She shouts at the kid in bursts. Her mouth moves and moves, then she pauses, giving the kid a chance to say only one or two words before starting in again.

Noah's phone rings. He lies down across the seats and answers. "Hi, Mr. Oakes. I—"

"Call me Baxter. Have you found her?"

"No, but I'm glad you called. I've got something for you."

"What is it?"

"Do you know a man named Tom Johnson?"

"No. Why?"

"He rented an ATV up here with his credit card the day Samantha disappeared, but he put my name on the rental log."

"That's strange. Are you sure?"

"Yes. I saw the receipt. Are you sure you don't know a Tom Johnson? You're the only one who knew I came up here."

"It sounds like a coincidence. You're not the only Noah in the world. This Tom Johnson probably rented it for a friend with the same name as you. Besides that, what does this have to do with anything?"

"Someone was riding around on an ATV the last time your daughter was seen. You know that woman you wanted me to check out?"

"Raine Harkins."

"Yes. You were right about her knowing something. She was the last one to see Samantha, and she heard an ATV just before—"

"It sounds pretty weak. What else does she know?"

"I really think I have a lead here."

"Did she say she *saw* an ATV?"

"No."

"Unless she saw Samantha riding away on a four-wheeler, I'd drop it. Where are you?"

"In Elko."

"You need to go back to the Haven and find out what else this Raine knows. What else did she see?"

"Nothing. I talked to her for a long time. Trust me. She doesn't know anything else."

"I need you to get my little girl back, Noah. This whole thing is killing me."

"I know, Baxter. I'm sorry. I'm doing my best. Are you absolutely sure you don't know someone named Tom Johnson? Did you tell anyone I was going to the Haven?"

"I've never heard of him."

"I think someone is trying to set me up."

"Look, I'm desperate. I don't want you to get distracted with all this ATV crap. Trust me, it's a coincidence. Were you even in Elko the day the vehicle was rented?"

The rental receipt showed April 19th. "Just a second." He checks the calendar on his phone. The nineteenth was a Friday. Noah arrived on a Saturday. "No."

"Okay. If this ever comes up, I'll explain you weren't there. In fact, I think you were in my office that day, weren't you?"

"I don't remember. Maybe."

"Look, I'll testify before God if I have to, just find my daughter and do it now!" He breathes into the phone. "I'm sorry, Noah, I—please focus on bringing her back, okay? Please? Nothing else matters."

CHAPTER THIRTY-TWO

DAVID

David sits in complete darkness. The moment he returned home from his walk, Monica insisted they have a private session with Sebastian. Thankfully, she didn't see him strolling through the Haven with Raine—sometimes walking hand-in-hand—but after yesterday, Monica has decided they must *work* on their relationship.

The trance room smells like rotten flowers, incense ashes, and candle wax. They've been sitting here, waiting for Terry and Kattrice, for at least thirty minutes. Until David convinced Monica to meditate, she'd been going on and on about what Sebastian might say and what questions they should ask. She kept pushing David to open up, demanding to know how he planned to make up for his selfish suicide attempt. Demanding to know how he will get his head back into the Teaching.

David doesn't plan to get his head back into the Teaching. Not her Teaching.

Kattrice opens the door, and light floods the trance room.

"Oh, good," Terry says. "They're already here."

David never realized what was really going on in these sessions before now. A private trance with Sebastian should lead one down the path to spiritual healing, but this is really couple's therapy. Marriage counseling. No, it's worse than marriage counseling. It's marriage counseling with in-laws as the counselors. There's nothing spiritual about that.

Monica grasps David's hand. "Hi, Mom."

David doesn't move.

"Hello." Kattrice lights a candle and sits on a pillow at the front of the room. She places the candle next to her side and uses the flame to ignite a stick of Nag Champa incense.

Terry assumes the Lotus position on his big red pillow and closes his eyes.

"Should we sing?" Monica asks.

"No," Kattrice says. "I don't think that will be necessary."

Terry's head rocks back, tilts left, then slumps forward. The candle flickers. His eyeballs move. His eyelids flutter. "Hello and welcome, me children."

"Hello, Sebastian," they say in unison.

"I be honored to speak to you, me children of the highest seas." Terry's chin rises. "The waters have been rough for you, have they not? Much pain has come into your lives, but do not worry. It be the ebb and the flow. The tide will rise again. Be you well, David?"

"Yep. I'm still here."

"Yes. Yes. And you know why. You know your time on the earth plane does not belong to you. It does not belong to your mind's will. You be here to learn what separation from God means. And you will return here again and again until you come to understand the currents of all souls lead to the same ocean. Sometimes the hardest lessons come in a soul's final lifetime, you know." Terry's head tilts to one side. "Do you know what I be saying to you?"

"Yes, Sebastian." David's automatic, robotic response leaves a sour taste in his mouth.

"I do not blame you for hiding the gun, David. Know that I love you. But also know, your actions, and your thoughts, yesterday . . . they hurt our family. They hurt your like-vibration. Monica, be you well?"

"I'm okay, Sebastian. David and I have been talking."

No they haven't. She's been talking, and he's been thinking about his future. About how Raine told him he must love himself before he can love anyone else.

"Good, good," Sebastian says.

"But I'm worried." Monica shifts in her seat. "I should have known he was going to do something like this. He's been acting strange for a long time. He's been avoiding the children and me, always taking off in his truck, going God knows where."

"The transmission's broken," David says.

"When did that happen?" she asks. "Are you going to fix it?"

"No."

"See? He's not in the Teaching. He's not talking to me. I don't know what to do to save him."

David pulls his hand away from hers.

"When you leave the earth plane for the final time," Sebastian says, "you become one with God. God be all things. God be all the souls ever before and ever after. You cannot join those souls unless you know how. On the earth plane, you learn how by loving your like-vibration. You cannot become one with God—you cannot avoid returning to the ape kingdom until you have learned to become one with your like-vibration."

"David doesn't love me," Monica sobs. "And he doesn't care about the kids or Samantha. Or me. If he did, he wouldn't have—"

"I have forgiven him." Sebastian raises his voice. "He knows this, don't you, David?"

"Yes, Sebastian." David is a robot. After years of auto-responding to Sebastian's questions, he can't help himself. He wants to argue. He wants to tell Sebastian he doesn't care if he learns to love his like-vibration, but living with her has been hell-on-earth. He'd rather die and come back than spend another moment listening to her, but if that means living another lifetime under her control . . . something tightens in his stomach. Sweat, cold and sudden, forms on his brow.

"Listen very carefully, me children. As you walk down the path of marriage, you will sometimes find the pain be too much to comprehend. Real pain goes beyond your mind and hurts your heart. Separation be dangerous. You must both—" He raises his voice. "Both of you must forgive each other. Monica?"

"Yes, Sebastian."

"Forgive him."

"But, I—"

"H-m-m. M-m-m"

Monica takes David's hand. "I forgive you, David."

Sebastian says. "David?"

"Yes, Sebastia—" No. No more robot. "I can't. I can't do this anymore." He pushes her hand away.

"See?" Monica says.

"You suffer, me son. It be okay. Know that I love you. Know that Monica loves you. Kattrice?"

"Yes?" Kattrice asks. "What was that?"

"I said, we love David, don't we?"

"Oh, yes. We do."

"Monica, David loves you. He loves the children and Samantha too, you know. He be a man, and men don't always show their feelings. I do not want you to blame him anymore. For anything. Do you understand what I be saying to you?"

"Yes, Sebastian."

"I want you to find a time in your relationship when you were sweet and kind to each other. Go back. Remember your love. Go back before your children be born. Before you wed, if you must. I want you to go on a trip and remember why you are like-vibrations. Enjoy your time on the earth plane together once again."

"A trip? A real trip?" Monica says.

"Yes, me child."

"Where?"

"Somewhere fun. Have fun. Go to Las Vegas." Terry's head tips back.

"Las Vegas?" she asks, her voice becoming excited.

"Yes. Go and have the fun."

"What about Jenny and Joseph?" David asks.

"Someone will watch over them. Do not worry."

"What about Samantha?" Monica says.

"Do not worry about her. Others are seeking her now. All will be well."

"Who?" Kattrice asks. "Isn't it David's responsibility to—"

Sebastian raises his voice. "David and Monica must unite, then all will be right. H-m-m. I rhymed. It's catchy, don't you think?" He laughs to himself. "David knows what to do. What says you, David? Do you want to take your bride to Las Vegas and have some fun?"

Fun? Yes.

With Monica? No.

But anywhere would be better than here. "I don't know. My truck is out of commission."

"Kattrice," Sebastian says, "tell Terry to let them use the Taurus."

"Yes, Sebastian."

"I still don't know," David says.

"Why worry, me son?"

David hesitates. His mouth is dry. "There's a lot of booze in Vegas."

"Yes, that be true." A smile creeps across the old man's face. "That be a good thing. Go. Drink the boozes. Have the fun. Don't worry. Be happy."

"I'm afraid Monica will have *too* much fun."

She pushes her elbow into his side, burying it in his ribs. He ignores her.

Sebastian says, "Monica has always known how to relax, but too much of the whiskey be bad for anyone. Not only does the liver die, you know, but the pancreas and the eyes suffer too. Believe me, though, it be good for her to drink, as long as it be for fun. The fear you have, David, comes from the disharmony in your marriage, not from the alcohols. Take your wife's hand and be children together, once again. Have the fun. Will you try?"

"Yes, Sebastian." The robot returns. It's easier to give in than to keep dragging this out.

"Monica," Sebastian says, "will you go and have fun?"

"I'm already looking forward to it."

"I'm tired, Kattrice," Sebastian says. "I'm going to leave you people now. I love you."

Terry's mouth gapes, and he gasps. His eyes fly open, he winces, and he covers his face with his hands like it hurts for Sebastian to leave his body.

Going away to Vegas, getting away from the Haven—this *is* a good idea. Going with Monica is a different story, but maybe Sebastian isn't wrong. It's been a long time since David had any fun and, a long, long time ago, he did have fun with his like-vibration.

Kattrice stands and helps Terry up. She rubs her eyes and motions to us. "Monica, could you come here a moment."

"Don't take too long," Terry says, dismounting his pillow. "Raine will be at the Shrine soon."

The sick-sweet odor of Nag Champa incense goes to war with David's nose when Terry passes by. He follows the stench of the old man outside and squints when the sunlight hits his eyes. Monica stays behind, gossiping with her mother. There was a time when David thought these little discussions were mother-daughter bonding moments, but not anymore. Now he believes they're in the trance room gossiping, plotting, demeaning members of the Haven. Demeaning him. Deciding who he is. Determining everyone's fate—declaring who *is* and who *isn't* in the Teaching.

Thinking back over the last several months—years—he sees a pattern. Things always get better after a private trance with Sebastian, but then they get worse again. He didn't want to have a private trance today. He didn't need it, not after talking with Raine, but now, things will get better. This is only because Kattrice and Monica will shift their focus to someone else. They had been working on Samantha before she left—trying to pull her into the Teaching—and then David drew attention to himself by locking himself in the shed.

He wonders who they're talking about now. Who are they going to fix next?

It's not the first time he's had thoughts like this. Suspected a pattern. But today, standing here on the stoop of the trance room with the sun on his face and the endless possibilities of what his life might become, it's the first time he's let these thoughts into his heart. This is how the Windhaven women use the Teaching. It's not right, and Sebastian isn't to blame. Sebastian is real, and he sees everything. He knows what these women do, but he must let them live out their karma.

And he must let David live out his karma.

What comes around goes around, and it's time David took control of his life. Vegas isn't just a good idea; it's the greatest idea anyone has ever had. Sebastian is right. It's not a sin to have fun. To live.

The day is young. If he left now, he could make it before sundown, but if he went alone, Monica would make his life hell forever. She might not let him see the kids when he came back.

David slowly opens the trance room door, it creaks, but he peers inside anyway.

" . . . lost his credit card," Monica says.

"I don't know if I believe that. I thought he wanted to know about the Teaching."

"I know."

"I don't like this Noah running around town, asking his questions."

"Mon," David says, "are you coming?"

"In a minute," she snaps. "Close the door."

"Okay."

Sounds like they're going to fix Noah. Poor bastard. He just got here.

David strolls into the garden area and finds Terry seated at the picnic table by the golden Buddha statue.

Terry needs his rest. Being a medium is hard on the human body, and it gets harder with age. Raine will ease Terry's burden when she learns to trance. She's going to be a great medium. So humble. She didn't even mention meeting Terry at the Shrine this afternoon.

Monica and Kattrice emerge from the trance room.

"What were you two talking about in there?" David asks.

"The weather," Monica says. "What do you think we were talking about?"

"I don't know. That's why I asked."

"We were talking about you. Us. You're not going to like it because you're so obsessed with money, but we need to go to Vegas soon. Like, today. Like, right now. Sebastian said—"

"Okay. Let's go." He walks past Terry, past the picnic table—past the Buddha.

"What? Wait up."

"Let's go. Now. I don't care about the money."

"Really?" She pulls up her yellow dress to keep it from snagging on the steppingstones. "Where do you want to stay?"

He can't tell if it's the upturn in the corner of her eye, or the cute scrunch on the bridge of her nose, or the shallow dimple on her left cheek, but something about her in this moment reminds him of the Monica he grew up with. The Monica who wouldn't let him go until he became hers. "I want to stay in the big pyramid."

"The Luxor?" She playfully slaps his arm. "That's what I was going to say."

"Do you want to call Shayla and see if she can take the kids now?"

Monica opens her mouth to answer, then pauses.

Far down the road, right before the bend, Raine steps out of the woods.

"Would you call her?" Monica asks.

"Shayla?"

She stops. "Yes. I need to go back for a minute. I forgot something."

"Why?"

"I forgot to tell my mom something." She turns toward the trance room. "I'll be right back."

David waves down the road to Raine. It feels good, so good to smile.

Raine waves back.

He doesn't wait for Monica.

The afternoon sun warms his face.

He heads for his cabin.

Vegas—with Monica.

Without Monica.

Either way.

It's is going to be great.

CHAPTER THIRTY-THREE

RAINE

I want to catch up with David and ask him how he's doing, but I don't want to be late for my trance lesson with Terry. I'm sure David's fine. I watch him hustle around the corner up ahead. He's heading for his cabin, head held high.

I pass by Terry's house and glance at the windows. No one's there, and he's not waiting for me by the wedding arch, so I go inside the Shrine.

A hundred candles and a thousand letters to God.

When I was a girl, I would sneak in here and play with the matches. No one suspected me, innocent little Raine Harkins. I'd take broken bricks and rocks, make a miniature fireplace, and start a fire. I was a careful kid. I always kicked dirt over the black spot when I was done, and no one ever caught me.

I could have burned the place down.

I'm glad I didn't, though.

It's so peaceful in here.

The pale blue walls extend up to the rafters. Slivers of light shine down through cracks in the roof's peak. The shelves hold more candles and photos now than when I was a child. Not much room for fires. I've heard Terry uses bar-b-cue tongs to remove old notes, making room for new ones. Letters to God. I suppose not all letters say nice things. I wouldn't want that negativity around me either.

Terry's late for our trance lesson. There's time to write a note, but I could also start a fire. One more foray into sin before I enter the enchanted world of Cecilia and all her wisdom. When I think about it like this, the whole thing seems ridiculous. Terry is the trance medium, not me. Sebastian is the ancient wise one. For all I know, my subconscious made up Cecilia just to please Terry. I have always been a pleaser.

But if Cecilia is real, maybe she can help me find Samantha. Maybe I can get a clue as to who is sending me those notes. Find out if it was Jace racing around on an ATV the day she disappeared.

"Raine." Terry steps inside the Shrine and puts his hand on my shoulder. "I am so sorry we didn't call you yesterday." His apology flows through his unblemished starry eyes. The man knows no guilt.

"It's okay," I say. "David and I talked this morning. I'm glad everything is all right."

"It is." He takes my hand and leads me into the sunlight toward his white wicker love seat. He's carrying a pen and paper. "It is better than okay. Kattrice said Sebastian has saved their marriage. It's a wonderful thing."

"Yes. I suppose it is."

"Please, sit." He gestures toward the lumpy pillow on the ground. "I apologize. I'm somewhat worn out from trancing earlier. As soon as we're finished here, I'm taking a nap."

I lift the pillow and remove the rock that was jamming

into my backside yesterday. The wedding arch over the love seat looks higher today than usual. He sits down, folds his legs, and flips his palms up, resting his forearms on his knees.

"We didn't get a chance to talk after the lesson yesterday," he says. "Did you hear a voice?"

"Yes. Cecilia spoke to me."

His face floods with joy. "Did you leave your body?"

"I think so. I'm not sure. It was a lot like meditating. I didn't feel my body, but I don't know if I left it."

"You did. I could tell."

"Did I—did she speak through me?"

"No. That comes later. Do you remember what she said?"

"Some of it."

"It's a shame we didn't get to finish, but that's okay. Things like that happen for a reason. I would have asked you to write everything down had we not been interrupted. What did your spirit voice sound like?"

"Her voice was deep and throaty. She kind of sounded like Sebastian, but her accent was different."

"Do you think you could talk like her?"

"Why?"

"When you've had more practice, you'll be able to completely relax your vocal cords, and she will speak through you. She will deliver a sermon—if that is the purpose of your trance—using your voice in real-time. But that is a long way off. First, we have to take baby steps." He holds up the pen and paper. "After every trance, write down what you can remember. Later, you can rewrite it and turn it into a sermon. At some point, with practice, you'll be able to write and trance at the same time, and then, with much practice, you won't need to write at all. Her voice will come through you, loud and clear for all to hear."

"Does Sebastian always speak through you while you're trancing?"

"On occasion." He looks away, dreamily. "It has happened a few times."

"But I've heard Sebastian hundreds of times."

"And I have meditated hundreds of times, listened to him, and written hundreds of sermons."

"What do you do with the sermons, again? I'm confused."

"I memorize them and speak as Sebastian for others to hear."

"But, during trance, who are you? Are you're pretending?"

"No. Not at all. It's his voice as much as it is mine. I have but one throat." The wrinkles around his eyes deepen. He narrows his gaze. "I speak the word of God as given to me by Sebastian through meditation, in his voice. This is the service I perform for the good of everyone. The message is not from me. I'm not pretending. I write, memorize, and deliver the sermons in an altered state of mind." He leans back. "Trust me, it's exhausting."

I used to confuse Santa with God. They look the same. When I was very young, I also confused Terry with God. Again, it's their appearance. Later, I confused Terry with Sebastian until I found out Sebastian was a bodiless spirit. Now, I'm just plain confused.

Terry is telling me that sometimes Sebastian speaks through him. Other times, he speaks using Sebastian's voice, delivering messages from previous meditations. It feels like I just found out Santa isn't real.

This changes everything.

I wonder who else knows about the sermons. Does Kattrice? What about my mother? What about all the other *wise* women?

David doesn't know. He believes so strongly in Sebastian,

and in the Teaching—this little factoid would ruin the Teaching for him. It would make him want to leave the Haven. Despite this, I don't want to leave, but someone wants me to. Those notes . . . I've got to find out who's sending them.

I wish Terry hadn't told me about his *sermons.*

Maybe Cecilia isn't real.

"Raine?" Terry asks. "Are you okay?"

"I don't know." I look away. "If you're reciting a sermon during Trance, are you really trancing?"

"Yes. I am. It's how it must be done, or Sebastian's message wouldn't come across the same. It does not matter if I've memorized his teachings and delivered them as him or if he speaks through me during a trance. What matters is that everyone has a chance to learn. You'll see. I'll teach you."

"It seems—"

"You said you heard your spirit voice, correct?"

"Yes."

"It would be a disservice not to share her wisdom with our community."

"But why do you have to talk like Sebastian? Why couldn't you just tell us what he said?"

"Like a preacher? Like Moses on the mount?" He tips his head back and laughs. "It would be a greater disservice to deliver *his* message as if it were me. *That* would be pretending. Besides, as I said, trancing isn't always done from sermons. He speaks through me directly sometimes, and your spirit will someday speak directly through you too, but until then, you'll need to practice meditating, writing sermons, and speaking with her voice."

Cecilia said a lot of good things yesterday. It was like a sermon. Explaining the difference between animal love and pure love to others could help them . . . but she also said for me to stop chasing men. To stop trying to fill the void left by my father. I wouldn't want that to come out during a trance. Maybe keeping control and relaying only the beneficial parts of a trance meditation is better.

"What do you think, Raine? I know you will be of great service if you'll practice."

"My spirit guide talked about past lives. How did I know—"

"You didn't. It wasn't you. It was her. Cecilia."

I stare at him. I am a believer. I have always believed in Sebastian, but Cecilia . . . me?

"I see your doubt. Do not worry. I also questioned the experience at first. Let's say, for the moment, that your spirit guide doesn't come from the astral. We can be completely scientific about this if that will help." A fleeting smirk crosses his lips. "There are researchers who claim past life experiences are nothing more than memories genetically passed from one generation to the next. It's possible to believe we each have the memories of a great, great, great ancestor residing in our brain cells. Genetic memories, as it were. These would be considered memories from past lives. Trancing unlocks your subconscious, opens these brain cells, and the memories of someone long deceased come to life." The love seat crackles as he shifts his position. "I've read this explanation, this scientific theory, but I don't necessarily believe in it. I believe in God, not science."

"Could it be both?"

His lips part in a wide grin. "I suppose so. I suppose it could."

If this scientific theory is true, then Cecilia *does* exist only in my head. She's stuck in a bunch of brain cells somewhere.

But I heard her.

No. I *thought* her.

But, in this way, she could be real. I know God is real. The story Cecilia told me about my past life in Bugarach—could it have come from my ancestor's genetic memories? Or did it come from the time I've spent staring at the map on my wall? From my subconscious yearnings for Bugarach. If so, that would explain how she knew so much about me. She is me. Me in the here and now. My genetic memories combined with my subconscious, warping and replaying my day-to-day thoughts, spinning them into a daytime dream.

"I haven't scared you away, have I?" he asks.

"No, not at all."

"Good. I want you to practice meditating and writing sermons before the next time we meet."

"Aren't we going to trance?"

"I'm sorry, but I am too weary to continue today."

I need answers. Ancient voice from the spirit world or not, I need to hear Cecilia. I need to know what she remembers about Samantha. What do have I buried in my subconscious?

I avert my eyes, not wanting to appear desperate.

The gardenias waver around the Shrine, giving in to the breeze, their sweet, heady scent clouding my thoughts.

"You are distressed," he says. "What is bothering you, my child?"

"It's that girl. Samantha. Cecilia said she wanted me to find her, just like you—or, I mean Sebastian. Sorry." He stares at me, unfazed. "Sebastian said I'm the only one who can find her."

He lowers his head, covers his eyes. "I am sorry, Raine. But I just can't today. Sebastian will make me pay for this later, but I'm just too tired." He scoots to the edge, making the wicker creak and hands me the pen and paper. "Write a letter to God, put it in the Shrine, then go home. Meditate. You'll get your answers."

The page is blank and the pen is heavy.

Terry gazes at me expectantly.

Let's see . . .

Dear God,

I want you to help me find Samantha. Please help me.

Ah, that's horrible. It's demanding and pathetic. Terry watches over me, exhausted but patient. I need to get this over with. The ink smears when I try to rub out the demanding *I want you to* part. Instead, I draw a line through the word *want* and write *would love* in its place. That's no better. I cross the whole thing out and—

Terry's eyes close. He collapses onto his side, sending flakes of paint into the air like a miniature snowstorm, nearly tipping the love seat over. "H-m-m. M-m-m." His eyeballs move beneath his lids like marbles in a leather bag.

"Are you okay? Terry?"

"Raine, you old soul," he sits up. His eyes stay closed. "How are you me child of the highest seas?"

"Sebastian?"

"Yes, yes. It be I. Sebastian."

"I'm fine. I—"

"No." Terry's arms rise and fall out of sync with each other. "You are not fine. You are incomplete. Listen to me. Do you know what I be saying to you?"

"Yes, Sebastian. I need to find Samantha."

"Let me see . . . M-m-m. H-m-m."

I wait for him to continue with bated breath, but—is this trancing real, or is it a "sermon" Terry memorized?

It feels real.

It might as well be real.

Santa Claus is real to those who believe in him.

Perhaps it's both, real and Terry's subconscious. If someone said something about Samantha when Terry was around, or if he saw something, then his subconscious could have gobbled it up for Sebastian to spit out later. His subconscious might know who wrote the notes.

. . . you should have run away with Samantha when you had a chance.

"I see . . ." Sebastian starts to say.

"Samantha? Do you see her?"

"No. I see a man. A very dangerous man. He is not who you think he is, this Noah."

"Noah? Did Terry see Noah do something?"

Terry's body shifts, and the wicker crackles. He looks uncomfortable. "Terry saw nothing. Do not believe the things me medium says when it comes to the mysteries of trance. I love him, but he can be a moron, you know. I lived many lifetimes, sailed many seas, all before I spoke through his body. He be a man, I be a spirit, and memories be nothing more than etchings on a vase. They're like a grocery list of the things Terry has done in this life. Nothing more. I am not Terry's subconscious. I am Sebastian."

"I'm sorry. I didn't mean to—"

"Goodbye for now, me sweet, sweet child."

"But—wait."

Terry's body slumps to the left. His shoulder lands on the armrest, and he jerks up, eyes wide. He gasps for air. His throat sounds like sandpaper in the wind. "I'm sorry, Raine. I—" His face turns red, and he stands. "I've got to go."

My scribbled letter to God, ugly with the word *want* crossed out, stares up at me.

I flip the paper over and try again.

> *God, I love you. I will give myself to you, no matter what happens, but if you could help me find Samantha, I think I could better serve your children.*

The placement of the letter in the Shrine doesn't matter, but there are so many in there already, I want God to find mine first. I put it on top of a children's book. Mary left it for her son's spirit to read. *There are no dead, and there is no dying.*

Raindrops suddenly pound the wooden roof as if the angels are applauding my letter. Stepping into the doorway, I see a raincloud zoom over the Haven.

I hunch my back and run into the torrent.

The grass is wet. My feet slip from side to side on the Windhaven's lawn, swimming in my Birkenstocks. Puddles form on the road, and I'm forced to scamper like I'm crossing a minefield. Up past the first big hill into the forest, the sun touches the treetops, but it's dark down here. I leave the road and take the shortcut through the woods toward my cabin.

It's even darker in the woods.

Every few steps, I'm blinded by the rain hitting my face. The trail jogs to the left. Black shadows, green leaves, bronze bark.

Eyes.

Someone is there.

I stop, wipe the water from my face, and the eyes are gone. There were eyes in that brush, I swear it. They looked right at me.

I wipe my face again.

An owl bursts into flight, flapping against the downpour,

splintering my heart with fear. I hold still and watch him fly against the torrent—small, strong, and determined. He escapes.

I run.

Crossing onto my road, the wind hits me, sending icy shivers down the backs of my arms. Up the steps, keys in hand, heart racing—I put my hand on the door and catch my breath. I'm reminded how far I've fallen from my exercise routine.

I miss running with Warren.

No, I don't.

Why do I always have to take on my boyfriend's hobbies? I hate minigolf.

Why did Sebastian say Noah is dangerous?

What has Terry heard? What has he seen?

The second I get inside, I strip off my shirt and close the door. "Java, I'm home." I grab a towel from the bathroom. "Java?"

She's not in the living room.

"Java, are you up there?"

The loft is motionless.

I check the kitchen.

Her food bowl is empty except for a white envelope with my name on it.

Outside, the rain pounds down.

I take the note out of the envelope, unfold it—swooping black letters.

You have defied God's will. Leave the Haven now, or Java dies.

A LETTER FROM THE SHRINE

Dear God,

I did it. I broke up with Jace, but you probably already knew that. You also know what he did, don't you? Please help me stay away from guys like him. He thought he was so badass, shooting his gun in the woods.

Sebastian is right. I don't need a man. I need a family. I need to tell them the truth, but we don't always get along. The Teaching says everyone should have as many babies as they can, but I don't want to keep it. I can't keep it. I'm so ashamed.

Will you take care of it if I get an abortion?

Love,
Samantha

CHAPTER THIRTY-FOUR

RAINE

Java is gone.

I sit on my sofa in a daze. Numb with misery. The rain left about an hour ago, but the clouds stayed. The setting sun fails to penetrate the gloom. Outside my living room window, residual raindrops fall from the roof and splash on the ground. My front door is locked, and I turned off the TV so I could hear if someone were prowling around outside. So I could hear Java if she came back, scratching at the front door.

Java is gone.

Though the rain stopped, I don't dare go looking for her. Not in the dark. Not alone.

I'm so alone.

I can't believe someone took my dog. She's everything to me. She's the only constant in my life, and now she's gone. What's worse, whoever took her wants me to leave the Haven. I can't leave without her, and I have no one to turn to—except Noah. But Sebastian said Noah isn't who I think he is.

Sebastian isn't who I thought he was.

Not always. Sometimes he's a "sermon."

So I sit here in a daze, thinking. Stuck in my mind.

A knock at the back door sends needles down my arms.

I grab my phone off the coffee table and glance at the threatening notes. Earlier, I lined them up in a row and studied the writing. They were definitely written by the same person, but that's all I could tell. I scoop them up, rush to the kitchen, and shove them into the junk drawer. My whistle hangs on the hook by the back door, and before I know it, I've got it around my neck.

I stick the whistle in my mouth and—

Breathe.

I need to think straight.

Blowing the whistle will only announce that I'm home.

Instead of blowing, I clutch it in my fist.

I've got to calm down.

The knock comes again.

Maybe it's Noah. Oh, please be Noah.

Slowly, I push the curtain aside. My mother stands there with her long gray hair, still damp from the rain, and her hands clasped together.

I open the door. "Come inside. You look like you're freezing."

"I'm fine." She brushes her hair back.

I go in for a hug, but she strides past me toward the living room. "We need to talk."

"What's going on?"

"This man you've been seeing. He's not who you think he is."

I glance at Java's food dish. The envelope from the last note lies where I dropped it on the floor. I casually shove it under the cupboard with my foot. "Mother, there's something I need to tell—"

"Sebastian said he could be dangerous."

"Wait." She disappears around the corner into the living room. "Was it Sebastian or Terry?"

"It was Sebastian." She raises her left eyebrow. "Kattrice said it was Sebastian. He's very concerned for you."

"Do you know how it works?"

"What?"

"Trancing."

"Sebastian gives us guidance from the spirit world. You know that." She sits down on the sofa. "Look, I don't want you seeing Noah anymore."

"You can't tell me who to date." I walk up to her. She folds her arms. Crosses her legs. "Just because Terry's suspicious doesn't mean—dammit, Mom. Java is gone."

She raises her voice. "Terry's not suspicious. It's not him, it's Sebastian, and he's not suspicious either. He's our teacher."

"You're not listening to me."

"You're not listening to me. I saw it for myself. This Noah's been going around town telling everyone about us. It's just like before when that private investigator came. Please, listen."

"So you think Noah's a private investigator now?" My jaw clenches. She's on my last nerve. "Fine. What did you see?"

"You know Edwin Baker? I saw Noah reading to him from his notebook at Pete's Kitchen about two weeks ago. I didn't think anything of it at the time, but then today, Monica said—"

"What were you doing eating at Pete's Kitchen? You hate that grease trap."

"I—" Her eyes go to the ceiling. "I was outside on my way to Walmart."

"So, you weren't *in* Pete's Kitchen. You were outside, spying. You don't know what they were talking about."

"I know what I saw." She looks away from me.

"Noah is writing a thesis for school. He was probably interviewing Edwin." I shake my head. "I can't believe this. Did you tell Terry you saw Noah talking to Edwin?"

"Yes."

"Was that before or after Sebastian said he was dangerous?"

She rises, meeting me eye to eye. "Has Noah ever read his thesis to you? When was the last time you saw him with his notebook?"

"What does that matter? He always has it with him. He—" He didn't have it with him when he stayed over last night. Did he? No. The last time I saw it was when he interviewed me before minigolf.

She sees my hesitation and grins. "If he *is* studying religion, why did Monica see him asking questions at that tractor place this morning? I'm telling you, he's not who you think—"

"Tractor place? What was Monica doing at a—"

A knock comes from the front door.

If Java were here, she would have barked. She would have warned us.

The hand of God is coming, Raine.

I don't move.

"Aren't you going to get that?" she asks.

"No. It's probably someone selling something."

"In the Haven?" She waves me away and heads for the door. "Don't be ridiculous."

"Stop. There's—"

She brushes the curtain aside. "It's him."

I peer through the living room window.

Noah stands on the front step, slightly bending his knees. He looks across the street. His pant legs are soaked, and the weight pulls his jeans tight. He shivers.

"What are you going to do?" she says. "He's dangerous."

"I can't just let him stand out there. He knows I'm here."

He knocks on the door again. "Raine? Are you home? It's important."

My mother struts over to the dining table.

I throw on the most delightful smile I can muster and open the door. His face glistens. The sky drizzles. Wet curls of sandy blond hair stick to his forehead, and his crooked tooth gleams when he smiles. He tries to hug me, but I lean to the left, revealing my mother.

She purses her lips.

"Noah," I say, "this is my mother. Have you met? You might have seen her at Trance."

"I did, but we didn't meet." He walks to her with his hand extended. "Hi, I'm Noah."

"Hello," she grasps his hand.

The energy in the room drops when they touch. It's cold. He glances at different parts of her face like she's a work of art, then fixates on her scar.

She furrows her brow and stops shaking his hand.

He turns to me. "Do you know a *Tom Johnson?*"

My mother steps behind the table. Terry has her so scared, telling her Noah is dangerous. What bullshit. She doesn't know Noah the way I do. "Why do you want to know?"

Before he can answer, my mother says, "Is this for your 'thesis?' "

Her sarcastic tone sickens me.

"Huh? No." He rubs his forehead. "Well, I mean, kind of. Why?"

She juts her chin out and shoots me a wide-eyed look. It's the same one she uses when she expects me to do something like say thank you to a waitress or hold the door for somebody.

She nods her head toward the front door.

"What's going on?" Noah asks, cracking a smile like we're playing a trick on him.

"Nothing," I stammer. "She was just leaving."

"No I wasn't. He's the one who—"

I put my hand on her shoulder. "You better go before the rain comes down in sheets again, Mother."

"Fine." She walks in an arc, keeping her distance from Noah. Poor guy. He's confused, and I'm embarrassed. She means well, but she can be so . . . what is it? Pious? Snooty? Judgmental?

"Why don't you ask him why he was talking to Edwin?" she says as she heads for the door.

Meddling. The word I was looking for was *meddling*.

"Who?" Noah asks.

She puts her hand on the doorknob and our eyes meet. "I'm not sure I should leave you alone with *him*."

I don't know if she lacks the ability to be subtle or if she's trying to embarrass me on purpose. "Just go."

She frowns.

I shouldn't have raised my voice, but I've had it. It's meddling. It's meddling and harassment. Noah is *not* dangerous.

She fumbles with the doorknob until the latch is free and steps into the night without another word.

I lock the door behind her, twisting the deadbolt.

"What was that all about?" he says.

"Nothing. Don't worry about her. She's crazy." I sit at the dining room table and put my head in my hands.

Noah joins me. "What's wrong?"

"They took her." I look him in the eyes. "Someone took Java."

"What?"

"They left another note. They're going to kill her if I don't leave the Haven." My eyes well up.

He reaches across the table and takes my hand. "We'll get her back."

"How?"

"We're going to find Samantha. I talked to a guy at a rental shop today and asked for the names of everyone who rented an ATV a couple of weeks ago. The clerk recognized each name, except for one. Mine."

"What?"

"Someone put my name on the rental log."

"Why would they do that?"

"I don't know. It might be a coincidence, but I think they were trying to make it look like I rented an ATV. I got ahold of the rental receipts, and the only name on the rental log that didn't match any of the receipts was Tom Johnson. Do you know him?"

"I've never heard of him, but I don't think it matters."

"Why?"

"David said his dad loaned an ATV to Jace. He was in the woods that day, riding around. I should have called you, but I was late for my trance lesson, and then—Java's gone, Noah. She's gone."

"I know." He squeezes my hand. "It's going to be okay. What else did David say?"

"Why?"

"I mean, is he okay?"

"Yes."

"He means a lot to you, doesn't he?"

"Yes."

Noah lets go of my hand. Gazes into the living room.

"We're just friends," I say.

"I know. I know."

"What's the problem then?"

"Jace might have been on the ATV, but David was the one with a gun, right? I mean, he has a gun."

"You said you'd stop accusing him."

"I'm not accusing him."

"You thought his name would be on the rental list, didn't you?"

"No. I—his name wasn't on the list. Mine was." He glances away. "Look, I'm just trying to figure out who was shooting the gun."

I grit my teeth. "It wasn't David."

"Okay, but you said he was in his shed with a gun yesterday. Where did he get it? Was it his?"

"No."

"Whose was it?"

"He found it in the woods."

Noah stands. "Really?"

"David's not a liar."

"I know. I don't think he did anything wrong. I just have to find out what happened to Samantha."

"Why? Why are you always so concerned about her?"

"For you. Because of the notes." His face reddens. "Because of Java."

"Don't bring her into this."

"Wasn't Terry missing his gun?"

"Yes, but that's not the one David found."

"How do you know?"

"David found a tan or beige something. A newer one. Terry's was an old revolver, like from an eighties crime show."

"Did you see it?"

"No."

He glances around. "Do you have a piece of paper? I need to write this down."

"Where's your notebook?" I hear my mother's sarcasm in my voice, but I can't help it.

"My—"

"For your thesis. Why don't you write it down in there?"

"What?"

"Your notebook. The one you use for school. The one with your notes on religion. On the Teaching. You know what I'm talking about, don't you?"

"Yes. Of course. I—"

"Noah, what were you doing talking to Edwin Baker?"

"Who?"

"My mother said she saw you talking to Edwin at Pete's Grill. She said you were taking notes in your notebook." I stand up. "What does Edwin know about religious studies?"

He raises his hands like I'm arresting him. "I'm sorry, Raine. I should have told you the truth."

"Get out."

"What?"

"I want you out." I grasp my whistle.

"Raine, wait. It's not what you think."

"You're not a student, are you?"

His face twists as though he can't handle the thoughts running through his head. He can't choose his next lie.

I should have listened to my mother from the beginning.

"You're right," he says. "I'm not a student."

"I knew it. Get out."

"But it's nothing bad."

"I said, get out."

He just stands there, staring at me.

I march to the back door, grasping my whistle.

"Where are you going?" he says.

"If you won't leave, then I have to."

"It's not what you think." He follows. "I'm trying to find Samantha for a friend."

My hand slips off the deadbolt. "I thought you were trying to find her for me."

His footsteps come up behind me.

I try the knob again and fail.

"I am." He puts his hand on my shoulder.

I spin around and slap his face. "Get away from me."

He steps back with his hand on his cheek, his eyes glistening but steady.

I lose it. "You're like everyone else in *the world*. You lie to get what you want and you don't care who you hurt."

"I didn't come here to hurt anyone."

"Why were you talking to Edwin then? What did you tell him?" A sucking hole of possibilities opens in my mind, the least of which includes cult-busters. People whose mission is to break up peaceful communities like mine, and I slept with one of them.

"I didn't tell Edwin anything."

"What about the police? Did you tell them the crazy cult people in the mountains kidnapped a girl?"

He tries to put his hand on my shoulder, and I shove it away.

"No." His face is flush. His beautiful brown eyes beg me to calm down. "I haven't told anyone about Samantha. I don't even care about her anymore. I only care about you. And Java."

"You're a liar."

I don't know who he is. He's not a student—he could be anyone.

I need to protect myself.

"Please, Raine."

I cross the kitchen and open the junk drawer. One of the notes falls onto the floor, and I pull out a pair of scissors. "Get out, liar."

"Whoa, wait." He raises his hands. "You're right. I'm a liar, but I didn't want to be. My friend said I had to lie or I'd be kicked out of the Haven. Think about it. If anyone knew I had come to bring Samantha back to Vegas, I wouldn't have been allowed to attend the trance meeting. Please understand, I didn't want to lie."

"Why should I believe that?" The scissors tremble.

"Because it's true."

"How do I know you're not making this up too? How do I know you're not some psycho? Maybe you're the one who left the notes? Maybe you wanted to scare Samantha away, and now you want to scare me away for some sick reason. Wait. I got it. You're a cult buster. You probably have Samantha held somewhere right now, *deprogramming* her."

"No. That's ridiculous. Raine, please. I'm sorry I made up that stuff about being a student. It's not like that. I promised to bring my friend's daughter back, sure, but I don't care about that anymore." His eyes shine with tears. "I only care about you. I think I love you."

My vision blurs, and I step backward toward the dining table, blinking. I'm not crying. I won't cry. "How do I know you didn't take Java?"

"Raine."

"Just go, Noah. I can't take any of this right now."

He walks toward me.

I step around the table.

He bends over and picks up the note.

Leave the Haven now, or Java dies.

"My God. I can't believe they took her." He locks his eyes on mine. "I'm going to get her back for you."

"Please, Noah. I want you to leave."

He shoves the paper into his pocket and heads for the door.

Am I making a mistake?

No.

He lied to me.

Everyone lied to me.

Noah probably never worked at a golf course. Or a hotel. Or as a bike courier.

He can't possibly love me. Not yet.

The rain pounds on the roof.

He opens the front door and steps outside.

Scissors in one hand, my whistle in the other—I watch as he drives away.

CHAPTER THIRTY-FIVE

NOAH

She won't answer his calls.

Noah puts his phone down on the hotel bathroom counter, picks up his razor, and drags the blade across his chin. Steam clings to the mirror.

He doesn't know what to do next.

Baxter hasn't been answering his phone, either, but that's okay. Noah has nothing good to tell him.

Yesterday was a manic blur. He spent the morning searching the Haven for Java—hanging missing dog signs, asking if anyone had seen her. He stopped by Raine's cabin over and over, but she was never home. Around noon, he gave up and returned to Elko.

Then he lost his mind.

He went everywhere—the diner, the library, two supermarkets, Starbucks, the Starbucks inside the two supermarkets. He asked everyone in his path if they'd seen a black-lab-shepherd mix. He showed them the photo of Samantha. He desperately pleaded for them to think hard, remember what they'd seen, and tell him everything they knew about the Haven.

Girl Scouts selling cookies outside Walmart said they'd seen a dog like Java, but they were lying. They were just trying to make a sale. Noah didn't fault them for that, but he didn't buy any cookies either.

The farm kid at Ted's Tractors Plus had never seen Samantha, and the manager didn't remember what the imposter with the Tom Johnson credit card looked like. The manager barely remembered working on April 19th, and he got mad at the kid for showing Noah the rental receipts. Noah pressed for more information, details, and the manager asked him to leave.

Raine had said Jace drove an ATV the day Samantha vanished. The rental place, the imposter, Tom Johnson—it's likely none of that matters. Jace didn't rent the ATV. He borrowed it from David's dad.

The steam from the shower evaporates off the mirror, and Noah washes his stubble down the drain. He puts his razor away and gazes at his face. His eyes are bloodshot from not having slept. Raine might never forgive him for lying. She might never talk to him again, but he promised her he'd find Java, and he will. He promised Baxter he would bring Samantha back, and he won't give up.

He slams his hands on the sink.

He promised to pay his loan shark back in one lump sum, and he will.

It's Wednesday, midmorning. Raine might be at work.

Why didn't he think of that yesterday? Of course. That's why she wasn't home.

The key turns easily in the ignition, and the minivan sputters to life. Four advertised law offices come up on his phone when he searches for *Elko Law*, and based on Raine's comments, he's able to narrow it down to the second listing. It only takes five minutes to get there.

The brown one-story building sits in the middle of an everyday neighborhood. It's covered in that gray Elko dust he's beginning to accept as normal. There's no open sign in the window, and no one's around. He gazes at the empty parking lot a moment before shoving the transmission into drive and peeling out onto the street.

Raine's got to be home.

The highway stretches across the desert like a black leather belt, then turns south, winding between the hills and mountains of northern Nevada. Ruby Dome watches over him in the rearview mirror. The sky recovered from yesterday's rain, but a new cluster of clouds float high above, threatening to descend. They're following him.

A cop car comes down the highway in the opposite direction. Raine would kill him if he flagged the officer down and asked about Samantha. He considers it anyway—he's asked everyone else, but he lets the car pass by. It's sad, the paranoia everyone in the community lives with.

Speeding through the Haven, he brakes only to dodge the mud puddles, hoping Raine is home. Rounding the corner to her A-frame, he sees her car.

He jumps out and bangs on the door.

"Raine. I'm sorry."

No answer.

Across the road, the trance building shows through the trees. There doesn't' appear to be anyone over there. He circles the A-frame, looking in every window. The back door is locked. Peering inside, he sees an empty hook. Raine's whistle is gone.

Think.

Where would she go?

Her car is here, so she must have walked somewhere.

He gazes into the forest.

"Raine?" he calls. "Are you out there?"

Standing on a large rock, he scans the hillside. Light breaks through the trees to his right, so he heads that way, trudging through sagebrush until he comes to the trail near the road.

He follows it into the woods.

The dirt is damp from the previous day's rain, but there are no discernable tracks until he comes to a small clearing near a broad band of sagebrush. The area appears to have been heavily trampled some time ago, but he can't tell how long.

Bending on one knee, he identifies a dog's footprint.

"Java?"

Maybe.

The trail splits, one path ascending a hill before turning west, and the other continuing straight toward an intersection. Again, at the intersection, the ground appears to have been trampled, but this time, tire tracks run down the middle.

It was an ATV.

The dirt is loose. Crumbly.

The trail weaves in between the pines, and Noah quickens his pace, keeping an eye on the tracks as he follows them deeper into the forest. He rounds a large boulder with silver streaks and stops.

His skin tingles when he sees it.

An ATV with a rack sits off to the side of the trail next to a burlap bag and a rope and a pile of rubber tie-downs.

He looks around, listens.

A bird coos in the distance.

Something rustles in the brush behind him, and he spins.

A gray squirrel sprints down the trail.

Noah steps toward the ATV, glancing this way and that, watching for movement in the trees.

The engine is still warm.

The key is in the ignition.

A scuffle comes from the woods to his left.

It's too far to see what's going on.

Then a dog barks.

Noah rushes in, following the barking—the yelping.

A gunshot shatters the air, and he ducks for a moment before breaking into an all-out sprint. His mind empties. He glances back, loses sight of the ATV.

Run.

More yelps. Cries for help.

"Stay still, you stupid bitch," a voice shouts.

There's a clearing up ahead, and on the other side, Java is tied to a dying lodgepole pine, cowering. She sees Noah and jerks left, banging her head against the trunk. The rope fastened to her collar is short. She struggles to get away.

Jace stands with his back to Noah and aims a gun at her head.

"No," Noah yells.

Jace whirls around and takes aim. His eyes narrow, his face tightens, the muzzle shakes.

Noah lurches behind a tree and presses his back against the trunk. His chest heaves. "Jace, what are you doing?"

"Go away." The teen's voice is shrill. "Man, please. Just go away."

"Let her go."

"I can't do that, man. I—"

Noah pulls out his cell phone and switches it on.

"—just go away."

There's no signal out here. "Jace, calm down."

"No. You're going to tell them. Shit."

"Tell them what?" Java's bark is panicky. "Tell them what, Jace? That you kidnapped a dog?"

"Yeah, that. Shit."

"Just put the gun down and walk away. I promise I won't say a word." Noah puts the phone in selfie-mode and holds it out to the side. The image is blurry, but he can see the clearing. Jace has both hands on the gun, and he's aiming in Noah's direction.

Java jerks, pulling the rope tight around the tree.

Noah pinches the screen and zooms in. The kid's chest hitches and his entire body quakes. He glances at Java, then focuses on Noah's hiding place.

"You don't have to do this, Jace."

"Yes, I do. What the hell are you—" He chokes. "Why don't you come out from behind that tree? I promise, man. I won't shoot."

Noah tries to zoom in on the gun with his phone, but he's reached maximum magnification. From this angle, he can't tell if the gun is black or tan. Is it Terry's or David's?

"Are you still there, man? Shit. I've had enough of this shit."

Noah coughs.

"Hey," Jace shouts. "What are you doing? Are you calling someone?"

Noah leans around the tree, trying to get a better look at the gun, and fire flashes from the muzzle. He jerks back, but not before tree bark pelts him in the face. The gunshot is deafening. Every muscle stiffens. He pats his head, his shoulder, his chest, searching for the bullet hole, but the bullet missed. His heart trumpets blood through his veins. He can't get enough oxygen, breathing in . . . and out . . . and in.

Java barks wildly.

"This shit isn't worth it," Jace yells. "I'd rather be homeless."

The fear comes in waves. Noah can't hold his hand still. The phone shakes, and he's terrified of getting his fingers shot off if he tries to take another look. "Jace?"

No response.

"Jace? Are you there?"

He counts to ten, gets a grip on himself, and a grip on the phone. The grainy image shows nothing but a terrified dog.

Jace is gone.

Noah comes out of hiding.

Java thrashes.

He attempts to grab her collar, but she lashes out at him. "Shh, girl. It's okay. It's me."

The sound of the ATV's engine coming to life echoes through the forest.

Noah goes behind Java's tree, unties the rope, and reels her in. The rope is knotted around her collar, choking her. He puts his hand out, palm down, and waits. She sniffs his fingers, and she lets him pet her. He straddles her back to hold her still and goes to work on the knot.

The whine of the ATV fades to a distant hum, then disappears entirely.

Java's rope comes free, and he grabs her by the collar, but the clasp breaks, and the whole thing comes off in his hand.

She races to the tree he'd hid behind, stops, and turns to face him.

"Come on, girl. It's me, Noah. I won't hurt you."

He takes one step forward, and she darts away, disappearing into the wilderness.

Noah slumps onto the ground and puts his hand over his heart. It's still racing from having been shot at. His lower back begins to cramp.

Java is gone. She's too fast. There's no way he could catch up to her.

Jace has a gun, and he's gone too.

Raine wasn't home. She never returned Noah's calls yesterday. Maybe she decided to heed the threats and leave the Haven.

Samantha is . . . no one knows. It's been almost two weeks since she went missing, and no one has seen her. Baxter's grief must be killing him by now.

And somewhere in Vegas, Titus is carrying a bat and asking if anyone has seen Noah.

The clouds that followed him into the Haven blanket the sky, but it's not raining.

Yet.

He made his promises, and he's going to keep them.

He stands up and spreads his arms.

The tension in his lower back wanes.

This isn't over.

CHAPTER THIRTY-SIX

DAVID

David checks the door to their hotel room. It's locked. Monica is already halfway to the elevator, running her hand along the railing as she goes. The Luxor's slanted walls make it look like an ancient pyramid, but the place is so enormous and odd, David feels unsteady. He checks the door again and thinks of Raine's tiny A-frame. Its slanted walls are quaint. Comforting.

The Haven is a far cry from Vegas.

David has never had vertigo, but from fifteen floors up, the open space between this side of the casino and the other makes him anxious. The railing is low. Someone could easily fall to their death and explode on the marble floor.

"Hurry," Monica says. "I'm hungry."

David walks along on the far wall, away from the casino canyon. "Do you want to eat here, or—"

"Yes. Here."

The elevator doors open, and they step inside.

On the ground floor, a Starbucks and an expensive-look-ing jewelry store encourage David to waste his money. Terry and Kattrice told him to treat Monica like a queen. Buy her anything she wants. Do it for his marriage. His kids. His soul.

Monica struts past the jewelry shop, heading toward the Pyramid Cafe. Palm trees and reed plants spring from raised gardens scattered throughout the casino. Amber stone statues of Pharaoh gods look down upon the gamblers with austere faces. People move in random directions, crossing in front of David, forcing him to stop, keeping him from catching up with Monica. She disappears around a corner. Laughter and cheers erupt from the opposite end of the casino—lights flash, electronic *beeps* and *boops* ping off the walls.

When he catches up with her, she's seated at a slot machine, hitting the SPIN button. "What are you doing, Mon? I thought we were going to eat." It's almost noon. They left the Haven late last night and went straight to bed after checking in. He hasn't eaten since then, and his stomach is making him pay for it.

"We're supposed to have fun," she says. "I only put in five dollars." She hits the BET MAX button. Three cherries come up. "We won."

"Good," he says. "Let's—"

She bets and spins again.

"I thought you were hungry."

"I am, but—"

"Drinks?" A waitress in a loose tank top, tight black shorts, and flesh-colored leggings holds an empty drink tray at eye-level.

"Yes," Monica says. "I'll have a margarita."

David fires her a look. "Don't you want to eat first?"

"We're supposed to be having fun."

"You want anything?" the waitress asks David, her listless eyes on his.

So this is how it's going to be. Fun. Watching Monica get sloshed and gamble all day. Real fun.

Monica leans back, touches his elbow. "Please, David. Remember how we used to be?"

For a split second, he sees the person he fell in love with a long time ago. It's startling and comforting all at once. In there, somewhere, lives the little girl with a passion for life, a passion for him; the one who showed up at his tenth birthday party when no one else would.

David shakes free of the memory.

If it's fun she wants . . . "Could I get a Jack and Coke, no ice?"

"Sorry. All the drinks have ice. House rules."

"Wait," he says. "How about a Bloody Mary? That comes with celery, right?"

"Sure." She departs.

Monica plays the slot machine. David watches. When she loses all her credits, she puts more money in. When those credits are gone, David suggests they try a different machine.

The drinks come.

David eats the celery.

More money goes in.

Once in a while, she wins.

She glances at him.

"Go ahead," he says. "Put more money in."

He orders a Jack and Coke.

She orders another margarita.

She wins again.

The drinks come. They order more.

They drink and order more.

The flashing lights on the slot machines are the most vivid

thing he's ever seen. Every pixel on every screen is distinct and alive. Sevens. Oranges. Golden bars. Dollar signs. Clown faces. Dice. Skulls. He belches Coke, and the whiskey burns his throat.

It feels good.

The games look amazing.

"Let's hit the strip," he says.

Cars stream up and down Las Vegas Boulevard beneath thousands of light bulbs in the middle of the day. Vegas is surreal. The sky is larger than usual. His face is hot, but it's a pleasant hot. It's a fast day. "How are we doing?"

"What do you mean?" she asks.

"Money-wise."

"I think we lost a lot." She flips through her billfold, checking every pocket. "I only have five dollars left."

"How much did your mom give you?"

She hesitates. "Three hundred. It was supposed to last all week, but before you get mad—"

"I'm not mad. Let's find an ATM." He runs ahead and turns around. "Come on. Let's have fun. Run." She's wearing a white blouse and blue stretch pants. He shouldn't have told her to run in those sandals. If she trips, he'll have to catch her. If she breaks her ankle, he'll have to carry her to urgent care. But . . . he can do that. He can do anything.

She runs to him, and she hasn't looked this good in years.

Beer goggles are great, but Jack and Coke lenses are spectacular.

In and out of the Tropicana. More drinks. In and out of the Aria. Two giant soft pretzels.

And more drinks.

He forgot to shave this morning. Maybe he'll grow a beard. What would he look like with a full beard?

Cream-colored leather borders the bar in the Bellagio. Elegance. Monica wants to try something other than slots. They rush over to a roulette table, and she puts a hundred-dollar chip on number twenty-two.

The roulette wheel spins, and the ball drops into slot number five.

A rake takes the chips away. The dealer's face is blank. That was a lot of money to lose so fast.

Monica bets again.

Time flies.

Monica bets again.

When did she get more chips?

"Drinks?" a waitress asks.

"I'll have a margarit—"

"No, thanks." David puts his hand on Monica's wrist. "We're good for now."

"Why did you—"

"Let's go somewhere else." He stumbles away from the table. The casino seems to move with him, countering every step he takes. He walks, leaning to the right, then farther to the right, loping sideways, lurching forward, trying to stay on his feet. He grasps a slot machine and pulls himself upright. The signs and the lights and the carpet—everything spins.

"Are you all right?" She grasps his elbow. He barely feels it. She helps him outside, he falters, grabs onto the railing, and leans over the edge. They're standing on a walkway overlooking the boulevard, but he doesn't remember going up an escalator. Cars cruise beneath them. He closes his eyes and prays for his stomach to stop churning. Spit pools in his cheeks, preparing for the oncoming vomit, but he swallows it back down. Fresh beads of sweat cover his face. "I think I'm okay."

"Good. Let's find a place to sit." They ride an escalator down to the street. "Over here." She eases him onto the ground beneath the walkway and sits down. "Do you have to throw up?"

It's cool. The shade covers him like a blanket. "No. I'm fine." He's aware of his slurring, but he doesn't care. There's nothing to care about. Despite his stomach, the day is great. It's moving fast and fun. Fun. Fun is a funny word.

"I thought you were going to lose your lunch up there," she says.

"We didn't eat lunch."

"We had those pretzels."

"You're right."

Her head rests on his shoulder. She smells like Tequila. Cinco de Mayo. Her hair is soft and bright blonde and fine in the early afternoon sun. Or has evening come?

"Were you angry about the money?" she asks. "The roulette table? You looked angry."

He sits up straight. "No. No. I'm fine."

"We're not going to have to worry about money."

"Why's that?"

"Mom and Dad are going to retire someday. Maybe soon. Trancing his hard on my dad's body. When he's done, we'll be in charge. All the tithings will go to us."

Daddy's princess, becoming a queen. That will never happen. She's so cute to dream. She still thinks she's going to become a trance medium.

A chuckle escapes him.

"What's so funny?" she asks.

"People don't have much to donate to the Teaching. Have you looked around the Haven? Ever really looked at it? At the people? They're not exactly millio—million . . . they're not rich."

"After tomorrow, we won't have to worry about money. At least not for a while." She stands up and holds out her hand.

David's head throbs. Another drink sounds good. Something to take that acrid taste out of his mouth. Something to fix this headache.

"My mom didn't want me to tell you this, but . . . " She hesitates. Wrinkles her nose.

"What?"

"You love me, don't you?"

"Yes. I *looove* you." His tongue is swollen, sour, and lispy. He takes her hand and pulls himself up off the ground. "Come on. Let's go over to the Flamingo. I want another drink."

It's like his feet are on autopilot. One foot in front of the other. Step, step, step.

She says, "There's a man here in Vegas. He's in big trouble. Spiritual trouble. We need to help him."

They ride the escalator up to the crosswalk then—step, step, step. Don't look down.

"My mom gave me his number. It's a great chance to share the Teaching."

What is Monica saying? Someone needs the Teaching? They ride down the escalator. "What's this guy's name?"

"Promise me you won't get mad."

"I won't. I won't get mad. I'm—"

"It's Baxter Oakes."

"Huh? Samantha's dad?"

"Yes. If we can help him, and he comes back to the Haven with us, it'll prove I—we—deserve to inherit everything."

"But Samantha ran away."

"I know. It's perfect. Just go along with it, okay?"

He's suddenly exhausted. "I don't know if it's a good idea." The Flamingo has palm trees and bushes and other plants out front. He leans against a pink sign—THE FLA-MINGO. "Why do we have to do it on vacation? Because your mom told you to?"

"No. I want to. Don't you want to?"

"I don't know. Sebastian says not to recruit. Why him? Won't he be mad we lost his daughter?"

"Maybe, but once he gets to know us, he'll find out we want to find Samantha as much as he does. And"—she lowers her voice—"we're not recruiting. We're sharing the Teaching. Sebastian *wants* us to share the Teaching."

"I don't know."

David watches a man in a dark blue suit strut out of the casino. The man's shoes shine like obsidian. They compete for attention with his silver cuff links. His hair is slicked back with something. David heard what they call that stuff on a reality show once. What was it? Product. The man has *product* in his hair and his watch twinkles in the sunlight. Diamonds.

It would be nice not to worry about money. Like now, not worrying about anything. Being drunk is great. What a great buzz. "Does he have money or something? Is that what this is about?"

"Yes, if you must know. He has a lot of money. Come on, David, we need his money. He could do a lot to help us. I mean, the community."

A sports car pulls up to the curb, and Mr. Hair Product gets in. It's a Maserati. No, it's a Ferrari. At eighty miles an hour, this kind of car roars. It doesn't rattle. Not like David's old Ford did. He bets this car can go twice as fast as his truck.

That would be a rush. That would be fun. "Okay. Sure. Let's recruit him. I'll help him. I'll give him the Teaching."

"Yay." She claps her hands together and grins. "Come on. Let's get drunk." She turns and heads for the Flamingo's entrance.

David waits. He wants to see the sports car take off.

Three.

The engine whirs.

Two.

The nose dips into the lane and waits for a break in the traffic.

One.

The car blasts down the strip, its engine buzzing in a crescendo, singing to David, blending with his buzz. His head hums. He turns to go, but across the street—across the four car lanes going this way and that—a teenager rides down an escalator. No. Make that two teenagers riding down the escalator.

"Monica. Wait."

David wipes his eyes. He tries to focus on the teens, but his eyes won't cooperate. In the distance, Caesar's Palace comes in crystal clear, but the foreground is a blur. "Do you see them?"

"Who?" She stumbles toward him. Bumps into his shoulder. Hangs on his arm.

"Over there." He points.

"I don't see—"

"That's Jace, isn't it? On the escalator?"

"Yeah. It looks like him."

David grabs her by the elbow and turns. "Can you see who's with him?"

She squints. Wrinkles her nose. "No. That guy is in the way."

"It's a girl, isn't it?" David turns back. "Shit. They're gone."

"So what?"

"Monica." He squeezes her arm. "That was Samantha."

Her face goes pale.

"That was Samantha with Jace."

CHAPTER THIRTY-SEVEN

RAINE

My mother went to bed about an hour ago.

I'm not sure I can handle another night in her trailer. It's so much worse than my cabin. The water reluctantly runs out of the tap and tastes like rotten eggs. Posters she bought at yard sales cover up holes in the paneling. A lone house plant hangs over her books, hiding the makeshift bookshelf—boards on cinder blocks. The carpet holds onto odors from the last occupants and the ones before them. From the '80s. Stale french fries and musty old incense—it makes me want to wash my clothes all the time.

I slowly open the front door, step outside, and close it behind me. The silhouettes of the trees in the distance look like jagged teeth against the dark blue horizon. My cabin is just beyond that ridge. It won't be long before the sun is completely gone, and another day will have passed. It's only been two days since someone took Java, but it feels like an eternity. I'm hiding out. Whoever left the notes won't kill her if they think I've left the Haven, but I can't stay here forever.

I hate it here.

I step off the porch and pace back and forth in front of the trailer, passing by my grandmother's rocking chair. The armrests are old and cracked. My mother hasn't gotten around to refinishing the chair yet, and she probably never will. Not unless God wills it. She really shouldn't leave it outside in the elements like this.

I pace.

I miss Java.

I've run out of places to look for her. At the risk of being seen, I spent the better part of yesterday and today wandering through the woods, calling her name. She's gotten away from me so many times that I hoped she had escaped on her own. My mother swears God has a plan, and Java will find her way back to the Haven, but she doesn't know about the notes.

Noah's been looking for Java too. I assume he's the one who hung the missing dog signs around the Haven. He blew up my phone, leaving messages, asking why I wasn't at home or at work. I don't think I'll be going back to the law office. My mother was right about Noah lying, and she was right about my work. I have no purpose there.

I sit in the rocking chair and glance at my phone. Eight new messages.

Damn Noah for lying, and damn him for being so concerned about Java. Sure, I overreacted, but he lied to me. He's a bold-faced liar.

But he loves me. He said he loved me.

I don't know what to believe. The way he left my cabin the other night—so determined to find Java. I didn't mean what I said. I don't think he wrote the notes, and he's not a cult buster. His story made sense. The Windhaven's would have asked him to leave immediately if they thought he was here to take Samantha back. It's not a cult thing. Sebastian says anyone can leave any-time they want. We're only protecting our community.

I listen to my phone messages. Noah sounds heartbroken and honest.

It doesn't feel right. Pushing people like Noah away for telling the truth in the name of protecting the community . . . maybe it *is* a cult thing.

Oh my God.

Maybe I do live in a cult.

I rock the chair. Take in the night air. I can't worry about whether I live in a cult or not right now. If I'm going to get Java back, I've got to find out who is leaving the notes, and that brings me back to finding Samantha.

Back to Jace.

I rock.

I gaze down the driveway toward Control Road.

Jace's mobile home lies nestled at the bottom of the hill, covered by a copse of pines. I can only see one end of the mobile home from here, and I've been watching for him. He wasn't around yesterday, but this morning I heard an ATV. I rushed outside to see where he was going, but I was too late.

It's after ten at night now, and I haven't heard him come back. Where was he all day?

I wonder if Noah had any luck searching for Java, and as if God were listening, my cell phone buzzes.

I take a deep breath.

It's time to let Noah off the hook, but it's not him.

"Hi. David?" There's some static, so I hold the receiver tight against my ear.

"Raine. Hi. It's me, David."

"I know. I'm surprised. What's going on?"

"Raine, you sound so . . . your voice sounds so . . . pretty. Have I ever told you that?"

His voice sounds rubbery. "No, you haven't. Have you been drinking?"

"Yep, yep, and . . . yep. I've had a few. I'm growing a beard, too. Monica and I are in Vegas fixing our marriage."

Nothing he says makes any sense, but I let it go. I've done enough judging lately. If they think getting drunk in Vegas is the cure for their marriage, then more power to them. "You sound like you're having fun."

He lowers his voice. "I'm having a great time. We're going to get rich."

"Really? Gambling?"

"Yep, or . . . nope. Maybe that way too. It depends on tomorrow. We're going to recruit—"

Monica yells in the background. "David, what are you doing? Come back to bed, lover."

"Thanks for calling, David. I've got to go."

He slurs into the phone. "Your voice is so pretty."

"Yes, and so is yours. Why don't you call me tomorrow and tell me more about your trip, okay?"

"Okay. That's a good idea—wait. I almost forgot why I called. We found Samantha."

"What? Oh my God, where?" I rock forward so hard, I almost tumble out of the chair. My feet skid across the ground.

"We saw her with Jace at—"

"Davy Bear, come back to bed. Mama's lonely." Monica sounds as drunk as he does. Drunker. *Davy Bear.* Disgusting.

He raises his voice and muffles the receiver. "Mon, what's the casino across from the Flamingo?"

"Who are you talking to?" Monica asks.

He hushes into the phone. "I've got to go."

"Don't. Did you talk to Samantha?"

"No, we tried to catch up to them, but there's a lot of people here. You'd love it, Raine. It's so much fun."

"Are you sure it was her?"

"I know it was Jace. It was definitely Jace—"

"David!"

Click.

Samantha is alive, and she's with Jace. In Las Vegas.

I pace back and forth.

Jace couldn't have ridden the ATV all the way to Vegas, could he? No. But he could have ridden it to town and gotten on a bus. Did Samantha go with him, or was she already there?

I call David back, but he doesn't answer. I pace, I call him again, and . . . no answer.

Maybe I've had it wrong all along. Maybe no one scared Samantha away. She and Jace could have gotten back together. Yes. She could have spent the last two weeks hiding out in his mobile home at the bottom of this hill, right in front of my face.

Or David is drunk and only thinks he saw Jace and Samantha.

The wind teases a low hum out of the trees, and I imagine a dog barking in the distance. A moaning. I stop and stare.

The day I saw Samantha, she didn't look like someone sneaking away to hide out at her boyfriend's house. She looked scared. Maybe Jace was chasing her on his ATV. Maybe he was trying to kidnap her, and . . . maybe he has held her captive this entire time. If he saw me in the woods with Samantha that day, he might have been afraid I saw him too. He might be the one behind the notes, trying to scare me away so I won't tell anyone.

I call David one last time. No answer. He must be too busy to pick up. He's probably in bed with Monica having drunk sex.

Ick.

I pace.

The more I pace, the more my mind takes over.

Worry, doubt, fear—all the feelings that block us from God. Emotions tumble inside my head like clothes in a dryer. I'm so in my mind about all this. David was so drunk I could smell his breath over the phone. Maybe he was seeing things. Samantha could be anywhere. Jace could be innocent. What do I really know?

I know Noah lied to me, but—

I must be going crazy. I believe Noah's story, but doubt is the devil's whisper. Noah could still be in on it. He could have left the notes, and Jace could be entirely innocent. Or Jace could be working with Noah on some grander plan. They did take off together the first day Noah came to Trance.

Stop it, Raine. You're going insane.

The wind picks up. My hair sweeps over my face, and I brush it away, but the wind blows it back.

Noah, Jace, David, Java, Samantha—

My mother's face appears in the kitchen window, and I jump back. Her hair rests on her shoulders like a funeral shroud. She slides the glass. "When are you coming inside?"

"Soon. Go back to bed."

She closes the window.

I walk to the other side of the trailer so she can't do that to me again. She's a spook.

It's pitch black back here.

The trees hide in the darkness.

I pull out my phone and tap on Noah's number.

It rings. Maybe he's asleep.

"Raine, hi. I've been trying to—"

"Stop. I know what you've been trying to do. You've been trying to break my phone with all your messages. Look, before you get too excited, this isn't a social call."

"Okay, okay. I—it's so good to hear your voice. I was worried something happened to you. I was about to call the police."

"You didn't call them, did you?" Suspicion, dread, fear— all the things men are made of.

"No."

"Good. Do you still want to find Samantha?"

"Yes, of course, but I was looking for Java, and—"

"Okay. Listen, I'm going to help you, but this doesn't mean we're getting back together. Do you understand?"

"I'm sorry I lied. I never wanted to—"

"You never wanted to hurt me. I know. I heard your messages." I walk to the edge of my mother's lot and try to distinguish Jace's mobile home from the trees. "I think I know where Samantha is. David and Monica went to Las Vegas to work on their marriage, and David said he saw Jace there. He said Jace was with Samantha."

"Jace and Samantha? In Vegas? That's impossible. I saw him this morning. He—"

"I heard his ATV this morning too, but that doesn't mean he couldn't have driven to town and hopped on a bus."

"Raine, he—"

"It doesn't matter how he got there. David said he saw him."

"I saw him too. Listen to me"—the wind dies down, quieting the woods, taking my breath away—"he had Java."

"He did? Where? Where did you see him? Do you have her?"

"No, she got away. Can I come see you?"

"Where were you?"

"In the woods. Where *are* you? I've been looking everywhere. Can't I come see you?"

"No. Tell me what happened."

"Okay, but—I'd really rather tell you in person."

"No. Tell me now. What happened?"

"Jace had Java tied to a tree, and he was pointing a gun at her. He was going to, you know, like the note said . . . kill her."

"Oh, shit. Is she okay?"

"I think so. Jace ran away, and I tried to catch her, but her collar came off in my hand."

Java's red leather collar. She's alive, but she's gone. My throat tightens.

"Are you sure David saw Jace?" he asks.

"Yes."

"With Samantha?"

"Yes." My mind's on fire. "If that asshole hurt my dog—"

"Did David say anything else? Did Samantha look like she was okay?"

"He didn't say. He wasn't exactly himself."

"Where were they?"

"By the . . . oh, wait. Dammit." All the casinos in Las Vegas are the same to me. "I think it was the one with the pink birds. The Flamingo. Yeah, he said Jace was across the street from the Flamingo."

"Caesar's Palace. Got it."

"Where did you see Java last?"

"If I tell you, will you promise not to go looking for her until I find Jace?"

"You're going to Vegas?"

"Yes. I'm leaving now. Do you promise?"

"Why should I?"

"Let me find Jace and Samantha and get the truth. I'll find out for sure if he left the notes."

"Who else would it be? You said Jace took Java. He was going to shoot her. You don't still think David—"

"No, I don't. I just want you to be safe. It would be horrible if we're wrong about Jace, or if he is working with someone else. Are you in a safe place?"

I'm not safe from boredom or my mother's nagging, but—"Yes. I'm safe."

"Okay. Stay there. I'll call you from Vegas. Promise me you'll stay there until I call."

"How long?"

"I'll be on the strip by morning."

"Noah—" my throat hitches.

"Don't worry, Raine. Java is going to be okay, and so are you, because you're not going to go look for her, right?"

CHAPTER THIRTY-EIGHT

NOAH

Slate gray clouds streak the Nevada sky over the taupe desert hills dotting the outskirts of Las Vegas. There's no resisting a yawn. Noah's bleary eyes welcome the sun on the horizon because there were times last night when, driving over the flatlands, the darkness overwhelmed him. It made him question if his eyes were still open, whether the earth was still round, and whether any of this—the cult, the kidnapping, the client, the beautiful woman and her dog . . . the Teaching—whether any of it was real.

But he's made it to the City of Second Chances now, and he's catching a second wind.

Who needs sleep?

The strip is quiet . . . for the strip. It's nearing eight in the morning on a weekday. Zombie gamblers who've lost all track of time wander up and down the sidewalks. There's no way Titus is out here this early, looking for Noah—looking to break some kneecaps. But Noah can't help it. He glances back and forth, watching out for the loan shark's trademark vermillion jacket.

He drives past the Luxor.

There's not much chance Jace is out here this early, either.

He pulls out his phone and calls Baxter, but again today, there's no answer. He tries Baxter's office, but it hasn't opened yet. He hasn't been able to get ahold of Mr. Oakes all week, but it's just as well. The conversation will go much better after he finds Samantha.

Raine said David saw Jace and Samantha across from the Flamingo, so that's where he starts. Caesar's Palace. He pulls down the palatial drive, watching the fountains send plumes of water into the air. He could go inside and ask if Jace was a registered guest. Ask if the teen somehow afforded a room here, but there's no way the clerk would tell him. He could try a bribe, use his someone-stole-my-credit-card trick, but none of that would work. It didn't work at the Hampton Inn in Elko, and it would never work here.

He pulls over and gazes at the boulevard. If he were a run-away teen in Vegas, where would he go? It depends. Did Samantha come with Jace willingly? Raine said the poor girl looked scared in the woods that day like someone was chasing her, but that doesn't mean it was Jace. Jace could have been rescuing her.

Save her from what? From who?

From whoever wrote those notes.

Jace could have helped Samantha leave the Haven. They could have gotten back together weeks ago. Lived in secrecy in his mobile home. Finding Jace in the woods with Java could have been the final straw. Jace, yelling, *this shit isn't worth it—I'd rather be homeless*. He and Samantha could have run away to Vegas together to . . .

To what?

To get married?

No. Probably not, but where else would they go? Jace couldn't possibly have enough money to gamble, and if he did, he wouldn't be out here doing it at eight in the morning.

But he could have decided to get married. He could have gotten married last night.

Noah drives down the strip and stops at the first wedding chapel he sees. It's open twenty-four hours a day. And so is the next chapel. And the next.

"Sorry, we haven't had any youngins in here with a spider-web tattoo. Not lately, anyway." The story is the same at each and every chapel. "You lookin' to stop a wedding?"

"Not exactly. I'm trying to find out if my friend got married."

Noah checks a few more. He enters a couple of cheap hotels near the strip. Walks through a casino.

Nothing.

The morning drifts into the afternoon. Vapors radiate off the pavement. The air is hot on his tongue and reality sets in. Vegas is too big. The buildings are too big. Jace is a needle in a gigantic haystack, and Samantha is no bigger.

He heads to Old Town where there's a smattering of quickie wedding chapels. It's his last resort, a last-ditch effort, and chapel after chapel, he finds nothing. Sitting in a parking lot, he realizes his apartment isn't far from here. Sleep would be good, but Titus might have his place staked out, looking to collect. Noah can't give up.

The heat from the sun penetrates the windshield. The dash is hot. He goes to a drive-thru and orders lunch. The Big Mac doesn't sit well, and the McFlurry melts before he can finish it.

Now his stomach hurts.

He should just go home. Take the risk. Maybe Titus has given up.

No. One more try, then he can give up.

Jace wasn't at Caesar's Palace earlier, but it wouldn't hurt to check again.

The sidewalks are more crowded along the strip now. He drives as slow as possible past the fountains. There are too many people walking this way and that. None of them are Jace or Samantha. He lumbers into the casino—flashing lights, chaotic *beeps* and *boops*. He wastes an hour wandering around on foot before driving back onto the boulevard.

A taxicab in front of him moves slowly. He stays behind it, glancing left and right, hoping against hope he'll see some sign of the teens. At the MGM, the cab turns down a side street, away from the strip.

Noah's eyes are heavy.

It's over.

He's not going to find them.

He turns in behind the cab and follows it. Home is this way. If the coast is clear, he can go inside, get a few belongings, and leave Vegas forever. Go somewhere Titus can't find him. He's so tired . . .

The cab passes by a Hard Rock Cafe and stops at a light.

Across the intersection, the doors to a wedding chapel open, and Jace steps outside.

Noah guns the accelerator, darts around the cab, and runs the light, focusing on the road, not on Jace. He goes fast, hoping Jace won't have time to recognize him. There's an alley behind the chapel. Noah cranks the steering wheel hard, his left rear tire bounces over the curb, and he slams on the brakes. Jumps out. Charges uphill toward the chapel.

A fleeting thought—Jace has a gun.

Noah closes in anyway.

Jace jumps and raises his hands. "I'm sorry, man. I'm sorry." He backs away.

"Where's Samantha?"

Jace looks at the front of the chapel.

The doors open, and a young girl with long blonde hair steps outside.

Jace waves to her. "Cori. Stay there." She has a wedding tiara in her hair and a bouquet in her hands.

"Why?" she says.

"I've got to talk to this guy a minute. I'll be right back." He starts down the hill toward the alley. "Come on, man. I've got something for you."

Noah gazes at the girl. It's not Samantha. It's the minigolf girl.

Shit.

"Come on, man." Jace gestures for Noah to follow.

"Stop. I'm not going anywhere with you. You shot at me."

"Christ." Jace turns around and trudges back up the hill. "I'm sorry, man. Honest." He closes in.

"Stay back." Noah raises his hands.

Jace ignores him.

Noah stands firm.

They come face to face. He put on too much cologne for his wedding, and it makes Noah's nose burn.

"Come into the alley with me," Jace whispers, "and I'll give it to you." He bends over and lifts his pant leg.

A gun grip sticks out of Jace's dress socks.

"Whoa." Noah steps back.

Jace covers the gun and stands up straight. His eyes are steady. His jaw is relaxed. Noah looks for other tells, but Jace isn't bluffing. "Why are you trying to give me that?"

The teen glances up the hill. "Just come with me, man." He turns toward the alley, and Noah waits a moment before following.

Cori stands on the chapel steps. "Jace? Where are you—"

"Hold on." Jace stops on the other side of the minivan. "Here. Take it."

The weight of the weapon is surprising. Polished, wooden grip. Black barrel. A revolver. It's got to be Terry's.

"That thing's caused me nothing but trouble, man. I can't keep hiding it from Cori."

Noah tucks the gun into his pants and covers the grip with his shirt. "How'd you get this?"

"That bitch, Monica. She gave it to me."

"Monica? When?"

"A few weeks ago. I don't know. It was when Samantha and I were dating. I didn't want it. She said Samantha liked guns, and I believed her." He looks down. "What dumb ass I was. That manipulative bitch."

"Samantha wasn't impressed?"

"No. She freaked out." He scoffs. "Chicks don't like guns, but you know what? She should have liked it."

"Why?"

"Because she had one of her own. What a hypocrite."

Noah can't keep his shock from showing. Monica must have stolen Terry's gun and given it to Jace. The other gun, the tan one, the one David found—it must have been Samantha's.

"Yeah, that's right," Jace says, "the little rich girl wasn't so innocent. You know what else?" He glances at the chapel. Cori's hair sways with the breeze. "She was pregnant."

"She—you didn't."

"No, I didn't. It isn't mine. No way, man." He puts his hands up. "But she was going to tell everyone it was if I didn't keep it a secret. The Haven would have made me raise it in the name of the Teaching. Can you imagine that? I'm not father material, man." He gazes at Cori. "Not yet."

"Did you ever see her gun? Do you know what it looked like?"

"I saw it once. It was newer than that one. It was all brown, and the bullets went in the handle."

"Light brown?"

"Yeah."

"If she wasn't impressed with the gun, why didn't you get rid of it?"

"I don't know, man. I should have. It all happened so fast. Samantha and I broke up. Terry said his gun was gone. Samantha threatened to tell everyone I was the father of her baby, and Monica threatened to tell everyone I stole the gun. I didn't know what to do. That place is a fucking nightmare."

Noah opens the cylinder. The muzzle swings in Jace's direction.

"Careful, man. It's loaded."

"Sorry." He points the gun down. "Why do you think she gave it to you?"

"Because she's an evil bitch, that's why. I thought she was being nice, but she used it against me. She made me do everything. It's what they all do there."

"Did she make you do something to Samantha?"

He raises his voice. "No. God no. I didn't hurt anyone.

Just"—his face scrunches—" the dog. I was talking about the dog. She made me take it and—just keep the gun and go, all right? I was out of mind. I'm sorry I shot at you."

"Why were you going to kill Java?"

Jace's eyes flare. He grips Noah's shoulder. "Look. You don't understand, man. What they do there—they make you think you can't live on your own. Anytime they can accuse someone of not being in the Teaching—it's horrible, man. Everyone looks down on you. They make you do 'service' night and day, and you think you have to do it or you won't go to heaven. They threaten to send you out into 'the world,' out into eternal damnation or some shit, and if you believe it, if you believe it, they can get you to do anything, man. I didn't want to hurt the dog. Really, I didn't."

He turns to go.

"Jace. Wait. Why didn't you call the police? If it was so horrible there, why didn't you call them? You could have shown them the gun. You could have told them what Monica did."

"Come on, man. Look at me. The police wouldn't help someone like me. Besides, if she or anyone else found out I called the cops that would have been it. I would've been thrown out of the Haven for sure. I would have had to be reborn and live this shitty life all over again." He looks up at the sky. "Man, that sounds crazy. I was so brainwashed. I am still brainwashed." His eyes narrow on Noah. "I'm not going back. You've got to understand. That's their control, man. Monica didn't think I had the guts to leave. She knew I didn't want to lose Cori, and she used it against me." He gazes up the hill, to the chapel, to his bride. "I never thought someone like Cori would run away with me, but she hated it there too." He turns his back. "Have a nice life, man."

"Just one more thing, Jace. Did Monica make you write those notes?"

"Notes?" His brow furrows.

"Yeah. The ones for Raine."

"I don't know what you're talking about."

He doesn't. The look on his face tells Noah everything he needs to know. Jace knows nothing about the notes. Monica wrote them.

Monica.

Seeing her at Yama's Powersports the other day wasn't a coincidence. She's a spy and a blackmailer . . . but the notes don't make sense. Why would she want to scare Raine away? Did she scare Samantha away with threatening notes? The Teaching wants everyone to stay in the Haven. It's a cult. They don't want people to leave.

It doesn't make sense.

"Jace. Wait."

"Come on, man. I've got to go."

"Did Monica tell you why she wanted you to kill Java?"

"She's a crazy bitch, that's why. They're all crazy—except for Cori."

"I don't understand. Monica and Raine are best friends. They've known each other since they were kids. Why would Monica do this to her?"

"Jace," Cori shouts from the chapel steps. "Can we go?"

Noah's mind races.

Jace heads up the hill.

Maybe Monica didn't scare Samantha away. Maybe she kidnapped her. Or maybe she did something worse. She *is* an alcoholic. Maybe she got into a fight with Samantha and flew into a drunken rage.

Noah catches up with Jace. "Hold on."

Jace turns around.

Sweat forms on Noah's brow.

"What is it?" Jace asks.

"Do you think Monica is capable of murder?"

Jace leans forward, puts his hand on Noah's shoulder. "Man, I think Monica is capable of anything."

CHAPTER THIRTY-NINE

RAINE

"You look miserable."

"Thanks, Mother." I lean back in my grandma's rocking chair. Dirt crunches beneath the wood runners.

My mother is standing on the steps of her trailer, handbag in hand. I haven't heard from Noah, and I fear the worst. I don't even know if he made it to Vegas. I promised him I wouldn't go looking for Java until he found Jace, and it's killing me. I regret it, but a promise is a promise.

The mountain air is warm. The sun's glare is stifling.

It's almost noon.

I can't sit around all day, doing nothing, waiting for a call. Java needs me.

If he doesn't call soon, I'm going to explode.

"Why don't you come with me?" my mother asks. "I'm going to town to get a few things for Ladies' Night."

"Vodka?"

She grins. "And tomato juice."

I rock the chair. "No, thanks."

"Will you come to Ladies' Night? You haven't come for a long time. Everyone would love to hear about your trance lessons."

No. You'd love to brag about your daughter. My *trance lessons.* I'm not a show pony.

All those old women, sitting around, ripping on everyone in the Haven. Or on people in Elko. Or on anyone *not* in the Teaching. The world. "I'd rather not. I'm fine right here."

She gives me that sad puppy look. "I'm worried. You've never taken a breakup this hard."

"It's not that. It's Java."

"Have you been to the Shrine this week?"

I look away. There's no way in hell I'm going to the Shrine.

"Why don't you invite Shayla or Monica over?"

I shake my head no.

"You need to spend more time with the women in the community. Reaffirm your place in God's plan. Let your feminine energy flow." She looks up at the sky. "If God intends for you to have more time on the earth plane with Java, then God will return her to you."

"How about you shut up about God and leave me alone?"

She stomps down the steps, clutching her handbag. "I'm going to talk to Kattrice about you. She'll know what to do. She'll get you out of this spiritual spiral."

I rock.

"You've been sitting there all day like a zombie, and I don't like it."

I don't care what she likes. She can go ahead and talk to Kattrice. Tell her I love my dog more than God's children. Maybe Terry will be in the next room when she does, listening, and the next time he meditates, Sebastian will tell him

I've fallen off God's path. Sebastian will tell him I'm not in the Teaching because animals are more important to me than the community, and Terry will write a sermon about it.

I don't care.

The way I feel right now, it's all bullshit.

I fold my arms over my chest.

She heads for her car. "I'm very disappointed in you."

That's it.

I launch out of the rocking chair. My feet hit the dirt, and she turns around.

"Stop," she says. "You're out of integrity!"

"Fuck you." I grab the rocking chair and sling at the trailer. "Fuck you and all the old women. Fuck Kattrice and Terry"—the chair bounces off the siding, and I kick it back—"and Monica and my father and—everyone." The chair breaks, and I stomp on the pieces. "And fuck God." I twist my foot, mashing spindles into the ground.

"God?"

"Yes. God." I jump on the seat, and it breaks in two.

"That was your grandmother's chair," she says, trembling.

I step toward her, and she backs away. Puts her hand on the car door handle. "Go to hell, Mother."

"You don't mean that."

"Oh, I mean it." I lower my head and step closer. "Fuck you and fuck the Teaching."

And fuck my father for leaving.

Tears threaten my eyes.

My life here is her fault. She made us stay when my dad didn't want to. He hated the Teaching. We could have had normal lives. I don't belong here. I never belonged here. I can't even remember my father's face.

She stole that from me so I could grow up in the Teaching. So I could grow up without a father.

And her face—I've never seen it this pale before. Contorting and twisting. She doesn't know what to do. What to say.

My vision blurs.

I take another step toward her, my eyes on fire.

She says, "You don't mean that."

"I mean it. Fuck you and fuck God. I want my dog back."

She opens the car door and puts it between us.

My phone rings.

It's Noah.

I stop. Wipe my face. "Noah? Where the hell are you?"

"I found Jace," he says.

"And Samantha?"

My mother gets inside her car. Starts the engine.

I flip her off.

"No. It wasn't her. It was that girl we saw him with at minigolf."

My mother glares at me as she backs out and turns the car around.

I flip her off again.

"They got married."

"Jace married Cori? Hold on a second." I catch my breath and sit on the front steps.

My mother drives away.

"What about Samantha?" I ask.

"He doesn't know where she is. Listen. He's not the one who left the notes." Noah's words fly through the receiver. Blood rushes through my ears. "He gave me the gun he was going to use to shoot Java. Raine. It's Terry's gun."

"What? He stole Terry's gun?"

"No. Are you sitting down?"

"Yes." Pieces of my grandmother's chair lay scattered at my feet. "What's going on?"

"Brace yourself. Monica took Terry's gun and gave it to Jace. Then she told him to kill Java or she'd kick him out of the Haven."

I stand up. "She wouldn't do that. She—"

"She wrote the notes, Raine, and I have the gun."

I pace.

"Raine?"

Monica wouldn't hurt me. She wouldn't hurt Java. She likes Java.

"Raine? Are you there?"

"Are you sure she wrote the notes?"

"Ninety-nine percent."

Why would Monica want to scare me away? We're friends. We've always been friends. I know she was jealous of my friendship with David, and because of what happened in high school, but—she can't be *this* jealous. We've grown apart, but—has she gone insane?

"You believe me, right?" he asks.

"I don't know. I need a minute."

"She's here in Vegas, right? With David?"

"Yes." *Davy Bear. Come back to bed. Mama's lonely.* "She's there. I heard her on the phone last night." I put my hand to my head and stop pacing.

The sun has made my forehead hot.

"Raine?"

"Just a minute." I close my eyes.

Breathe.

The other day, David said she would lose her mind if

Terry taught him how to trance. He said it was a good thing that *I* was the chosen one, not him.

It's not a good thing.

Monica wants to be the chosen one.

She has always wanted to take over the community from her father.

Oh my God.

She has lost her mind. She must think I'm taking over, and—that's why she wrote the notes.

"Are you okay?"

"You might be right." My throat swells, and I swallow.

"Good. I'm glad you believe me."

Dirt shifts and slides beneath my shoes as I tromp down the hill. The swooping handwriting, delicate and disturbing. Feminine. She wrote the notes. She broke into my house and walked right up to Java. Java would have willingly gone with her. Female. She told Jace to kill my dog.

I seethe.

"And she's here in Vegas," Noah says, "so you're safe, right?"

"She's not going to hurt me," I growl.

"You're breaking up a little. Are you going somewhere?"

"I'm going home. Just a minute." I pick up my pace. "Can you hear me now?"

"Yes."

I charge past Jace's mobile home. "Sorry about that. I'm going home to get Java's leash and see if I can find her."

"Right now?"

"Yes, now. What are you going to do?"

"I have to tell my friend I couldn't find his daughter. Then I'm coming back to the Haven."

"Right." My lips tense. "I forgot about your *friend.*"

"I'm sorry. Look, I don't want to search for Samantha anymore. Not until after I help you find Java. That's all that matters to me."

"Sure." I march onto Control Road.

"But I've got to tell my friend in person. I owe him that."

"Of course."

He breathes into the phone. "I don't know what I'm going to say, Raine. Do you think Monica wanted Samantha to run away? Do you think she wrote notes to scare her too?"

"No. I don't think so. I can see why she wants me to leave, but it's so against the Teaching to push a new person away. Especially a kid."

"Then I've got nothing to tell Baxter."

"You've got your problems, and I've got mine."

"I'm coming back to help you find Java as soon as I can. I'll be there day after tomorrow."

I walk past the Shrine. "I don't need your help." I glance up at Terry and Kattrice's house. Terry stands in a second-story window. What would he do if he knew about his daughter? What would he do if he knew she stole his gun? Wrote those notes?

He slips behind a curtain.

"Give me a chance, Raine. Please? All I'm asking is, you give me a chance."

The shortcut to my house comes up on my left. "I'm going into some trees. I might lose you again."

"Wait."

In the distance, an ATV buzzes through the woods. "You there? Noah? Can you hear me?"

Nothing.

The sound of the ATV fades away.

Noah wants to help me. Genuinely. I heard it in his voice. He wants a chance.

Picturing him sneaking around town, telling everyone he was a student . . . it still makes my neck hot, but—

It is by self-forgetting that we find.

It is by forgiving that we are forgiven.

I step out of the trees and onto my road.

"Raine? You there?"

"Yes. You can come back, but only to look for Java, and only if I haven't found her first."

"Okay."

"Goodbye, Noah."

"Wait. There's something else. Did you know Samantha was pregnant?"

"No. Was it Jace?"

"He swears he's not the father, and I believe him. Do you think it was someone else in the Haven?"

"I don't know." My head spins. I can't think about Samantha. I've got to find Java.

"Do you think she left because she was pregnant? Would David and Monica have gotten mad at her?"

"No. The Teaching tells us to have as many children as we can. If anything, Monica would have made Samantha stay and have the baby to score points with Sebastian."

"Then why did she leave?"

CHAPTER FORTY

NOAH

The Oakes Land and Building Development office clings to Las Vegas like a leech on skin. So many buildings—big, expensive buildings. Baxter's business has done well. It would have been great to join him. To have been Baxter's right-hand man, and maybe it's not too late, but Noah isn't holding his breath.

The elevator doors open. Noah steps inside and presses the button for the seventh floor.

He's got to tell Baxter he couldn't bring Samantha back. Not only did he fail to bring her back, he completely lost her. After two weeks, he has no idea where she went, and the news he has isn't good.

She's pregnant.

The elevator passes the fourth floor.

He practices his speech.

Hi, Baxter. I searched everywhere, and I got close to that woman, Raine Harkins, like you asked, but I haven't been able to find Samantha. I'm so sorry, but hey, there's some good news. Congratulations, you're going to be a grandfather!

The doors open into a long hallway. The light fixtures are from a 1940s film—dangling chrome chandeliers—but everything else is sleek and modern. Prints of tall buildings hang on the walls, architectural achievements of years past. Smooth white baseboards separate the walls from the plush sable carpeting . Suite 707 lies at the far end between two ferns. The French doors to the suite host eight panes of frosted glass and two platinum handles.

Fancy.

He hesitates to gather his thoughts. Prepare for the confrontation. Jace said Monica was capable of anything, and Raine said she was in Vegas, so Noah brought the gun. He likes the way it feels to have that kind of power tucked just below his waistline, but it also makes him anxious. He's never carried a weapon before.

He can't wait until this whole thing is over.

Baxter Oakes is a tough, down-to-business kind of guy, but he's also a loving father. He's used to getting what he wants, and he wants his daughter back. The last few times Noah talked to him on the phone, Baxter came close to breaking down.

This news is going to kill him.

Both French doors are closed.

He takes a deep breath, puts his hand on the door handle, and a familiar voice comes from behind. " . . . no, he's not here. Wasn't he supposed to be here?" It's a woman. "How would I know where he is?"

It sounds like Monica.

He crouches behind a fern.

The woman's voice gets louder. "Don't worry, I'll find him . . . yes, I know how much to ask for, but what if he doesn't believe me? What if he thinks we don't have her?"

Through the fronds, at the end of the hall, the woman steps into view. She presses a cell phone to her head.

It *is* Monica.

Noah backs around the corner into the hallway before she can see him.

"You're right," she says. "I forgot that. But I have some pictures of her on my phone to prove it . . . I know. I know. I also brought some torn clothes to show him we mean business."

She's talking about Samantha. She's got to be. The Johansen's kidnapped Samantha, and now Monica is trying to collect a ransom. Maybe Terry and Kattrice are in on it too. Everything the community was accused of years ago—kidnapping that little girl—it's actually happening this time.

"We're getting along," she says. "Yesterday was great, but he's been grumpy today . . . no, he thinks we're here to recruit her father . . . I'm telling you, no. That's all he knows. . . . don't worry. I can handle David."

Noah bursts from hiding and charges toward her. The gun slides down his thigh, and he stops to adjust his pants.

Monica startles, shoves her phone into her pocket, and turns to go.

"Stop." He gets the gun back in place without taking it out. "Where are you hiding Samantha?"

"Shouldn't you be in school?" she sneers. "Oh, wait. You're not a student, are you?"

"I heard what you said. Where is she?"

"You didn't hear me. I wasn't talking about Samantha."

"Don't lie." He reads her. She's holding aces and claiming

a gentleman's hand. She's got nothing. "Jace told me every-thing. The gun. The notes. Where is she?"

"Who the hell do you think you are? You're the liar. UNLV, my ass." She turns to go, her beach bag swinging on her shoulder.

Noah grabs the bag. They tussle. He grabs her arm.

"Let go of me."

"Hey." David comes running down the hall. "Let go of my wife."

Noah steps back.

David is pissed and puffy. Stubble covers his face. Mis-shapen bags hang under his bloodshot eyes.

Monica wraps her arms around him. Her savior.

David doesn't hug her back.

"What are you doing here?" David asks.

"I overheard her. You kidnapped Samantha."

"No we didn't."

Noah points at Monica's shoulder. "Then what's in the bag?"

"Ignore him, David. Let's go."

"No," Noah says. "She's got Samantha's clothes in there. She was just on the phone planning a ransom."

"I was not."

David looks at her. "What's he talking about?"

"I don't know. Honest."

"Look in the bag," Noah says.

David reaches for it, and she pulls away. "Open the bag, Mon."

Her eyes go from David to Noah and back to David. "No."

"Monica," David says, "why are we really here?"

Noah takes a step forward, and David raises his hand. "Back off."

"Mr. Oakes needs our help," she says. "He needs the Teaching."

David rips the bag out of her hands and begins tossing her things onto the floor. A romance novel. Sunglasses. Lotion. He holds up a faded teal sweatshirt three sizes too small to fit her. It's torn in the middle. "Whose is this? Samantha's?"

"Yes," she stammers. "But no one kidnapped her. No one—"

"Why'd you bring this?" David thrusts the sweatshirt in her face.

"He needs our help, David." She grabs the sweatshirt and throws it on the floor. "And we need his. If he doesn't want to come back to the Haven with us, we need to convince him Samantha is there."

"Does Terry know you're doing this? Lying like this?"

"Where's Samantha?" Noah asks.

Monica yells, "We don't have her. We—"

Noah trembles. He considers pulling the gun out and shoving it in her face for all the pain she put Raine through. For all the notes. Java. "Where are you holding her?"

"Back off," David says. "We're not holding anyone. Let me think." He puts his hand over his forehead and rubs his temples. It's obvious he has no idea what Monica is up to. "No one kidnapped Samantha. Terry wouldn't have allowed it, and I would've known. I would've seen something." He glares at Monica. "You were going to lie and say we kidnapped her to get her father to come to the Haven, weren't you?"

"No . . . well, I—"

"Where's Samantha?" Noah demands.

David grits his teeth. "We don't know."

Noah backs away. Eases off. "Do you know what your wife has been doing? Do you know she blackmailed Jace? Made him kidnap Raine's dog?"

"I did no such thing."

"What?" David says. "Why the hell do you think she did that?"

"Because Jace said so, and he gave me—he showed me the gun he used. It was Terry's gun. She stole it and started leaving notes on Raine's cabin, threatening her. She's been trying to scare Raine out of the Haven for the last two weeks, but when it didn't work, she threatened to kill Java, but she didn't want to do it herself." Noah glares at Monica. "She blackmailed Jace and made him do it."

"Java's dead?" David asks.

"No. I saved her."

"Is any of this true, Mon?"

She looks him square in the eyes, unblinking. "No."

He glares. "Monica . . ."

"Okay. It's partly true. I left a couple of notes on her cabin, alright? But it's not—I was drunk." She averts her eyes. "Remember that night we were listening to Johnny Cash? Remember that song, the one with 'sooner or later, God's going to run you down?' I thought it would be funny to leave Raine a note as a joke. I wasn't trying to *scare* her away."

"Yes, you were." Noah reaches into his pocket, pulls out a piece of paper, and hands it to David.

You have defied God's will. Leave the Haven now, or Java dies.

David stares at the page. "This is your handwriting, Mon. Your fancy, *greeting card* writing."

She takes a step back.

"When Raine didn't leave the Haven," Noah says, "your wife kidnapped Java. She made Jace take her, and—"

"How?"

"I didn't make Jace do anything."

"Shut up and let him talk."

Noah continues. "Monica stole Terry's gun and gave it to Jace to impress Samantha. Then she said she'd tell everyone he stole it if he didn't kill Java. She threatened to get him kicked out of the community. When I found him with Java in the woods, he was about to do it. He was about to shoot her with Terry's gun."

"But," David says, "he's here in Vegas. I saw him yesterday."

"He ran away right after I found him. He must have come straight here."

"Why should I believe you?"

Noah lifts his shirt and exposes the butt end of Terry's revolver. "Because Jace gave me this." Monica cowers. "And she wrote that note. You said so yourself. That's her handwriting."

David turns pale. "You sadistic, jealous bitch. How could you?"

Monica looks away.

"What else have you been doing?"

"Nothing."

"Where's Samantha?" Noah asks.

Her face turns red, and she stares at the floor.

David steps toward her, his body shaking, his lips tightening, his jaw muscles pulsating. Noah can hear David's teeth grinding. "Monica. Do you know where Samantha is?"

"No. I don't." She looks up at him, her eyes unyielding.

"I really don't. Really, I—I don't know where she is. She just ran away. I swear."

David turns his back and heads for the elevators.

"David," she calls out, "wait. We still need to—"

"Shut up. *We* don't need to do anything. You're a robot. You're your mom's puppet. I can't believe anything you say."

"David."

Noah glances down the hall toward Baxter's suite. A woman stands on the other side of the French doors, watching through the frosted glass.

"You're out of integrity," David says. "You and your mother are both out of integrity." He pushes the down button on the elevator.

The woman sees Noah looking at her and walks away from the doors.

"Wait." Monica points at Noah. "He's the liar. Listen to me. He's not a student."

"Shut up."

"Aren't you curious why he's here? Why he keeps asking about Samantha?"

David gazes at Noah.

"He came to destroy our community," she stammers. "He's a cult buster."

"Christ." David leaves the elevator, trudges toward her. "And how would you know that, *Mon*?" The elevator dings.

"Sebastian told me. Sebastian knows everything. He is wise."

"Bullshit." The cords in David's neck tighten. "If Sebastian thought Noah was a threat to the community, Terry wouldn't have let him come to Trance. Tell me the truth."

"I did. It was Sebastian, and—"

"She's been spying on me," Noah says.

"Don't listen to him."

"How do you know he's a cult buster?"

"Okay." She takes a deep breath. "I wasn't spying on him, but I did look him up on the internet. There's nothing about him ever going to UNLV. He's been pretending to be a student, but he's really been trying to break up our community." She glowers at Noah. "He's the liar."

"Monica," David says, looming over her, "You're a fucking spy. You and your mother, and Ally, and all the other women—always running around, making shit up. That's what you guys do when you're not drinking, isn't it? You spy on people and tell Terry, and then Sebastian suddenly knows everything about everyone."

"No," she says. "That's not true." She points at Noah. "He's trying to destroy our community. He's a cult buster. Look at him. The Teaching tells us—"

"Shut up about the Teaching." David makes fists. "Just shut the fuck up."

She draws back, wide-eyed and shaking.

"It's true," Noah says. "I'm not a student, but I'm not a cult buster either. I actually like your community," he eyes Monica.

David glances at the elevators, the floor, the suite at the end of the hall. "What *are* you doing here, Noah?"

"My uncle is a friend of Mr. Oakes. He introduced us a few weeks ago. Mr. Oakes asked if I would go to the Haven and bring his daughter back, but then she ran away. I'm here to talk to him about it. That's all. "

"He's not here," Monica mumbles.

David shoots her a look. "I told you to shut up."

She puts her hand on David's arm. "Davy, please. What about our trip? We were doing so well, healing our relationship. Remember last night?"

"This trip is a lie. You. Your mother. Your father. The three of you drove me to suicide." He shoves her away.

"Davy, don't say that."

He faces Noah. "I don't know where Samantha is. Tell her father I'm sorry."

"I will." Noah heads for the suite. He's wasted enough time on them.

Monica says something to David, and he rips into her. They argue.

As Noah approaches the French doors, he notices a placard hiding behind one of the ferns.

OAKES LAND AND BUILDING DEVELOPMENT

BAXTER OAKES, CEO

MARCUS JAMESON, CFO

SAMUEL RUTHON, COO

TIFFANY SWORALES, MARKETING

THOMAS H. JOHNSON, BUSINESS DEVELOPMENT

Thomas H. Johnson . . .

Tom Johnson.

The name from the ATV rental shop.

That can't be right. Baxter said he'd never heard of a Tom Johnson.

But Tom Johnson paid for an ATV rental under Noah's name, and he works for Baxter.

Someone right under Baxter's nose was in the woods the day Samantha disappeared.

Noah opens the door and steps inside.

CHAPTER FORTY-ONE

NOAH

The woman Noah saw through the frosted French doors earlier sits behind a glass-topped desk beneath an aluminum sign reading OAKES LAND AND BUILDING DEVELOPMENT. A silver barrette holds her chopped black hair in place, and she wears a white blouse with red buttons. The buttons match her lips and fingernails, and she makes a sour face when he approaches.

"Is Mr. Oakes in?" He puts his hands on the desk and leans forward. "It's urgent I talk to him."

"No." She scoots her chair back. "He's not here."

"Where is he? I need to talk to him."

She speaks with a thick, urban Italian accent. "What you doing here, barging in like this? You want I call security?"

"Where is he?"

Her features harden. "I'm not telling you nothing, scumbag. The door's over there."

"Tell me where he is."

She glances at the desk phone.

"Don't do it," Noah says.

She reaches for the phone, and he pulls it off the desk.

"I'm sorry," he says, "but this could be a matter of life and death. It's about his daughter. I've got to know—"

She stands. Shoves the chair away. "He's not here!"

"Is Tom Johnson here?"

She cocks her head. "Who?"

"Tom—Thomas Johnson. Is he here somewhere?"

"You don't know what you're getting yourself into, asshole. You'd better leave."

"Who is Thomas Johnson?" Noah demands. "His name is on the wall outside."

"Are you the IRS?"

"No."

"Then get the hell out of here. I don't have to talk to you."

"I'm not leaving until you tell me who Tom Johnson is."

"He's no one. Now leave, or you'll be sorry."

The door to the office opens, and David sticks his head inside. "What's going on in here?"

"Come on in, David. Close the door."

She shakes her head. "You're going to be sorry."

David walks up to the desk. "Noah. What are you—"

Noah pulls the gun out of his pants. His right hand trembles until he steadies it with his left. He points the barrel at the woman.

She backs against the wall.

David raises his hands and steps away. "Oh, shit. Noah."

"Where's Mr. Oakes?" Noah yells. "Where's Tom Johnson?"

"You're with Scarlucci, aren't you?" She raises her hands. "Tell him he's going to have to do better than you if he wants out of the deal."

"I'm not with anyone. I don't want to hurt anyone. Please, I'm begging you, tell me who Tom Johnson is."

Her eyes narrow, and her lips tighten. "You're serious, ain't you? You don't know who Scarlucci is, do you?"

"No. I don't. I just need to know who—"

"There is no Thomas Johnson," she says. "He's a fugazi."

"What do you mean?"

"He's not real. He doesn't exist. You know, for tax reasons. He has a credit card, a bank account, a residence in his name, but he doesn't exist. Okay? You want to put that thing away now?"

Tom Johnson doesn't exist, but—"Who uses his credit card? Who?"

"Mr. Oakes."

"Noah," David says.

"Where's Mr. Oakes? Tell me." He waves the muzzle. "Now."

"Noah," David says. "Calm down. Put the gun down. You don't have to—"

"There's no time, David. Raine could be in trouble." He lowers his head toward the gun. Takes aim at the woman's chest. "Tell me where Mr. Oakes is."

She grimaces. "He went camping in the mountains. He hasn't been here all week."

"Where in the mountains?"

"Up by Elko somewhere. I don't know exactly."

David puts his hand on Noah's shoulder.

Noah's brain is on fire.

Two weeks ago, Tom Johnson rented an ATV in Elko, but it wasn't Tom Johnson.

It was Baxter.

The next day, Samantha went missing.

"Put the gun down, Noah." David sounds like he's far away. Noah's heart pounds. "Please."

"No," Noah says. "Listen. I need to figure this out. Her boss, Baxter Oakes—he rented an ATV under my name the day before Samantha went missing, but he must not have had any cash because he paid for it with Tom Johnson's credit card. Raine heard an ATV in the forest that day. Until now, we thought my name on the rental log had to be a coincidence because Jace had your dad's ATV. We thought he was the one riding around the forest, but it wasn't him. It was Baxter on a rental."

"What are you saying?"

"Baxter Oakes was in the woods the day Raine saw Samantha run away."

"So?"

"So, I don't know why he was there, but—shit."

"What you gonna do?" the woman asks. "How long you gonna point that thing at me?"

"Shut up," Noah says. "I need to think."

"Noah, let's go."

"Shit. Oh, shit. Baxter was always asking me about Raine. He always wanted to know what she knew. He insisted he didn't know anyone named Tom Johnson, and I believed him. He . . . oh, shit. He did something to Samantha, and he thinks Raine saw him do it."

"What did you tell him?" David asks.

"Everything. I told him Raine was the last to see Samantha, but he must have already known that. He must have seen her in the forest that day—shit." Noah glances at the clock on the wall. "He hasn't answered his phone or been in the office all week. Not since I told him about Raine. Not since I asked about Tom Johnson."

"You think he kidnapped his own daughter?" David asks.

"I don't know."

"You think he's going to hurt Raine?"

"Yes."

The woman steps toward the desk.

"Stop." Noah readjusts his aim. "Your boss went camping near Elko, right? When?"

"He left Tuesday."

"Are you sure? Are you sure he's there now?"

"Yes."

"David, we've got to warn Raine."

David pulls out his phone, taps the screen—puts it to his ear.

"Who's Raine?" the woman asks.

Noah glances at David. "Well?"

"There's no answer. It went to voicemail."

CHAPTER FORTY-TWO

SAMANTHA

Two Weeks Ago . . .

Samantha Oakes sucks her belly in and stares at the mirror in disbelief. She sucks it in harder, leans forward, pats it down, pushes on it, and lets it go. It pooches out. She turns sideways and pulls her hair away from her neck. Acne is forming below her ear.

A bubble forms in her throat.

She shouldn't have pushed so hard on her stomach.

Today is the first day she couldn't get her baby bump to disappear in the mirror. It's the beginning of the end.

She crouches down by the toilet.

The house shakes.

She grasps the bowl.

"Are you going to be in there much longer?" Monica bangs on the door. "I've got to go."

"Just a—" She heaves into the toilet.

"Are you okay?"

Tangy acid drips from her lips. "I'm fine." She heaves again. Partially digested granola splashes into the water. She flushes the toilet and watches her breakfast disappear. Slowly, she opens the door, keeping her head down. Monica's wearing those hideous purple flip-flops again, blocking the hallway.

"Are you sick or something?" Monica asks.

"No, I'm fine." She squeezes past and strides down the hall.

"Hey, careful." Monica smiles. "You shouldn't push your new mom like that." She enters the bathroom and closes the door.

Mom.

How ironic.

Samantha is going to be a new mom, too, but she doesn't want to be. Not with this child.

She sits on the couch in the living room and rips a page from one of Jenny's coloring books.

Her new dad is over at Terry's, fixing a toilet. She wishes he were here so she could say goodbye.

She holds the page with both hands and closes her eyes. She tries to pray, but it doesn't come easy; not the way it does for everyone else in the Haven. Sebastian says she'll get better at it over time, but her time has run out. She can't stay here. Her baby bump is too big. When they find out what happened, they'll make her keep the baby.

Using a crayon, she writes a letter to God.

Dear God,

> *This is my last note . . .*

The toilet flushes, and Monica sashays down the hall.

Samantha shoves the letter into her pocket.

"What are you doing?" Monica asks.

"Nothing."

"Your room is a mess, and the kitchen needs cleaning. You've got to start doing more service."

"Fine." She stands up and pushes her way past Monica into the hall. "I'll clean my room right now."

"Wait. You've got to stop pushing me."

"I'm sorry." Samantha closes the door to the laundry room—her *bedroom*. She listens.

Monica doesn't follow.

The room is a mess. The kitchen is a mess. The whole house is a mess, but it doesn't matter anymore.

She unzips her backpack and stuffs her things inside it. When she first came to the Haven, everything she had fit in there, but now, it's too small. She'll have to leave behind some clothes, that religious book Kattrice gave her, that stuffed animal from Jace.

What a jerk.

The blender in the kitchen whirs to life. Good. Monica won't be coming in here anytime soon.

She unzips the outer pocket of her backpack and makes sure the gun is still there. It's a good thing she didn't get rid of it, but the sight of it . . . she'll need it on the road, but—she scrunches her eyes shut. Her hate for *him* burns like acid on an ulcer.

She wants to vomit again.

To touch his gun is to touch *him*.

She zips the pocket shut.

The backpack is cumbersome. Unwieldy. It weighs her down, but she can do this. If she can get out of the Haven with her things, she can make it to Washington.

The hallway is clear, so she foots it to the front door.

"Where are you going?" Monica's behind the kitchen counter, holding a drink.

"Hiking. I'll be back in a while."

"Where are you *really* going?"

"Hiking." She opens the door.

"You didn't clean the kitchen, and now you're leaving?"

"I—"

"Saying you'll do something and then not doing it is the same as lying. You're not in the Teaching."

The Teaching.

No, Samantha isn't in the Teaching.

Everyone would damn her if they knew what she let *him* do. She can't be in the Teaching, as much as she wants to be, as much as she wants a new life, a safe life, away from *him* forever, but after all those years, and then this . . . she places her hand on her stomach. If they knew, they would damn her.

"Monica?" she says softly.

"What?"

"Thank you for taking me in."

"What?" Monica puts her drink down on the kitchen counter.

Samantha bounds down the steps outside.

The tears come.

Jenny and Joseph are playing in the front yard.

Goodbye, little adopted brother. Goodbye, little adopted sister.

She breaks into a run, water streaming from her eyes. At the bend, she stops. She wills the tears to stop. Enough is enough. She's going to rip the Haven off like a bandage. It's tough, but she's tougher. She's run away before, and she can do it again.

Monica yells something, but Samantha is already too far to hear what she's saying.

She's doing the right thing.

If her father were to come here looking for her . . . stop it. Don't think about *him*.

But if *he* did come to the Haven . . .

Stop it.

The Shrine stands amid the white gardenias and lodgepole pines, a gateway to God. She glances around to see if anyone is watching before going inside. Her pocket crumpled the letter when she ran, but God won't mind. She places it on top of a children's book next to another letter. It's a sin to read other people's letters.

She picks up a matchbox and shakes it. The sticks rattle. If she can't hitch a ride to Elko from a stranger, she might need to camp out tonight. She might need to light a fire to keep warm.

But it's bad karma to steal from the Shrine.

She puts the matchbox down.

I love you, God. Please watch over me.

The backpack forces her to lean forward as she makes the trek up Control Road toward the highway. The straps cut into her shoulders. Loosening them doesn't help. It only makes the pack hang lower and rub against her back. At the top of the hill, she sees Terry and Kattrice walking hand-in-hand in the distance.

They're coming toward her.

She'll have to talk to them, and Terry, with his penetrating stare, he'll know what she's doing.

She changes direction and heads toward the trail to the firepit.

She's got to get away, unseen. At least in the woods, if someone else comes, she can hide.

Running away from Las Vegas was easier. All she had to do was get on her phone, pull up Uber, and get a ride to the bus station. She got off in Elko, but, other than finding a new family, that was a mistake. It wasn't far enough. This time, she's going to Seattle. It's easier to hide in a big city, and they have free clinics there.

It's just a procedure. Women have them all the time.

The trail leading to the firepit looks different in the daylight, but it's the right one. Last time she was here she had the best time of her life. Sitting around the fire, watching everyone else get drunk. For a few fleeting moments, she had a future. Why did Jace have to turn out to be such an asshole? They could have been a real item, but he *had* to have a gun, didn't he? He had to wave it around, reminding her of her father—all those nights, crying herself to sleep . . .

If you try to get out of that bed, Sammy, I'll have to shoot you. Now don't move.

She walks through the woods, watching shadows play over the rocks, the logs, the trail, like silky black sheets—cool, dark, and dry. The trail meanders through the trees, and the shade feels good. It feels good to be out of the sun, but her face is hot.

Her face burns with hate for *him.*

Her stomach churns.

This is all her father's fault. She wouldn't be going through this if it weren't for *him.*

Like an all-consuming fire, the hate sucks the air out of her lungs, and she can't . . . stop . . . the hate.

She tries to stay calm and think, but all her nice thoughts, her positive self-talk—nothing works. She struggles to breathe. She struggles—*remember to breathe*—but she hates him so much, her heart thunders inside. Fury rages like a forest fire, taking all the oxygen.

There's no air.

Breathe.

She crouches behind a colossal granite boulder near a swathe of sagebrush, gasping.

Make it go away.

Focus on the silver veins running through the boulder.

Think nice thoughts.

Breathe.

This is all *his* fault. She wishes he were dead. She wishes her mother hadn't left. Gina the Vagina, the needle-freak—yet, living with her would have been better than living with *him*.

This is our little secret, Sammy. Remember, if you try to get out of bed, I'll shoot you dead. Don't move.

She scrunches her eyes shut. She's seven years old. He comes into her room and it's just a game. Like cops and robbers. Now she's twelve, and he shows her how his gun matches his suntan. He buys her black silk sheets to hide the blood, and he makes her take sleeping pills when she can't stop crying. She's fifteen now, and he won't wear a condom.

Samantha opens her eyes.

Her face burns, her palms itch. Something smells strange, and she wipes her nose.

Why couldn't he have worn a condom?

Stop it.

Think nice thoughts.

Focus on the boulder.

Think nice thoughts.

She closes her eyes and—

Why won't it stop? The memories keep coming . . . the light shining into her bedroom when he would crack her door, come inside, and crawl into her bed. His breath. His skin against her face. His sharp stubble gouging her pores, and his cologne . . . the memories are so real, she can smell his cologne.

She can smell his cologne.

Here, in the woods, she smells his—no. It's not possible, but—yes. It's here.

She smells his cologne.

She smells *him*.

He's—

A noise comes from the other side of the boulder.

He's here. Oh, shit. Shit. He's here.

She slips her backpack off and fumbles for the zipper to the outer pocket.

A gunshot shatters the air, making her world—the sagebrush, the boulder, the ground—shake with terrifying force. She collapses onto the backpack, covering it with her body, shoving her hand into the pocket, gripping the gun.

"Hello?" A woman peers around the boulder. She looks familiar.

Samantha releases her grip on the gun and puts her hand on her chest. "You scared me."

"I'm sorry," the woman says. "Did you hear that?"

Breathe. "The gun? Yeah, I heard it." She stands, trying not to shake, trying to hold her hands steady, conscious that her belly is getting bigger all the time. It's so noticeable.

The woman's gentle blue eyes stare curiously at her. "Are you okay?"

"I'm fine."

"You're Samantha, right?" The woman comes around the boulder.

"Yes, I . . . look, I—"

A dog barks in the distance. "It's okay. That's my dog."

It's time to get out of here. This woman smells like *his* cologne, and it's creeping her out.

Samantha puts her backpack on.

"My name is Raine." She holds out her hand. "We haven't officially met. Will you help me find my dog? Her name is Java."

Samantha glances down the trail. It's a long way to Elko. She wishes she'd taken the matches from the Shrine. "I'm sorry, I—" She takes off, but the woman grabs her arm.

"Wait," the woman says, "we can help you."

"No. You're one of them." She pulls her arm free and runs. "Please. Leave me alone."

"Someone's shooting a gun out here. It's not safe to go that way."

Samantha sprints through the trees, purposely changing direction every few feet, crushing pine-needles in her wake.

Raine.

Samantha remembers her now. She's Monica's friend.

Raine yells something, but she's too far away for Samantha to understand her.

She glances back and sees Raine coming after her.

She speeds up, crests the hilltop, and sprints down the other side. The backpack pulls on her shoulders, and her belly bounces. She hides behind a tree, catches her breath, and listens.

Nothing.

Raine must have given up.

All is quiet for a moment, then she hears footsteps.

She peers around the corner.

Raine stands on top of the hill with her hands on her hips, bent over, gasping for air.

Samantha holds her breath.

"Java," Raine calls. "Where are you?"

The barking stopped.

Raine turns around and disappears back the way she came.

Samantha exhales.

"Shh. Don't move," a man whispers.

There isn't time to yell before the reek of his cologne, the memories of all those nights, the terror, the black sheets, the stinging of his unshaven face pressing against her lips—

Her throat closes.

Her vision blurs.

"Stay right there," he says. "Don't move."

She can't see him.

Everything comes crashing down.

Shadows crisscross over the forest floor in front of her, stretching from one pine to another, unmoving. Moving. Still as death, yet fast.

Everything is moving so fast.

Everything is a blur.

She struggles to speak. "Dad? Is that you?"

"Sammy. Don't move."

A LETTER FROM THE SHRINE

Dear God,

This is my last note to you. This is Goodbye. Thank you for giving me a new family, but I have to leave them. The Teaching says everyone should love children, but that's why I have to leave. I'm going to Washington. I can't love this baby. It's his, and I hate him. Sebastian says love is forgiveness, but I hate him so much. I'll never forgive him. I wish he were dead.

Because of him, I'll never know love.

Maybe in my next life, I'll find peace.

Please watch over me.

Love,

Samantha

CHAPTER FORTY-THREE

SAMANTHA

She stands with her back against a tree, trying to suppress the memories. The dark nights. The smell of his cologne. His touch. It's too much. She thinks happy thoughts to make the memories go away, but—

But this isn't a flashback.

He's found her.

She's alone.

In the woods.

And he's here . . . somewhere.

She rubs her eyes, and the woods come into focus. She searches each pine, each branch, each pine needle—

His cologne fills the air.

She leans around the tree and—

"Sammy, I said don't move."

Gasping, she jerks back.

If only she'd run away earlier this morning. Or last night.

If only she'd gone with that woman, Raine, to find that dog.

If only—

"I'm not going to hurt you," he says.

She wriggles out of the backpack and lets it fall to the ground.

He steps out from behind a tree not ten feet away. His hair is messed up, uncombed, and his jeans have holes. He wears a flannel shirt like he's from around here. It's quite the disguise.

"Don't move," he says, raising one hand. "I'm—"

"Leave me alone."

"You know I can't do that."

She crouches down and clutches the backpack to her chest.

"It's time for you to come home."

Fire floods her face. She clenches the canvas covering so hard her knuckles ache.

He takes a step closer. Tears form in *his* eyes, but he—he never cries.

He's never cried before.

The Devil isn't capable of tears, but here he is . . . sobbing. "Sammy—"

"I'm not going anywhere with you."

He forces a smile. "Sweetheart, it's time to come home."

He reaches for her, and she scoots back against the tree. "Go to hell."

"Please, don't be this way. I'm sorry."

She reaches into her backpack. "Leave me alone, or I'll tell everyone what you did."

"But . . . it's our little secret."

This is our little secret, Sammy. Remember, if you try to get out of that bed, I'll shoot you dead. Now don't move.

His hand is pale. He steps closer. His long fingers stretch out toward her.

Her fingers find the gun in the backpack, but she can't bring herself to pull it out of the pocket. She's not a murderer, and he's her father, and there's got to be another way.

But there isn't.

She squeezes the grip, but . . . she . . . can't . . . do it. "I'll tell everyone you raped me. I'll make sure everyone knows. You'll go out of business. I'll go on the internet and—"

"If you do that, everyone will know about you, too." A tear runs down his cheek. "They'll know you're having my baby. My grandchild." He stops reaching for her and wipes the tear away like it never existed.

"I don't care who knows," she says.

If he comes any closer, she'll shoot him.

She's got no choice.

She should shoot him now, but she can't. Why is this so hard? She's dreamed of this moment forever, imagining it over and over, night after night, but now that the time has come—it's different. He's different. He's crying.

Why is he crying?

Is it the baby?

Is it because she's pregnant?

"I'm sorry, Sammy. I'm so sorry." He covers his face with his hands. Sobs. "I'm not going to hurt you anymore. I want you to have the baby. I want a second chance as a father."

"No."

He lowers his hands and lunges forward, his arms outstretched.

The gun catches on the pocket. She can't get it out.

His hands hit her shoulders.

She raises the backpack, shoves it in his face, but he bats it away, and—he's on her. The backpack lands next to her head, and the gun comes tumbling out, sending plumes of dust near a sprawling cluster of sagebrush.

She can't reach it.

He grabs her hair, slams her head into the ground, then pulls her face close to his. He hasn't shaved today. His eyes, so dark they are almost black, fill her vision, and he presses his lips against hers.

She screams, claws at his eyes, kicks, twists, slaps, and—

"I'm sorry, Sammy. I'm so sorry." He wraps his fingers around her throat and pins her to the ground.

She . . . can't . . . breathe.

Breathe.

The gun is just out of reach. She stretches her arm out but—

His fingers tighten around her throat. They're so strong. She can't breathe.

"I'm sorry, Sammy. It's you or me. If they find out about the baby, the deal won't go through. They'll kill me. I'm . . . so . . . sorry." He squeezes hard, and something in her neck pops. "I'm sorry."

Her head tilts sideways, and she stares at the gun.

She brushes the muzzle with the tip of her finger, but that only pushes it farther away.

She feels dizzy.

The gun is a soft, light brown color. Much lighter than the dark red dirt surrounding it. If she can see it, someone else will see it.

Her throat collapses.

Dear God, let this be over soon.

Let him finish.

Soon.

A copper taste pours into her mouth.

Like all those dark nights—*let him finish, soon.*

Just let him finish and . . . let her go to heaven.

Darkness comes.

She doesn't know how to pray, not like those in the Teaching, but she tries.

Please, God, let someone find his gun.

Please . . . let someone find his gun.

And when they do, let them shoot him with it.

Let him die.

Please, God.

Please.

Let it be done.

CHAPTER FORTY-FOUR

NOAH

Noah's footsteps echo in the stairwell of Baxter's office building, reverberating off the concrete walls.

Three more flights to the bottom.

He grasps the railing and flies around the corner.

Mr. Oakes—Mr. Baxter Oakes—land developer, father, kidnapper. Killer?

"Noah, wait." David comes, bounding down the stairs behind him.

There's no time to wait.

Raine is in trouble.

Noah reaches the bottom floor and takes out his cell phone.

David stops one flight up, bends over, and gasps for air.

Raine's got to answer. *Please, answer.*

He tells himself to be calm. There's no reason to scare her, just tell her to go somewhere else.

The phone rings.

He'll ask her where she's at and when she can leave. Then

he'll tell her to get the hell out of there. If she wants to know why, he'll make up a story about—no. No more stories. No more lies.

He's got to tell her the truth. Baxter Oakes is coming for her.

Raine doesn't answer the phone.

The sign on the door lever reads EMERGENCY EXIT ONLY. Noah pushes the lever anyway, the door opens, and an alarm sounds.

He bursts outside.

"Noah," David yells. "Wait for me."

The hot air assaults his senses. Heat emanates from the setting sun and distorts the casinos in the distance. He runs toward his minivan. He can get to the Haven by one in the morning if he hurries. If Raine still hasn't answered her phone by then.

He's got to make it.

This is his fault.

Baxter sent him to the Haven to find Samantha, but he found Raine instead. That's what Baxter really wanted, and Noah fell for it. He told Baxter Raine's name. Her full name. He verified where she lived and what she looked like. He handed her to Baxter on a silver platter.

The building alarm stops.

He reaches the van.

"Noah." David runs across the lot. "Hold up." He puts his hand on the hood.

Noah opens the driver's side door.

"Where are you going?" David asks. "To the Haven?"

"Yes. Watch out."

David rubs his face. "Tonight?"

"Yes. You need to move."

"David," Monica shouts from across the parking lot. She marches toward them, waving her arms in the air.

David glances at her, then eyes Noah. "I'm coming with you."

Monica speeds up. "David."

"Get in," Noah says.

David runs around the front of the minivan.

"Where are you going?" She breaks into an all-out run. "David. Stop."

He opens the passenger door, and Noah starts the engine.

She stops in front of the minivan and peers over the hood. Her bloodshot eyes. Her veiny cheeks.

"Get out of the way, Monica." David fumes.

"Not until you tell me what you're doing."

"I'm going back to the Haven with Noah. Raine needs my help. Now get out of the way."

"You can't just leave me here. I'm not driving all the way back by myself."

David gets in and slams the door shut, shattering the passenger window.

"Don't worry about it," Noah says. "It already didn't work."

A white seventies Buick with black tinted windows pulls into the lot.

"Shit," Noah says.

David yells, "Get out of the way, Monica."

Noah hits the horn.

She puts both hands on the hood. Leans forward.

The Buick parks near the building, and the driver's door opens.

Noah puts the van in drive and lets it lurch forward an inch, shoving Monica backward.

She stumbles, catches her balance, and balls her hands into fists. "You're not in the Teaching, David. You're out of integrity. You're thinking about Raine instead of me. I'm your like-vibration, not her. I'm the love of your life, not her. If you leave me here, you're leaving the Haven. I'll make sure of that. You'll never be allowed back. You'll be doomed. Doomed!"

"Go fuck yourself," David yells.

Noah presses the accelerator.

She tries to move out of the way, slips, and falls down.

He hits the brakes.

A man in a vermillion suit jacket gets out of the Buick and strides across the lot.

"Oh, shit," Noah says.

"What?"

"That's Titus. He—" Noah throws the van in reverse and guns it. "I owe him some money."

Monica gets to her feet.

Noah spins the wheel, brakes, and the minivan rocks to a stop, sitting sideways in the lot.

Titus approaches Monica from behind. He undoes a button. His jacket flies open, and he pulls out a gun. His tree-trunk legs propel him forward. He dwarfs her from behind. Before she can turn around, he wraps his free arm around her chest and puts the gun to her head. "Noah! Let's talk."

"About what?" He puts the minivan in drive.

"What are you doing?" David asks.

"What should I do?"

David gazes at his wife.

"I'm serious," Titus shouts. "Give me my money, or"—He presses the muzzle against Monica's cheekbone—"she gets it."

Monica screams.

"What do you want me to do, David?"

David puts his hand on Noah's shoulder. "I want you to leave."

Noah hits the gas. The engine's whine blends with Monica's screaming.

They speed toward the road.

"What's he doing?" Noah asks.

David turns. Looks out the back window. "He let go of her. He's running back to his car."

Noah stops at the intersection and glances in the rearview mirror while waiting for a car to pass.

Monica is on her knees with one arm in the air, yelling something.

"How much money do you owe that guy?" David asks.

"Not as much as you might think." He pulls out and heads for the strip. "Can you call Raine?"

David puts his phone to his ear.

"Anything?" Noah asks.

"No. She's not answering."

Within minutes, Noah has the minivan going full speed on the freeway, cruising north. He glances at the side mirror. "Any sign of Titus?"

"No," David says. "How fast can this thing go?"

"I don't know, but I've got to be careful. It's seen better days." He tightens his grip on the steering wheel. "Why don't you try calling Raine again."

David does.

No answer.

"She's going to be okay," David says. "Relax. We have a long road ahead of us."

The dark orange skyline fades to purple, then black.

Partway through the state, Noah turns off the freeway onto a two-lane road. An hour goes by, then two. Then three. The night hides the horizon. The monotonously straight highway threatens to go on forever. Nothing but darkness lies beyond the headlights.

The minivan isn't moving fast enough.

Noah presses on the accelerator, but he's already hit maximum velocity.

David is right. He needs to relax or they won't make it. "With luck, we should get there around one."

"Yep." David gazes out the passenger window.

"Maybe she'll answer now. Try again."

David calls.

Nothing.

Noah slams his hand on the wheel.

"Don't worry," David says. "She's going to be okay. She's probably asleep by now."

"No. You don't understand. She's gone to find Java. I'm sure of it. She won't stop looking until she finds her." He wipes his face. "She's not asleep. She's out in the woods. Dammit. She's out there, wandering around in the woods right now, and if Baxter hasn't found her yet, he's going to. And when he does—"

"Stop it. You've got to—" David points out the window. "Watch out!"

Two eyes dart onto the road.

Noah turns the wheel, but he's too late, and something bounces into the undercarriage with a *flwumpf*.

The check engine light comes on.

He hits the brakes. Pulls onto the shoulder.

Steam boils over the hood.

"What the hell was that?" Noah asks.

"It looked like a red fox."

Noah puts his head in his hands. "A red fox. Really? You saw the color?"

"No, that's the kind of fox it is. It's a red fox."

"Oh."

"Do you have any tools in here?" David turns toward the back of the minivan. "We're not going to get very far with it overheating like this."

CHAPTER FORTY-FIVE

RAINE

I crack my eyes just enough to gauge the time of day. It's still dark out. So dark, I can't see the tack marking the small village of Bugarach on my map. I must have slept only a couple hours.

I close my eyes.

It feels good to be home, waking up in my own bed. The smell of my dirty laundry instead of my mother's deodorized cling-free dryer sheets. After our fight, I don't ever want to go back there. I pull my blanket up to my chin and roll over. My mind drifts, and I'm caught between a dream and consciousness.

Then reality sneaks up behind me and says, *boo*.

Java is still gone.

I couldn't find her.

I spent the evening walking the Haven, the woods—everywhere—until my feet revolted. Blisters formed. My running shoes weren't made for that kind of hiking. Sometime around midnight, I realized how futile it was to continue looking for her in the dark, stumbling over bushes and rocks half awake. I barely remember coming home and flopping down in the loft.

She never came when I called. Poor thing. She must be so scared. She's probably hiding.

But I won't stop. I'm awake now, and she's out there. Somewhere.

I stretch my arms out over my head, point my toes, and my body shakes.

What time is it?

My cell phone isn't where I keep it on my nightstand. Vaguely, I remember the moment I discovered it was gone. I was standing at the trailhead near the firepit. I had only just begun to search for her, and I had my phone with me when I left the house, but maybe not. Maybe I left it on the kitchen counter.

Soreness creeps up the backs of my legs as I come down the stairs.

My phone isn't on the counter.

I search the kitchen but stop after opening the drawer with the notes from Monica. To think, I was so terrified, I actually considered leaving the Haven because of her. Negative energy lingers around the drawer like smoke over a doused fire. I pull the letters out and throw them in the wastebasket. Good riddance.

There's no sign of my phone. I guess I lost it for good.

I'm starving.

Corn Pops and coffee, that's all I need. I sit at the dining table with a bowl and a cup. A soft orange haze creeps in through the windows, waking up the walls. It's the dawn of a new day. It's going to be a great day, because today, I am going to find Java.

Damn Monica.

This is all her fault.

I shovel a spoonful into my mouth.

This is all Monica's fault, but I can't let hate rule me. Hate won't find my dog.

I put the spoon down and close my eyes. I've got to push the past aside and move on. Find forgiveness so I can escape the hate. Being a Windhaven, Monica had it better than most people in the community, but it wasn't always easy for her, growing up the daughter of a trance medium. She naturally wanted to take over for her father, but she let jealousy rule her heart. She wanted to be the next trance medium and resented me.

Then she kidnapped my dog.

She is truly sick.

She is not in the Teaching.

But, doesn't everyone deserve forgiveness?

I take my bowl to the living room and sit on the sofa where Java used to sit. Her doggy scent rises out of the cushions. Old Fritos and dusty leather. She would sit here with me while I meditated in the mornings, patiently waiting for me to take her for a walk. How she loved to go for walks.

Dammit.

How can I forgive Monica for what she's done?

I've got to find Java.

I stare out the window, waiting for dawn to finish breaking, waiting for the day to eat the morning haze and bask in the sun's glory. A faint, surreal light shines through the trees, and I wait.

Java is still out there somewhere. I don't worry whether she is hungry because she lived on her own for a year before I adopted her. I worry she is alone. Scared. Lost.

I worry someone has taken her.

That's it. Time to go.

I cross the floor, and a blister pops as if to warn me not to wear my running shoes. I throw on my Birkenstocks, step out the back door, bound down the steps, and—stop. It's still a little dark out. Do I need a flashlight? No. The sun will rise higher soon and push the shadows aside.

The morning air is refreshing, but the stillness reminds me of last night. The endless trudging through the darkness, the occasional, unexplainable sounds in the trees . . . I jog back to my cabin and grab my whistle off the hook.

It's all I need.

I trudge down the road.

God, I'm tired.

My eyes burn when I blink, so I keep them open, letting the cool air soothe. It's quiet. Serene. Java is probably hiding in the trees, but I decide to eliminate the Haven first. Stay out of the gloomy woods until the sun comes up.

"Java."

I attempt to call her quietly, not wanting to wake anyone up, but it's hard. The lights in the cabins and trailers are off, and a gentle wind blows through the trees. The Haven is beautiful this time of day. As I near Terry and Kattrice's, an upstairs light comes on. It shines through the sheer white curtains, but there's no movement inside. Nothing I can see from here.

"U-m-m. M-m-m."

My heart jumps.

Below the window, a chair slides across the deck, screeching as it scrapes against the wood.

Terry emerges from the shadows and puts his hands on the railing. His long white hair faintly aglow. His cardinal red robe. The collar cradling his neck. His light blue eyes, unwavering. "My dear Raine. I'm sorry. I didn't mean to frighten you."

"That's okay."

"I"—he takes a deep breath—"want to tell you again how pleased I am you're learning to trance, but why haven't you come back for another lesson? Where have you been all week?"

"Nowhere. I was spending time with my mother."

"Good." He lifts his chin, gazes at the dying stars. "It's good for you to spend time with her. You should spend more time with her. You should spend more time with all the women. Remember, you're born into your blood family to learn what you've forgotten in your last life, but you'll be with your spirit family for all eternity."

He thinks he's part of my spirit family. I don't have time for this. "Okay. I'll let you get back to trancing or whatever—"

"You haven't found her yet, have you?." He lowers his head. "That's why you're out here, yelling before sun-up."

"Oh, you heard me. I'm sorry."

"No, no, my dear. It is quite all right . . . this time. But next time, you should wait until it's lighter out."

"I wasn't trying to wake anyone up."

"I believe you. I'm more concerned about your well-being than I am everyone's sleep. It's not necessarily safe out here this early. There are animals in the woods."

I glance up the road. A light comes on in a cabin.

Terry drifts away from the railing and walks down the steps. "Perhaps I should come with you to look for her. At least until the sun has risen."

"That's okay." I grasp my whistle. "I'll be okay. You haven't seen her, have you?"

"No, I have not."

I take a step back.

He stops. "Sebastian is concerned about you. He says your love for Java may be clouding your true purpose on the earth plane. Whenever your dog runs away, you seem to abandon the Teaching."

Sebastian can go to hell. I want my dog back.

"I love her."

"I know you do, dear." He gazes directly at me and takes a deep, satisfying breath. "It's your karma, I suppose. Just promise me you'll be careful."

"I will."

He turns and walks up the steps. "Yes. You will." The light up the road goes out. "Yes. Thy will be done."

I stride past the Shrine. In my last letter to God, I asked for help finding Samantha, not Java. But Terry pushed me to write that letter.

Animal love versus true love.

Animal love *is* true love. That's my Teaching.

"Java!"

Past the Shrine, past the tall lodgepole pines, nothing moves except the branches in the breeze.

I hope Noah's talk with his friend went well. I long to see him. Yesterday was embarrassing. I was tired, angry, and sick of staying with my mother, but that's no excuse for the way I talked to him on the phone. He was so wonderful, offering to come back and help me find Java. I may never be able to forgive Monica, but Noah is forgiven. It puts me at peace.

I pass by the trance room.

I should forgive Terry also. Until I saw him just now, I hadn't realized how angry I'd become over the whole trance thing. Who am I to judge how he delivers Sebastian's message to the world? The world is beautiful and mysterious. Knowing about the sermons, and the genetic memory theory, doesn't necessarily make Sebastian any less real. It just makes him more a part of Terry than the astral. Terry is forgivable. The Teaching, on the other hand . . . after I find Java, I'm going to reevaluate my belief system.

"Java!"

Coming around the bend, I see the trail leading to the firepit. I remember having my phone with me here last night, but I don't see it anywhere now. The shadows in the woods aren't as ominous as they were an hour ago, but it's still a little dark.

I grasp my whistle and head into the trees.

High above, birds twerp. The breeze picks up and hisses through the branches. The fragrance of sage, soil, and pine blend together, making life on the earth plane pleasant. I'm safe. My mind relaxes, and I walk on God's playground freely. The trail meanders through the forest in the same way it always has, but this time it will lead me to Java, unlike last night.

I'm going to find her.

"Java!"

I reach the boulder where I saw Samantha after the gun went off two weeks ago. I'm not far from where Noah said he saw Java. The boulder's silvery veins run through it like streamers hanging from the wedding arch. Had I known David and Monica were adopting Samantha, had I known she was pregnant, I wouldn't have let her get away. I would have tried harder.

"Java!"

I'm struck by a strange odor. The intensity, the chemical

intensity, makes me wince. It's not natural. The forest's earthy scent lingers, but there's a stronger, more medicinal fragrance taking over. It's hypnotic, but not in a good way. Not like the essential oils I use for meditation.

Something snaps, and I spin around.

"Java?"

Another crack sounds, and I turn back toward the boulder. It came from the other side.

The pungent yet clean odor hits me again.

Then I realize what the odor is.

It's a man's cologne.

CHAPTER FORTY-SIX

DAVID

Another hour and they'll be in the Haven.

The rising sun shines through the broken passenger window, blinding David. Noah's minivan is worse than David's truck. If there'd been any tools in here at all, he could have fixed the water hose himself, but Noah's not the kind of guy to have tools. Noah is a thinker, not a doer. And he's a worrier. It's been painful watching Noah stress over Raine these last several hours. Noah keeps talking about what will happen if the minivan breaks down again. That's his only valid concern. The red fox they ran over shouldn't have been big enough to break the water hose clamp, but it was.

David rubs his eyes. These have been the longest two days he can remember, and he still feels hungover. Exhausted.

Noah glances at the clock in the dash. Grimaces.

"We're going to make it," David says. "We'll get there, and Raine will be asleep in her loft. She's fine. We only lost about four hours."

"We lost more than that. The sun is coming up."

A Lady Gaga song comes on the radio.

David presses the seek button until he hears The Doors. Jim Morrison sings about eternal rewards and wasting the dawn. "We're going to make it. Try to relax."

"I hope so. How are you holding up?"

"I've been better. I don't know. I'm" —he gazes out the open window— "catching a second wind."

"Are you still hungover?"

"Yep. I won't be drinking like that again for a long time."

Getting drunk on the strip with Monica was the best, but it was temporary. She's a nightmare. He's not sure what he was thinking, agreeing to recruit Baxter for the cult. And that is what it is—a cult.

It's a cult. I grew up in a cult.

He's spent his entire life letting the Windhaven's twist his thinking, squeezing him for money in tithing, making him work for free. All in the name of service. Service to his like-vibration. Service to God.

God. Guilt. Manipulation.

The Teaching.

He wipes his face. Feels the scruff of his burgeoning beard. Wishes he was home in bed.

"I hope you don't mind me asking," Noah says, "but what are you going to do?"

"About what?"

"Monica."

"I'm going to leave the community before she gets back." He looks down at his boots. "As soon as we know Raine is okay, I'm packing up and leaving."

"I'm sorry."

"Don't be. It's been coming for a long time."

"What about your kids?"

"I'm taking them with me."

"And the Teaching?"

"What about it?"

"Aren't you—you're a teacher, right?"

"I'm leaving the Haven, not the Teaching. The Teaching will always be with me . . . the good parts anyway."

Noah glances at David, hesitates, then asks, "Is trancing for real?"

"It's real to me."

"You really believe Sebastian speaks through Terry?"

"Yep. Sebastian is as real as you are."

"How do you know Terry isn't faking it?"

"I don't, but it doesn't matter." Silhouettes on the horizon slowly turn into mountains. "If you believe in something, then it's real. I've always believed in Sebastian." A groove in the road pulls the minivan to the side.

Noah counters. He centers the van in the lane.

David continues. "Sebastian saved my life last week. Terry did too. I'm going to miss them."

The heater comes on, weakly pushing warm air through the vents.

"I think it's a good thing you're getting out of there. I'm sorry about your wife. She needs help—" Noah's phone buzzes. "Oh, shit."

"What?"

"It's Baxter Oakes."

Dawn breaks over the mountains. The sun's glare rapes the windshield. Hides the road. David squints. He can't believe he stayed awake all night, but suddenly, he's not tired.

The phone buzzes.

"Answer it," David says.

"I—"

"Answer it."

"What if he's—"

David takes the phone. "Hello?"

"Who's this?"

"A friend of Noah's."

Noah puts his hand on David's shoulder. "Ask about Raine."

David covers the receiver. "No."

"Put Noah on," Baxter says. "I need to talk to him. Is he there?"

Noah's lips pinch together, and his cheeks turn red. "Let me talk to him." He lets go of the steering wheel with one hand and reaches for the phone.

David leans away.

The minivan swerves.

"Are you there?" Baxter asks.

"I'm here," David says.

"Keep him on the phone," Noah says. "If he's talking to you, then he's not hurting Raine."

"Shh."

"Where is he?" Baxter asks.

"He's right here, but he can't talk right now. He—"

"You tell him I don't want him looking for Samantha anymore. You got that?"

"Why?"

"I just got a message from my assistant. Apparently, he threatened her with a gun yesterday. You tell him I don't do business with people like that. Tell him it's over."

"What about your daughter?"

"What about her? Who is this?"

"It's David Johansen. Don't you want your daughter back?"

"Do you know where she—wait." He huffs into the phone. "Johansen? You're one of them, aren't you?"

"I don't know where she is, but we should talk. Can we meet? Are you in Elko?"

"How'd you know where I was?"

"Your assistant told us. Look, we can be there in less than an hour. Can you meet us downtown at the—"

"No. It's over. Tell Noah to mind his own business. I don't need his help anymore."

"Ask about Tom Johnson," Noah whispers. "Do it. Do it."

David grits his teeth. "We know about Tom Johnson. I think you should meet with us."

Baxter breathes into the phone. "What do you think you know?"

"We know you're Tom Johnson. We know about the ATV."

Silence.

"What's he saying?" Noah asks.

"Nothing."

Noah snatches the phone out of David's hand. "Where are you? What are you doing?"

David takes the phone back.

Baxter says, "I think you know what I'm doing, Noah. I'm cleaning up loose ends."

CHAPTER FORTY-SEVEN

RAINE

My hand rests on the tall, granite boulder. I don't remember putting it there. The surface is cold, rough, and hard, and I listen while the veins in the back of my hand pulsate faster and faster.

I could have sworn I heard someone walking around on the other side. Snapping branches beneath their feet. Mumbling.

But I haven't heard anything for a while.

But the smell.

A man's cologne.

It's still there.

An odd thought occurs to me. What if it's Samantha? What if after two weeks, I found her where I lost her, hiding behind this boulder.

I glance down at my Birkenstock's. My blisters burn.

I sniff.

The cologne lingers.

A primal alarm sounds in my head, and I want to run, but I'm frozen in place.

Run. Stay quiet. Go. Escape. Scream.

Panic strikes, and I slowly take my hand off the rock. One move at a time—careful, easy, take it slow. Wait. Listen. The birds tweet, they twerp, their wings flapping in the trees. The noise is infuriating. I take a step back, listen, and—there it is.

Something moves on the other side.

Footsteps, soft and light.

I lean away from the boulder until I'm about to fall, then I break into a run. Better safe than sorry. My sandals fly off behind me. The dusty trail actually feels good on my feet until I step on a sharp rock. I'm leaving a string of blood behind me now. Halfway up the hill to the firepit, I stop. It's too wide open over there. I've got to hide. I've got to go off the trail and find a bush or a rock outcropping. Somewhere.

I've got to find somewhere to hide.

Stepping between the trees, over thistles and weeds, I leave the trail. My feet crush God's earth, and he punishes me for losing my sandals. Pine needles, knapweed, sticks, coarse debris—my arches ache. Rocks hiding in the shade cut my feet. I stumble along the ridge, grabbing at branches for balance, crossing over the unforgiving ground.

"Excuse me," a man calls out. "Don't go. I didn't mean to scare you."

I lurch behind a pine. The hill ahead steepens. Rocks surrounded by thick sage jut out of the ground, making an escape this way impossible. I would have to crawl, and he would grab me by the ankle if I tried.

I peer around the pine.

He stands at the bottom of the hill, right where the trail widens and splits—one path leading back the way I came, the other up the hill. He's older, but not old. Fifty-ish. His hair is slicked back, exposing a deep widow's peak. He would look like an insurance salesman if it weren't for the brown flannel hunting shirt he's wearing. And the ripped jeans.

He's not from the Haven, and his cologne stinks.

"Are you from around here?" he says. "My name's Baxter. You lost your sandals." He holds them up, smiling.

My blisters burn.

"Come on down," he says. "I need your help."

"What do you want?"

"I'm looking for a girl. She's about fifteen—blond. Have you seen her?"

I say nothing. My heart thunders in my chest like I'm still running.

He walks up the hill toward the point where I abandoned the trail. His hiking boots have no scars. "She's my daughter. I really need to find her." He watches me as he negotiates the incline, bending his knees, pushing down on his thighs with his hands. With every step he takes, he keeps his eyes fixed on me.

I'm a hot mess. I'm hiding behind a tree, sweating, my feet covered in blood and dirt like some hillbilly. My hair is a disaster. He must think I'm insane. "I haven't seen her."

"I apologize," he says. "I didn't mean to scare you." He steps off the trail into the brush, stumbles, grabs a branch for balance. "I'm not used to the outdoors."

"Well, you did scare me. You scared the hell out of me."

"I'm sorry, but I'm desperate. Her name's Samantha. Do you know her?"

"Yes."

A sheen coats his eyes. "Please, don't be afraid."

I come out from behind the tree.

His lips quiver and he forces a smile. "When was the last time you saw her?"

"Two weeks ago. I don't think she's out here anymore, but you could check the firepit. It's that way."

"Where did you see her last?" He takes a step forward.

"Not far from here." I point. "Back around that bend."

He turns and wipes his forehead. "I was just over there. She wasn't there."

He's getting too close. I step sideways, edge down the hill, and my foot slips.

"Here, let me help you." He rushes forward, holding out his hand.

My foot slips again, and I grasp him by the wrist to keep from falling.

He grips my wrist in return. His hand is soft but strong. I step back up the hill. He's got her eyes. There's definitely a resemblance. Deep, dark brown, shiny obsidian eyes, filling with tears.

I stand up straight and let go of his wrist.

"I'm sorry," he says, still holding onto me.

"Why?" I pull, but he doesn't let go.

"I'm so sorry."

I jerk my arm, but his grip tightens. "Let go of me."

His other hand comes up fast, reaching for my throat.

I duck and ram my fist into his groin.

He yells and lets go.

I scramble up the hill, my bloody feet aching, my hands clawing at bark and dirt and sagebrush. Sticks. I cast the debris behind me, hoping to hit him in the face, hoping to blind him. To make him stop.

"I'm sorry," he says, reaching for my ankle.

I kick.

He falters.

I get some traction, and I go.

The top of the hill is right there. The firepit is on the other side. If I can make it, I can run.

He grasps my ankle.

My chest hits the ground. I pull on a rock, but my hand slips off, and I roll onto my back.

His lips are parted, exposing his teeth, and he pulls on my leg, his eyes shining like he's crying.

"I'm sorry," he says.

I kick at him with my free leg and connect. His head rocks back, but he doesn't let go. I kick again, but he dodges, and I miss.

And he won't let go.

He's too big. Too strong.

He moves up on me.

Oh, God. He's on me.

My fist finds his face, but it makes no difference.

He sits up, his hips straddling my waist.

I'm pinned.

He wipes his lips and looks at his fingers.

A drop of blood falls from his hand and lands on my chest.

"I'm sorry," he says. "I didn't want to do this."

I reach inside my shirt, pull out my whistle, and put it in my mouth.

He puts his hands around my neck and shakes it. "Don't move. It'll be over soon."

I blow into the whistle.

I close my eyes, and I blow.

CHAPTER FORTY-EIGHT

NOAH

The back corner of Noah's minivan slips off the dirt road as they careen around the bend toward Raine's A-frame.

David puts his hand on the dashboard.

Noah hits the gas.

Raine's car is in the driveway. Maybe she's home. Maybe Baxter hasn't found her.

Noah slams the brakes and slides to a stop, cock-eyed in the road. He reaches across David, opens the glove compartment, and takes out the gun. Terry's old black revolver.

In a beat, he's at Raine's front door, knocking.

David runs around back.

"Raine? Are you in there?" Noah knocks once more and tries the knob. She shouldn't have left it unlocked. What was she thinking?

He steps inside. "Raine, are you in here?"

The sofa—empty. The dining table—empty. Java's bowl—empty and upside down.

David comes in through the back door. "Is she here?"

Noah attacks the stairs to her loft—dresser, dirty clothes, bed, blankets . . .

No Raine.

He hides the gun in his pants and slams his hand on the railing.

"Is she up there?" David asks.

"No." He rushes down the stairs.

"She's not in the bathroom either." David disappears into the kitchen.

"She wouldn't have left this early. She's not an early riser." Horrible thoughts cascade over him. He pictures Jace's ATV with the rope and the bag. Raine tied to a tree, crying, being held at gunpoint by Baxter, the way Jace held Java.

"I can't believe I married this," David says, standing by the wastebasket, holding a piece of paper. "Look at what she wrote."

Swooping black letters. *The hand of God is coming, Raine.*

"I know."

"If she hadn't left these notes, Raine would be here now. She'd be safe. I bet she's out looking for Java."

Noah strides into the living room. Looks out the front window. Raine could be anywhere. She could be over there inside the trance room. Or at one of her friends' houses. She could have gone back to wherever she was when he talked to her yesterday, but—dammit. David's right. She's out there looking for Java.

She's in the woods.

He races past the TV into the kitchen.

David goes to the back door and pulls the curtain aside.

"See anything," Noah asks.

"No."

"He's got her, David. I know it. I just know it."

"Calm down. You don't know anything. Maybe I'm wrong. Maybe she went to her mother's."

"No. After I told her Monica wrote the notes, all she wanted to do was find Java." He puts his hands on the counter and leans forward. "She's probably been out there looking for her since yesterday, unless . . ."

"Unless what?"

"Unless Baxter was here when she got home. Unless he kidnapped her."

David glances around. "I doubt it. There's no sign of a struggle."

Noah points to the hook by the door. "Her whistle is gone, but that doesn't mean anything. She always—"

"Wait." David puts his hand up. "Shh."

"What?"

"Shh."

Silence.

"I must be losing my mind," David says. "I thought I heard a whistle."

"I don't hear anything."

"It's probably because you mentioned it. God I'm tired." He opens the back door and steps outside.

Noah follows him down the steps.

The woods sprawl for miles.

"She could be anywhere," David says.

"You're not losing your mind. Listen."

A faint, high-pitch sound escapes the trees.

Noah reaches into his waistband and pulls out Terry's gun.

The sound comes again.

It's a whistle.

David puts his hand on Noah's shoulder. "You lead the way."

CHAPTER FORTY-NINE

RAINE

Samantha's father sticks his hand in my mouth and tries to take my whistle.

I bite him.

He hits me in the face so hard everything goes black. When I open my eyes, he rips the whistle out of my mouth and jerks it until the chain snaps. The back of my neck burns. I take a swing at him, but he blocks it and throws my whistle over his shoulder.

The only thing my father ever gave me bounces off a rock and lands in a tree.

His fingers wrap around my neck, and he begins to squeeze. His hands are enormous. Powerful. I bring my knees up, but he's too high on my torso. I can't kick him. His weight presses on my abdomen, and my throat collapses.

I cough, slap, twist, raise my head forward, reach for his hair—he pulls my neck off the ground and slams it back down. The back of my head smashes against the earth. God's great earth.

"I'm sorry," he says.

Something in my throat makes a cracking sound. I slap at his ear. Weak. Too late. Pressure builds in my lungs, behind my eyes. I don't have much time. Holding onto his flannel shirt with my left hand, I grab his ear with my right. I squeeze hard and extend my thumb over his cheekbone. With as much force as I can muster, I jam it into his eye.

He arches his back and lifts his chin, dislodging my thumb from his eye socket.

I flail.

He smacks me hard. His hair flops forward over his brow. His lips part. He puts both hands on my neck, and he grits his teeth. He flexes his forearms.

He crushes my throat.

I can't bear to look at him.

He's hideous.

I refuse to let this monster's scowl haunt me for all of eternity.

I won't do it.

He lowers his face near mine.

A drop of sweat falls into my eye.

I turn my head and search the hilltop for something beautiful. Something to take with me to the astral.

And then I see her . . .

Java bounds over the hill, tongue lolling, black fur shining in the morning light.

She leaps at him, baring her teeth, and he falls backward onto my ankles. Good dog. She goes for his throat, and I kick myself free. I sit up and try to breathe, but I can only get a trickle of air through my throat. Tears fill my eyes. I grasp my neck and pinch it. It's like I have rocks in my larynx. I push and prod, but my throat won't open up. The pain is unbearable. God help me.

Java is on him, growling. Gnashing at his face.

He screams and flails and swears.

Something gives, and my throat pops open. A blast of air bursts from my lungs, sending agonizing spikes of pain up my neck.

I wheeze.

Java yelps.

Shooting stars block my vision, and I rub my eyes.

Everything is a blur.

Java yelps again.

I rub my eyes. I blink and rub, and my vision clears in time to see him pin Java's neck to the ground with one massive hand. He balls the other in a fist and slams it into her face. She cries, and he hits her again. His gigantic fist hits her again. Again and again. Blood flies off his knuckles, and he hits her again.

I scream at the top of my lungs, but all that comes out is a rasping, "No. Stop."

I lunge forward and grab his arm—his swinging arm—and I pull, but gravity pulls harder, and I lose my balance. I overshoot him, spin sideways, and slide down the hill on my back, helpless.

A sound comes from the hilltop.

He strikes her again.

There's something red rustling in the bushes behind him.

My whistle—hanging from a branch above the bushes—begins to sway.

He raises his fist high in the air, setting up the final blow. She can't take another hit. I reach out in vain, and—

"Stop!" Terry, wearing his cardinal red robe, emerges from the bushes, holding a gun with both hands. He trembles. He points the gun at Samantha's father. "Stop."

The man lowers his fist. Glares at Terry. "What are you going to do?"

Terry takes a step forward. "Don't move."

The man takes his hand off Java's neck.

She lies there, motionless, her face bleeding.

He raises his arms.

Terry strides down the hill. "Are you okay, Raine?"

I stand. Put my hand on my throat.

Terry keeps the gun on the man, stepping sideways around him. "Raine?"

I try, but I can't speak.

Terry glances at me, and the man lunges forward. He slaps the gun out of Terry's hand. Terry falters, slips, hits the ground. The man leaps upon him and takes a swing. Terry folds his arms over his face to block the blow.

The gun slides down the hill, stopping at my feet.

The man connects, and Terry's head swings to the side.

I pick up the gun. Hold it with both hands and aim at the man's chest.

Java lies on the hill. Motionless.

The man raises his fist, and I pull the trigger.

A flash of light.

A deafening boom.

My wrists compress and pain shoots up my arms.

The man's face explodes, spraying the hill with bone and blood. His fist falls, his shoulders go limp, and his body slumps forward, hangs there for a moment, then collapses onto the ground and slides down the hill, coming to rest at my feet.

Terry rolls over. Faces me with wide eyes.

Java stirs. Her ribcage flexes.

She's breathing.

She's alive, and she's breathing.

I take a step back, shaking, and aim at the man's head.

There's no point. His face is gone.

I take another step back.

Pieces of brain are strewn across the rocks and brush. My stomach does a double-flip and I want to scream, but my throat won't allow it.

"Raine," Terry says. "Don't shoot."

I let go of the gun—filthy thing—and scurry up the hill to Java. I kneel. Put my hand on her. Pray. She opens one eye, looks at me without raising her head, and pants.

I hear Terry get to his feet, and I tear my eyes off Java. "Are you okay?"

"I believe I am." He goes to the gun. Picks it up and shakes his head. "Thy will be done." He stands over the dead man, his light blue eyes ablaze with an unearthly intensity. "Thy will be done." He wipes the gun with his robe, removing my fingerprints. "Oh, God of the highest seas. Thy will be done." A breeze lifts his long white hair off his shoulders, and he kneels.

I stroke Java's fur. She wags her tail and kicks her hind legs, and she tries to stand. I caress her shoulder and hold her down. "It's okay, baby. You're okay. Just wait."

Terry pries one of the man's hands open. He places the grip in the man's palm and closes the long, sinewy fingers around it. The tan barrel blends in with the man's skin like it belongs there.

"Raine!" Noah and David come running out of the forest below. Noah's got a gun in his hand, but he's too late.

Terry tries to stand, stumbles forward, then sits back on the hill.

"Oh my God," Noah says. He attempts to rush forward, but David puts his hand on Noah's chest. "What the hell happened? Raine, are you okay?"

Terry raises his hand. "Shh."

"But—"

"H-m-m. M-m-m." Terry suddenly rocks forward. Then back. His spine arches, his eyes close, and he places his palms on the ground, bracing himself against the hill.

Java escapes my hold and stands. Blood drips from her face, and she barks. I wrap my arms around her.

I love her.

"Hello, me children of the most high seas." Sebastian's voice flows from Terry. "Do not fear me medium. Terry be living out his karma, you know. He sits high upon God's vessel, watching from the crow's nest." Terry's legs cross. His upper body sways. Sebastian speaks. "This evil man," Terry's hand swings through the air, dipping dangerously close to the man's gaping head wound, "this Baxter Oakes. He has reaped his karma. He has passed over to the spirit world now—I see him here—but he did not pass over by the hand of me children. No. He passed over by the bullet of his own gun."

A bead of sweat runs down the back of my neck, giving me chills.

"There be no dead, and there be no dying," Sebastian continues, "but this man be doomed. Doomed to return."

His voice lowers, takes on a guttural, animal tone. "This man's crimes against God, against his own child . . . " He wavers. "His beautiful little girl, poisoned by his seed, abused, driven from her home to us, driven toward Washington where you know, she be driven to consider the most heinous of acts. To murder a baby. No. This man's sins—h-m-m—he will re-embody, and next time, he will suffer far worse than this." Terry's arms stretch toward the sky. "Samantha Oakes . . . you be free now. The gun was found. The Devil was shot. God has answered your prayer."

Terry slumps forward, then falls back against the hill.

David goes to him.

Noah runs to me.

I hold onto Java.

Noah holds onto me.

EPILOGUE

RAINE

It was a suicide. Baxter Oakes killed himself.

That's what everyone believes. Noah and David didn't see me shoot the gun, and Terry never said a word. He didn't lie. Okay, he lied in silence, but I saved his life. For that, I think he'll be eternally grateful. In a way, Baxter did kill himself. Karma killed him. Everyone—Noah, David, the community, the police—they all believed it was suicide. They wanted to believe it.

Belief is reality, and everyone believes Baxter Oakes attacked me, then attacked my dog. Terry appeared and stopped him by sharing the Teaching. Terry made him realize his wrongs, and upon hearing God's word, Baxter fell prey to his own guilt. He overpowered Terry, took the gun, and there was nothing Terry, God, nor the Teaching could do.

Remorse filled Baxter's soul, and he shot himself.

Everyone believes this.

Belief is reality.

The police found the gun in Baxter's hand, and it was

registered to him. They didn't ask a lot of questions, and the community didn't offer a lot of answers. I love this place, but the time has come to leave. It's been two months since the shooting, and I've come to realize "the world" is no worse than the community. For me, the Teaching has become a personal way of life. It's no longer a set of Sebastian's commandments, and I can take it with me anywhere I go.

Java pulls me down the front steps of my A-frame into the yard. I jerk on her leash to let her know I'm still the boss, and she spins toward me, tongue lolling. She's beautiful. You'd never know Baxter punched her face.

I take a deep breath.

There isn't a cloud in the sky. There hasn't been one for weeks. A thin layer of sweat cools my forehead.

She pulls me toward my A-frame. I'm going to miss this place. "Can you lock the door?"

"Of course." Noah twists the lock.

The morning sun blasts through the trees. I put on my sunglasses, and we head for Terry and Kattrice's house.

"Are you sure you want to ask for help?" Noah asks. "I have *some* money saved up. It's close to what I owe Titus."

"You said he was going to break your kneecaps if you didn't pay in full. Besides, we need something to live on until we get jobs."

My foot slips off my sandal and touches the road. The dirt burns. I'm sick of this heat. The temperature drops at night, but not enough to keep me from waking up in sweat most mornings. My freckles have turned dark brown, and everyone's lawn is dying.

Everyone's except Terry's.

"What do you think he will say?" Noah asks.

"He'll say yes. I've paid tithes to the community my entire life. Besides that, he owes me. They still have plenty of money."

"Do you think they get that it's over?"

"I'm sure Sebastian has a plan."

It's sad, but since the "suicide," Terry and Kattrice have lost their hold on the Haven. The community has become a clan of cavemen, unthawing to discover a new world after being frozen for millions of years. A new reality. Even the Pliskins are planning to leave.

"Does your mother know what we're doing?"

"Yes. Not about the money, but I told her we were moving to Las Vegas last night."

"How'd she take it?"

"Not good, but she decided it was God's will, not mine. She made a brave face and said she'd cry about it later."

"I'm sorry."

"Don't be. She's fine. I got the feeling she was actually happy for us. For the first time ever, she suggested I try to find my father."

"Really?"

"Yes, I know. Everyone is changing."

We pass the trail to the firepit. David came up from Las Vegas two weeks ago, and we went up there for old time's sake, but it wasn't like old times. I don't like the taste of cheap beer like I did when I was a teenager. Maybe I never did, I'm not sure. Noah came and tried to fit in. I floated the idea of a trip to the upside-down mountain—Bugarach—and Shayla teased David for having product in his hair. He looks like a Vegas socialite these days.

We didn't talk about Monica.

Later that night, Shayla asked about Samantha. Everyone is still talking about what happened. Baxter Oakes's suicide and the story of his missing daughter dominated the local newspapers for weeks. The residents of Elko pointed their fingers at us, claiming the evil cult must have done something to the poor girl. Hid her. Brainwashed her. The tension became unbearable until a couple hitchhiking north from Las Vegas found an odd-shaped mound in the desert.

It was Samantha.

She'd been buried in a black garbage bag along with her unborn child. Strangled. The marks on her neck matched Baxter Oakes's unusually large hands, and the cult accusations ended. He murdered his daughter in the Haven and buried her on his way home to Vegas not far from the highway. At first, no one knew why. We had our little theories, but none of them were true. When the newspapers published the results of the unborn child's paternity test, things became clearer.

What a monster.

I spent the first two weeks after the attack meditating, letting go of my hate for him. Letting go of the hate for what he'd done to Java, and I was almost there when I learned what he'd done to Samantha.

Monster.

I've spent the last two months meditating on forgiveness, and I'm still not there. Forgiveness heals the forgiver, and I need to heal, but my meditations always turn into a replay of the shooting. Baxter's dead body on the hillside . . . picturing this brings me peace and makes me anxious at the same time.

He deserved worse.

Once or twice, I tried to trance Cecilia, seeking guidance from the other side. It didn't work. Looking back on my trance lessons, I think Terry may have used hypnosis to trick me into believing she was real.

Belief is reality.

Noah's phone buzzes. He glances at the screen. Grasps my arm. "It's them."

"Answer it."

"Hello? . . . yes, this is he . . . no, that works great . . . yes, I'll be there first thing Monday morning."

"Did you get it?"

He shoves his phone in his pocket and tries to hold back a smile, but his crooked tooth escapes, and he beams. "Yes!" He wraps his arms around me. Picks me up. Swings me around.

My sandals fall off, and my feet burn when he puts me down, but I don't care.

His eyes are ablaze. "You're looking at the new administrative assistant to Mark Whalen, Vice President, Moorehead Acquisition LLP. I'm going to be his right-hand man."

"That's great." I bend over to put my sandals back on. "But—"

"He's only a VP right now, but it's still a good place to start. He'll be as rich as Samantha's father was, someday."

Dread knocks at my door. I kick a rock down the road.

"What's wrong?" he asks.

"How much do you know about this guy?"

"It's okay, Raine. He's not like Baxter Oakes."

"Are you sure?"

"Yes. My uncle has known this guy for a long time. A lot better than he knew Baxter, and it's a straight-up job. I'm not being sent off to find a missing girl." He smiles. "I'm going to be a simple administrative assistant. All I have to do is schedule meetings, plan events. Get him answers. It's going to be cake. Don't worry."

"Okay. You're right. I'm just paranoid."

We stroll down Control Road, and Java barks at David's old cabin. Monica stands in the front window. A white nightshirt covered in cartoon rainbows hangs off her gaunt shoulders. She sees us coming and steps to the side. The weeds have taken over her yard. She slides the curtain shut and vanishes into the recesses of her broken marriage. Jenny and Joseph must be with David this weekend. Otherwise, they'd be outside playing before the day heats up.

Monica lives in a bottle.

I've forgiven her, but I haven't forgotten what she did.

I'm so happy for David, though. He got a construction job in Vegas one week after the shooting and left her. Their babysitter, Cori, ran away with Jace to California or somewhere. Except for the kids, Monica is alone. Kattrice and Terry avoid her because she's not in the Teaching anymore. She stopped going to Trance. The last time she went to Ladies' Brunch, my mother ripped her apart for writing the letters. She denied everything, going as far as to claim she never blackmailed Jace.

No one believed her.

They all believed my mother.

Belief is reality.

I miss our friendship, but I can't change the past. I still wish I'd stopped Samantha from running away that day. Sometimes, when I walk in the forest, I see her hiding behind that boulder. Trembling. Burdened by that overstuffed backpack. If only I'd known Baxter was there too, I wouldn't have let her get away.

But I didn't know. If I had known what was going through her head, I would have run faster. But no one knew, except for Sebastian. And by association, Terry.

The things Sebastian said right after the shooting—the prayer, the gun. Washington. He said Samantha was running away to Washington . . . he couldn't have known these things unless Samantha had told him, and I doubt she did.

He is wise.

Or he cheated.

Mrs. Pliskin was the first to suggest Terry might have gone into the Shrine and read everyone's letters to God. She didn't mean to start anything, but the paranoia spread, and soon, everyone began doubting Terry and Kattrice. They stopped writing letters to God. A week or so later, the Shrine burned to the ground. Terry said it was kids playing with matches— like I used to do—but I don't think so. I think Samantha must have written a letter to God about Washington.

The Windhaven's house stands tall in the sweltering heat. Their green lawn runs up to the deck, lapping up water from a lone sprinkler in the middle.

"There he is." Noah points to the deck.

Terry stands. Puts his hands on the railing. "Hello, Raine. Noah. Please, come inside."

We follow him into the kitchen. The oak dining table runs parallel to their long marble serving counter. Their stainless-steel sink, triple-door refrigerator-freezer, gas range, and double dutch oven—it's the most beautiful kitchen in the Haven.

My tithings paid for this kitchen.

The sound of a toilet flushing comes from the hall, and Kattrice appears in the entryway. Her sweatshirt hangs from her shoulders and folds over her hips like melted cheese. She's never worn make-up, but she should do something. The lines in her face have deepened over these last few weeks. "Get that dog out here."

"We'll only be a minute," I say.

"Terry," she says, "Are you going to do something about this?" She waves her hand as if to shoo a fly.

"I'm sorry, Raine," Terry says. "I should have asked you to tie Java up outside before we came in. Could you?"

"Sure."

When I return, Kattrice isn't there. Thank God for small favors.

I sit next to Noah at the kitchen table.

Terry sits across from us, his hands clasped on the wooden surface.

"We can't stay long," I say. "We're here to ask for the community's help."

"I apologize for my like-vibration." Terry nods toward the hall. "She's never liked animals." His gaze is filled with peace. His starry eyes forever blue. His smile forever welcoming. "How can the community help you?"

I hesitate.

Noah takes my hand beneath the table.

"Terry." I close my eyes and tip my head forward. "I love you, but—I love the Teaching, too, but . . . we're leaving the Haven."

He says nothing.

I open my eyes.

He sits there, unphased by my news. "Where are you going, my child?"

"I'm—" Noah squeezes my hand. "We're moving to Las

Vegas. Noah just got a job there, and I'm going to—" This is harder than I thought. He's staring at me like a child on Christmas morning, and I'm about to tell him I don't believe in Santa.

"It's okay, Raine. You know how we feel. People are free to leave anytime they want. You can take the Teaching with you. When you come back, we'll still be here."

"Thank you. I know."

"But this isn't all you wanted to tell me, is it?"

"No."

"Did you want to talk to Sebastian?"

"No," I blurt it out. There's a tingle in my chest. I have a strange urge to laugh, but I keep it together. "I don't need to talk to him. I—we need money."

Terry leans back in his chair. This does phase him. "Are you sure you don't want to talk to Sebastian? Don't want to say goodbye?"

"No. We just need some money to get started in Vegas."

"I'm sorry, Raine."

"But I've paid tithings to the community my whole life."

He shakes his head. "That's not how it works. The community isn't a bank account. Your tithings have been spent to support the Teaching." I glance at the dishwasher. Most people in the Haven do their dishes by hand. "There's nothing for you to withdraw."

"What do you mean, 'support the Teaching?' " Noah asks.

"Money is love in motion," Terry says. "Money from the tithings flows to those in the community who need it, when they need it, according to God's will. According to his love."

I love Noah. I love everything about him, including his kneecaps. We need this money. "Noah can't go back to Las Vegas without the community's help."

"Are you in the Teaching, Noah?"

"I—"

I squeeze Noah's hand. "If he says yes, will you give him the money? Or is it God's will to only give money to those in the Teaching? Doesn't God love everyone on the earth plane equally?"

"Raine," Terry pleads. "You know that's not what I meant."

I stand. "I know God loves everyone, but if money is love in motion, then you'll help keep Noah safe."

"Why can't he go back to Vegas with the money he has?" Terry raises his hands. "He doesn't look poor." Noah glances down at his dress shirt. "Why does he need money to be safe?"

"Why don't you ask Sebastian?" I can't keep the sarcasm out of my voice. "Doesn't Sebastian know everything?"

Kattrice appears in the doorway. "You two can leave now. When things don't work out for you in sin city, you can come back to the community. We'll still take you in."

Noah stands. "Let's go, Raine. They're a cult. A destructive cult. They aren't going to help us."

"Ha," Kattrice says. "Some cult we are. Everybody's leaving, but do you see us crying about it? We don't care. We've never cared who comes and who goes."

"You seemed to care a lot about Baxter Oakes," Noah says. "You sent your daughter to recruit him. That didn't have anything to do with the fact he was a millionaire, did it?"

My eyes connect with Terry's.

Terry looks away.

"Tell the truth," Noah says. "You sent Monica after Baxter's money, didn't you?" He eyes Kattrice. "I know you did. I heard it from Monica herself. You recruit rich people. You're a cult. You were trying to get Baxter's money, and if he hadn't killed himself, he might have killed Raine. It's your fault he came here. You made Samantha live with your daughter and arranged for her adoption just so you could get your hands on Baxter's money."

Terry turns red. Stands. Puts both hands on the table. "And you came to the Haven to impress him. You wanted to be his right-hand man, didn't you?"

"How did you know—"

I put my hand on Noah's shoulder. "My mother must have told them." Damn spy. "Terry, are you going to help us or not?"

"You,"—Terry points his finger at Noah—"wanted Baxter's money. You lied to us to get it. You said you were a student. You told us you were studying religion. How is it you're not a cult, *Noah*?"

"That's enough," I say. "Are you going to help us or not?"

"You're not in the Teaching," Kattrice says.

I stare into Terry's eyes. "Does she know?"

"Does she know what?" Terry asks.

"Do I know what?" She steps toward me.

"About the sermons? About how you really trance?"

Terry turns white. For a moment, the fear of God appears on his face, then he wipes it away.

"Terry," I say, "I helped you. I saved you. Don't you think you can put love in motion to save Noah?"

"What is she talking about?" demands Kattrice.

"You're right." He stands. "The Teaching is for everyone. God loves everyone." He walks behind the serving counter and opens a drawer.

"What are you doing?" Kattrice asks. "What's going on?"

He returns with a checkbook and a pen. "How much love does Noah need to be safe?"

"Five-thousand," Noah says.

"Stop," Kattrice yells.

Terry begins to write. "It doesn't matter anymore. Every-one is leaving. We might as well—"

"Wait," I say.

He looks up at me.

Kattrice exhales.

"My tithings over the years add up to at least fifteen thou-sand. I know that's a lot of love, but I think ten would be fair. We need the extra to get started."

He nods and finishes writing.

"Don't you dare." Kattrice reaches for the checkbook. "Don't you give them anything."

He tears out the check and hands it to Noah.

"Thank you," I say. "I love you."

"How much did you give her?" Kattrice asks.

Noah heads for the door.

Terry spreads his arms. "We're going to miss you."

I give him a hug. "I'm going to miss you, too. Thanks for saving Java. And Noah."

The distance returns to his starry blue eyes. "Take the Teaching with you, will you? Tell others about it?"

"I will, but only the good parts."

He puts his hand on my shoulder. "Thank you, Raine."

Kattrice's body shakes. "Why did you give her that money?" Her sweatshirt threatens to fall off her shoulders.

I follow Noah outside.

Poor Terry. Kattrice yells at him while I untie Java.

"We should stop at the bank on our way to Vegas," Noah says. "She might change Terry's mind. He could cancel the check."

"I don't think so." I put on my sunglasses.

Half the wedding arch is gone. It burned along with the Shrine. There's nothing next to it except a black spot where the letters to God used to be.

All those prayers—gone.

Java jumps on me.

I kneel to pet her.

She saved my life.

Terry saved hers, and I saved his, yet she's closer to God than any of us ever will be.

She's not ruled by power, or sex, or money.

She's ruled by love.

AUTHOR'S NOTE

Thank you so much for reading *The Teaching*. I am over-joyed to have shared my cult experience with you in this fictional way. For me, this story began decades ago, back in the early 1990s.

The room was pitch black. My future wife and I stood in the basement of a suburban home, listening to the spirit's voice for the first time that Christmas. Yes, they celebrated Christmas. They celebrated all the usual holidays. They shopped in all the same stores, wore all the same clothes, and worked in all the same places as everyone else in "the world." They drank beer, smoked cigarettes, and prayed. Before returning home, we wondered, *Is listening to a spirit speak through a trance medium different than listening to a priest read from an ancient black book?* Thousands of societies have practiced medium-ship. We weren't sure what to believe.

Fourteen years later, after a series of tragic events, we returned to the community. We became a part of "the cult of beer and cigarettes." We did not believe living in a communal society and attending Trance made us cult members. We were not recruited. The leaders did not prepare us for the "end-of-days" common to other, more popularly known cults. No one was forced to stay, including us. After three years, we left on good terms, and we left on our own.

The term "cult" can be defined as a social group with

unusual religious, spiritual, or philosophical beliefs. By this definition, we lived in a cult. Most people consider this term pejorative, but it's not necessarily so. A group of people with unusual beliefs and practices are not necessarily evil. Evil comes from the sacrifice of one's morals to fill out-of-balance needs. Greed, sloth, envy—you know the list. Threats, lies, and other destructively influential acts are used by evil persons, whether they belong to a cult or not. If you help influence people to murder a movie star, or break into a government building, or fly an airplane into a building, does it mean you are part of a cult? It depends on what you choose to believe. When you wake up tomorrow, ask yourself what you believe in, then ask yourself where those beliefs came from. You might be surprised.

Thank you again for reading *The Teaching*. Please feel free to connect with me on my website at www.topaine.com, on Twitter @TOPaine, or on my Facebook author page: www. facebook.com/TOPaineAuthor.

Warm regards,
T. O.

ACKNOWLEDGEMENTS

First and foremost, thanks to you, the reader. I am eternally grateful for the time you spent reading The Teaching.

Thank you to my author and writers conference heroes, J.D. Barker, Robert Dugoni, Steven James, Hallie Ephron, Larry Brooks, C.J. Tudor, Joel Burcat, Boyd Morrison, Donald Maass, Cherry Adair, Jonas Saul, Elizabeth Lyon, and the many others who not only set an example for aspiring authors, but also devote their time, energy, and talent to lifting others up.

Elena Hartwell Taylor for her editing prowess and effervescent encouragement.

Those brave souls, my first readers, whose feedback improved this work of fiction and motivated me to forge ahead, draft after draft. Special thanks to Amy Neswald, Patricia Hutto, and Kev North.

My family and friends, notably Jess Caudill for his words of encouragement, and his bravery as the first to sign up for my newsletter.

And finally, to the first reader of The Teaching and everything else in my life, my like-vibration, my love, Kim.

CPSIA information can be obtained
at www.ICGtesting.com
Printed in the USA
LVHW092241230322
714262LV00005B/198